The Sari Shop Widow

Also by Shobhan Bantwal

THE FORBIDDEN DAUGHTER

THE DOWRY BRIDE

Published by Kensington Publishing Corporation

The Sari Shop Widow

SHOBHAN BANTWAL

KENSINGTON BOOKS
http://www.kensingtonbooks.com

KENSINGTON BOOKS are published by

Kensington Publishing Corp.
119 West 40th Street
New York, NY 10018

All Kensington titles, imprints, and distributed lines are available at special quantity discounts for bulk purchases for sales promotion, premiums, fund-raising, educational, or institutional use.

Special book excerpts or customized printings can also be created to fit specific needs. For details, write or phone the office of the Kensington Special Sales Manager: Kensington Publishing Corp., 119 West 40th Street, New York, NY 10018. Attn. Special Sales Department. Phone: 1-800-221-2647.

Kensington and the K logo Reg. U.S. Pat. & TM Off.

ISBN-13: 978-0-7582-3202-1
ISBN-10: 0-7582-3202-0

First Kensington Trade Paperback Printing: September 2009
10 9 8 7 6 5 4 3 2 1

Printed in the United States of America

Acknowledgments

As always, at the beginning of a new venture, I offer a prayer of thanks to Lord Ganesh, the remover of obstacles.

My heartfelt appreciation goes to my generous, warm, and supportive editor, Audrey LaFehr, who has placed her faith in me time and again. The friendly and efficient editorial, production, public relations, and marketing folks at Kensington Publishing richly deserve my gratitude for a job well done. I look forward to working with you on my future projects.

To my agents, Stephanie Lehmann and Elaine Koster, thank you for your invaluable help and guidance at every step.

I am greatly indebted to my critique partners, Teri Bozowski and Carol Aloisi. They are gentle in their criticism but right on target.

The Writers' Exchange at Barnes & Noble in Princeton, New Jersey, and the Writers' Group at the Plainsboro Public Library deserve my thanks for their insightful comments and suggestions.

I offer a grateful hug to my many friends, who also serve as tireless cheerleaders, marketers, and promoters of my books.

To my family, whose love and support I could not survive without. They are my constant source of inspiration.

The Sari Shop Widow

Chapter 1

For the second time in ten years her life was beginning to come apart. Anjali Kapadia stood still for a minute, trying to absorb the news. Could it possibly be a mistake? But it wasn't; she'd heard it clearly. Despite her best efforts to curb it, the initial shock wave refused to ebb. The seemingly harmless bit of information was all it had taken to shatter the image of a satisfying lifestyle and career.

Her mind in overdrive, she started to pace the length of the tasteful and elegant boutique. Her boutique—her baby—her artistic and inventive skills put to optimum use in creating a fairytale store worthy of movie stars, models, and beauty queens.

Technically the business belonged to her and her parents as equal partners, but it was Anjali's creativity and vision that had turned it into a classy and successful enterprise—at least until recently. It stood apart like a *maharani*, a queen amongst the ordinary, plain vanilla sari and clothing shops of New Jersey's "Little India."

The area known as Little India, located in Edison, was crammed with sari shops, jewelry stores, restaurants, grocery markets, and souvenir shops. It was a small slice of India buried in central New Jersey, a quaint neighborhood that smelled of pungent curry, fried onions, ripe mangoes, incense, and *masala chai*, strong tea laced with spices and oodles of thick, creamy milk.

Even the store's name was Anjali's brainstorm. Overrun with ho-hum and even dumpy names and ugly storefronts, Little India was badly in need of some class. So she'd called her store Silk & Sapphires. It had a nice ring to it, and according to Hindu astrology, a sapphire supposedly dispelled the destructive influence of the fiery planet *Shanee*. Saturn. The store's window displayed the most elegant mannequins and rare jewelry to give it a boutique flavor rather than just a sari-cum-bauble shop.

The interior was done in soft cream and shimmering blue to fit the name. Teardrop crystal chandeliers hung from a vaulted ceiling. Strategically placed recessed lights highlighted the displays, mirrored walls created the illusion of space and light, and dense cream carpeting covered the sales floor and fitting rooms. No harsh music with screeching falsetto voices was allowed to tarnish the store's atmosphere either. Only soft instrumental pieces by both Indian and other masters were piped in through the sound system.

Shopping at Silk & Sapphires was meant to be a unique and indulgent experience.

The boutique also carried jewelry—one-of-a-kind creations of precious and semiprecious gems fit for an empress or a blushing bride. It was all custom-made in India by her uncles, Anjali's mom's brothers, two of whom were in the jewelry business in the state of Gujarat in northwestern India.

Nearly every piece of clothing the store sold was designed by Anjali, each outfit envisioned, then meticulously planned, cut, sewn, and embellished to her demanding specifications. She took pride in finding the right fabrics, trimmings, and tailors to make her designs evolve from an idea swirling in her brain to divine ensembles. Granted, her clothes and accessories were far more expensive than some, but they were worth the money. Every design was exclusive. Many of them were award winners in fashion shows and competitions.

She glanced at them and exhaled a long sigh. The colorful silks, the clingy chiffons, and the gossamer tissue-crepes were draped in an exquisite array on their pretty satin hangers—row upon row of lush, costly clothes. The pearls, the rainbow of beads, and the jewel-tone sequins lovingly sewn into the borders, sleeves, necklines, and bodices of the sleek garments sparkled and winked at her as she strode up and down the aisles, again and again.

What had gone wrong? How? When?

Could she be kissing her dress design business and her beloved store good-bye? If so, how soon? Catching her reflection in the mirrored wall behind the row of clothes, she realized her eyes were filled with resentment and frustration. Darn it! She rarely let bitterness prevail over her, and she wouldn't do so now. She was a woman who liked to laugh, although there hadn't been much to laugh about in the last decade—not since she'd cremated Vikram.

How could her parents have concealed such a significant problem from her for so long? And how could they even dream up something so preposterous to address the problem? How could they jeopardize her career as well as theirs with one phone call?

She wouldn't stand for it. She couldn't. She'd get a loan from a bank to bail them out of their financial mess, or even beg and borrow from friends and acquaintances before she'd give in to her parents' harebrained plan.

Turning on the narrow heel of her tan sandals, she trudged back to the long glass display counter behind which her parents stood. They'd been mutely watching her pace like a caged panther all this time. Now the mildly optimistic look on their faces told her they hoped her dark mood had passed, or at least diminished to some degree.

Well, no such luck. The distress was still spiraling inside her like a mad January blizzard. She raised her troubled eyes to them. "Why didn't you guys tell me about the problem sooner?"

Her father, Mohan Kapadia, a wiry man with glasses and a heavy mop of graying hair, gave a helpless shrug. "We didn't want to upset you. And I honestly thought your mother and I could handle it by now."

"But we're equal partners in this. I'm not a child who needs to be protected from bad news." She took a deep breath to steady her tremulous voice. "I know I nearly lost my mind some years ago, but I don't need coddling anymore."

"I know that, Anju, but I'm upset at myself for not being a better businessman." He sent Anjali a rueful look. "I suppose I didn't want to believe it myself at first. It's not easy admitting to one's daughter that one is . . . uh . . . a failure."

She immediately regretted her outburst. "I'm sorry, Dad. You're not a failure. It's not all your fault. We're all in this together."

"But still . . ."

"I'm just as much to blame," she said. "I should have kept an eye on our finances a bit more. What I can't believe is why you went to Jeevan of all people for help."

"Jeevan is my eldest brother. Who else could I go to when we're in financial trouble?" He combed his long, skinny fingers through his hair for the fourth time since Anjali had walked into the store minutes ago. His nervous raking was making his hair stand up in stiff peaks, making him look like one of those troll dolls sold in novelty stores. His starched blue shirt and gray slacks paired with sensible black shoes did little to improve the troll image.

"You could have gone to that old man, the Indian capitalist with three wives . . . What's his name . . . Harikishan."

Usha Kapadia, Anjali's mother, gave a derisive, unladylike snort. "After killing off his first two wives, old Harikishan has met his match. His third wife is young and pretty and smart. She keeps him . . . um . . . occupied," she remarked, clearing her throat. "He's not interested in pursuing the financing business anymore."

"How about Naren-kaka?" Naren Kapadia was her father's youngest brother.

Her father shook his head. "Naren has a large debt on his motel. You know that."

"Then why not go to a legitimate bank?" Anjali suggested.

"Instead, you called your other brother Jeevan, in India?" She still couldn't make sense of her parents' wacky decision.

"Your uncle's got the best business brain in the world," her father argued.

"But Jeevan's a dictator."

Her mother, trim and elegant in a shell-pink chiffon sari, and tiny pearls at her throat and ears, threw her a scorching look. "Anju, Jeevan is your oldest uncle. Show your elders some respect. And stop referring to him as Jeevan. To you he's Jeevan-kaka, just like he's Jeevan-bhai to your father and me."

"I'm sorry." Anjali sighed. From her mother's tone one would think Anjali was a teenager or young adult at most. Their family business, essentially their livelihood, was headed for ruin, and her mother was lecturing her, a grown woman, on the old-fashioned Gujarati way of talking about one's uncle. "You know as well as I that Jeevan-kaka is bad news, Mom." He was a short, tubby, beady-eyed scoundrel who sat atop a mountain of money. He was rich and mean and sly and unscrupulous—a lethal combination.

Jeevan was the oldest of three brothers and two sisters, and never let his siblings forget it. In his eyes, he was only one small step below God. At the mention of his name, the family trembled with fear. With a simple phone call he could reduce some of them to tears. Most often, when someone in the family mentioned Jeevan's name, it was preceded by "Oh, God," and rightfully so.

Mohan shook his head. "Jeevan-bhai is a little bit on the strict side. That doesn't mean he's unkind."

"*Little* bit strict?" Anjali groaned. Was her father living on the same planet as she? She looked at him. The shape and deep brown tint of their eyes were similar, and the thick black lashes were definitely something she'd inherited from him. In fact, most of her sharp features were her father's, but her complexion and straight black hair were genetic traits from her mother's side of the family. "After the beating you took from him as the middle brother, you still choose to defend him, Dad?"

This time Mohan's eyes glinted with irritation. "You of all people, with your fancy college degrees, should realize we have major financial problems. We need some serious help and advice. Who better than your uncle to give it? Everything your uncle touches turns to gold."

Her mom gave another scornful snort. "That's why they call him *Bada saheb*." Big boss. Despite admonishing Anjali about her lack of respect for Jeevan, her mom had plenty of contempt for her eldest and most feared brother-in-law. But then Usha always had a different set of rules for herself. And they changed frequently according to her convenience and mood.

Having expressed her sentiments, her mother turned around to cast a quick glance in the mirrored wall and patted her hair, which was swept back into a simple but elegant chignon. Then she went back to arranging the new shipment of jewelry in the display case—earrings, bracelets, and rings made of rare yellow diamonds.

Anjali watched her mom's dainty fingers gently lift each piece and arrange it over the sapphire blue velvet spread. Having grown up in a family of jewelers, Usha knew her gems well. And at fifty-nine she looked wonderful—much younger than her age.

"Whatever my brother's faults, he has the knowledge and money to help us," said Mohan, picking up his calculator and gathering up the day's receipts. "And his advice is free."

Anjali mulled over the issue for a minute. There had to be another, less drastic solution than the insufferable Jeevan. "Can't you call him again and tell him you were wrong?"

"No." Her father shook his head emphatically.

"Say you made an error in judgment and that everything's just fine?"

Mohan gave her a bland look. "I can't. He's arriving here next week."

"What?" A dull thud jolted both Anjali and her father. Usha had dropped a box on the counter and turned dark, accusing eyes on her husband. "You didn't tell me your brother was coming *here*."

"I thought I did." Mohan's tone was mildly apologetic.

"Not true, Mohan," Usha reminded him. "This morning, when you called your brother, you said you were asking for a little advice and nothing more. You didn't say anything about him coming to New Jersey."

"Slipped my mind . . . I guess." Ordinarily a resolute man with a good head for business, Anjali's father seemed to turn to putty when his beloved Usha was around. Despite her sweet face, dimpled smile, and her preference for soft colors and understated accessories, she wielded the gavel like a seasoned judge. It was a good thing, too, because Anjali's dad was too softhearted. If it were up to him, he'd give away half the store to someone he thought was needy.

She watched the angry color rise in her mother's amazingly unlined face. "Slipped your mind? Something as important as that?"

"But . . . but he said he wanted to come. How could I say no?"

"Exactly when is Jeevan-bhai arriving?" Usha demanded. "Or were you planning to tell me after he arrived at Newark Airport?"

Anjali had a feeling her father had deliberately kept his brother's visit a secret. She felt a twinge of sympathy for her dad. The poor man was caught between his loyalties to his brother on the one hand and his wife and kids on the other.

"But there's still one more week," he mumbled weakly. "He's arriving next Monday."

"Next Monday is only five days away, not one week," reminded Usha.

Mohan ran his fingers through his hair yet again. What little hair had been lying flat now stood at attention. "Jeevan-bhai is family. Why are you getting so upset?"

Usha's look of annoyance turned to disbelief. "Your brother is not some ordinary family member like the others; he is a god. Once he descends from his chariot he wants everything perfect, from homemade vegetarian food cooked in clarified butter and spotless white sheets to his newspaper available at a precise time every morning. And don't forget hot *masala chai* five times a day. I'll have to dedicate myself to serving him hand and foot."

If there was one thing Anjali couldn't picture her mother doing, it was waiting on someone hand and foot. Raised in indulged affluence in the city of Ahmedabad, and being the only girl in a family with four boys, she was a prima donna. Her brothers doted on her.

Though Usha was a good cook, she preferred working in the store and depended on restaurant food to feed the family most of the time. It was the simplest and most efficient thing to do, anyway, with literally dozens of Indian restaurants serving any kind of reasonably priced multiregional cuisine, literally within walking distance from their store.

Every night, after locking up, Anjali and her parents, too exhausted to worry about cooking, bought restaurant food and toted it home. After eating, they barely had energy left to get changed and head for their beds in their modest house in neighboring Iselin. Despite keeping the store closed on Mondays, the boutique was a 24/7 commitment for the three of them. It was their whole life.

Anjali couldn't bear to think of any other way of life. She'd had her own home and a career separate from her parents many moons ago, while she'd been married to Vikram Gandhi. But after Vik's death, heartbroken and depressed, she'd decided to pool all her savings with her parents' and upgrade their struggling sari shop in Edison.

Now the boutique was everything to her, a place where she'd buried her grief and more or less resurrected herself. It had helped to have a challenging business to keep her mind occupied, the best kind of therapy for a grieving young widow.

Her brother, Nilesh, a sophomore at Rutgers University, had always distanced himself from the clothing business. Nearly eighteen years younger than she, and an unexpected late-life baby for her parents, he could be a joy as well as an annoyance.

Nilesh was both her brother and her baby in so many ways.

She'd babysat him, changed his diapers, held him when he'd been sick, and bottle-fed him. And yet she and Nilesh argued and snarled and threw barbs at each other like any other siblings. She loved him to pieces. She'd never had children of her own, so he was still her baby. Of course, there'd been no opportunity for Anjali to think about having babies, not when Vik had died of a brain aneurysm within two years of their marriage.

"Anju." Usha's voice forced her thoughts back to the cold reality of their present situation. "Could you come here and finish this display for me? I have to get busy cleaning up the house." She threw her husband a meaningful look. "Since Jeevan-bhai is arriving in five . . . no . . . four and a half days," she said with a glance at her wristwatch, "I have to clean, shop, cook, and launder . . . and iron."

Anjali noticed her father's harried expression. *Poor Dad.*

Usha strode away in a huff to the back of the store, then returned a minute later with her pocketbook on her arm and the car keys jangling in her hand. Putting on her driving glasses, she swept out the front door. Anjali and her father watched her disappear into the parking lot, then exchanged a troubled glance.

In about two hours her mother would have shopped for the essentials, stored them away in the kitchen, cleaned and vacuumed the house, and aired the guest room mattress. Usha Kapadia was like a tornado when she was on a mission, especially when she was upset or angry. And Jeevan's visit definitely qualified as both upsetting and annoying. Besides, Anjali knew exactly how her mother felt; she felt the same way herself. The last time Jeevan had visited some five years ago, her mother, just recovering from a hysterectomy, had nearly suffered a mental breakdown.

After a four-week visit, it had been the most blessed relief to put the chubby Jeevan and his wife on a jet bound for India.

Anjali observed her father pull up a stool and sit down with his elbows parked on the counter. "So, Dad, what exactly is Jeevan-kaka coming all the way to the U.S. to do?" she asked.

Mohan's expression was one of tired resignation. His messy hair tugged gently at Anjali's heart. "He's going to take a look at the boutique, then decide what we should do. He promised he'll help us financially, too."

"His fortune's in rupees, so how's he going to help in dollars?"

"Rupees can easily be converted to any foreign currency these days."

Anjali's chin instinctively snapped up. "We're not going to accept his charity, I hope?"

Mohan gave a wry laugh. "Jeevan-bhai believes in loans, not charitable contributions. He's a businessman, Anju, not a philanthropist."

"So do you think we might be able to save the store?"

He shrugged. "I don't know. I really hope so. This store is all I have. All *we* have."

"I'm sorry, Dad. Until last year, things had looked pretty good. Our profit margin wasn't great, but it wasn't critical."

Rising from his stool, Mohan went to the open display case where his wife had been working and started emptying out the small jewelry boxes onto the counter. "Too much competition in the immediate area. Other stores have started to copy our boutique concept and exclusive designs. The trouble is they get both their materials and manufacturing much cheaper from India."

"I know." Anjali and her parents got their goods from Bangkok, the U.S., and Hong Kong. It made a huge difference in pricing. "But their quality and style are nowhere near ours, Dad. Their stores are merely gaudy imitations. It's like comparing a diamond to rhinestones."

"Even then—"

"Wasn't it just the other day that a customer was complaining that something she bought from one of our competitors lost its color and most of its beads after a single cleaning?"

"But most customers go for surface looks. When they can pay $500 instead of $1,500 for an outfit, the last thing they think of is color loss or the beads falling off. How many times

do people take such fancy garments to the cleaners anyway?"
He positioned the last diamond ring in between a necklace and
its matching bracelet, then shut the glass door and locked it.

Her father was right. Even before he'd explained it, she knew
what the problem was. She just didn't want to admit it. They'd
overextended themselves with the present year's inventory, too.
The store was packed with beautiful things, but not enough customers to buy them. Most of it was her fault. On seeing the
striking new silks in Thailand, she'd gone a bit overboard with
her orders for *chania-choli* outfits. Long flowing skirts with
matching blouses. Then she'd requested her uncles in India to
craft jewelry to match those ensembles.

Despite her training, she'd made the grave mistake of neglect-
ing the financial end of the business and left it entirely to her father. He was a smart businessman but she still should have kept
her eye on the bottom line.

Unfortunately, her heart was in creating pretty things and not
in finances. But no matter what her reasons, it was still partly
her fault. It wasn't fair to let her father take the blame.

Mohan returned to his bookkeeping chores, so Anjali moved
to the sari section and started to unpack the new boxes of
Benaresi silk saris that had arrived that morning. Even before
she could slit the carton with a box-cutter, she knew the goods
would be beautiful. She'd hand-picked every one of them during
her recent trip to India and supervised the packaging herself.

Reverently she unwrapped each exquisite sari from its tissue
paper and placed it inside the glass cabinet. This place used to be
just a sari shop at one time—boring, bland, dimly lit—one of count-
less such shops that lined Oak Tree Road. Her parents had sold
Japanese-made synthetic saris wound in bolts and crammed
onto shelves alongside the most uninspiring mass-produced clothes.

Back in the 1970s, as a child, Anjali had enjoyed going to her
parents' old Jackson Heights store in New York City. Every afternoon, after school, she'd done her homework in the crowded
back room. That cramped space had also served as her parents'
office. A desk and chair, a file cabinet, and a portable electric

stove for warming up lunch and making *chai* had left room for little else. She'd loved wandering around the shop, touching the fabrics and draping them over herself, slipping into the high-heeled and jeweled sandals on display, pretending she was a fashion model.

Then her parents had relocated to Edison in the 1980s because it was a brand-new Indian enclave with more promise and less competition. However, even after the move, the store's name and general appearance had remained the same. Her parents were bright people, but creativity was not their strong point. She was a teenager by then and had come to view the business more objectively. It needed to be much more than Kapadia's Sari Emporium.

Somewhere between the ninth and tenth grades, she'd decided to try her hand at dress designing. Helping her parents at the shop combined with her eye for color and shapes had naturally progressed into a degree in apparel design and merchandising, and further into plans for joining her parents' business someday.

But fate had taken her on a slight detour. Soon after graduate school she'd met Vikram Gandhi, fallen for his boyish good looks and sunny nature, and then married him. His career was in New York, so instead of working for her parents she'd found a job at an advertising agency in the city.

She'd been happy, though, content with her condo in Queens, her marriage to Vik, and life in general. Back then she'd had big dreams of owning several elegant boutiques all over the country—maybe in other countries, too. With typical youthful enthusiasm she'd had it all figured out.

Although Vik was an electronics engineer by profession, he had encouraged her retail dreams, even shared in them. And just when they thought they'd saved enough money to start working on bringing those dreams to reality, Vik had collapsed at his office, and died soon after. His only symptom had been waking up with a severe headache that morning.

They'd had no idea that a silent killer had been stalking Vik for many years. He had swallowed a couple of aspirin and gone to work despite the acute headache. By the time the ambulance had arrived, he'd hemorrhaged to death. All her dreams had died with him. So much for drawing up a neat blueprint of her life. The only solace was that he hadn't suffered too long.

Seeing her drowning in grief, her parents had encouraged her to quit her job in New York, sell her condo, live with them, and help them with the store, which was best suited for her training and disposition anyway. Even Vik's parents had seen the logic in that and supported her decision. Little by little she'd overcome her sorrow and made her parents' business a success.

Unfortunately, along the way, she'd drifted away from Vik's parents and his married sister. Anyhow, Florida was too far to visit often.

Eventually she'd sunk all of her and Vik's joint savings into upgrading and glamorizing the store, and making it a show-piece—Silk & Sapphires. The grand opening was written about in all the local newspapers. Magazines had run articles about the new ethnic dream store in the heart of Little India. With all that helpful buzz customers had crowded in, and the business had done extremely well.

But now it looked like all that hype and hard work were for naught. Anjali and her parents were in danger of losing their boutique. Her dad had estimated that if they didn't start turning a profit within the next six to nine months, they might have to sell, or worse, declare bankruptcy.

They'd never been exactly rich, but they'd been comfortable. Her education had been entirely paid for by her parents, and at this late age they were paying Nilesh's college bills.

They still lived in a decent home and drove late-model cars. Going from relative middle-class comfort to possible bank-ruptcy was inconceivable to Anjali. What in heaven's name were they going to do if things got really bad?

She closed her eyes and tried to dispel the dark image of po-tential poverty. *No. Please, God, no.*

Despite all her initial ranting at the idea of having the autocratic Jeevan come down to stick his large nose into their private affairs, when faced with the frightening prospect of bankruptcy, Anjali was beginning to have second thoughts. She'd also had a little while to simmer down.

Maybe the old curmudgeon would be of some use after all. Her dad was right. There was never any doubt that Jeevan had a gift for business. He had the uncanny combined instincts of a lion, a bloodhound, and a fox.

Placing the last sari in the cabinet, Anjali looked at her wristwatch. It was nearly closing time. She needed to get her mind off work and business—and her uncle's impending visit. Maybe she'd call Kip and meet him later over a drink. He'd help her relax.

For lack of a better term, she thought of Kip as her boyfriend. He was her friend for sure, a patient pal, her lover, and a comfort to have at times. But he wasn't a boyfriend in the true sense of the word. Their relationship was neither sweet nor romantic. It didn't involve whispered sweet nothings, flowers or chocolates, holding hands, or walks in the moonlight. It was just a friendship with some free drinks and sex thrown in when it was mutually convenient.

She'd been seeing Kip Rowling secretly for nearly two years, mainly because widowhood was lonely and frustrating. All her Indian girlfriends were married and enjoying husbands, homes, and children. They were involved in a variety of careers, too. As a single woman who worked seven days a week, Anjali didn't fit into their social circle anymore. She was the odd one out, the one to be pitied and condescended, and occasionally the one to be eyed with suspicion as a potential husband snatcher.

She had some non-Indian girlfriends—women she'd gone to college with. They were single like her, but they'd never been married. She got together with them for drinks or dinner once in a while. But she didn't have any close friends. Her work was her life.

Although she was a mature woman, in charge of her own life, if her parents ever found out about Kip, a white Protestant guy who owned a bar and lounge in the heart of New Brunswick, had little formal education, and wore an earring in one ear, she'd be in deep trouble. Respectable Gujarati women with solid family values, especially thirty-seven-year-old Hindu widows, weren't expected to fraternize with barkeepers.

She was lucky to be born and raised in the U.S. If this was India, she'd probably have to live the semi-reclusive life of a widow. Widows were supposed to keep their inauspicious shadow from falling over the rest of society and bringing a similar curse upon it. Indian society had evolved considerably in the past decade or so, but widows still had a rough life over there.

All the Indian guys her parents and relatives tried to fix her up with wanted marriage, but she was afraid of marriage after what had happened to Vik. A few of those men were widowed, or even divorced, but almost all of them had kids, and she didn't want to play mom to anyone's children, not when her life was consumed by business.

It wasn't that she disliked children. She'd hoped to have her own when she was married to Vik, but that dream, too, had become a blur and then vanished.

Besides, so far, every Gujarati man she'd been introduced to had turned out as interesting as plain boiled potatoes. They all lacked sophistication. *Desis*—countrymen—as Indians in America affectionately referred to themselves, were a homogenous bunch of people—essentially decent, honest, hardworking, and obsessively goal-oriented, but the one thing about them that bored Anjali to tears was their lack of humor. They laughed at others and felt no guilt at ridiculing the guy next door, but they could never poke fun at themselves.

Vik was different. She had yet to meet another Indian man with a self-deprecating sense of humor like Vik's. Because of his highly recognizable last name, folks had often asked him if he was related to Mahatma Gandhi or Indira Gandhi. His stock answer used to be, "I'm related to both, except no one seemed to recognize my potential for political greatness or martyrdom, so I ended up in engineering school." With his deadpan response, he'd always ended up getting a chuckle out of people.

And now there was Kip Rowling—a fun guy. He could make

an idiot of himself and then laugh about it. She liked that about him, not to mention the fact that he was sexy as hell and made her bones melt into a puddle of warm soup with a single touch. She hadn't experienced that kind of sexual high in years. At the moment, though, she badly needed a good belly laugh. And a roll between the sheets sounded pretty good, too.

Noticing her father still engrossed in his receipts, she quietly pulled her cell phone out of her pocket and slinked away through the rear door out into the parking lot. And she dialed Kip's number.

Chapter 2

Anjali maneuvered her compact black sedan around Oak Tree Road's busiest intersection. Even this late on a Wednesday evening, when most of the businesses were either closed or in the process of closing, the street was thick with traffic.

Pedestrians crossed the street at leisure and she had to keep a careful eye on them. Many of them behaved as if they were still in their native India, where traffic rules were made mostly to be disregarded. Some even appeared to derive perverse joy out of thumbing their noses at pedestrian crossing signs and honking cars. The same people who were willing to obey the laws two miles outside this neighborhood seemed to lose all sense of civic awareness when they set foot in Little India.

By the time she got to New Brunswick, a mild headache was beginning to set in, probably because she hadn't eaten since breakfast. She'd lied to her parents that she was going to meet some friends for dinner.

An old Beatles tune greeted her as she entered the Rowling Rok Bar & Lounge. The air inside was warm and humid. The bitter, yeasty smell of beer and a mix of perfumes hung in the air. Wednesday was "Ladies' Night." Women could buy drinks for half price. The place was comfortably filled with females of various ages but very few men. The hum of chatter was loud enough to muffle the music. The giant TV screen was off.

She headed straight for the bar that Kip was tending. He grinned and waved at her, motioning to her to grab a stool at the counter. A few seconds later, he put a tall glass of rum and cola in her hand. It was the only thing she drank and he knew it well.

"Hi, Angelface. You look a bit peaked," he said and pinched her cheek briefly. "Hungry?" He pushed a bowl of pretzels toward her. "Want Billy to fry you some mozzarella sticks?"

Shaking her head, she gratefully took a thirsty gulp of her drink along with an aspirin tablet she'd dug out of her pocketbook. Mixing aspirin, cola, and alcohol wasn't very prudent, but she was too tired to care about prudence this evening. In about twenty minutes her headache was likely to fade away.

She observed Kip return to his task and deftly handle several orders. He was so darn good at that. She often wondered how he could remember the recipes for all those exotic cocktails and stay even-tempered on the busiest of days. He always served with a smile and a friendly word. Even the most difficult customers, including the inebriated and abusive ones, turned to putty in his large, capable hands.

Kip had a way with people. With the number of customers in the bar tonight, it didn't seem like he'd have much time for her. Just as well, she concluded. She wasn't in much of a social mood. Maybe she shouldn't have come at all. Why impose her drab sentiments on Kip?

But when there was a slight lull at the bar, Kip returned to her. Twirling a lock of her long dark hair around his index finger, he tugged gently. "What's the matter? Had a bad day?"

She took a sip from her glass and stared vacantly at the crowded display of liquor bottles on the long shelf with its mirrored backsplash. She'd come here to forget her woes, but neither the prattling crowd in the bar nor the rum in her cola had helped so far.

A drink with more punch to it would have been nice to get smashed with, but common sense told her it would solve nothing. In fact, she'd be hungover and even more miserable the next day. And facing her mom and dad's looks of shocked disappointment at seeing her drunk would be a whole lot worse. Instead she brought her gaze back to focus on Kip. "Sorry. I'm rotten company tonight."

"Something bothering you?"

"A little."

"Want to talk about it?"

"It's just some . . . well . . . family stuff. I'm not sure I should burden you with it, Kip."

"What are friends for, babe?" He leaned forward, elbows braced on the counter, his face cupped in his hands, his eyes studying hers. "About this family stuff, let me guess. Did your old man tell you to pitch in with the housework?"

"Not even close." Kip always teased her about what a pampered life she led.

"Um . . . let's see. Your parents aren't having another baby, are they?" His bright green eyes twinkled with suppressed humor. The fact that she had a brother nearly young enough to be her son seemed to amuse Kip.

"Not funny." Tonight she wasn't in a mood for Kip's sardonic wit. His tall, athletic build and raw masculinity rarely failed to heat her blood, but at the moment she looked with little interest at the way his T-shirt stretched across his wide chest and shoulders, or the way his snug jeans hugged his slim hips and sinewy legs. "I have real problems."

"Sorry." His voice turned serious. "Why don't you tell Uncle Kip? He's got a nice big shoulder to cry on."

After a quick survey of the room, she shook her head. "Too many people. I think I'll just go home." She didn't want to yell to be heard above the buzz, despite Kip's offer of a sympathetic ear. Just because she was feeling blue it wasn't fair to expect him to drop everything and console her.

"Don't go yet. I could ask Billy to watch the bar for a few minutes," he suggested. Despite his laid-back ways, he was a perceptive man. He must have guessed she was in genuine distress.

"Uh . . . if you're sure." Anjali slid off the stool and picked up her glass. "Shall I wait for you at the empty corner booth?"

"No, let's go out to the patio in the back. It's too damn hot in here." He pressed a button on the intercom system located beneath the counter and called the guy in the kitchen. When he heard Billy's muffled response, he said, "Can you cover for me for a little bit?"

"Yeah. Be there in a minute," was the reply.

Meanwhile Kip went to the coffeemaker and poured himself a cup.

Anjali cast an eye around the lounge. The patrons were scattered in small groups. One of the tables was occupied by what looked like young Indian women, most likely graduate students. They'd been eyeing her curiously since the moment she'd walked in. But she was used to it, that puzzled look reserved for a brown-skinned woman who walked into a bar alone and then sat on a bar stool and flirted with the bartender.

Rowling Rok wasn't very large, but it was lucrative. From what Kip had told her, he'd inherited it from his late grandfather.

The business seemed to have worked out great for him. He had renovated the ancient bar, put in the giant television set for sports fans, and introduced live music on weekends to replace the old jukebox. Several performers including different types of amateur bands performed regularly to cater to the diverse ethnic groups that frequented his bar. He even had an Indian *Bhangra* group once a month. The pulsing beat of north Indian *Bhangra* music was perfect for fast dancing.

Billy came out of the kitchen, wiping the sweat off his brow with a napkin. Billy Rowling was a stocky blond man in his early forties, with a deceptively mean sneer on his round face. Maybe it came from having served in the Marine Corps for many years. In reality he was a sweet but reserved man. He served as short-order cook, bouncer, and substitute bartender. He was Kip's cousin, right-hand man, friend, and business partner, all rolled into one handy package.

Billy cracked a rare smile at Anjali. "Hi, didn't know you were here."

Anjali returned the greeting. "Good to see you, Billy."

"Likewise," he said before turning to a customer claiming his attention.

Kip flipped open the hinged counter flap meant for employees to get behind the bar and pulled her in, then ushered her through the cluttered kitchen and out the back door. The aroma of mozzarella sticks and roasted peanuts followed them outside.

The rear patio was a small but neat square of concrete, enclosed by a six-foot-high brick wall. A picnic table and two benches were the only outdoor furniture. The temperature outside was refreshingly cool. Kip was right: it was too hot inside although it was only June and summer had barely begun.

They sat on a bench side by side, leaning against the edge of the table, their backs to the building. Anjali still nursed her drink while Kip sipped his coffee and stretched his long legs out in front of him, crossed at the ankles. He never drank alcohol while on duty and expected his staff to do the same.

He slipped a comforting arm around her shoulders. "So what's bugging you, kid?"

She stared at the row of trash cans lined up like dark sentries standing guard against the wall and took a deep, shuddering breath. "We might lose the store, Kip."

"Your old man's selling the place?"

"He might be forced to," she said. "Financial problems."

His arm tightened around her. "How did *that* happen?"

"It's been happening for a while. We've been expanding our inventory, hoping the increase in Indian weddings and upscale parties would mean more business, but that hasn't happened. Sales are low. I was too careless to notice and my dad was too optimistic to take it seriously until now."

"I thought your shop was booming. Every year there are more Indian people moving into Jersey, aren't there? I see them everywhere."

"That also means more competition," she reminded him. "Other stores like ours have mushroomed. Ours was the only exclusive boutique at first, but now there are copycats within a stone's throw. Dad says if we don't turn a profit soon, we'll go bankrupt." Her voice cracked a little. The tears were hovering close to the surface.

Kip remained silent for a minute or two. "Your dad's a smart businessman. I'm sure he'll think of a way," he said softly.

He sounded warm and sympathetic and Anjali instinctively leaned closer against him. Kip was right. He had a big shoulder to cry on, but she quelled the urge to burst into noisy sobs. It would ruin her makeup and make her eyes look like boiled shrimp. She knew she had a passably attractive face and nice eyes, but she just couldn't cry prettily like some women.

Kip smelled of his usual spicy cologne and coffee and cigarette smoke—a blended scent that she'd come to like a lot. It was potent and very male. Very arousing. "Yeah, Dad thought of a way all right. It'll kill us all."

"He's hired someone to torch the place?" Kip turned to her with wide, stunned eyes.

"No!" She threw him a horrified frown. "How could you even think that?"

"Well, I figured—"

"You figured wrong," she retorted, interrupting him. "My dad's a decent and principled guy. He'd never dream of arson and insurance fraud."

"I grew up in a rough neighborhood; my thinking's warped." Kip squeezed her arm. "I apologize."

She slumped against him once again. "In some ways it's worse than torching the place. My rich uncle, Dad's eldest brother, is arriving next week from India to assess the situation."

"All the way from India?"

"He's some kind of business mastermind."

"Well, that explains it." Kip chuckled. "A nice, rich uncle—Daddy Warbucks, or is it Uncle Warbucks? I thought rich uncles were a cliché. Most of us don't have one of those, you know."

"No, some of us have rich grandfathers who hand down flourishing bars," she mocked.

Kip's chuckle turned into a laugh, a rich masculine sound

that was both droll and seductive. "Guess I deserved that. So what can Uncle Warbucks do that your father can't?"

"Dad thinks his brother might have some fresh ideas to save the business and even pump some money into it. Strictly a loan, of course. My uncle's a notorious Scrooge."

"Rich *and* stingy?"

"Jeevan Kapadia's not rich; he's loaded."

"Is that what's getting you down?" He ruffled her hair with his fingers.

"That and everything else. Mom's going to be impossible to live with as long as my uncle Jeevan is here. The last time he came to stay, she nearly ended up in an institution."

Kip let out a low whistle. "Mean son of a bitch. Want me to get rid of him for you?"

"Don't start planting ideas in my head, Kip."

"I have connections."

"It sounds awfully tempting, but he's not *that* bad," she replied on a laugh, realizing she was feeling a little better. The headache was finally wearing off. Kip's warm hand traveled from her shoulder to the nape of her neck and made firm, circular motions that she found deeply soothing. "Mmm . . . that feels great." She sighed as he continued to rub and knead her skin and follow a downward path all the way to the small of her back. Kip had great hands, large and hard but not too rough. At the moment he was making her purr like a well-coddled kitten.

Suddenly her breath came to a standstill before lurching back into a jerky rhythm. His hand had circled around her rib cage and wound itself about her right breast. She turned her head and looked up at him. Sure enough, he was staring at her with a gleam in his eyes. The tiny diamond in his earlobe glinted in the muted glow cast by the streetlight beyond the wall. "You are one hell of a beautiful woman, Angelface," he murmured.

Anjali shivered. Lord, but Kip had a way of getting her excited. With his long fingers caressing her through the thin fabric of her silk blouse and lacy bra, and the expression on his face looking like he wanted to devour her whole, it was hard not to surrender to the urge to let him have her.

So she did. Somehow she always did—despite the lectures on caution she delivered to herself time and again.

Kip had a breathless effect on her. He was different. At forty-six, a full nine years older than she, he was a suave, practiced lover who knew how to pleasure a woman while pleasing himself in the process. She'd never asked him how many women he'd slept with. As long as he wore protection, what did it matter?

He was her one outlet from long hours of work and the strict, puritanical atmosphere of her home. Her parents would never understand something like the basic, carnal needs of a young woman. All they knew was how not to talk about sex and to satisfy anything remotely sexual within the sanctity of a nice, neat marriage bed concealed behind locked doors.

And Anjali didn't have that luxury.

She wasn't in love with Kip, thank goodness. Her feelings for him were based on lust and genuine affection. He was a confirmed bachelor and way too independent for her to think about anything permanent with him. Besides, in her old-fashioned Gujarati environment, Kip would stick out like Mount Everest planted amidst gentle, rolling hills.

And Kip never concealed the fact that he liked women—all colors, nationalities and religious affiliations included. His only criterion seemed to be beauty. As long as he thought a woman looked good, and she was able and willing to put out, Kip was available.

How had she, a second-generation Indian-American widow raised in a conservative family, ended up with a Don Juan like Kip?

She had stepped into Rowling Rok one night with two of her girlfriends on a Ladies' Night. She'd been wearing one of her own designs, a sleek peach silk dress that did wonders for her complexion and long dark hair.

When she'd gone up to the bar for a refill, Kip had flirted wildly with her. "So, are you an angel descended from heaven or am I dreaming?" he'd asked with a wicked glint of humor in his eyes. They were a rich shade of green she'd never seen before.

"I'm very human, thank you," she'd replied warily, despite the heady feeling of being thoroughly surveyed by a pair of sexy, roving eyes that had turned warm with appreciation, like liquid emeralds.

"So, what's your name, pretty lady?"

"Why do you want to know?" she'd challenged him, trying to put as much starch into her voice as possible. She wasn't about to give her name or anything else to a flirtatious wolf with the most beautifully sculpted body and an incredible smile.

He had chuckled, the sound making Anjali want to reach across the counter and touch his face to see if it was as delightfully raspy as it looked with its late-evening shadow. "I make it my business to find out who comes into my lair."

There, she was right: he was a wicked wolf. "So you own this . . . lair?" She'd pretended to throw a casually critical glance around the room. Although she'd liked the warm, polished oak paneling, the friendly atmosphere, the framed prints of the Jersey coast, and the cozy lighting, she'd managed to appear indifferent.

"Yeah, I'm Kip Rowling, lord and keeper of Rowling Rok," he'd replied and put his hand forward for a handshake.

There was no way to avoid a friendly gesture like that. So with her slim hand placed in his large, hard grasp, she'd aimed a hesitant smile at him. "I'm Anjali Kapadia. Nice to meet you, lord and keeper of Rowling Rok."

He'd pretended to clutch his heart and gasp, making her giggle. "An-ja-li? As in An-gel-face? I knew it. I knew you were an angel from heaven."

After the introduction he'd invited her to sit at the bar stool instead of returning immediately to her table and they'd talked for several minutes. He was a delectable surprise, a much-needed one after a very long dry spell with no men and no amusement in her life. Despite her efforts to keep a rein on her emotions, she'd lost a bit of her heart to Kip that night. And given him her cell phone number.

Following the entertaining chatter with Kip, she'd returned to her table, only to be teased mercilessly by her friends about the cute bartender with the kissable mouth and gorgeous eyes. Then, surprisingly, Kip had called her the following week and invited her to his bar once again for drinks. Within a short time she'd found herself visiting him at least twice a week after work.

She always told her parents she was going out with her girlfriends, and they didn't seem to mind as long as she got home by midnight and was at the store before ten o'clock the next morning. They were naïve enough to believe she was merely enjoying the company of other single women.

Within months of getting to know Kip, Anjali had wound up in his bed. And she wasn't surprised at all. Kip was that kind of guy—all masculine charm, hard muscle, and the sexual finesse of a male courtesan. He could seduce a woman with a mere lift of an eyebrow.

The first time it had happened she'd been drinking too much. It wasn't a legitimate excuse but she liked to think it was. It was a lapse in judgment—and it happened more often than her conscience was comfortable with.

Now, as always, Kip led her upstairs to his apartment. It was no more than a small office with an adjoining bedroom and bath—his home away from home. It was a place to do his bookkeeping, to rest, to unwind. His love nest.

At first she'd felt awkward and embarrassed about sleeping with a man who had no sense of morality. He'd made no promises to her and never tried to hide the fact that the comfortable, king-sized bed in that room saw plenty of action. But then she'd realized she was no better, especially when compared with other *Desi* women her own age.

Some thirty minutes later, feeling somewhat less stressed and wearing the glow of recent sex—scorching, toe-tingling, mind-numbing sex—she kissed Kip good-bye. "Thanks, I feel a lot better."

He chuckled. "My pleasure, Angelface."

She descended the stairs and went around the side of the building to the parking lot. As always, after one of her trysts with Kip, she felt a deep sense of shame and guilt sweep over her. She was a sensible businesswoman raised in an orthodox

Hindu household, and yet it seemed like she was seeking out cheap thrills.

What was the matter with her? Was it only loneliness that goaded her into a secret liaison with a man like Kip? Or was she a nymphomaniac? How did other women cope with what she was going through?

If she paid heed to her parents' advice and married a decent man, she could have all the sex she wanted and put an end to the loneliness. She could have love and warmth and a sense of belonging. And yet, lifelong commitment was not what she wanted at this time. *Face it, Anjali,* she told herself. *You're different from other Indian women. You're free-spirited and your libido is a tad too active. Learn to live with it.*

Slipping behind the wheel of her car, she turned on the ignition. At the moment there were more pressing things to worry about than her seemingly out-of-control libido.

A large asteroid named Jeevan was hurtling toward the United States. And she had to brace herself for the impact.

Chapter 3

By early Monday morning, Usha had the house in order. Every dust bunny and cobweb had been eradicated, the carpets professionally cleaned, and the guest bed had fresh white sheets and pillows and a brand-new blanket and bedspread.

Lunch was prepared and waiting on the stove. The refrigerator was stocked with fresh vegetables and fruit, plenty of milk and yogurt. A glass jar of pure *ghee*—clarified butter—sat on the kitchen counter, cooling off.

Anjali stood in the kitchen doorway and watched her mother scrub the pan in which she'd made the *ghee*. The entire house was imbued with its sweet scent.

Poor Mom. She looked like she'd lost weight in the past few days from working like a fiend in both the store and the house before Jeevan-kaka's scheduled arrival later that morning. Anjali had done her part to help out, but her mother was a perfectionist and preferred to do most of it herself. She also liked playing the martyr.

The June sky looked overcast. It suited the mood in the Kapadia home, except for Anjali's father. His eyes seemed to glow in anticipation of seeing his brother after a five-year interval.

Probably sensing her presence, her mother turned around to give her a quick glance. "Your father's whistling," she sniffed.

"Yes." Anjali had distinctly heard him whistling a jolly tune upstairs a little while ago. She'd hoped her mother hadn't heard the buoyant sound, something they weren't accustomed to hearing from the serious Mohan. Now it only served to make her mother crankier. But at least her dad was in a jubilant mood.

Anjali walked up to the pantry, poured a bowl of cornflakes and a glass of orange juice.

Setting the washed pot in the dish drainer, her mother dried her hands and studied Anjali. "You were out late last night."

"I . . . saw my friends after a long time . . . and we talked." Since when had lying come so easily to her? After her return from seeing Kip, once again, she'd sneaked up to her room. She had tried to convince herself that she wasn't hurting anyone. Both Kip and she were single; they were free to enjoy each other with no strings attached. And this was America, where consensual sex between responsible adults was the norm. However, sleep had still eluded her.

"You don't look all that well." Her mother's assessing look lingered on her.

"I'm okay, Mom. You're the one who looks beat."

Usha took off her apron and sank into the kitchen chair opposite Anjali's. "Jeevan-bhai is enough to make anyone weary."

Anjali poured milk over her cornflakes and added a spoonful of sugar. "Why don't you eat some breakfast? It'll make you feel better."

Ever conscious of maintaining her figure, Usha shook her head. "Every morsel makes me fat. Ever since that hysterectomy, my metabolism seems to have shut down. I think I'll have another cup of tea instead."

"You drink too much tea and don't eat enough. It's not good for you, Mom."

"Oh, stop fussing about my diet, Anju. Do you want a cup of tea or not?" When Anjali shook her head Usha got up and walked toward the foot of the staircase to call out to her husband. "Mohan, do you want a cup of tea?"

"Yes," replied Mohan from upstairs. Moments later he strode into the kitchen, shaved, showered, dressed, and smelling of his favorite cologne—some inexpensive brand bought at the drugstore. In his peppy walk and the way he pulled the chair out and sat down with the morning paper, Anjali could detect an air of expectancy.

Usha placed a mug of tea before him and got one for herself. "What time are you leaving for the airport?" she asked him wearily.

He checked his wristwatch. "In about fifteen minutes." Lowering his newspaper, he peered at Usha through his gold-rimmed glasses. "Don't worry so much. He has changed a lot in the last few years. Jeevan-bhai is almost seventy-seven now—more flexible."

Usha took a slow sip of the fragrant spiced tea. "Jeevan-bhai's not likely to change, no matter what his age."

Perhaps trying to avoid a confrontation with his peeved wife, Mohan quietly drank his tea and returned to reading the paper. A little later he put on his shoes and went out the front door.

Anjali and her mother exchanged a silent look. The show was about to begin.

An hour later, the sound of the car pulling into the driveway had Anjali and Usha rushing to the entry foyer. Anjali smiled inwardly when she noticed her mother taking a quick peek at herself in the framed mirror hanging on the wall. As far as she could see, her mom looked perfect.

Usha had on a butter-yellow sari with a daisy print. Today she wore her old-fashioned *mangalsutra*, the necklace that symbolized marriage in the Hindu culture, and old-fashioned diamond cluster earrings. It wouldn't do to wear any of the delicate, contemporary jewelry that her mother favored. Jeevan-kaka did not tolerate married women in the family wearing anything but traditional garb. They were supposed to take pride in the Kapadia name.

Somewhat nervous herself, Anjali wore a sensible pastel blue *salwar-kameez* suit that covered most of her arms and legs. The *kameez* was a loose shirt that hung below her knees, effectively making her look shapeless. The *salwar* pants and the *chunni*, the matching boa-like accessory, were modest, too. The outfit was in direct contrast to her usual form-fitting slacks, skirts, dresses, trendy blouses, and snug sweaters.

Her father didn't approve of her wardrobe because she was a woman on the wrong side of thirty-five, and her marital status had to be considered. But that didn't stop her from enjoying her slim and youthful figure.

People always told her she looked ten years younger, and it felt good to wear clothes that suited her. Besides, the owner of a fashionable boutique couldn't afford to wear frumpy clothes. She had to set the right tone for the business.

The front door opened and her dad walked in, carrying two large suitcases, his face aglow. "Usha, Anju, Jeevan-bhai is here," he announced cheerfully.

As if they needed reminding. The house had been buzzing with nothing but Jeevan Kapadia's arrival for the past few days. And the suitcases! They were the size of mature hogs, which didn't bode well at all. Her uncle was here to stay a long, long time.

Expecting to see the roly-poly Jeevan-kaka following on her father's heels, Anjali's jaw dropped when a considerably slimmer man walked in. She heard her mother draw in a shocked breath.

Good Lord, who *was* this man?

He had Jeevan-kaka's eyes, his shaggy, squirrel-tail eyebrows, and bulbous nose, but this man was only two-thirds his size. His khaki pants were about two sizes too large and were bunched up and held together at the waist with a thick black belt. He had lost more hair than ever and his once-smooth face looked wrinkled. One tooth on the bottom was missing, too. Talk about age catching up. Five years had made an astounding difference.

Then he spoke to her mother. "Ahh, Usha! *Kem chho?* How are you, little sister?"

It was her uncle all right. For a slimmed-down man, the voice was still robust and commanding. It had suited the chubby Jeevan, but not this one. Whatever happened to make him lose weight? Maybe he'd gone on some kind of diet and exercise program?

Anjali watched her mother flash her most cordial smile and bend down to touch Jeevan's feet in the conservative way of greeting an elder. So she followed her mother's example and did the same. It'd be best if she played the passive little Hindu woman—for the moment.

Grinning from ear to ear, Jeevan-kaka first blessed his sister-in-law and then caught Anjali in an exuberant hug. She nearly got smothered in the embrace, her nose squashed against his soft cream cotton shirt and the smell of his basil-scented cologne.

He held her away from him for a second and studied her, his shrewd black eyes seemingly taking in every inch while Anjali tried not to squirm. "Anju, how big-big you have become. Looking lovely-lovely also, huh?"

Well, at least he thought she looked lovely. And thank goodness, *big* in his vocabulary meant grown-up. She had news for him: she'd become a voting adult some nineteen years ago.

Just as she thought the surprise and the official welcoming ceremony were over, and they could now settle into the routine of having her uncle around for the next several weeks or months, another shock followed.

A strange man came in through the door, a giant suitcase in each hand. Anjali's head snapped up to study him. She could almost feel her mother's back stiffening alongside her own.

He certainly didn't look like the average cab or limo driver. He was tall and broad-shouldered. With her eye for fashion, the first thing Anjali took in was his attire. He wore an open-neck tan shirt and tobacco dress slacks, both beautifully tailored and very expensive looking. The shoes were glossy brown wing tips. He had smooth white skin. His hair was dense, dark, and neatly groomed. A scar was visible just beneath his left eyebrow, making the eyelid look swollen. His eyes were . . . gray.

He couldn't be Indian—not with that complexion and those eyes. And yet, there was something very Indian about him. Anjali could sense his Indian-ness, sniff it. One *Desi* could always spot another.

"Come inside, Rishi," Jeevan-kaka ordered the man, beaming at him.

Rishi? It was an Indian name, Sanskrit for sage or wise man.

"Put the suitcases down and meet everyone, *beta*," instructed Jeevan-kaka. Although *beta* meant son, most often the term was used affectionately for a child of either sex, so it probably meant nothing in this case. Jeevan-kaka's sons were about this man's age, especially his youngest, but none of them were this fair or impressive looking. And none was called Rishi either.

Something odd came to mind. Jeevan-kaka couldn't possibly have a love-child, could he? The old man was even more puritanical than her father. She couldn't picture him fathering an illegitimate son. But then, his wife, Chandrika, was unattractive, and there was a remote possibility that Jeevan-kaka could have strayed. Although why any woman in her right mind, no matter how desperate, would go for Jeevan was beyond Anjali's imagination. Nonetheless he was loaded, and money was a magnet to certain types of females.

The stranger put the suitcases on the floor and dutifully joined his palms to greet Anjali and her mother in the traditional way. "*Namaste*," he said with an accent she couldn't quite place. He had an interesting baritone voice.

For a split second her mother's eyes connected with hers and Anjali clearly saw the look of puzzled wariness in them.

Who *was* this man? Anjali tried to take a few silent guesses. He certainly didn't look like any of her other cousins. Maybe he was a friend of Jeevan-kaka's?

Her father solved the mystery to some extent when he said, "Usha, Anju, this is Rishi Shah, Jeevan-bhai's business partner from London." But then he immediately proceeded to drop another bombshell. "Rishi will be staying with us."

Anjali's mind went into a tailspin. It was bad enough that her autocratic uncle had arrived, but he'd also come with a partner. And since when had her independent-minded uncle decided to take on a sidekick? And if he had, how come it wasn't some older man like himself? Instead here was someone who looked young enough to be his son—even a grandson.

As good hosts, Mohan and Usha welcomed Rishi Shah and Jeevan into their home and ushered them into the living room. As Anjali followed them she happened to notice the younger man's gait. He seemed to favor his right leg a little—an almost imperceptible limp.

Jeevan-kaka cast a glance around the room before settling on the old blue couch. "You need new paint on the walls, Mohan."

Anjali exchanged another look with her mother. He'd been here all of two minutes and already he was voicing criticisms. But he was right. The walls did need a coat of paint. Nothing escaped those coyote eyes.

"How about some hot *chai*, Jeevan-bhai?" asked Usha, obviously trying to steer his attention away from the walls.

"No, Usha, *chai* does not agree with me these days. You can make me a hot cup of *masala doodh*—nonfat milk with saffron, cardamom, a little bit clove, and almond paste."

Her mom's brow settled into a troubled frown. Anjali could almost see the thoughts churning in her mind. Almonds, saffron, cardamom, and a hint of clove to be ground fine and added to boiling skim milk. Jeevan's crazy demands had already begun. Thank goodness they happened to have skim milk in the house because of her mother's strict diet.

"What would you like to drink, Rishi?" Mohan smiled at the stranger, clearly trying to be an attentive host. Maybe Mohan could feel the negative vibes emanating from his wife and daughter and felt he had to do something to intercept them, stop them from reaching their guest.

Rishi Shah was busy checking out the house, his gaze wandering over every painting, photograph, pillow, and carpet fiber. He looked up when addressed. "Something cold would be welcome, if you don't mind, sir."

Then she recognized the accent. British, very clipped and proper—the Queen's English. How interesting was that? And he'd addressed her father as *sir*.

"Cola is okay?" her father asked, and the man nodded, looking as serious as ever.

While her parents escaped into the kitchen to fill the drink orders, Anjali sat stiffly in one of the chairs, preferring not to raise her eyes. Her uncle always had that effect on her.

Jeevan-kaka chuckled, sounding smug. "Rishi, what did I tell you, huh? Our Anju is lovely or what?"

Anjali slowly lifted her head to look at Rishi Shah and saw him nod silently at Jeevan-kaka's comment. Her uncle telling a stranger to agree with his biased opinion about her looks was embarrassing. Then the man looked across the room at her, his assessing eyes intense beams of gray that rattled her a little.

He would've been a good-looking man but for the unsmiling mouth that made him seem cold and remote, like a monolith standing alone, distant, watchful. Intimidating. She wondered what his real opinion of her was. From his expression she could tell nothing.

Perhaps to keep the conversation going, Jeevan-kaka asked her about her work and where she had traveled in recent months. That was easy. She loved her work and her travels and she told him about all she'd been doing. Only after she'd finished talking about her latest trips to India and Bangkok did she realize she was babbling and using her hands to carry on an animated dialogue. Suddenly sensing Rishi Shah's solemn gaze on her, she lapsed into silence.

"So, when are you getting married again, *beta*?" asked Jeevan-kaka.

She cleared her throat. "Excuse me!"

"You need a good husband. You are now what, thirty-five?"

Discussing her age was outrageous enough, but to question her about remarriage was crass. Why was the older generation so hung up on marriage? However, when it came to her uncle, there was nothing she could do but give him a straightforward answer. "I'm thirty-seven, Jeevan-kaka. And I don't plan on marrying anytime soon. I'm too busy."

Jeevan's bushy eyebrows rose high. "What does busy have to do with marriage? Every girl has to be married at a proper age, otherwise how will she have children?" He made a dismissive gesture with his hands. "Life is always busy, Anju. You should settle down, *beta*. Finding a good husband is the best cure for everything."

"But I'm not ill. Widowhood is not a disease." Anjali tried to keep her voice even, but her distress was beginning to rise. A stranger was sitting in the room, watching her, listening to her uncle's discourse on marriage, and specifically her private life.

But a quick glance at the man sitting next to him surprised her. A hint of hilarity flashed in his eyes. He seemed amused by her response to her uncle's opinionated remarks. So, he had a sense of humor hidden under that aloofness, did he? Her own lips twitched in response.

Her uncle wiggled his eyebrows and grinned. "I can find you a nice-nice Gujarati man. Our town has some rich men who are looking for a pretty wife like you."

"Thanks, Jeevan-kaka, but I'm not interested. If I change my mind about marriage in the future, I'd like to find my own man."

"You have modern ideas." Jeevan barked out a patronizing laugh. "So when are you coming to the farm, *beta*? You are going all over India but you're not coming to see me and Chandrika."

Anjali took a cleansing breath and smiled at her uncle. At least he was off the subject of marriage. "Perhaps next time. You know how it is when most of my business is in Delhi and Mumbai." Traveling to his remote farm near Gamdi, a few miles outside the city of Anand, wasn't easy.

"Oh yes, I know all about business demands," he said, rolling his eyes.

With another agreeable nod Anjali subsided into silence. All this time Rishi Shah had merely sat in his corner, not having said a single word, but she could feel the discomfort emanating from him. With his exclusive clothes, his fancy accent, and his cool reserve, he looked out of place in their small, suburban home with its well-worn furniture, the lingering odors of spicy food, and its ten-year-old carpeting and paint.

But if he didn't want to be here, why had he bothered to accompany her uncle?

Thankfully her father arrived with a glass of soda for Shah, who accepted it with a word of thanks. The awkward silence was broken by her father and uncle starting a conversation. She made a convenient escape to the kitchen to help her mother.

Usha turned a troubled gaze toward her. "Not only does he come with enough clothes for an entire year, he brings a guest in the bargain," she whispered.

"Hmm," agreed Anjali. They both watched the milk in the pan come to a rolling boil while another pan brewed the strong tea with its aromatic mixture of spices. "Who is he? I mean, what's he to Jeevan-kaka other than a business partner?"

Shrugging, Usha stirred the milk with a long-handled spoon. "How should I know? I just met him. Did you notice how fair he is?"

"And the eyes—they're a rare shade of gray." Those eyes were amazing. Anjali brought out cups and saucers and placed them on a tray. "And Jeevan-kaka treats him like family, not a business associate."

"I noticed that. I hope that young man is not as difficult as your uncle, or I'll have two big problems on my hands." Usha strained the tea into three cups and poured the *masala* milk into another.

"Since he's planning to stay with us, which room does he get?" Theirs wasn't a big house and guests always created a bit of a problem.

"Nilesh's room. Where else can I put him?"

Anjali stared at her mother. "What about Nilesh?"

"I'll have to ask him to move to the basement, on the sofa bed."

"But that's not fair to Nilesh," protested Anjali. "You should at least ask him first." Nilesh's room was next to hers. That meant some stranger was going to be sleeping in the bed some ten feet away from her—separated by a wall, of course. But the thought was unsettling.

In the living room, her father, Jeevan-kaka, and Shah were deep in conversation about the store. Her eyes went to Rishi Shah. He was explaining something to the two men. He was very articulate. Where was he educated? England? Some upscale English school in India?

Jeevan-kaka lifted his cup and sniffed suspiciously. Then after a single cautious sip he closed his eyes tight and grimaced. "Uh-oh! Usha, did you put sugar in this? I am a diabetic now. I cannot take sugar."

"I'm sorry, Jeevan-bhai," murmured Usha. "I had no idea you were diabetic. Should I make another cup without sugar?"

Jeevan shook his head. "I will finish this, but next time, remember, no sugar in anything."

Anjali stared wide-eyed at her uncle. This was unexpected. The old Jeevan would have had a minor fit if he was given something that didn't meet his stringent requirements. Her mother, too, was looking strangely at him. The man had changed. Maybe her dad was right. Perhaps Jeevan wasn't as rigid as he used to be. Was age catching up with him?

But in the next moment the supposition was tossed out. "Usha. I hope you did not put coconut in my lunch," he said.

Usha bit her lower lip. "Oh dear, I sprinkled it over the *khaman*," she said, referring to the little square steamed cakes made of ground chickpeas, green chili peppers, and ginger, and then garnished with roasted mustard seeds, grated coconut, and fresh coriander.

"Tsk-tsk," clucked her uncle. "Coconut is giving me intestinal problems lately."

"I'll make sure to brush the coconut off your *khaman*," assured Usha. It seemed to ease Jeevan's concerns for the moment.

Once the drinks were finished, the talk turned purely to business. In that respect, the old Jeevan-kaka was still the same. He ate, slept, breathed, and dreamed business. He owned a cloth mill, a chain of food stores, clothing shops, a dairy farm, and his latest acquisition, a hotel in Ahmedabad.

"So, let us discuss your store problem now. What exactly is wrong?" Jeevan finished the last of his milk, then settled back in the chair with his hands clasped over his middle. He looked like a rural judge about to hear a case and hand down a verdict.

And a verdict it would be, Anjali reflected. He loved analyzing business data and diagnosing problems. Troubleshooting was his forte. She wasn't sure how the other, younger guy fit into all of this. Was he going to bulldoze into their store like her uncle surely would, and dictate to them?

She turned her attention to the conversation. Her father explained the situation in great detail to the two men.

Jeevan-kaka gestured toward Shah. "Rishi is a genius in solving business problems. He has an MBA from Oxford University and he specializes in saving failing businesses. He goes to different parts of Asia and Europe for doing this type of consulting work. He knows everything."

Mohan turned to Shah with what bordered on surprised delight. "That is impressive, Rishi. We should consider ourselves lucky to have your advice."

"Extremely lucky," chirped Jeevan-kaka. "For outsiders he charges big consulting fees, but for family it is free." He looked pleased with himself.

So Rishi Shah was offering them free business advice? Why? But then, he was probably going to stay with them for a long time, so it wasn't really free advice. They'd be giving him room and board in return. But God knew what his going rate was.

What surprised Anjali was her mother's expression. Despite her earlier resentment, she too was smiling a bit. It was probably the word *free* that did it. "How did you and Jeevan-bhai hook up with each other, Mr. Shah?"

Shah cracked the first real smile of the day. His gray eyes lost their iciness and thawed somewhat. "Jeevan-kaka has known me all my life. I'm fortunate to be his partner, Mrs. Kapadia. He has taught me most everything I know."

Mohan laughed. "Rishi, we're quite informal around here. Don't call us Mr. and Mrs. Kapadia. And there's no need to address me as sir, either."

"Uncle Mohan and Auntie Usha will do fine, if it's okay with you," added Usha.

Finishing the last of his soda, Shah nodded. "Uncle and Auntie, then." He rose to his feet. "I'd like to freshen up a bit if it's all right with you folks. Maybe we can see the store after that?" He glanced questioningly at Jeevan, and got a nod from the older man.

Anjali's father jumped to his feet to help Shah carry the suitcases upstairs and get the two guests settled. "Jeevan-bhai, you will take the guest room and Rishi can have Nilesh's room."

"But I'd hate to impose, Uncle," said Shah in a mild protest. "I'll be happy to sleep on your settee."

"Oh, no, *beta*, Nilesh can sleep in the basement," insisted her father.

Anjali glanced at the men's backs as they went up the stairs, then turned to her mother. "You and Dad just gave away Nilesh's room to a stranger. Poor Nilesh is at school at the moment and doesn't even have a chance to say anything about it."

"That's the Indian way, Anju. We always honor a guest in our home." Usha brushed off Anjali's concerns. "I'm sure Nilesh won't mind."

"I wouldn't be too sure about that." Anjali bent down to pick up the empty cups. This was typical Indian hospitality and no matter what her thoughts on the subject, no one was going to pay any attention to her. Her brother would be relegated to the basement.

She washed the cups and glanced at her mother. "Mom, did you notice how the Shah guy said Jeevan-kaka's known him all his life but he avoided saying how they became a team?"

"He's very clever, isn't he, like a politician? But he seems like a nice, well-mannered young man." Usha inclined her head upward. "Let's give the men a few minutes to get settled. Then we better get ready to take them to the store. Jeevan-bhai's dying to see it, I'm sure."

"You go ahead, Mom. I'll be up in a little bit." Anjali needed a moment to catch her breath. All of a sudden the house felt crowded. She wasn't likely to have much solitude for some time to come.

After several minutes of brooding she headed upstairs to her room to get changed. She couldn't wait to get out of the shape-less *salwar-kameez* and into a pair of slacks and a shirt. If Jeevan-kaka had a problem with her American wardrobe, so be it. And if he was going to be a long-term guest, he'd have to get used to seeing her in her usual clothes.

In the hallway outside her room, she came across Rishi Shah as he stepped out of Nilesh's room, looking a lot less travel-weary. His wide shoulders seemed to take up the width of the hallway. "I beg your pardon, Miss Kapadia," he murmured and stood aside to let her pass.

Anjali noticed his crisp white linen shirt and elegant dove gray trousers. His nearly black hair was neatly combed and his face looked freshly shaved. She got a whiff of his aftershave. It was masculine and pleasant.

She quickly stepped into her room and shut the door. *Miss Kapadia?* The last time someone had called her that, she was an undergrad. And the man who'd used that handle was an old man who wore a bow tie and tweeds.

So, how long did Rishi Shah plan to stay with them?

Chapter 4

Anjali prepared herself for the ride to the store. They piled into her father's van, which was generally used for hauling merchandise and such to and from the store, but when they had company, it served as a passenger vehicle.

Jeevan sat in the front, next to his brother, while Anjali, her mother, and Shah got into the backseat, with her mother sandwiched between Shah and herself. Shah's long legs looked crowded in the small space.

It was typical New Jersey weather in late spring—hovering on hot and just turning humid. The earlier cloud cover had parted, giving way to sunshine. Despite the air-conditioning going full blast, the cramped ten-minute ride felt sticky and long.

She was also seething about her uncle's remark. "Anju, what kind of clothes are you wearing?" he'd asked. "Why did you change from *salwar-kameez* to pants?"

"This is typical American attire, Jeevan-kaka," she'd replied. "Most women my age wear clothes like these." All she had on was a simple navy silk shirt and ecru slacks. What was wrong with that? After her brusque response she'd braced herself for a scathing comeback from her uncle.

Instead Jeevan had stunned them all once again when he'd laughed and patted her head. "Young lady, you have become very naughty lately or what?"

She'd let that one go with a smile.

Jeevan had some comments about how much the neighborhood had changed since his last visit. "Oh, how many *Desi* restaurants do you have here, Mohan? This is so *pukka* Mumbai and Ahmedabad." His eyes went wide at the number of clothing stores that had sprung up within the last couple of years. "So many sari shops!"

"That's precisely our problem, Jeevan-bhai," Usha said to him. "Excessive competition."

Shah was quietly surveying the neighborhood, his eyes hidden behind super-dark sunglasses. Anjali was curious to know how he viewed this ethnic landscape that looked like a piece of India transplanted into the United States. How did it compare with the *Desi* neighborhoods in London and other cities?

They parked behind the store as usual. While the rest of them went toward the back door, Anjali noticed Shah stayed by the van. Ignoring the door held open by her father, he crossed the parking lot instead, and sauntered up to the sidewalk. Then he stood with his hands in his trouser pockets to study Silk & Sapphires' storefront, or at least that's what it looked like from the angle of his head. From his posture she could tell he was looking critically at the display, the store sign, just about everything.

He didn't look impressed.

Well, she wouldn't let that bother her. She couldn't put stock in what some stranger who had arrived in New Jersey less than two hours ago thought about her boutique.

Jeevan-kaka, after waiting impatiently at the door for Shah, gave up and crossed the street to join him. Anjali and her parents went inside the store and left the two men to their devices.

Immediately Anjali crossed the length of the store and gravitated toward the glass panel in the front door to observe the men outside. The two of them started to gesture and talk. Shah had to bend his head low to be on a level with her uncle's.

She couldn't hear a word of their conversation, but she could imagine what it was. They were probably analyzing her store bit by bit and wondering how they could transform it, or worse, make it theirs. Her uncle acquired businesses at about the same frequency he bought underwear.

The thought sent a mild tremor of alarm through her. She'd have to find some way to keep what was hers.

Her father interrupted her thoughts. "Can you unlock the front door, Anju? They can come inside that way instead of walking all the way to the back."

"Sure, Dad." She unlocked the front door and watched her father head directly to the back office, probably to pull out the financial reports for his brother's review.

Then she got busy tidying up the shop. Hastily she stowed away the empty sari carton she had left behind the previous night. She picked up the odds and ends she and her parents had inadvertently left here and there and shoved all the items into the appropriate drawers behind the cash register.

It was a good thing today was Monday and the store was officially closed. At least they didn't have to worry about customers in addition to giving Jeevan-kaka and Shah the grand tour. From all indications her uncle's inspection was already getting off to a bad start. She glanced out the window again and found the two men still standing in the same spot, deep in discussion.

Her mother came up behind her, took a peek outside, and shook her head. "I don't know what those two are doing out there. Let's make sure everything is neat before they come in."

Anjali shot her mother a reassuring look. "I took care of it. I haven't had a chance to look at the back rooms, though."

"Then let's get to it."

In five minutes flat the women had the two small fitting rooms and the restroom looking as neat as they could manage. Anjali observed her father sitting at the computer, furiously clicking away, a slight frown on his face. The laser printer on the desk was spitting out page after page of reports. Despite his earlier elation at having his brother here, her father now seemed just as nervous as Anjali and her mother.

A moment later the security bell attached to the front door chimed, announcing the arrival of Jeevan and Shah. Anjali heard them talking.

"But what if that fellow refuses to sell, Rishi?" her uncle asked.

"We'll offer him a fair price. No one refuses a good offer." Anjali heard cool confidence in Shah's voice. "You know that as well as I."

And what exactly did that mean, she wondered? Offer someone a fair price? All of a sudden her stomach lurched. Was Shah talking about her father? Were her uncle and Shah planning to buy the boutique from them? But then her uncle had mentioned some *fellow*.

Meaning to question them about their intentions, Anjali stepped out of the office and onto the sales floor. She came to a standstill when she noticed the men stopping at one of the displays. They were studying it carefully. It was a bride-and-groom duo of mannequins sporting Anjali's latest bridal wear. She had the mannequins posing under a wedding *mandap*—the ceremonial Hindu marriage canopy.

The bride was dressed in traditional red and gold, with a *chunni* over her head, but the dress was designed somewhat like an American bridal gown, with slightly puffed sleeves and a low neckline that showed a hint of cleavage and showcased the ruby-and-pearl necklace to perfection. The groom wore a cream silk, tuxedo-style jacket over matching trousers paired with cream and gold hand-sewn *mojdis*, the traditional formal shoes.

Anjali was particularly proud of those designs. She'd had at least three bridal couples who'd fallen in love with that display and ordered similar outfits in recent months.

Itching to hear the men's comments, she hid behind one of the tall clothing racks to eavesdrop on their conversation. From her vantage point she could just about see their profiles.

Shah had his dark glasses hooked over his shirt pocket. He touched the embroidered sleeve on the bride's outfit. "This is good, Jeevan-kaka, elegant . . . clever."

"All designed by our Anju, Rishi. She is very talented in these things, you know."

A brief smile touched Anjali's face at the warm pride in Jeevan-kaka's voice. She had to admit that despite his cantankerous ways, he was genuinely fond of his nieces and nephews. He was a true family man.

"I can see that," said Shah. "Everything here is quite impressive. But design and display are not the problem, are they? We have to come up with a plan to expand this into something that's even better, a more one-stop, one-of-a-kind type of store. Right now it appears to be competing with a dozen or more stores that do more or less similar things and sell similar products."

Anjali nearly gave herself away by gasping. Do similar things and sell similar products? Hardly! There was no comparison between her boutique and those other shops. And what was that remark about one-stop shopping? She reflected over it for a moment. Then it sank in.

They were going to buy her and her parents out and then turn her exclusive boutique into a run-of-the-mill department store. Good grief!

How could a man who dressed like a million dollars and spoke impeccable English dream up such bourgeois ideas? Jeevan-kaka was capable of coming up with classless notions, but Shah seemed urbane—a man who shopped at the best stores. He had the aura of money about him. Even the way he held his soda glass or greeted people or simply stood up reeked of refinement. He was a good example of how deceptive appearances could be.

She held her breath, inched closer, desperate to hear more of what they were saying.

"That is true, Rishi, but what if that fellow will not sell?"

Shah paused. "There's no harm in asking, is there?" He laid a large hand on the old man's shoulder. "Jeevan-kaka, when was the last time you and I couldn't convince someone to sell?"

Jeevan grinned. "Okay, we will ask."

As the two men made their way toward the office, Anjali shifted gently so they wouldn't see her. Seconds later she jumped when a voice close to her, much too close, whispered, "You may come out now, Miss Kapadia."

"Oh!" Hot blood rose in Anjali's cheeks at the sight of Rishi

Shah standing behind her with his arms crossed over his chest, staring down at her exactly the way Mr. Goldstein, her high school principal, had done when he'd caught her cutting class. She felt like she was sixteen again. And she didn't like the trapped feeling one bit.

"M-Mr. Shah!" When and how had the man crept up on her so quickly? She'd seen him and her uncle walking away. "Are you spying on me?" He'd managed to make her feel like a thief in her own store.

"Not at all."

"Sneaking up on me like that? I'd call that spying."

"I beg to differ, Miss Kapadia."

"But—"

"*You* were spying on Jeevan-kaka and me," he interrupted her dryly, his accent more clipped than ever.

Shah looked enviably cool. He was standing so close she could see the scar on his eyelid clearly, and the thin, black rim around his steel gray irises. Steel gray—that's what the shade was. And just as cold and hard as the metal. She shivered a little. Mr. Goldstein came to mind again.

Finding no suitable words against his accusation, she did what came instinctively. She turned defensive. "I was merely walking around *my* property, checking on *my* things when you and my uncle happened to walk in."

"One of the drawbacks of having mirrored walls is that one can see everything around in a single glance," he said. "I saw you emerge from the office and stop when you spied us. I clearly observed you tiptoeing and assuming a position behind the *chania-cholis*."

"Like I said, I was checking on the *chania-cholis*."

"You, Miss Kapadia, wanted to find out exactly what Jeevan-kaka and I were discussing." His dark eyebrows shot way up, challenging her.

"Maybe. Besides, it's *my* store, and I have a right to know what you two are planning to do with it."

A glint of humor, both astonishing and sudden, appeared in

his eyes, making the steel turn to a softer gray, more like pewter. "Since you eavesdropped, you heard it all."

To give her shaking hands something to do, she pretended to adjust the scarf on a mannequin. "All I gathered was that you're planning on turning my boutique into some type of department store."

He became silent for a moment before breaking into an amused smile. "Department store? Where did you get that idea?"

Much to her chagrin, her lower lip started to tremble. The scarf slipped out of her hands and glided to the floor. "How can you do this? You and Jeevan-kaka charge in here like a pair of Indian bulls, criticize everything, and then plan to turn an elegant shop into a cheap mockery."

"That's not the way it is," he said, sounding like a patient schoolteacher. He bent down to pick up the scarf and handed it to her. "Without knowing the details of our plan, you're simply jumping to conclusions."

Carefully placing the scarf back around the mannequin's neck, she started to move toward the office. "Then why don't you and Jeevan-kaka enlighten me and my parents? Let's hear what your grand plan is all about." She generally didn't make barbed remarks, but she couldn't help saying, "Buy-one-get-one-free specials on rare diamonds from South Africa? *Chania-cholis* and *shervanis* made of polyester and rayon? Blue-light specials on Myanmar rubies?"

"Blue-light specials?" He laughed. "Is that an American marketing concept?"

"Not funny, Mr. Shah." She was trying hard not to burst into tears.

"It wasn't meant to be funny." He wasn't laughing anymore. "I'm trying to learn some American merchandising terms."

She stopped in her tracks abruptly. "Look, I'm sorry. It's nothing personal, but my parents and I are under a lot of stress at the moment. My sense of humor is on . . . vacation."

"I understand. Mine frequently takes a holiday," he said with a self-deprecating smile. The left eye, with its puffy lid, looked smaller than the right when he smiled.

She realized something. The flash of humor in his face was like a mantle lifting away from him. A human being existed underneath that cold, granite-like façade. And she wasn't sure whether she liked or disliked the discovery.

Her uncle saw them approaching. "Here they are." He motioned to them to step inside the office. "Rishi, I was waiting for you so we could tell them together what you and I were discussing."

Anjali looked at her parents. It was hard to judge what her father was thinking; he wore a puzzled frown. Her mother looked tense, brittle enough to shatter.

"Rishi, tell them, *beta*," said Jeevan, looking pleased and paternal. "He has a brilliant plan, Mohan," he assured his brother.

Shah stood with his hands in his pockets and surveyed the room for a moment, once again seemingly studying every detail, down to the last thumbtack holding up a newspaper cutting on the wall. "You have a marvelous store here. Jeevan-kaka and I are impressed. It has some unique designs and it shows great promise."

"But?" Anjali cut in.

"But . . . I think it needs something more."

"More what?" demanded Anjali.

"It could use some upgrading."

"How much upgrading?" Usha asked, clearly suspicious.

"Considerable," said Shah, looking somewhat uncomfortable. "My recommendation is a complete overhaul—an expansion, if you will."

"Expansion?" said Usha in an astonished whisper.

"We're up to our eyeballs in debt," Anjali said. "The last thing we need is to sink more money into the business."

"But Jeevan-kaka and I—"

"We need to clear out our present inventory," Anjali cut in, "not add to it."

He offered her a reassuring smile. "You don't need to worry on that count, Miss Kapadia. Jeevan-kaka and I are planning to finance this operation."

"You're loaning us the money?"

He shook his head. "We'll be your partners. We'll take on fifty-one percent of the debt."

She frowned. "That means . . . you'll own fifty-one percent of the business."

Anjali felt the carpet being jerked out from under her feet.

Chapter 5

Rishi noted the expression on Anjali Kapadia's face. She had turned pale and her mouth was quivering. Her breath had quickened, making her chest rise and fall visibly beneath that soft-looking silk blouse that clung to her breasts. And a pretty bosom it was, too—full and proud.

Her mother looked like she was about to explode. And her father seemed just plain stunned. What was worse was that they had all slipped into silence.

Rishi was prepared to field angry rebuttals, protests, and arguments, but not utter quiet. It was rather . . . disquieting, he reflected with a wry inward grimace at his own play on words.

The three American Kapadias looked frozen like a tableau. Jeevan was the only Kapadia who seemed unaffected. In fact, he looked jubilant. A smile hovered over his face, making his nose look larger than ever. But then Jeevan had heard Rishi's ideas in some detail and he approved of them wholeheartedly.

Finding a spare folding chair resting against the wall, Rishi unfolded it and gestured to Anjali to sit down. She looked rather fragile, and he didn't want her passing out or something. But she ignored him and continued to stare at the floor as if fascinated by the pattern on the tiles.

He cleared his throat. "I'm sorry, folks. I realize this is a bit of a surprise, but believe me, what the store needs at this time is shock therapy."

Mohan Kapadia was the first to respond. He combed his fingers through his hair. "I'm not sure about this expansion idea, Rishi."

"I'll explain in a moment, Uncle," Rishi assured him. It wasn't a promising sign that the two women continued to maintain their silence. From what he'd gathered during the last couple of hours and from Jeevan-kaka's description of the family, it was Usha who more or less ruled the roost. Anjali was the creative mind and the visionary behind the business. He'd managed to antagonize the two main players.

It was probably a mistake on his part to present his ideas with such haste. A little more tact would have helped as well. Unfortunately, being used to direct and tough business negotiations most of the time, he wasn't prepared for this kind of delicate, dance-around-the-issue type of situation.

Perhaps he should have waited a little, prepared them to some degree and introduced his plan bit by bit. Instead, he'd delivered it in one quick stroke. But it wasn't all his fault, damn it. Miss Kapadia, with her pretty eyes and the distrust and sadness alternating in them, had made him lose his sense of balance.

And he very rarely lost his sense of balance.

Usha turned her head and fixed her gaze on her brother-in-law. "Jeevan-bhai, I agree with Mohan and Anju. I can't imagine how expanding a failing business is going to help. We'll only end up deeper in debt."

Jeevan Kapadia raised an imperious hand and motioned for the three of them to calm down. "Why are you jumping to conclusions? At least *listen* to Rishi first."

Rishi sighed. Jeevan-kaka, despite his brilliant mind, had little sense of timing or diplomacy. Once he latched on to an idea, he ran at top speed with no thought for caution—like those bulls Miss Kapadia had alluded to. But then, he was in no position to judge Jeevan-kaka when he himself had behaved in exactly that fashion.

It was time for damage control.

"This is what I propose," he started. "We approach the person who owns the wholesale grocery shop next door. From the looks of the storefront, it's not a thriving business. I want to find out if he's willing to sell his space to us. Jeevan-kaka tells me you currently own half of the building. If we can buy that man out, then we can join the two halves, essentially doubling its size and at the same time owning a larger, more desirable property."

Mohan shook his head. "The township zoning department may not allow that kind of restructuring of what was originally a duplex home—two houses joined by a wall."

"I'll look into it. All we may have to do is apply for a permit to fuse the two parts. As it stands, it's a single building made into two stores with a firewall in between."

"That will be very expensive," cautioned Usha.

"Don't worry about funding, Auntie. That's our problem—mine and Jeevan-kaka's," replied Rishi gently. "The advantage of owning both portions of the building is that we can refurbish both as one, modernize it, and make it attractive."

Usha didn't respond, but continued to frown.

"That run-down store next door is single-handedly decreasing the value of your property as well as your sales volume," said Rishi, putting on his most convincing voice. "It's common knowledge that an unsightly property brings down the value of everything around it. The very appearance of *that* store prevents customers from coming to *yours*."

"We're aware of that," said Usha, telling Rishi that she was sensitive about the aesthetics of her business. "We've tried several times to get Mr. Tejmal to clean up his storefront, but he just doesn't seem to care. So we're stuck with him."

"That's why we need to buy him out. Then you can have a corner building with its own large parking lot and separate entrances from two different streets," he explained. "Obviously parking is at a premium in this neighborhood. This will be perfect to house a trendy boutique with no ugly elements on either side to spoil its exclusive look."

Mohan chewed his lower lip. "Sounds good in theory, but . . ."

"Go ahead, Uncle." Rishi shifted and gave him a questioning look. "Tell us what's on your mind."

"Tejmal will not sell, Rishi. He has owned that store for years. He bought it when real estate here was cheap because the neighborhood was not very desirable. In fact, when I bought my half some years ago, Tejmal's portion had already doubled in value. Now it's worth even more. Why would he want to sell a hot property?"

"Precisely because it *is* hot property, Uncle. Real estate here peaked a while ago, then reached a plateau, and is now in decline. It's the perfect time for him to sell."

"How do *you* know all this?" Anjali spoke for the first time in several minutes, surprising Rishi. But she still looked somewhat dazed.

He turned his attention to her. "Research."

Usha shook her head. "Still, Tejmal may not *want* to sell. That store is his life."

A disdainful roar of laughter came from Jeevan. "Have you seen that man's display window? It is full of dust and cobwebs—and one pane is cracked. Like Rishi says, it is making your classy store look cheap. He is ruining the quality of the entire neighborhood." He pulled a face. "If he does not sell that place, or at least refurbish it, he is dead, I'm telling you."

Anjali turned to her uncle, looking horrified. "You can't mean that!"

"Why are you looking so shocked, Anju? I'm just stating a fact."

"You're not going to . . . threaten Mr. Tejmal's life or . . . something, are you?"

In reply she got a blank look from Jeevan. "Why would I do that?"

Rishi suppressed his urge to laugh. Was this woman serious? Did she really think her uncle had the potential to terrorize or put a contract out on some harmless old shopkeeper? Jeevan was notorious for his strong-arm business tactics, but they didn't extend to such outlandish practices. He winked at Jeevan. "I think Miss Kapadia's been seeing too many Hindi movies."

"That's not true!" Anjali protested. "Jeevan-kaka can be . . . well, I was only wondering if . . . Never mind." This time she did collapse onto the chair Rishi had pulled up earlier and her hands descended in her lap in a limp, hopeless gesture. "I'm tired of this whole affair."

She did look tired, Rishi noticed. More than tired, she looked dejected. He felt a strong pang of sympathy for her, but the disciplined businessman in him dispelled the emotion. She appeared to be a woman who was obviously used to having her own way. Well, it was about time she learned a lesson or two.

Life was not always neat and uncomplicated. And it didn't come in pure shades of black and white either. Owning and running a business definitely involved innumerable shades of gray—and the sooner she learned that, the better. Time for the fairy princess to emerge from her sheltered castle, he told himself.

But his gentler feelings of compassion still clouded the pragmatic ones.

Since there were no more chairs left, he shifted again and leaned against the wall. It was crowded with tacked-on lists of phone numbers, store ads, pizza shop coupons, and pictures of Indian outfits. This tiny office appeared to be Mohan's domain, very different from the neat and organized shop floor run by the two women.

He directed his gaze toward Anjali. "I own successful boutiques in London, Delhi, Mumbai, Hong Kong, and Singapore, so I know what I'm talking about, Miss Kapadia. If you'll just listen for a moment, I'll tell you all about it."

He heard no protests, so he continued. "The one-stop-shopping concept comprises taking what you already have here, an exclusive boutique, then adding to it a classy beauty salon, an on-site photo studio, event planning and decorating, floral design, and an upscale coffee shop that sells *chai*, gourmet coffees, pastries, a variety of snacks, et cetera. A shopping experience like that is entirely different from the other operations around here. Am I correct?" He looked for affirmation at Mohan Kapadia, who was still gnawing on his lower lip.

"Sounds risky," Usha murmured and glanced at her husband, who nodded.

Just then the sound of the bell alerted them to the front door being opened. Someone had entered the store.

Anjali, who had sat like a statue all this time, sprang to her feet. "Wonder who it is. Everyone knows we're closed on Mondays." She immediately started striding out to the shop floor.

Rishi asked the older Kapadias to stay put. "I'll go with her. You folks can talk to Jeevan-kaka for a bit."

He followed Anjali out the office door. He needed a chance to talk to her privately, convince her that he wasn't her enemy. She seemed to be the most seriously affected by his plans, and he didn't want to upset her any more than he already had. He'd be working with her very closely for the foreseeable future and it would be difficult if she continued to regard him with such fear and distrust.

She zipped through the aisles, sure-footed and agile—confident in her own milieu. She walked with a sexy, catwalk kind of swagger. He wondered if she'd picked that up from the fashion models who showcased her clothes.

He knew Anjali's designs well. He'd studied them since Jeevan-kaka had mentioned this unexpected trip to the U.S. He'd read everything on the store's Web site, apparently designed by her young brother. With Jeevan-kaka's input, Rishi had a good idea of their balance sheet, too.

Naturally the models were good looking, but he hadn't known the creator of those delightful clothes was equally attractive. He had to admit that despite her defensiveness and underlying hostility, she was a pretty woman. He'd been surprised to hear she was thirty-seven. She looked much younger.

Jeevan-kaka had been singing her praises in the past, and more so during the last couple of days. The old fox was clearly trying to do some matchmaking between Rishi and his niece. He'd told him a few times how Anjali would make the perfect wife. Since Jeevan-kaka had a tendency to exaggerate and even fib at times to suit his purposes, Rishi hadn't paid much attention to his bragging about how appealing and bright his niece was.

Well, this time the old man hadn't lied or exaggerated.

The smooth fit of her slacks showed off a slim waist, gently curved hips, and shapely legs. She wasn't tall, but she had a lithe, athletic body. About her being bright, he'd have to wait and see. So far he'd only seen one or two sides of her personality. He was an excellent judge of character, and if he'd guessed right, there were other, less prickly facets to her. He meant to discover them all—sooner or later.

It would be to his advantage to find out *everything* about Miss Kapadia.

His eyes went to the front door. A petite young woman stood near it, taking in the room with dark, curious eyes. Dressed in designer jeans, electric blue shirt, and high-heeled sandals nearly six inches high, she seemed to be a customer. He saw her turn to the approaching Anjali with an apologetic smile. "Sorry, I know you're closed today, but I thought I'd take a chance."

"Not a problem," Anjali replied.

"I was just driving by and everything in your window looked so beautiful," said the young lady with a guilty grin and a shrug. "I couldn't resist trying the door . . . and it was unlocked . . ."

Rishi decided to stay a few steps behind and observe. Although he couldn't see Anjali's smile, he could hear it in her voice. "That's perfectly all right. You're welcome to come inside and look." She shook hands with the woman. "I'm Anjali Kapadia."

The young lady's eyes warmed up. "I'm Roopa Singh. You're sure I'm not imposing on your day off?"

"Not at all. Customers are always welcome."

"Thanks. That's kind of you." She let her gaze wander around the store for a moment. "I'm looking for bridal wear."

Ah, newly engaged and eager to shop for a wedding trousseau, Rishi reflected with a sense of satisfaction. *Excellent potential.*

"You're at the right place, then," said Anjali. "I'll show you where the bridal nook is."

When she turned around and saw Rishi standing by the jewelry case, her smile immediately vanished. It was like a bright light had been put out.

"I thought I'd come out and help," he said, explaining his

presence. It wasn't really important how Anjali reacted to him, but it did sting a little. She had every right to distrust him. Her uncle, who was known to be authoritarian, had swooped down on them and then foisted Rishi on them as an unexpected and unpleasant surprise. He'd seen it in both Anjali's and her mother's faces—the shock of seeing a stranger they hadn't anticipated, their quick exchange of bewildered looks.

He'd immediately felt like an intruder. But he was planning on remedying that within the next day or two. He meant to find himself a hotel room as soon as he could convince Jeevan-kaka that as much as he was thrilled to be considered part of the Kapadia family, he didn't belong in their cramped house.

Usurping Nilesh Kapadia's room was beyond intrusion. He hadn't even met the young man yet and the poor boy didn't know his room had been casually offered to a stranger. Rishi's main cause for discomfort was the Kapadia women, especially Anjali. She wasn't unwelcoming as such, but there was that cool politeness that was like an invisible barrier.

Well, he was here strictly for business purposes, and if his future *business* partners didn't like the fact or like him, that was their problem. And he wouldn't have been here if Jeevan Kapadia hadn't asked for his assistance. Rishi would do anything for the old man. He owed Jeevan a lot. Much more than a lot.

The two women disappeared amongst the bridal outfits and he followed them. He wanted to observe how Anjali Kapadia did business. He also needed to know the typical client that shopped at Silk & Sapphires if he was to make the upgrades meaningful. In fact, he considered it serendipitous that a promising customer had stopped in while he was here for his initial assessment.

This particular shopper appeared quite wealthy. The latest designer handbag and the fashionable sandals hadn't escaped Rishi's experienced eye; neither had the gleaming black German import parked right outside the door. He stepped forward and positioned himself practically next to Anjali. He didn't want her to think he was a voyeur on top of everything else.

He introduced himself to the customer. "Hello. I'm Rishi

Shah, an associate of Miss Kapadia's," he said, offering his hand to Ms. Singh.

Roopa Singh accepted his handshake and looked at both him and Anjali by turns. "So you two are like . . . uh . . . both owners of the store?"

Rishi knew it was his Caucasian looks and British accent combined with the Indian name that had the young lady mystified. She was probably wondering what a white-skinned Brit called Shah was doing in a business partnership with a purely *Desi* woman in New Jersey. It happened all the time when he and Jeevan-kaka introduced themselves as partners.

Nonetheless he smiled, trying to summon all the charm he could muster. "Yes, Miss Kapadia and I will be co-owners soon."

Anjali glanced at him briefly before turning on the goodwill for the bride-to-be. "So, when is the wedding, Miss Singh?"

"Please call me Roopa. The wedding is set for a year from now. Mid June."

"Beautiful and popular time of year for a wedding," said Anjali. "All those roses and petunias in bloom—can't beat that for outdoor photographs."

"Exactly. And I'm a teacher, so I can have all summer off right after the wedding . . . for an extra-long honeymoon." Roopa Singh dimpled prettily.

Anjali smiled. "Perfect timing, then."

"I'm looking for something that's kind of light and summery and yet Indian . . . you know . . ." Roopa made a helpless gesture with a dainty, manicured hand and Rishi noticed the diamond engagement ring, an impressive solitaire set in platinum—two carats or thereabout.

Anjali promptly brought out a writing pad and pen. "Okay, are you going to have a ceremonial Hindu wedding or . . ." She deliberately let that hang, Rishi realized, so the customer would tell her if her fiancé was Indian or of some other faith. Clever.

"Ajit and I want a nice East-West mix." She looked longingly at the display Rishi had admired earlier. "I love that. Is it possible to have something along those lines?"

"No problem," assured Anjali, already busy taking notes.

"We can design something for both of you in coordination, and for anybody else in the bridal party, too. What color did you have in mind?"

"The usual red and gold for the ceremony, of course." Roopa bit her lower lip in that cute way some women did when they were undecided or befuddled. She looked around at the racks and shook her head. "For the reception, I don't know yet." She turned to Anjali. "I'm open to suggestions."

Anjali studied Roopa critically for a minute. Rishi could almost sense the wheels turning in her brain. "I think I know exactly what would look good. A rosy peach would be perfect . . . almost like apricot, only lighter."

The customer looked skeptical. "You really think it would be a good color for me? I'm usually partial to blues and greens."

"I'm positive." Anjali nudged Roopa to one of the racks that held the more elaborate and glitzy *salwar-kameez* outfits. She pulled one down that was indeed a rare color.

Rishi thought light apricot sounded about right to describe it.

"This is the shade I'm talking about." With a quick flick of her wrist Anjali plucked the *chunni* and draped it around the young lady's neck, then turned her around to face the mirrored wall. "What do you think?"

Roopa Singh stared at herself for a moment, then turned this way and that several times. "I think I like it. A lot!"

"Looks great on you. It emphasizes your lovely complexion and brown eyes." Anjali walked back a few steps and eyed the image for a second. "I could design something special for you in that color."

"You can do that?"

"I've designed all the clothes in the store myself. They're exclusively made for Silk & Sapphires." She picked up her pad and pencil again. "Let me show you what I have in mind." With a few bold strokes Anjali began to draw a simple yet elegant design.

Rishi watched her sketch, fascinated by the deft hand and the imagination. She was good at this design thing. Damn good.

Roopa looked at the picture and her eyes went wide with delight. "That's cute! I love it." She gave it a moment's thought. "I think I want exactly that."

"You're sure you don't need to discuss it with your fiancé . . . or your parents?" Anjali seemed to be throwing in the practical and cautionary hints.

Mentally Rishi approved of Anjali's sales strategy. It was good to remind eager young shoppers of the costs involved. Wedding clothes were expensive and the bride's parents were most likely paying for them.

But young Roopa shook her head. "Nah, my parents and Ajit want me to pick whatever I like. But Ajit will have to come in here himself and see what he wants in the groom-wear area." She was already off and fingering other outfits.

Rishi moved to a portion of the wall where he could lean back and observe the transaction. His knee was beginning to ache again, and standing for long periods of time left it feeling worse. Having sat in a plane for hours earlier and with jet lag beginning to set in, he'd already put his leg under a lot of stress. Absently he bent his right leg, rested the heel flat against the wall, and rubbed the knee.

Nearly an hour later, the two young ladies had discussed bride and groom attire and Roopa had settled on her wedding and reception costumes, and they moved to the jewelry display area. Rishi once again casually sauntered to get closer to them.

When Anjali had Roopa convinced that rubies would go perfectly with the red ensemble while pink corals with pearl accents were the right jewelry to set off her reception outfit, the sale was more or less concluded.

Roopa Singh looked thoroughly pleased with herself. "It's a good thing I walked in here on your day off. I got individualized service and everything just like I wanted," she said with a smug grin. "I'll bring Ajit here soon."

"Excellent," said Anjali. "We can design something for him that harmonizes perfectly with your ensembles."

Roopa looked questioningly at Anjali. "Do you know any good salons around here that do hair and bridal makeup, *mehndi* and all that?"

"I can give you the names of several places around here," Anjali replied.

Mehndi referred to the henna designs that women, especially brides, decorated their hands and feet with. It was traditional for brides in India, but now the West had discovered it and it was all the rage, especially with second-generation Indian-Brits and Indian-Americans. In London, Rishi had introduced a full-time *mehndi* artist in one of his stores, and she was kept busy.

That's exactly what this place needs, he reflected, as he moved forward to join the two women. "Miss Singh, may I offer a suggestion?"

Roopa glanced at him. "Sure."

Anjali threw him another distressed look. He ignored it and said to Roopa, "We plan to put a salon on the premises very soon. It will offer makeup, hairstyling, nails, *mehndi,* and just about everything a bride or a party guest would need. We'll be adding on a full-service photo studio and printing options, wedding and party decorations, flowers. All our services will be first-class, just like the clothing and jewelry you just selected. You might want to wait a few weeks and stop by again?"

Roopa gave him an eager nod while she pulled out a checkbook from her handbag. "I can wait. That'll be great—everything under one roof. It's such a hassle going to ten different places to plan a wedding."

Rishi turned his gaze on Anjali. *I told you so.* But all he got was a bland look. She wasn't about to allow him his moment of triumph. He wished she'd loosen up a little.

Meanwhile Roopa cast a skeptical glance around the store. "Isn't this place a bit small to include a salon and studio, though?"

Anjali tossed him a glance this time. *I told you so.*

"But we're planning to expand soon," Rishi said. "We'll be taking over the space next door. The whole building will become one large boutique." Privately he hoped he hadn't counted his chickens even before they were eggs. Now he'd really have to work hard on Mr. Tejmal.

Perhaps sensing the undercurrent of dissension between Rishi and Anjali, Roopa looked speculatively first at one and then the other. "I'll come back in the next couple of days with Ajit and maybe we can all discuss this some more." She lifted a thin, tweezed eyebrow at Anjali. "How much deposit do you need for today?"

Rishi heard the amount Anjali quoted. With an inward smile he realized Anjali had just concluded a substantial sale to this rich young woman with a fat checkbook. Not bad for a day's worth of business—and on a day they were supposed to be closed, too.

Earlier he had told himself he'd wait and see how bright Anjali Kapadia was. He was slowly beginning to recognize that Jeevan-kaka was right about her.

Anjali printed up an invoice on her computer. "I'm going to order the fabrics tomorrow and when they come in, I'd like you to see them . . . just to make sure that's what you really want. If you approve, then I'll have our best seamstress start work on it," she said with a warm smile. "In the meantime, if you have any questions or concerns, please don't hesitate to call. Here's my card."

Roopa threw the card in her handbag. She studied the invoice and didn't seem particularly concerned with the price of the items. It too went into the bag. Extending a hand to Anjali and then to Rishi, she said, "Thanks, you guys. I think your store is beautiful. With the expansion you mentioned, I think it'll be fabulous."

Rishi nodded. "Thanks. I hope you'll recommend us to your friends?"

The young lady threw him a dimpled smile. "If everything goes perfectly, we'll definitely recommend you to others."

"Fair enough," Rishi said, returning her smile.

Both Rishi and Anjali watched Roopa Singh walk out of the store, put on her sunglasses, and get behind the wheel of her car.

Rishi turned to Anjali. "You handled that beautifully. Jolly good work."

"Just doing my job," she murmured and strode to the front door. After making sure it was locked, she hurried directly back to the office in silence.

He saw the look of total defeat in her eyes, as if her world was coming apart and she was rapidly falling through the fissure.

Was he totally wrong in his calculations? In the end, would he end up hurting this woman instead of helping her and her family like he was supposed to?

Chapter 6

Lunch was a minor disaster, in Anjali's opinion. Jeevan-kaka predictably found everything wrong with the food. The potato and beans were too spicy; the *dal* or lentils were not cooked soft enough for his liking; the *rotlis*—rolled whole-wheat bread—was not thin enough. And despite her mother's efforts to remove every speck of coconut from the *khaman*, her uncle complained that the mere smell of it was likely to cause him intestinal distress.

Surprisingly, Rishi Shah complimented Anjali's mother on the food. And she knew it wasn't merely lip service, because he ate second and third helpings, making Anjali believe his praise was genuine. But all his kind words about her mother's cooking weren't about to lessen her suspicions about him. And she was still curious about who he was and about his strange looks.

Anjali's father did his best to keep the peace at the table by telling his brother that the evening meal would be less spicy and the *dal* cooked softer. That didn't endear Mohan to his wife much, but then the guest and elder were always right.

And to everyone's amazement, Jeevan-kaka had actually apologized in his own way to his sister-in-law. "Your cooking is not bad, Usha. It is quite good, but I am getting old, you know. These days my stomach is giving me trouble, and I have to eat less spicy."

"I'll put very little chili in the food tonight," she had assured him through clenched teeth.

After the meal was over, Anjali did her best to soothe her mother's bruised ego. "Mom, don't pay attention to his comments. He's just an old man with no social graces."

Usha shrugged it off, but Anjali could see the pain in her mom's expressive eyes. How could her uncle be so thoughtless and cruel?

She rubbed her mother's shoulders. "Hopefully just a few more days, Mom, and then they'll both be gone." Anjali knew for a fact that she was trying to convince herself more than her mother. She could only pray the nightmare would be over soon. Maybe after the store was up and running smoothly, the two men would return to their respective homes.

Soon the preparations for dinner began. Her mother was already pulling out produce from the vegetable bin in the refrigerator. Anjali could feel the tension humming around Usha. This would be their daily routine from now on: cooking and cleaning and cooking and cleaning, because Jeevan-kaka refused to eat anything but home-cooked food.

Anjali's father's other brother, Naren Kapadia, and his family were invited to dinner. The good thing was, Naren being the youngest of the siblings, he was just as intimidated by Jeevan as everyone else in the family. Naren-kaka's wife, Varsha-kaki, barely tolerated Jeevan. And their daughter, Sejal, who worked part-time at the boutique, was so scared of him that as a little girl she had wet her panties in his presence once.

Meanwhile, Anjali and her mother had a brief reprieve since the old man had taken himself upstairs for a nap. The house was blissfully quiet.

Rishi Shah and her dad had gone into town so Shah could rent a car. At least that was the excuse Shah had used to get out of the house. And renting a car for his exclusive use was a brilliant idea as far as Anjali was concerned. At least she and her parents wouldn't have to chauffeur him around, and hopefully he'd take the old man in his car as much as possible.

Anjali was dicing zucchini when her brother walked in the door, looking hopelessly disheveled as usual. Nilesh wore an old cocoa brown T-shirt, faded jeans, and ratty-looking sneakers that were scuffed to the max. A bulging black backpack was slung on his right shoulder.

"Mom, Anju, what time is Jeevan-kaka arriving?" he asked. From Anjali's and Usha's expressions he must have guessed the answer. "He's here already!"

Anjali nodded. "You got *that* right."

"So where is the old dinosaur?"

"Shh, he's taking a nap," Anjali whispered, warning Nilesh to pipe down. "He's tired after picking on Mom's cooking, the walls in our home, my clothes, and of course the store."

Nilesh frowned and looked at the kitchen clock. "All of that? What time did the guy get in? The crack of dawn?"

"Close enough."

"No wonder Mom looks like shit." At his mother's vexed expression, Nilesh bit his tongue. "Sorry."

Anjali shook her head at her brother, silently telling him not to kid around with their mother. *"Pissed off,"* she mouthed to him and he nodded his understanding.

Tall and lean, Nilesh was a pleasant-looking young man, but his clothes always looked like they had just come out of the wringer—which they generally had. He never bothered to iron them. His dark, straight hair was a bit long since he let months slide between haircuts. He considered good grooming a waste of time.

Mostly Nilesh's time was devoted to the computer. Between his homework assignments, working on new software programs, the Internet, and riveting computer games, he could sit in front of a computer for hours without batting an eyelash.

He tossed his backpack on the breakfast table, opened the refrigerator, and studied the shelves for a few seconds. "I'm starving. Any leftovers from lunch, or did Jeevan-kaka polish off everything?" His face broke into a smile. "Man, I remember, that guy can really eat."

"You'll be surprised when you see him, Nil," Anjali added. "He's eating a lot less and he's lost weight."

"Lost weight? You're shitting me!"

"Watch your language, Nilesh," his mother warned. "He'll

twist your ears if he hears words like that. Remember the last time you used foul language in his presence?"

Nilesh grinned. "That was five years ago. I'm several inches taller than him now and I work out. Let him try twisting my ears this time."

Usha pointed to the lowest shelf of the refrigerator. "Leftovers are in those covered dishes. Just put whatever you want on a plate and microwave it."

Grabbing a plate from the cabinet, Nilesh set it on the counter and piled it high with food. While it warmed in the microwave, he turned to Anjali. "Why the long face? It can't be all that crappy."

Anjali snickered. "You won't be saying that when you find out what happened to your room, buddy."

Nilesh froze in place, ignoring the microwave's shrill beeps. "What do you mean?"

"It means as of today you don't have a room in this house."

Nilesh gave his mother a stunned look. "The old geezer got my room?"

Usha cleared her throat. "Well . . . he . . ."

"Why didn't you put him in the guest room?"

Again Anjali snickered. "He *is* in the guest room, but he brought a surprise."

Nilesh's thick eyebrows descended in a knot. "What?"

"Shh, keep your voice down." Usha went to the microwave and pulled out the steaming plate of food. "Your uncle has brought his business partner with him—a young man from England."

"England?" Nilesh paused. "What's his name?"

"Rishi Shah."

"Since when did Jeevan-kaka start taking on partners?" asked Nilesh, the frown still intact.

"Since now," said Anjali.

"He's a loner," argued Nilesh. "And nobody could stand having him for a partner."

Usha put the plate on the table. "Well, he has a partner now. And since Rishi Shah is staying with us, we asked him to take your room. I'm afraid you'll have to sleep on the sofa bed in the basement."

Nilesh pulled a face. "Oh fu . . . bummer! Why didn't you put that dude in Anju's room?"

"When you meet him you'll see why they couldn't," said Anjali and slid the mound of diced zucchini off the cutting board into a mixing bowl. "He's a forty-ish white-skinned guy with an interesting British accent. He wears Armani and Gucci."

"Fashionable girly type, you mean?" Nilesh asked with frank contempt.

"Hardly. He's real macho. I doubt that he'd like to sleep in a feminine bedroom with lavender sheets, gardenia-scented candles, and lace curtains on the windows."

"Put him in the basement, then," growled Nilesh. "That's manly enough."

Anjali shook her head. "He looks more like he belongs in a suite at the Waldorf."

"Enough, you two." Usha held up a spatula. "Anju, finish chopping the zucchini. Nilesh, you know we don't treat guests that way in this house. Now sit down and eat your lunch."

Everything went quiet. For about two seconds.

Grumbling about being treated like dirt in his own home, Nilesh sat down to eat his meal. Nothing distracted him from eating, though. Despite his slender physique the kid could pack away an awful lot of food. Over the next several minutes he polished off his lunch, followed by a banana and an apple, while Anjali and her mother worked on getting things ready for dinner.

Nilesh must have felt better after eating and mulling over the situation, because he rose to his feet and placed his empty plate in the sink. "So is that Shah guy napping in my room right now or can I go in and get my stuff out of there?"

His mother turned around from the stove where something was simmering in a pot. "You better transfer your things to the basement right now. Rishi has gone out with your father to rent a car. He'll be back soon."

"Fine, I'll go now." Nilesh picked up his backpack and wandered out of the kitchen, his shoulders hunched in peevish resignation.

He looked like a little boy again, thought Anjali, recalling the times when he was refused an expensive toy and he'd go sulking to his room. She turned at her mother. "I told you Nilesh would get upset."

Giving the fragrant, simmering spinach *saag* a vigorous stir, Usha replied, "He'll get over it. As long as he has his precious computer, he can manage."

With a shrug Anjali returned to her task. Some ten minutes later she heard automobiles in the driveway. Then the front door opened and her father walked in.

Curious, Anjali discarded her apron and stepped out into the foyer. "Did Mr. Shah get his rental car, Dad?" She was hoping the answer was yes.

Her father nodded. "He leased a very nice luxury SUV."

Hearing a low whistle emerge from the staircase, Anjali looked up. Nilesh was coming down the steps, his laptop and a bundle of clothes tucked under his arm. "Luxury SUV? That son-of-a-gun must be filthy rich."

Mohan frowned at his son and motioned to him to shut up. Unfortunately it didn't do much good because Rishi Shah was already approaching the front door and had heard every word of what Nilesh had uttered.

Anjali noticed the frozen expression on Nilesh's face. He seemed to be stuck on stair number three. "Shit!" he murmured under his breath. Then to Shah he said, "I—I'm sorry. That . . . wasn't a very . . . uh . . . nice thing to say."

Seemingly unmoved by Nilesh's embarrassment, Shah stepped forward to shake his hand. "Hello. You must be Nilesh? I'm Rishi Shah." He seemed cool and in control.

Nilesh transferred the laptop and clothes to his left armpit and took Shah's hand. "Yeah, I'm Nilesh." He managed to look sufficiently contrite. "Sorry . . . Didn't mean to insult you or anything. It's just, well . . . it's the SUV."

Mild amusement seemed to flit across Shah's face. "Not to

worry. I've been called a lot worse than a filthy rich son-of-a-gun."

"No kidding?" Nilesh looked incredulous.

Shah shook his head. "Significantly worse. Besides, I'm the one who should apologize for usurping your room."

Perhaps because he'd been so easily forgiven for his faux pas, Nilesh made a magnanimous gesture with his long, slim hand. "Hey, no problem, Rishi. I'll transfer some of my stuff from the room to the basement and then it's all yours."

"That's mighty generous of you."

Nilesh was too busy craning his neck to get a better look at the shiny black automobile parked in the driveway to pay attention to Shah's gratitude. "That's awesome. I'd kill to own one of those babies." He threw a meaningful look at his father, and Anjali suppressed the urge to smile. Her brother was positively bubbling. Boy, was he easy to manipulate. The wimp.

Anjali's father started walking toward the kitchen. "One of those babies is worth more than two years of your college tuition, Nilesh. I can hardly afford to maintain your mom's old sedan and my delivery van right now."

Nilesh rolled his eyes.

Shah offered Nilesh a friendly grin and inclined his head toward the driveway. "Want to give that *baby* a test drive?"

Anjali's heart skipped a tiny beat. The man was capable of grinning? In fact, he had a great grin. It transformed his face completely. His eyes crinkled at the corners and the steel in them definitely turned to a warm, smoky tint. He had nice, even teeth and a tiny dimple in his right cheek.

She hated to admit it, but Rishi Shah was a great-looking man, at least when he let his hair down and smiled a little. Even better when he grinned.

Nilesh's eyes lit up like twin candles. "You mean . . . like right now?"

"Yes. We can go for a quick spin if you'd like." Shah pulled the keys from his pocket and tossed them at Nilesh, who deftly caught them with one hand in midair. "Go get your driver's license, Nilesh. I'd like you to show me the neighborhood. I want to familiarize myself with this area. And," he added with a laugh, "get used to driving on the wrong side of the road."

"All right!" Nilesh turned and raced up the steps to get his license.

Anjali watched his jean-clad legs disappear over the landing. A weird kind of feeling was beginning to bloom in her stomach. She looked up to see Shah studying her. She felt the heat rising in her neck and face.

Fortunately, a minute later Nilesh was bounding down the staircase. "I'll show you some really cool places to hang out, Rishi."

"Jolly good." Shah lifted a dark eyebrow at Anjali. "Miss Kapadia, would you care to join Nilesh and me?" The ice in his voice was brittle enough to crack.

How could he be so nice and friendly to her brother and so cold and distant with her? Anjali shook her head. "No, thanks."

"We'll be back in a short while."

"I'm helping my mother make dinner."

Nilesh was already out the door. Anjali watched Shah follow him. His limp seemed a bit more pronounced now than it was that morning. She wondered if he was in pain. What exactly was the matter with his leg?

As they reached the vehicle Nilesh said something to him. She couldn't hear their conversation, but it must have been something ridiculously male-bonding, because she saw Nilesh and Rishi do a quick high-five. They looked like teenagers going off to meet their girlfriends for a double date. Then the two of them laughed and climbed into the vehicle.

Anjali felt a twinge of something shoot through her brain. She couldn't quite put her finger on it. It felt almost like . . . envy. But that was entirely absurd. What was there to be envious about? So her young and impressionable brother was awed by a good-looking and wealthy man some two decades older than himself—a man who seemed to be sophisticated and well traveled and knowledgeable about business. So what?

Besides, Nilesh was more dazzled by the SUV than the man who'd leased it.

No, she concluded, it wasn't envy. Perhaps it was the insignificant detail that he called everyone else by a friendlier handle than he did her. She was Miss Kapadia to him. She turned that over for a second. Oh well, that was fine with her. It kept a certain distance between them.

She shut the front door and returned to the kitchen. But Shah's mysterious limp and its cause kept her thinking.

Chapter 7

Anjali nearly choked on her food. Jeevan-kaka had just pulled out a gun from his pocket and was brandishing it like a mad highwayman. His short, stubby fingers were amazingly nimble as he twirled it, allowing the folks around the dinner table to get a good look at his toy. He looked like a little kid with his first ever birthday present.

Her hands shook so much she had to put her water glass down so it wouldn't slide out of her grip. She'd never seen a gun up close—only in movies and TV. Almost everyone at the dinner table silently watched Jeevan's dramatic gesture with a mixture of awe and fear, except Rishi Shah, who continued to eat his dinner with no more than a casual glance at Jeevan.

Nilesh looked positively giddy with delight. "Way to go, Jeevan-kaka!" he exclaimed, his eyes ablaze. "That could blow a nice little hole in a guy's head."

Jeevan-kaka looked like Danny DeVito trying to play John Wayne. "Beautiful gun, huh, Nilesh? You want to look at it?" The old man started to lean across the table with the gun held out.

"No!" Usha's voice cracked like a whip, making Nilesh's spoon clatter onto his plate and Jeevan withdraw his hand. "Nilesh is not allowed to touch a gun. Not in *this* house."

"Mom!" Nilesh exploded at his mother. "I just wanted to look at it, okay? I'm not exactly planning to go on a wild shooting spree."

Usha tossed him a blistering glance. "No. Guns are not to be taken lightly." Then she sent her brother-in-law a dark look. "I would appreciate it if you don't let my son anywhere near that . . . that thing, Jeevan-bhai."

Cousin Sejal's pretty face was frozen in wide-eyed wonder. Anjali hoped Sejal wasn't going to pee in her pants. At four it was understandable, but at twenty-four it would be a major embarrassment. Anjali's aunt, Varsha-kaki, was nervously trying to brush imaginary hair off her face. Not a single loose tendril was to be seen anywhere in the vicinity of her round, fair, moonlike face.

"Jeevan-kaka, what are you doing with a gun?" Anjali managed to ask after she'd had a few seconds to recover.

Her uncle flashed a grin. "This is protection, Anju. If anybody tries funny business with me, I will shoot his brains with my pistol."

Naren-kaka looked like he was about to throw up. "Jeevan-bhai, p-please put that thing down. It is making me n-nervous." Naren-kaka was a slim man who resembled Anjali's father quite a bit. The two brothers had the same sharp features, high cheekbones, and dense mop of hair, except Naren was shorter than his brother, and his hair was not entirely gray yet.

Jeevan of course was in a league of his own—no resemblance whatsoever to the siblings, physical, mental, emotional, or intellectual.

Anjali's father kept swallowing large quantities of water while her mother looked like she was ready to pick up the nearest saucepan and hit Jeevan over the head. Usha spoke in a quietly authoritative voice. "Jeevan-bhai, this is a safe neighborhood and nobody's going to try any funny business with you. Please put that thing away."

"See how it is making everybody nervous? It always works. Even murderers are afraid of my gun." Jeevan-kaka's glee was unmistakable.

Until a little while ago, her Indian uncle was merely a crusty old man, Anjali reflected. He was still a crusty old man, but now he was armed and dangerous. He was turning into a demon.

Where had he acquired a gun? And if he'd had it all along, how had he brought it with him all the way from India? Security at airports these days was extremely tight. Did he have a permit to carry one of those things?

Mohan glanced warily at his oldest brother. "Why do you need that kind of protection?"

Jeevan-kaka's eyes had a feral gleam in them. "Do you know what life in rural India is for some of us? There are bandits roaming the countryside these days. They break into people's houses in the middle of the night."

"Bandits in *this* century?" asked Mohan.

"Oh yes. They're heavily armed. The only solution for their victims is a gun, Mohan."

"That might be the case in India, but not here," Anjali protested. "We live in a civilized society."

"Doesn't *Amreeka* have the worst crime rate?" sneered Jeevan. "Almost every television show has *Amreekan* people getting robbed and murdered and raped—even worse than India."

"You're talking about fictional crime dramas and movies." Anjali was losing her patience with him. "Real life isn't like that."

"What are you talking about, Anju? I read newspapers and watch TV news all the time. Somebody is murdering somebody every day. *Amreeka* has the most guns in the world."

"But that is in some inner cities only," Mohan explained patiently. "Ours is a quiet suburban area. There is practically no violent crime here."

Perhaps noting the fearful expressions on everyone's face, Rishi Shah intervened. "They're right, Jeevan-kaka. This seems like a safe area. I went out with Nilesh for a ride earlier. I didn't notice anything dangerous. Why don't you put that thing away for now?" When Jeevan-kaka hesitated, he quietly added, "Please."

"All right." Jeevan deposited the gun on the table and went back to finishing his meal, astounding Anjali once again. Five years ago, he would have done exactly as he pleased, but now he'd actually agreed to abide by his young partner's request.

What sort of hold did Shah have over her uncle? No one else had that kind of influence over the old man. But whatever it was, it worked, and she was grateful. For now, the gun was safely out of her uncle's hands.

Anjali sent Rishi Shah a silent look of thanks across the table. He acknowledged it with a nod and went back to eating. The food was terribly bland this time around because of Jeevan-kaka's gastric problems, but nobody was complaining—not even Jeevan-kaka.

The rest of the folks still seemed a bit on edge. Sejal and her mother threw quick, nervous glances at the gun. Nilesh was still sulking from his mother's reprimand.

Anjali felt her stomach tremble at the thought of having a firearm in the house, in the hands of a madman like her uncle. She wasn't sure if he knew how to use it properly. She also wondered how Shah put up with that sort of thing. Unless . . . he carried a gun, too? Was that why he was serenely polishing off the food on his plate, like a gun on the dining table was an everyday occurrence?

Her uncle had said he needed a firearm to protect himself in present-day rural India. Anjali had often wondered why her uncle had moved from his spacious city home in Anand to his farm in the country, and why he'd continued to live there when all his siblings lived either in the U.S. or the U.K. But then he had a lot of his money invested in Gujarat, a legacy that had come down from his father, Anjali's grandfather, who'd started out as a clerk but had worked hard to start a small cloth mill and eventually succeeded.

As the meal came to an end, Anjali was somewhat grateful for the gun episode because it had diverted her uncle's attention from the food. Another round of critical comments about her mother's cooking would have resulted in some major fireworks. Although the rest of the group was made up of family, Rishi Shah was an outsider and she didn't want the embarrassment of a family feud in his presence.

A little later, her mother brought out dessert—*doodh paak*. She had remembered to make a separate batch with low-fat milk and a sugar substitute for Jeevan-kaka. Anjali watched him finish two helpings of the rice pudding garnished with almonds and pistachios.

Anjali's aunt and cousin helped wash the dishes and when the kitchen was neat and clean once again, everyone settled down in the family room to chat over a cup of *chai*.

What caught Anjali's eye was her cousin Sejal slanting coy glances at Rishi Shah. Was shy little Sejal beginning to develop a mild crush on Shah? It was understandable, of course. Sejal was raised in a very strict home and not allowed any real social contact with men except the nice and nerdy Gujarati guys her parents tried to fix her up with.

Shah, on the other hand, was an entirely different species of male: suave, successful, older, and far more mature than the men Sejal was used to. He exuded cool confidence—exactly what Sejal would consider sexy and a bit of a challenge. And his unusual Caucasian looks were probably enticing, too. More disturbing was Shah catching Sejal's eye once or twice and smiling—just a quiet hint of a smile, but a smile nevertheless.

Sejal blushed violently each time.

Anjali bristled. Shah was flirting with her young cousin. If he thought he could find some free entertainment in Sejal during his visit to the U.S. he was sadly mistaken. He could even be married, with kids. Well, if he made a move on Sejal, Anjali would tell Jeevan-kaka about him and have Shah properly chastised.

But somehow Anjali doubted if anything or anyone could intimidate Shah. He looked much too self-assured to be easily scared away, and looked entirely too comfortable in the U.S.

Chapter 8

Anjali came awake to the ear-shattering sound of a bell ringing. What the heck was that? Then it struck her. The house was on fire! She shot out of bed, the adrenaline instantly spiking in her blood. It was dark in her room and she groped frantically for the light switch till she found it. At least the electricity was still on.

With no thought other than to get herself and everyone in the family out of the house, she opened the bedroom door and ran down the hallway yelling, "Fire, you guys! Get out!"

Her heartbeat thundering in her ears, she managed to turn on the hallway light and sped down the stairs. Downstairs in the foyer, she skidded to a stop. Oh God! Nilesh was sleeping in the basement. What if the fire had started there? That boy was so careless sometimes.

She ran to the kitchen, opened the door that led to the basement, and stumbled downstairs in the dark, yelling again. "Nil! Honey, get out! Fire!"

Turning on the basement light with shaking fingers, she looked around. Nilesh was stretched out on his stomach, his head buried under the pillow. Her heart skipped a beat. Was her baby brother unconscious from breathing carbon monoxide fumes? She rushed up to the sofa bed and poked a finger at the long, hairy leg that stuck out of the covers. "Nil?" No response. "Nilesh?"

Nilesh stirred a little, shifted, and went right back to sleep.

Fear zipped through her chest. He wasn't waking up. Oh boy! That wasn't a good sign. She poked him hard in the back this time. "Nil . . . baby . . ."

"Damn it!" Nilesh turned onto his back and tore the pillow off his face. "What the fuck are you doing?" He squinted at her.

She bent down and peered at him. He seemed okay. "There's a fire, you silly boy. Get out of bed. Now!"

He frowned at her and snorted like a cantankerous horse. "What fire?"

"Don't you hear the alarm? It's been screaming for several minutes."

He sat up groggily. "What the—" He shook his head. "That's not what our fire alarm sounds like. That sounds like . . ." He listened more carefully. "Like temple bells."

Several sets of quick footsteps could be heard stomping on the floor above. The others had obviously woken up and rushed downstairs. Anjali cocked her ears. "You're right; it does sound like bells."

Her father came down, his hair standing on end and his hunter green pajamas looking rumpled. "What are you two doing? Your mom and I are trying to get some sleep."

Nilesh pointed an accusing finger at Anjali. "It's *her* fault. She's running around screaming like a damn lunatic. She stabbed me in the back and disturbed my sleep, too."

"Oh stop it, you big crybaby. I didn't stab you." Anjali turned to her father with a sheepish look. "It sounded like a fire alarm, so I decided to wake everyone up."

"And you did a fine job! Now we're all up." Her father ran all ten fingers through his hair and stared at her.

Before Anjali could say anything else, her mother appeared on the steps, wrapped in a pretty pink robe, frowning delicately. "What is all this commotion about?"

Anjali glanced at her mother, wondering how she could look so good at such an ungodly hour while her father looked like a troll. "Mom, what on earth is that sound if it's not the fire alarm?"

Usha sighed long and loud. "It's your uncle doing his morning *pooja*. He has brought a big brass bell for the purpose. I forgot to tell you last night."

"Oh man, I should have known it was Jeevan-kaka. The guy's a menace." Nilesh stuck his fingers in his ears and fell back on his bed. "Just shut the fucking door, you guys, and let me get some sleep."

"No need for obscenities," Usha warned Nilesh, then turned around and started up the stairs, with Mohan in tow. "Let's all get some sleep. It's only four-fifty in the morning."

Anjali stood still for a second, the clanging bell wreaking havoc on her already frayed nerves. "Oh, Jeevan-kaka, what am I going to do with you?" She stomped up the stairs and shut off the stairway light before closing the door. "The man needs to be brought under control," she murmured to herself.

The sound of the bell was coming from the family room and the light was on in there, so she headed toward it, fully prepared to deliver a lecture to her uncle.

She found Jeevan-kaka dressed in nothing but white pajamas. Sitting cross-legged on the floor with his bare, hairy back to her, he looked like a hunched-up teddy bear. His bald head was sprinkled with age spots of various sizes and shades of brown. A low stool with silver idols of Krishna and Ganesh was placed in front of him. In his right hand he had a huge bell that he was swinging with all his might.

He was chanting something in a low murmur and seemed entirely immersed in his ritualistic homage to the gods. An incense stick burned in a small silver holder, perfuming the air with some sort of tropical floral scent, and a tea light flickered before the idols.

Anjali was tempted to rush in, seize the bell from his hand, and toss it out the window, but something stopped her. Her uncle looked peaceful, despite the racket created by the bell. All the rest of the noise—her yelling and the family running up and down the stairs—had apparently not made a dent in his concentration.

She stood in the doorway, contemplating. Since when had the wily fox become so spiritual anyway? Five years ago he wasn't into anything religious. She'd have remembered the bell, if nothing else. Back then, all he had cared about was money. How to make lots of it. And how to keep all of it.

Gradually her irritation receded. He was just an odd old man praying. A bit extreme to conduct one's *pooja* in such a thoughtless manner, but he was still being a devout Hindu. What could she do but overlook it?

With a resigned sigh she headed back upstairs. With any luck, she'd be able to stuff some cotton balls in her ears and get a couple of hours of sleep. The *pooja* had to end at some point. She hadn't been able to fall asleep until well after midnight. Jeevan-kaka's gun and Rishi Shah's silent flirtation with Sejal had bothered her.

Speaking of Shah, as she reached the landing she saw him leaning against the frame of his bedroom door, arms folded across his middle. Other than the navy robe, worn over navy pajamas, and big bare feet, there was no other sign of his having been awakened unexpectedly. His hair looked neat and even the dark shadow of beard didn't look all that out of place. His gaze was fixed on her. "Is the fire emergency over, Miss Kapadia?"

She sent him an apologetic look. "Sorry, but Jeevan-kaka's bell sounded like the fire alarm. It was a gut reaction on my part."

To her surprise, Shah smiled, sending a mild and unexpected flutter through her system. "I don't blame you. It is rather loud."

"It's enough to bust one's eardrums. I don't know when he became so religious. He wasn't into this kind of stuff the last time he stayed with us."

"He's been at it for a while now. And you're not the first to mistake his bell for a fire alarm."

"No?" She wasn't a lunatic after all.

"We were in a hotel in Singapore last year and several of the guests on our floor ran out into the corridor half naked and screaming bloody fire because of his bell."

Anjali couldn't help chuckling. "He performed his *pooja* in a hotel room?"

"He takes his morning worship very seriously. I was in the bathroom when his bell pealed and I rushed out with just a towel covering me. I made a complete idiot of myself and sent one nice old English lady into a dead faint."

Despite her misgivings about Shah, Anjali burst out laughing. "A serious attack of the vapors, as some old-fashioned Brits would say." She couldn't stop laughing. Maybe because of the lingering effects of the adrenaline, she nearly doubled over with mirth.

She could only imagine the chaos in a grand hotel, with those prim and proper rich folks running around, distressed about being seen in all their semi-naked glory. Her hilarity abruptly subsided when she remembered the last part of his anecdote. "You didn't really run outside with just a . . . towel, did you?"

His eyes danced with humor. "I did, and I must have looked like a clown, too. I had shaving cream over half my face."

Anjali's stomach clenched. Holy cow, he looked good when he laughed. His eyes turned to pure smoke. She couldn't help the hot color rising in her cheeks. She was picturing him wearing nothing but a scrap of cloth, and the image was . . . driving her pulse rate up. "W-what did you do?"

"I convinced Jeevan-kaka to use a smaller and less boisterous bell. I even went out and bought him a small bell from a souvenir shop."

"Did the old tyrant agree to use it?"

Shah drew a dramatic breath. "Yes, a bit reluctantly. But then we had another catastrophe the next morning."

"No!"

"His incense sticks, those jasmine *agarbattis* he uses, set off the real smoke alarm and it was bedlam once again at five A.M. in the hotel."

She went into a hysterical fit of laughter again. She could picture the pandemonium the second time around. "So what happened then?"

"We very nearly got ousted from the hotel, but I had a talk with the hotel's management. The owner happens to be an acquaintance of mine."

"Damage control, huh?" Suddenly conscious that her hair was a complete mess and she was dressed in a skimpy, emerald green nightgown with no sleeves and a low neck, she moved quickly toward her bedroom door. The hemline barely came down to mid-thigh and her legs were completely bare. Now *she* felt almost naked. "I . . . uh . . . think I'll try to get some sleep now. You might want to do the same."

"Miss Kapadia."

"Hmm?"

"You have splendid legs."

She drew in a sharp breath. "Oh." She frowned. "Oh." She had no idea how to handle that.

"A modern American woman like you ought to be able to handle a simple compliment." The amusement still lurked in his eyes.

She stepped inside her room and shut the door, then stood leaning against it, shaking. He was definitely a very strange man.

But he sure looked good in his monogrammed silk robe, and his smile was brilliant. And best of all, he'd laughed at himself when he'd recounted his hotel escapade and Jeevan-kaka's bells. Now that she thought about it, she wasn't sure if Shah had made it all up just to amuse her.

She had a weakness for men with a self-deprecating sense of humor. And oh boy, she couldn't get the nearly nude image of him out of her mind.

Groaning, she went back to her bed. She wasn't supposed to like Rishi Shah. He was the man who had exploded into her life when she'd least expected it. He was the guy who was going to take over her business and turn her graceful Silk & Sapphires into something gaudy and grotesque.

No, she couldn't like Shah. Or could she?

Chapter 9

Rishi emerged from the shower feeling considerably more refreshed than he'd felt an hour ago. His leg felt slightly better, too. The cursed knee was acting up again. He had tossed and turned on the narrow single bed belonging to Nilesh. It wasn't uncomfortable, but Rishi was used to more lavish beds at his townhouse in London and his apartment in Delhi.

And Jeevan-kaka's bell had created the worst sort of disturbance, giving him a headache to match the throbbing in his leg.

Besides, it wasn't the feel of the bed or the level of the air-conditioning that had left him with practically no sleep. It was the whole bloody setup. He was a stranger to these people. They had been kind and hospitable to him, and young Nilesh was already treating him like a mentor of sorts, an older friend.

The Kapadias were a nice, wholesome family, but he was imposing on them. If Jeevan-kaka hadn't insisted that Rishi stay here instead of at a hotel, this never would have happened. He hated hurting Jeevan-kaka's feelings and that meant staying here at least for a few days.

Plus, the pretty and intriguing Anjali's presence only a few feet from where he slept was mildly disquieting. He didn't like the fact that she was stealing his thoughts away from Samantha, his girlfriend in London. He'd promised Samantha he'd invite her to join him soon so they could take a much-needed holiday.

Maybe he could take Samantha to one of the Caribbean island resorts where they could swim in a crystal-blue ocean, lie on the beach for hours and bake themselves till they turned the color of lightly grilled pork chops. And Samantha looked magnificent in a bikini—especially that little white number with the tiny black bows.

Lately he hadn't had time for lying idle anywhere. His life was mostly work-work-work and travel-travel-travel. He'd been so busy tending to his multiple stores and offering consulting services to other businesses that he hadn't given a thought to anything else.

All the money he was raking in was nice, but sometime in the near future he'd have to slow down and give himself a moment to enjoy some of it. Jeevan-kaka had been lecturing him on acquiring a wife. But Rishi had come to the conclusion that Samantha wasn't the wifely sort. She was good in bed, efficient as a business associate, marvelous as the woman on his arm at business and social functions, but she was certainly not the wife-and-mother type.

Oh well, for now he wasn't keen on marriage anyway. He had no time for a wife. Besides, he was too old for marriage and too set in his ways. Forty-two was rather late to think about a wife and a family, wasn't it? However, Jeevan-kaka was convinced otherwise. The old man thought forty-two was not in the least unrealistic to get married and start a family. Maybe he was right. The old fox often was.

Rishi grabbed a towel. The Kapadias apparently had two full-size bathrooms upstairs and a small powder room downstairs. Assuming the master bath was exclusively for Mohan and Usha's use, Rishi would obviously be sharing this bathroom with Jeevan-kaka, Anjali, and Nilesh. Though she was cute and alluring, sharing a bathroom with Anjali was a bit too intimate for him.

However, at the moment, as he dried himself, he was experiencing some cheap voyeuristic thrills in looking at her toiletries sitting on the counter: lotions, creams, and cleansers with ingredients like honey, yogurt, and wild berries; a purple razor with a rosebud on the handle; a hair dryer; a couple of brushes. Next to the tub were more scented shampoos and conditioners, and a shaving cream for women. The bathroom smelled like Anjali—a combination of . . . what was it? Strawberries and . . . gardenias was his guess.

The house was quiet and the sun was already brightening the sky as he slipped back into Nilesh's room and got dressed. It promised to be a hot day.

Fortunately he had found an ironing board and an iron in the closet the previous evening, so he didn't have to worry about wearing clothes wrinkled from having traveled in a suitcase. The iron was brand new and was still in its original box. When he'd seen Nilesh he'd realized why. The boy looked like he wouldn't know what an iron was.

Rishi couldn't help smiling as he recalled meeting Nilesh the previous afternoon. The boy was a spoiled brat, but he was bright. He also had potential, at least in the technical field.

Minutes later, dressed in a lightweight gray suit and a cream shirt and coordinated tie, Rishi tiptoed downstairs in search of a cup of tea. It was 7:13 A.M. The rest of the household was obviously sleeping after the morning's perceived fire scare. He found Jeevan sitting bare-chested in white pajamas at the kitchen table, reading a newspaper.

"Good morning," he said to the older man.

Jeevan looked up over his reading glasses. "Good morning, *beta*. You are up early."

"Jet lag," Rishi replied.

"Me, too. That is why I got up at dawn and finished my *pooja*."

Well before dawn. Rishi smiled. "I know. Your bell caused a bit of a stir in the house."

Jeevan appeared clueless. "You want some *chai*?"

"*Chai* was exactly what I had in mind, but you don't drink *chai* anymore," said Rishi, wondering if he should say something about Jeevan disturbing the household before sunup.

After a moment he decided it was best to let Mohan Kapadia handle his big brother on his own.

Pointing to a stainless steel pan on the stove, Jeevan-kaka said, "I made *masala* milk for myself and *chai* for you. Cups are in the cabinet on the right. Help yourself."

Taking a sip of the thick, aromatic brew, Rishi turned to Jeevan with a pleased grin. "Not bad, sir . . . not bad at all."

"Rishi, I know how to make the best *chai*. I used to make it for my brothers and sisters when I was young and unmarried." He pointed a finger toward the ceiling. "I think Usha is in the bad habit of waking up late. So I made the milk and *chai* myself."

"I appreciate that." It was very thoughtful of the old man— thoughtful and unexpected, but entirely inconsiderate in disturbing everyone with his bell, and unkind in his remarks about Usha. But then that was Jeevan-kaka—a man of contradictions.

"Poor Auntie Usha was up late and she'd been slogging in the kitchen all day," Rishi said in her defense. He raised his brows at Jeevan. "So, what are our plans for today? Personally, I think we should approach Mr. Tejmal first thing this morning and talk business."

"Perfect. I had the same thing in mind." Jeevan folded the paper and laid it on the table. "I want you to take care of it."

"Are you sure?" Privately, Rishi had been hoping to do it on his own. Jeevan-kaka was about as subtle as a steamroller with a row of sharp steel teeth. He tended to put potential sellers on the defensive. Jeevan nodded, so he said, "Excellent. What time do the stores open in this area?"

"I think around ten o'clock."

Rishi looked at his watch. "I'll see if I can find a fitness club around here somewhere and sign up for a membership. If I don't get some exercise soon, my leg is going to fall asleep."

A concerned expression came over Jeevan's face. "Rishi, the long plane ride must have been bad for the leg?"

"That's all right. I travel all over the world. I can deal with it."

"Thank you, *beta*. You don't know how important this is to me."

"I have some idea."

"If my brother and his family are having problems, it is my duty to help them. And I trust you to come up with a good plan for them."

Rising to put his cup in the sink, Rishi patted Jeevan's shoulder. "I'd been planning to talk to you about expanding our market into the U.S. sometime in the future. This presents an opportunity."

"It does?"

"And it's rather fortunate that your brother already has a business and knows something about U.S. import-export laws."

Jeevan peeled off his glasses and laid them on the table, then rubbed his eyes with his palms. "You are right." He looked at his wristwatch. "I think I will go upstairs and get dressed now."

Rishi wandered over to the family room and the telephone. Locating a telephone directory, he opened the blinds on the window and sat down on the couch. As he was unfamiliar with American directories, it took him a couple of minutes to find what he was looking for.

He found several gyms and fitness centers and jotted down the addresses and phone numbers for a few that seemed to be within the immediate area. Later, when Nilesh was up, he would ask him for recommendations. The boy looked like he worked out. He had to know a gym or two. Come to think of it, Anjali's trim, athletic figure probably owed something to working out regularly, too.

Feeling restless, Rishi picked up the remote control and flicked channels on the small but serviceable television set until he found BBC News and settled down to watch what was happening around the world. A few minutes later, Jeevan-kaka joined him.

The two men sat companionably on the couch and watched the news for a while, then shut off the TV and returned to discussing business. Rishi pulled out a small notebook and pen from his pocket and made notes.

Half an hour later, Usha Kapadia appeared, dressed in a pastel blue cotton sari. She looked well groomed and ready to face the day. "Sorry, I overslept this morning," she murmured and headed straight for the kitchen.

"Usha, I already made milk for myself and *chai* for Rishi," Jeevan informed her.

Usha turned around and gaped at the old man. "Since when did *you* start making *chai?*"

"I always knew how to make it." Jeevan grinned. "Whenever it becomes necessary, I still make it."

"Good for you, Jeevan-bhai." Usha strode into the kitchen and very soon the appetizing aroma of onions sizzling in oil wafted into the family room.

Rishi's stomach rumbled. By his body clock it was lunchtime, and whatever she was making in there smelled jolly good.

By the time Usha had breakfast on the table, it was close to 9:00 A.M. and Mohan had joined the two men in the family room.

Just as they were about to start eating the wonderful looking *powha*—beaten rice seasoned with mustard seeds, onions, hot chilis and potato chunks, Anjali put in an appearance. Rishi's mind went on full alert as the sweet strawberry-gardenia scent reached him.

This morning she was dressed in a narrow tan skirt that reached just below her knees and a shirt in a very becoming blue. Her hair looked soft and freshly washed. The lady had class.

Amazing, Rishi reflected. She didn't look like she'd had very little sleep. She seemed full of pep laced with the usual dose of guarded reserve. He watched her open the refrigerator, pour a glass of orange juice for herself, and take a dainty sip.

Mentally he tried to toss Anjali out of his mind and replace the image with Samantha. Right about now it was early afternoon in London and Samantha would be at work in her crowded advertising office, looking very efficient in one of her designer suits and issuing orders to her staff.

Strangely, the thought of Samantha didn't stir a single amorous sentiment this morning, like it used to at one time. Instead, his eyes traveled to Anjali, who was still standing at the kitchen counter, sipping her orange juice, pretending to ignore him and everyone else at the table. She tried hard to keep up the cool image, but he didn't believe it for one moment.

He could sense a lot of heated emotions churning in that pretty head of hers. It seemed like behind all that wariness there was sadness. The wounded look had taken him by surprise when he'd caught a flash of it the previous day. It was a brief glimpse but it was definitely there. She was unhappy inside. But she didn't want anyone to know it. He wondered if she ever showed that side to her parents—or to anyone.

Breakfast was quiet. Jeevan-kaka didn't make a bit of fuss. He ate in quiet contemplation. Rishi had a feeling the old man was a little nervous about the prospect of Mr. Tejmal's willingness to sell.

When Nilesh finally showed up for breakfast, red-eyed, unshaven, and scruffy, Rishi asked him about local gyms. Just as he'd guessed, the young man knew quite a bit and recommended one that was only a mile from the house.

Rishi thanked his hostess for an excellent breakfast and rose from his chair. "I'm going to sign up for a temporary membership at the gym. I'll meet you folks at the store later," he informed them and headed out.

All the way to the gym, Rishi mulled over his imminent meeting with Tejmal. Having done his research, Rishi knew exactly what kind of a price he would offer. He believed in fair business practices. Buying and selling had to be a satisfactory experience for both parties. Negotiations could get rough depending on the old man's attitude and business savvy. If the old chap was anything like Jeevan-kaka, God help him.

As the large, single-story building that housed the gym came into view, he slowed down, found a spot in the parking lot, and parked his vehicle. Several cars were already there. It looked like the place opened early.

Perfect, he thought with a satisfied nod. It suited him well—the earlier the better.

Chapter 10

"Hi, Anjali, it's me again." The girlish voice sounded cheerful and eager.

Anjali, who was bending down to pick up some packaging material off the floor, straightened up and pushed the hair out of her eyes. Her face broke into a smile of recognition. "Roopa!"

"I brought Ajit this time." Roopa Singh was dressed in a white miniskirt and a white shirt with bold neon green and blue splashes. She wore the same white sandals that she'd worn the previous day and carried the same white handbag. Her hair was tied back in a ponytail. She could easily be mistaken for a carefree teenager instead of a responsible schoolteacher.

"Welcome to Silk & Sapphires." Anjali offered her hand to Roopa's fiancé. "I'm Anjali Kapadia. So you're the lucky groom."

"I'm Ajit Sahni." The man shook her hand with a lighthearted grin. "I'm the lucky guy who's going to be footing Roopa's shopping bills after May of next year," he added and playfully tugged on Roopa's ponytail.

"Congratulations." Anjali noticed he was at least a foot taller than the petite Miss Singh. He was a slim man with a narrow face and a dark mustache and goatee. He wore glasses that gave him a serious, owlish look. But the friendly grin seemed to change that image at once. It bordered on cute. She could see why any young woman would find him irresistible.

Her next hour was spent with the couple, going over sketches, designs, and styles, just like she had the previous day with Roopa.

She observed the groom-to-be whip out his platinum American Express card to pay for the deposit on his purchases. His elegantly fitted clothes and the sleek imported sports car parked outside convinced her that theirs would be an ultra-expensive wedding. The bridal clothes and accessories would probably be a drop in the bucket where these two happy young people were concerned, so she didn't particularly feel guilty about selling them her top-of-the-line items. Ajit and Roopa were doing their part in keeping the store from plunging into bankruptcy, God bless them. And hopefully showcase her designs well enough to bring their friends to her store.

A slight pang of envy struck her, though, as she watched Ajit Sahni put a possessive arm around Roopa's slim waist and give it a squeeze. While Anjali rang up the sale, she caught a quick glimpse of the intimate look that passed between the couple. They were in love.

Ah, love—such a beautiful thing. And so fleeting. Anjali would probably never again experience the feeling of being completely and foolishly in love. She was too old and too jaded for that sort of sentimental mush anymore.

She considered herself a dedicated businesswoman and designer. Making beautiful clothes and selling them to folks who appreciated them and wore them with the same sense of awe that she felt in creating them were her main interests in life now. Love and marriage were not something she paid attention to, although her parents would have loved it if she did.

But now that Jeevan-kaka was here with his old-fashioned ideas about marriage, the subject was likely to rear its head again. She'd have to find new ways to avoid it.

The credit card receipt sputtered out of the register, interrupting her thoughts. She handed it to Ajit for his signature. "We'll let you guys know when our other bridal services are up and running."

"I can't wait to get the bridal hair and makeup demonstration," said Roopa, trying to get a peek at the receipt her fiancé was signing.

"There'll be an elegant *chai* and coffee shop on the premises, by the way."

Ajit raised his jet-black eyebrows. "Pretty fancy. You hear that, babe?" he teased his fiancée. "You could practically live here during the summer."

"We aim to please," said Anjali with a chuckle and put the signed receipt away. "A unique shopping experience for brides, grooms, and everyone in between . . . for any occasion." She was surprised to find herself peddling, or rather *almost* peddling the one-stop concept herself, although she didn't have too much faith in it.

But she had no choice other than to market the notion actively and hope it would succeed.

"Thanks, Anjali," said Ajit. "I'll stop by in February for my first fitting, then. Here's my business card if you need to reach me." Pocketing the invoice and the credit card receipt, Ajit wrapped his arm around Roopa once again. "You ready for lunch, sweetheart?"

Roopa nodded, the stars in her eyes even brighter than they were an hour ago. "Shopping makes me hungry."

Ajit winked at Anjali over Roopa's head. "Shopping makes her hungry; it makes me lose my shirt." When Roopa threw him a look of mock indignation, he grinned and steered her toward the exit.

People in love, thought Anjali with an indulgent shake of her head. She promised herself she'd make it a lovely wedding for them—something they'd remember forever. She chuckled over Ajit's droll remark about losing his shirt.

"You should laugh more often; it suits you."

Anjali looked up and her laughter faded. Rishi Shah stood a few feet away, his suit still looking good after hours of wear. He must have come in through the rear entrance because she would have seen him if he'd walked in the front door. "Mr. Shah, I thought you were going to be out on important business all day." She'd been looking forward to a day of peace and quiet.

"Don't you wish? That's what I'd expected, too, but the old man, Tejmal, was too bloody easy to convince." Rishi Shah smiled that rare, amused smile.

"You mean easy to manipulate."

"Same thing." His confidence was enviable.

"I guess that means Tejmal is willing to sell?"

"Willing, ready, and eager," he replied. "Not much of a challenge, if you ask me. Within the week we can close the deal and that space becomes ours." He pointed at the wall on Tejmal's side.

Week? Anjali felt her heart drop very slowly. She'd hoped it would take months, at least weeks before anything jelled, so she could have a little more time to get used to the idea. Exactly how much money had Shah offered the old man to make him so anxious to give up his property?

She raised an eyebrow. "You managed to get financing arranged that quickly? No wonder they call you a business whiz."

"We're paying cash. That's what attracted Tejmal in the first place. He was rather hesitant in the beginning, but I mentioned cash and his cataract-riddled eyes lit up."

"Tejmal has cataracts?"

"One of the many reasons he wants to get out of the grocery business and retire. He told me he'd been putting off having eye surgery for the last couple of years. Now he can go ahead and schedule his operation," said Rishi.

"I see." Anjali noticed that typical British and Indian way of pronouncing *schedule*. It always intrigued her.

"It's just a matter of arranging for our London bank to transfer the funds. Then we can set up an appointment with Tejmal's lawyer and accountant and yours."

"Oh."

"That's all you have to say, Miss Kapadia? I thought you'd have some choice words for a man who browbeats old men like Tejmal into submission."

"Would it matter? You and Jeevan-kaka have everything locked away. The store is yours now."

"Wait a minute. That's not true."

She gave a long sigh. "Fifty-one percent ownership means you own most of it, Mr. Shah."

"I realize Jeevan-kaka and I look like bullies at the moment, but I hope in time you'll realize that once the refurbishing and setup are complete, we'll leave everything to you and your parents. The store is still very much yours. We'll only be silent partners. We don't plan to interfere unless it becomes necessary, Anjali."

"You mean when we screw up completely, like we did this past year?" She realized he'd used her first name.

He eyed her for a moment. "We don't believe any of you *screwed up*, as you choose to put it. Business decisions are not always perfect. We all make mistakes. And we learn from them."

"I must be the exception."

"Don't be so hard on yourself, Anjali." As if he'd suddenly realized he'd called her by her first name, he tilted his head. "May I call you Anjali?"

"Of course, Mr. Shah."

"I wish you'd call me Rishi, especially since we'll be partners soon."

She shrugged. "As you wish."

He abruptly moved in behind the counter to where she stood, crowding her between himself and the cash register, taking her by surprise. "Anjali, please don't pretend indifference. If we are to work together for a while to make this shop a success, you have to start showing a modicum of interest. All this is more yours than it ever will be mine or your uncle's." He took a step closer, literally squeezing her against the register. "You understand what I'm saying?"

Anjali struggled for breath. It took a moment to realize the breathlessness was caused by his nearness. She could smell his aftershave, clearly see the small scar just beneath his right eyebrow, and literally count the number of hairs in his thick, short eyelashes. Dear Lord, but the man had a disturbing presence.

She swallowed hard, but managed to breathe and hold his gaze. "Y-yes," she finally managed to choke out.

"So, do we have an understanding?"

"Uh-huh."

He still towered over her. "Will you start addressing me as Rishi?"

Feeling limp and still out of breath, she nodded. She could see his shoulders ease a little.

"I'm sorry," he murmured. Unexpectedly he raised a hand to touch her face—a gentle, fleeting touch. "I didn't mean to frighten you. I'm not the sort of chap who hurts women."

"I—I'm not frightened." She didn't think he was dangerous. That's probably why she hadn't made a single move to escape when he'd come too close. He was intense, a ruthless business-man, perhaps, but he didn't come across as a violent man.

He backed away several paces and then moved back to the other side of the counter before extending a hand. "Truce?"

She nodded and placed a damp hand in his large, dry one. She still couldn't speak. Her insides were tingling.

"Ah, there you are." Jeevan-kaka's voice interrupted them as he emerged from the back and approached them. "Did you tell Anju the good news, Rishi?"

Rishi nodded. "I did, and she's thrilled." He turned to Anjali with a smile. There was no hint of what had just occurred be-tween them. "Aren't you, Anjali?"

"Yes," Anjali murmured, her voice still unsteady. This was ridiculous. She was reacting like she'd just stepped off a roller coaster. But then Rishi Shah had managed to twist her nerves into tight knots during that brief minute when he'd pressed against her. He, on the other hand, looked unruffled.

"Good. Next thing on the agenda is interviewing the building contractors." Jeevan-kaka looked like a kid in a candy shop as he rubbed his hands together in anticipation. He obviously lived for this kind of business planning.

"I was thinking of having Anjali design the interior and then bring in an architect and contractor to follow her ideas," replied

Rishi. He must have heard Anjali's gasp of surprise. He turned his gaze to her. "Why do you look stunned?"

"Why . . . would you want *me* to design the new store? I'm sure you have some fancy interior designer in London or Hong Kong you'd prefer to work with."

Rishi shook his head. "Your father tells me you designed the store's interior and the display window, and both Jeevan-kaka and I think you did a remarkable job."

"Really?"

"We've been discussing it since early this morning. I believe you were still sleeping at the time." His amused look was his way of reminding her of the hue and cry she'd raised about that imaginary fire.

Predictably she felt the warmth seep into her neck and face. She tried to keep her thoughts focused on what they were discussing at the moment. "So you'll allow me to work on the interior design?"

"Of course, *beta*," chirped Jeevan. "You are good at that. Why would we pay for an expensive designer when we have talent in our family?" he said, always the guy with his eye on the bottom line.

"Not only will we allow it, Anjali, we'll consider it an honor." Rishi picked up the pen and writing tablet lying on the counter and drew a crude rectangle to indicate the rough layout.

"Thanks." Despite their compliments she still had misgivings.

The sound of the door opening had the three of them looking up. Sejal strode in, looking a little flushed from the hot day outside.

"Hi, guys," she called in her usual cheery note. "Sorry I'm late. There was some kind of accident on Route One and the traffic was . . ." She stopped and looked at the faces around her. "Did I interrupt something?"

Jeevan-kaka shot Sejal a magnanimous smile. "No, Sejal. You should hear this exciting news. We are buying the neighbor's store and making this store bigger and better and nicenice."

"You mean like . . . the whole building?" Sejal's face lit up by slow degrees.

Anjali gave her a nod.

"Cool! Then maybe I can work here full-time after graduation?"

"There's a good chance that could happen."

"I can be like you, Anju. I can become a full-time designer and fashion consultant." She had a grin on her face. "Wait till I tell my classmates. They're going to be soooo envious."

Rishi chuckled indulgently before he started drawing smaller rectangles within his large rectangle. He pushed it closer to Anjali. "Here, take a look at some ideas I have. This represents the two stores combined, after the wall is demolished."

"Hmm."

He pointed to a corner. "This far area over here would be ideal for the café, close to Tejmal's back door. It facilitates grocery deliveries and pickups, and venting the kitchen stove and its odors directly into the back. The opposite corner over here, which now houses the children's outfits, can become the beauty salon. It has good southern exposure with lots of sunlight. We could put in some skylights in the roof to bring in additional natural light."

As Anjali listened to his voice explain things to her, the reality of it all began to sink in. It was happening too fast; it was happening nonetheless. Three optimistic pairs of eyes were focused on her. But instead of her nervousness diminishing, it went up a notch.

She was drowning.

Chapter 11

"They've taken over our lives, Kip." Anjali sat on her usual bar stool and sipped her rum and cola. "They're all over our house and our store. Even my bathroom isn't mine anymore. My poor brother's been uprooted from his room and installed in the basement."

Kip gave her his most sympathetic look as he filled two large mugs with beer from the tap. "Sorry to hear that."

"No sorrier than I am." She played with a cardboard coaster with the black-and-red Rowling Rok logo. "They're buying fifty-one percent of the business and expanding it."

Delivering the two foam-topped mugs to the men at the other end of the counter, Kip returned to her. "Sounds a bit risky, doesn't it, especially if you're already in the hole?"

She nodded. "You'd think, right? But Rishi and my uncle have it all figured out. They tell me he's got a number of upscale one-stop stores all over the globe and they're doing fantastically well, so the American one's going to be an even bigger success."

"So this dude's rich?"

"Seems to be. He always wears European designer labels, and he just leased a luxury SUV."

Kip let out a low whistle. "Sounds like serious money to me, Angelface. Then why are you so down in the dumps? They're putting up the money. All you have to do is what you do best: design your pretty togs and jewels and sell them with that sweet smile of yours."

"Easy for you to say," she retorted. "There's no one buying up more than half your bar and telling you how to run your business."

"True, but isn't it better for someone to save your business rather than let it die a slow death?"

She took a thoughtful sip of her drink. "I suppose, but at the moment I'm not feeling particularly optimistic. It's a lot of money they're sinking into this venture."

"Then just do your job and let *them* worry about the finances."

"Wish it were that easy. Believe me, there's so much conviction in those gray eyes, it's hard to say no."

"Gray eyes?"

"Yep, gray eyes, jet-black hair, and skin as white as yours. Go figure that."

"What's this guy's name?" Kip had a comical look of confusion.

"Rishi Shah. It's a purely Gujarati name. He looks and talks like a Brit, behaves like one, and he and my Indian uncle are thick as thieves. Business partners supposedly. There's something very fishy about their relationship, Kip."

"Like what? Your uncle and the British dude are hired goons for the Indian mafia or something?"

"It's possible, especially since my uncle's carrying a handgun these days."

"An old Indian guy with a gun?" He smiled. "It's probably a fake."

"Uh-uh. It's real. He's so proud of it, too, brandishing it like a cowboy and all."

Someone yelled for service at the other end of the bar and Kip turned away. "Sorry, got to go, babe."

Anjali finished her drink, placed the glass on the counter, and looked around. It was a busy night for Kip. The two waitresses, Jean and Maggie, who served the customers at the tables were hopping, too. It was time for her to leave. She waited until he returned. "Kip, I'm going home. Looks like it's a busy night for you."

"Sure is." He leaned over the counter, cupped her face in both his hands, and kissed her full on the mouth. "We'll talk later in the week, Angelface."

"Thanks for the drink and pep talk." Reluctantly she slid off the stool and turned around. When she looked up she froze.

Rishi Shah stood just inside the entry door, his hands in his pockets, looking squarely at her. She stood rooted to her spot and stared at him, unable to do anything else. He had obviously witnessed the kiss. Rebellion kicked in after a second or two. So what if he'd seen Kip kissing her? What she did with her personal life was none of his business.

But it was possible he could rat on her to Jeevan-kaka and her parents. That could pose a major problem. The thought was scary. She could never face her mother under the circumstances. And Jeevan-kaka? His potential reaction made her legs feel weak.

Taking a deep breath, she started walking toward the door. Shah started moving in her direction at the same time. They met halfway.

"Hello, Anjali."

"Hello, Rishi," she replied, hating the way her voice sounded wobbly. "I was just leaving." She tried to walk past him but he interrupted her progress with a piercing look.

"What's the hurry? Why don't you have a drink with me?"

She clutched her pocketbook harder. Why did he make her feel so uncomfortable? It wasn't as if she was a minor caught drinking behind her parents' backs. "I can't. I have to . . . go home."

"Can't or won't?" A slight smile touched his lips.

"I'm not very good company at the moment." And that was the truth.

"Come on, Anjali, I thought we came to an understanding today."

"Yes, but . . ." A few people were staring at them, maybe because they were blocking the entryway.

"We're partners now, so let's drink to a long and healthy partnership, shall we?" he suggested.

"I already had a drink."

This time his smile was warmer, once again making her wonder how a simple movement of the facial muscles could transform his face. "Then come sit with me while I have my drink. We need to discuss some business."

She nodded. "Fine, I'll stay for a few minutes."

"Thank you." He signaled Maggie for service. "Could we have a table for two, please?" His smile for Maggie was his most charming yet.

"Sure thing." Young Maggie seemed dazzled by him. She gawked at him for a second before recovering enough to lead the way to one of two empty tables. Rishi didn't look anything like Rowling Rok's average customer.

Anjali wondered about the ease with which Rishi made himself at home. How did he do it? He seemed to exude power with his looks and fancy clothes, and the way he turned on the charm with women.

Maggie gave them time to seat themselves and disappeared, promising to return soon for their orders.

Rishi pulled Anjali's chair out for her before taking his seat. He was quite the gentleman. No surprise there. She looked around and caught Kip's eye. He stood still for an instant and gave her a questioning lift of his brows. She gave him a slight nod. *Yeah, that's him, the Brit.*

A chuckle from Rishi made her turn toward him. "What's so amusing?"

"I hope I'm not making your friend behind the bar jealous."

She frowned. "I don't know what you're talking about."

"Is everyone in America that affable with each other in a pub?"

"What do you mean?"

"Is kissing the patrons part of customer service?" He cocked a single dark eyebrow. "Or is that exclusive to friendly bartenders?"

A warm surge of blood to her face made Anjali look away. "Kip happens to be a good friend besides being the owner of this place."

"A good friend who's on kissing terms with you."

Maggie showed up to take their drink orders, putting an end to their odd conversation. Rishi asked for a scotch and soda. "You sure you don't want anything, Anjali?"

She shook her head. "Like I said, I already had one drink and I have to drive back."

"Very sensible," he said. Then he sent Maggie another smile. "Well, looks like just the scotch and soda, miss."

"My name's Maggie," she said with a girlish giggle, probably finding his accent irresistible.

"Thank you kindly, Maggie," he said, taking in Maggie's slim, boyish figure dressed in a short black skirt and bosom-hugging purple blouse. The admiring glance elicited another pleased giggle from Maggie, who practically ran to get his drink.

That's when it hit Anjali. What was Rishi doing here, in a bar located miles away from Iselin? "How did you find this place?"

"Nilesh told me about it."

She narrowed her eyes at him. "Nilesh knows nothing about this place. It's some distance from where we live, and he's too young to know much about bars."

He laughed, looking thoroughly amused. "Nilesh is a typical college boy. He happens to know every bar within a thirty-mile radius." He shook his head at her, at what he probably considered her hopeless naïveté. "And your brother also seems to know that you come here often."

"He does?" Did Nilesh also know about her relationship with Kip? How come he'd never said a word to her?

His drink arrived and he thanked Maggie.

"Don't look so stunned," he advised Anjali. "It's a small world. Look around you. There are several Indian men and women here. Don't you think one or two just might happen to know who you are? Anyone could have mentioned your visits to your brother."

He was right. She'd never paid attention to the other Indians in this place. As long as she hadn't recognized anyone, she'd thought she could remain anonymous. With her youthful looks she'd assumed she could pass for a graduate or doctoral student from nearby Rutgers University. Besides, she'd seen plenty of young Indian men and women flirting and necking with their respective Caucasian, Hispanic, and African-American girlfriends and boyfriends in the bar and the parking lot. Unfortunately, because of the relaxed atmosphere she hadn't seen the need to be careful.

Well, no more carelessness. From now on, she'd have to meet Kip in his apartment by coming in the back door.

As if he'd read her mind, Rishi took a sip of his scotch and smiled. "Making alternate plans for your future rendezvous with the Rolling Stone?"

"Mr. Shah, what I do with my private life is my business." She couldn't imagine why she felt the need to defend herself. It truly was her concern, not this man's, and not even her family's. Even though she lived with her parents for the sake of convenience and economy, at her age she was free to come and go as she pleased.

Her defensive remarks only seemed to amuse him further. "I thought you agreed to call me Rishi." When she remained silent, he put his hand across the table to cover hers. "Didn't you, Anjali?"

"I guess so." His hand touching hers was very disturbing. Just nerves, she told herself. She was a bit jumpy at being caught kissing, that's all. So she pulled her hand out from under his and decided to turn the tables on him. "So, why are you here in New Brunswick when there are any number of bars within a mile or two of our home?"

He gave the place an assessing look. "I wanted to explore Rolling Stone for myself. Just curious to see what it is about this particular pub that draws the talented and discerning Miss Anjali Kapadia so frequently."

"It's Rowling Rok with a W in the first word and no C in the second," she informed him. "By the way, we call them bars here, not pubs."

"I stand corrected." He sipped his drink, appearing as nonchalant as ever. Meanwhile Maggie stopped by once again to ask if he needed another drink, giving him her undivided attention. She wasn't fooling either Rishi or Anjali about her interest in him.

Another peek at the bar and Anjali found Kip staring at Rishi and herself. She looked away hastily, only to find Rishi gazing at her with similar intensity. What the heck was going on here? Two men looking at her like she was some freak of nature? Feeling very uncomfortable under Rishi's close scrutiny, Anjali pushed back her chair and got to her feet. "I have to go now. It's getting late and Mom will have dinner waiting."

"You're right. I'm leaving soon myself." He rose from his chair. "I'll see you in a bit, then?"

"I guess," she said over her shoulder and strode out of the bar. She could feel Rishi Shah's eyes following her all the way out.

Inside her car, she sat behind the wheel and let her mind settle a bit before she turned on the ignition. Why exactly had Rishi followed her to the bar? He'd made no bones about the fact that he knew she was there. At least he hadn't pretended it was sheer accident that they'd bumped into each other. He'd succeeded in making her feel like a schoolgirl caught breaking curfew.

And why was Kip staring at them all that time? Was he jealous like Rishi had surmised? Oh well, she had other things, more important things than men to worry about.

She backed the car out of the parking spot and drove home.

Chapter 12

Rishi sipped his scotch at leisure and observed the scene: Anjali gliding toward the exit door and Kip Rowling keeping his eyes glued on her back. A hungry, slightly possessive look lurked in Rowling's eyes. Then the barkeeper turned his gaze to Rishi. No open hostility seemed evident there, but it wasn't mere curiosity reserved for strangers either. It was more the territorial look of a male guarding his domain.

Interesting. From the nature of the kiss Rishi had witnessed between those two, he could tell they were lovers. That level of intimacy couldn't exist between friends.

So, it looked like the enigmatic and pretty Anjali was having an affair with a pub owner. Since Rishi had already become quite familiar with the Kapadia family and realized how conservative they were, he could only assume her parents had no knowledge of Kip Rowling or his relationship with their daughter.

Even Nilesh had no idea what his sister was up to. Although it was Nilesh who had informed him about Anjali's habit of visiting the Rowling Rok Bar & Lounge frequently, Rishi doubted that the boy knew what went on there. Nilesh had simply said, "She meets her girlfriends there for drinks. I think she needs to get away from the shop and my parents sometimes."

Rishi's reason for coming to the pub to seek out Anjali was to talk to her in private—hopefully over a friendly drink. A fair

amount of his business was conducted in the relaxing, casual atmosphere of a London pub.

A few minutes with her was all he was looking for, just
enough to explain his position. And to apologize for his un-
gentlemanly behavior that morning. No matter how cold she
was toward him, he had no right to invade her space and intimidate her. So his only recourse was to talk to her alone. Around
the home and the store they were constantly surrounded by
family.

Ever since he'd met her he'd felt the urge to take her aside and
clarify some things to her. For some odd reason she seemed to be
under the impression that he and Jeevan-kaka were here to take
what belonged to her. Why hadn't someone told her the truth—
that they were simply helping her and nothing more? But then,
Jeevan-kaka's actions were often hasty and impulsive, with little
to no explanation given. His despotic attitude often translated
into *do as I say and don't ask questions.*

It certainly was a hell of a shock to walk into the pub and
find Anjali kissing the bartender instead of having a drink with
her women friends. But he wasn't the only one astonished.
When she'd turned around from the bar and found him at the
door, her face had registered both surprise—and guilt.

His astonishing discovery had dispelled all other thoughts
from his mind. Therefore he'd never had a chance to have that
talk. Suddenly she'd gone on the defensive and he'd started
needling her. Then she'd walked out on him. Instead of smoothing those ruffled feathers like he'd meant to, he had managed to
turn a mildly antagonistic Anjali into an infuriated one. Once
again, it was his own fault for handling things badly.

He had no right to judge her. It was none of his business what
the lady did in her spare time. His main concern was her commitment to the store, and from what he'd observed so far, she
was dedicated to it one hundred percent. In fact, she seemed obsessed with it, afraid to let anyone near it, like a mother guarding an ailing child.

Now that he'd seen her with another man he wondered about

her personal life. Did she still mourn for her dead husband? What kind of marriage had she had? Had she been happy? A lot of questions about her suddenly popped up in his mind. It would be interesting to find out.

Maggie the waitress came back to ask if he wanted more scotch. He shook his head. He paid her for the drink and included enough money for a generous tip, then walked out of the bar. He got another one of those cool, guarded looks from Rowling before he stepped out.

Dinner at the Kapadia home was quieter than the previous night, Anjali noted with some satisfaction. Naren-kaka and his family were absent, for one thing, and so was Nilesh. He was at the library, studying for an exam. He wasn't taking the summer off from school.

Jeevan-kaka's handgun was nowhere in sight, thank goodness. Anjali had a feeling Rishi Shah had advised him to keep it out of sight.

She ate her dinner in silence and watched everyone else talk at the table. Naturally it was all about the business. Her parents were both surprised and excited that Tejmal had agreed to sell his place. Until now Anjali hadn't really thought about it, but she was going to miss that quaint old man. He'd been a bit of a pain in the rear with his sloppy ways and his refusal to clean up his eyesore of a shop, but he was a decent man and he'd been a kind neighbor.

Earlier, as they'd sat down to dinner, Anjali had been afraid that Rishi might bring up their meeting at the bar, but he'd kept his mouth shut. He must have noticed her discomfort because less than five minutes into the meal his eyes had connected briefly with hers across the table, and she'd known right away that her secret was safe. She'd thrown him a grateful look and gone back to her food.

"Why are you so quiet, Anju?" said Jeevan-kaka, drawing her out of her reverie.

"I'm listening to all of you talk," she said absently.

Jeevan-kaka gave her a benign smile. "Tomorrow your father, Rishi, and I will be talking to some contractors for estimates."

"I see." As usual her uncle had assumed it was a man's place to deal with the contractors. She and her mother hadn't been invited to the talks.

Rishi was the one who stunned her. "Anjali and Auntie are equal partners in the business. They should be involved in the meeting," he said.

Her uncle frowned at Rishi. "But this is men's work."

Rishi shook his head. "The two of them manage a large portion of the business, and a lot of Anjali's money is tied up in the store. She's the main driving force behind Silk & Sapphires. We need both the ladies' input on everything." He glanced at her. "Don't you want to be involved, Anjali?"

"Of course I do!" she snapped. And immediately regretted it. It wasn't his fault that her uncle was a chauvinist. "Thank you for including Mom and me, Rishi," she said, "although Jeevan-kaka seems to think women have no place in such matters." She had to admit Rishi was being fair. Besides, he hadn't given away her secret.

Surprisingly, Jeevan accepted the women's involvement with no further protest. The man had changed so much. The old Jeevan would have fought it tooth and nail.

Her mother looked a bit more at ease, too. She was smiling at something and seemed completely immersed in the conversation. Secretly Anjali hoped her uncle would continue to stay on his best behavior as long as he was in the U.S.

After the meal, she and her mother washed and dried the dishes. Since it was late, her parents went directly to bed and so did Jeevan-kaka. Rishi announced that he was going for a walk and took off.

She decided to watch a little television on her own, catch the late news, hoping she could unwind a little. Perhaps Nilesh would come home before she went to bed. She was curious to find out how he knew about Rowling Rok and the fact that she went there often.

She didn't know how long she'd been on the couch before falling asleep. She woke up with a start when someone touched her shoulder. She blinked at the dark shadow outlined against the light coming from the TV. She smiled. "Hi, Nil."

"Anjali." It wasn't her brother.

"Rishi?" Realizing she was stretched out on the couch, she quickly sat up.

"Sorry to wake you," he whispered. "But shouldn't you be sleeping in your bed?"

"I must have dozed off watching the news."

"You must be very tired. Why don't you go on up? I'll take care of shutting off the lights. I've already checked the locks."

"Thanks. Did you have a good walk?"

"Yes. It's an interesting neighborhood. And the weather's nice tonight—not too hot."

"You must find our summer weather unbearable after London's cool humidity."

He shrugged. "I'm used to Hong Kong, Singapore, and India, too."

"Oh, of course." She glanced at the wall clock. "Do you know if Nilesh is home yet?"

"His car isn't in the driveway. He must be studying hard for his exam."

"Poor kid," she said. "I remember the days when I crammed for an exam at the last minute and drove myself nuts. Feels like so long ago."

Instead of walking away, Rishi raised a brow at her. "Mind if I sit with you and talk for a bit?"

"Be my guest."

He sat down beside her on the couch. "I remember the frenzied days and nights before exams, too. Although for me it's been even longer than you. I feel old when I look at Nilesh and all his energy."

"I know what you mean. Sometimes I feel like Nil's mother and not his sister."

Rishi chuckled. "You don't at all look like his mother. You look much too young for that."

"Thanks, but I'm eighteen years older than Nil, you know."

"Couldn't tell by your looks. You could pass for a university student."

"You don't look so old yourself." She meant it, too. He didn't have a single wrinkle or gray hair. He had a body most men half his age would kill for. He was probably in his . . . late thirties or perhaps forty from what she'd gathered so far.

"I'm forty-two, Anjali. That's five years older than you are." He stared thoughtfully at the TV for a second. "I'm old enough to be Nilesh's father."

"My father was older than you when Nil was born." Seeing his brows raised in surprise, she said, "And my mother was nearly forty."

"Is that right? They must be a very . . . um . . . romantic couple," he said with a mischievous grin.

She smothered a snicker. "Romantic in their own way—in private. Looking at them you'd never know, though. They don't even touch each other in public."

"Most old-fashioned Indian folks are that way." He gazed at the TV again for a bit. "Tell me, how did you feel about having a newborn sibling at eighteen?"

"I hated it. Can you imagine the shock of discovering your parents are having a baby when you're just about ready to enter college?"

"I wouldn't know. I don't have any brothers or sisters."

"Lucky you."

"I suppose it was a bit embarrassing for you. What would your friends say and all that?"

Anjali rolled her eyes. "I didn't even tell my friends for the longest time. I didn't want my mother to be seen in that condition."

A deep, rumbling chuckle emerged from him. "Poor little Anjali. You were no longer the only child."

"And what's worse, the baby turned out to be a boy. In our culture a boy is only one or two tiny steps below God."

"I know that," said Rishi. "Despite my looks I'm half Indian."

"Although I must admit I didn't know how good I had it then," she said wistfully. "Life was so much simpler when Mom and Dad could worry about the business and the finances and my job was just to be a good student and earn good grades."

"And did you?"

"Did I what?"

"Earn good grades?" He seemed very intense all of a sudden.

She felt her breath get a little shaky at his closeness. He sat only a couple of feet away. "Mostly As and an occasional B. My GPA was around 3.8."

"That's very good."

"How about you? Were you an A student at Oxford, Rishi?" She was surprised at how easily his name glided off her tongue, now that she'd accepted it.

"Not always, but I managed to get my master's degree if that's what you're asking."

"But Jeevan-kaka says you're a business whiz, a genius."

Rishi leaned back, locked his hands behind him and rested his head on them. "Have you noticed how real life has very little to do with what you learn in a classroom, Anjali?"

"Uh-huh."

"Well, that's what this is. I like what I do and discovered at an early age that I had a head for business. The advanced degree was simply something to build up my credentials. I could have done well enough without it, but in the world of business consulting it helps to have that beside my name."

"I know what you mean. It's impressive to have an Oxford MBA on your business card when you're meeting the CEO of a corporation."

"Exactly." He turned to her with a smile.

Seeing that transforming smile once again, Anjali realized that she was actually having an amiable conversation with this guy. When had that started to happen? Only hours ago she'd been sitting in a bar with him, resenting his having witnessed her kiss a man in public. But here she was now, sharing memories of college days with him like an old friend.

Looking at the clock, she rose to her feet. "I better go to bed."

Rishi got to his feet, too. "Anjali."

"Hmm?"

"I've been meaning to explain something to you . . . in private."

"Oh?"

"Since we're alone now I'd like to make it clear that neither Jeevan-kaka nor I have any plans to stay here permanently or tell you how to run your boutique. The business is yours and we'll leave it entirely up to you once the expansion is complete."

"I see." This evening was filled with surprises.

"Just thought you should know that." He absently rubbed the back of his neck. "By the way, were you afraid I'd spill the beans? About your boyfriend, I mean?"

She stiffened immediately. Now why did he have to go and spoil a perfectly friendly moment, a brief moment of bonding? "Yes, I was." She was terrified, actually.

"You know I wouldn't do something like that. You can trust me."

"I don't really know you."

"You're *getting* to know me, aren't you?" He gave her one of those laser-beam looks that left her feeling exposed.

"I suppose."

"And are you beginning to at least accept the idea that I'm here to help and not take away what's yours?"

She gave herself a second to answer that one as honestly as she could. "I'm trying."

"Fair enough," he said and shut off the television and the lamp beside the couch. "I can't ask for more than that." He waited for her to go upstairs first and then followed her. They wished each other good night, went into their separate rooms, and closed their doors.

A little while later, just as Anjali settled into bed, she heard Nilesh come in and head for the basement. She breathed a sigh of relief. Despite what she'd said to Rishi earlier, she loved her brother dearly. Life would have been quite bland without Nilesh.

That night, Anjali dreamed of Vikram. It had been a while since she'd had a dream about him. When she woke up, she could almost feel Vik's presence in the room. At times she felt she could reach out and touch Vik sleeping next to her.

Did every woman who'd loved her husband and lost him feel like she did? Even when she slept with Kip, her mind always conjured up an image of Vik's face. It was always Vik loving her, making her feel alive. She could still visualize the cleft in his chin, eyes that slanted upward, the expressions that flitted across his face. She could recall some of their conversations word for word.

Had she hooked up with Kip because the way he made love was reminiscent of Vik's style? Did his sense of humor remind her of Vik? Every once in a while, on lonely nights, she pulled out photo albums of their life together and gazed at the pictures. So many years, and he still haunted her dreams and her waking moments. And the tears still came—drenching tears that sometimes didn't subside for a long time.

Would she ever be able to let go of Vik?

Chapter 13

The closing on Tejmal's store occurred less than a week later. Anjali studied the legal document. The five of them were now partners in the new venture. She had come to accept that fact. And to be honest, Jeevan-kaka wasn't quite as bad to live with as she'd imagined.

Even her mother's nerves were beginning to settle and they had all slipped into a routine. As long as Jeevan-kaka got his saffron milk three times a day along with his insipid food, he was fine. His gun hadn't been seen since that first day and he'd agreed to use her mother's small silver bell for his morning *pooja* instead of the humongous brass one that had awakened them that first morning.

On the evening of the closing, as they sat down to dinner, Rishi made a surprise announcement. "I want to tell you folks something," he said. "You've been most kind to put me up all these days, but I feel I should move into a hotel."

Anjali's head snapped up. She could feel the others' attention immediately aroused, too.

Jeevan was the first to speak. "Why?"

Rishi looked at him. "Uncle and Auntie have been very generous in accommodating me, a total stranger, with no advance notice whatsoever. But I dislike taking advantage of them. Now that we all know I'll be required to be here for some time, I've decided that a hotel room would be best."

"It's so much easier for us to discuss business in this house. We're all here . . . together." Jeevan-kaka seemed reluctant to see the younger man leave.

Anjali wondered once again about the relationship between those two. Why was her uncle so dependent on Rishi? For a stubborn, independent old man, Jeevan-kaka was like a fretting, clinging child when it came to Rishi.

"I'm not going too far," replied Rishi, "only a phone call away. We'll all be spending some eight or ten hours at the store together every day."

Mohan glanced at Rishi. "Are you uncomfortable here, *beta?*"

"Not at all, Uncle. On the contrary, I'm getting very spoiled by all this delicious home-cooked food and a nice room to myself. But Nilesh shouldn't have to give up his space permanently. It would be most inconsiderate of me to take advantage of his good nature."

Nilesh had joined them at the dinner table that evening. "Hey, it's no problem, man," he said. "It's not like I spend a lot of time at home anyway."

"That's not the point, Nilesh. It's your room, and the longer I stay the longer I'm imposing on you and your family. Besides, you're a student and you need your own quiet area to study."

Good for Rishi, Anjali mentally applauded. She'd been wondering how long she'd have to share a bathroom with a stranger. It was bad enough that her uncle was going to be around for months.

And then she had to be careful how she dressed in her own home at nights and how she behaved. Since that comment Rishi had made about her legs, she'd made sure to wear pajamas to bed instead of her short nightgowns. But she had to admit he'd been a gentleman since then. Come to think of it, even that particular remark hadn't been really lewd. It was more like a clinical assessment. She'd read too much into it for some reason.

He seemed to be considerate about some things. He took all his laundry to the cleaners, preferring not to hog up their washer and dryer. Of course, all those expensive clothes he wore had to be professionally cleaned. He ate whatever her mother put on the table and never complained about anything. He often brought home snacks, fruit, pastries, and desserts that the whole family enjoyed. In most ways he was the ideal guest.

But it would be a relief to have him out of her house, mainly because he made her so uneasy. All kinds of weird emotions that had been buried for years were creeping up on her again and she didn't want them to complicate her life.

Her mother seemed upset at Rishi's news, too, surprising Anjali. Usha had been the unhappiest of them all at having to entertain a stranger.

"But you're always welcome at our house, Rishi," Usha said. "You may not be family, but you're like family to us. We enjoy having you here."

Rishi reached across the table and patted Usha's hand. "Likewise, Auntie, I enjoy being here, but I respect your privacy." He paused. "And I don't want to outstay my welcome. I'll move into a hotel tomorrow."

Jeevan-kaka gave Rishi a thoroughly disgruntled look. "I thought we agreed that you and I would be together while we worked on this project."

Rishi sent the old man an indulgent smile. "Who says we won't be together while we work? The hotel room is mainly for bed and bath."

Sufficiently mollified, Jeevan-kaka went back to his meal.

The thought of Rishi leaving them seemed to bring a certain contemplative air to the table. The rest of the meal was unusually quiet, with only a few minor references to the day's business. After dinner, Nilesh excused himself and left for the library.

After the dishes were cleared and the kitchen cleaned up, Rishi said to Anjali, "I think we should talk about the ideas for the store's interior. Didn't you say you've drawn some sketches already?"

Anjali nodded and ran to her room to fetch them. But she

was hesitant about sharing them with the others. Her expertise was in clothing and jewelry design and she knew nothing about building plans or blueprints. All she had was a rough idea of where everything should be placed based on the crude rectangles Rishi had drawn the other day.

By the time she came back downstairs her mother had cleared the dining table of its pickle jars and condiments so Anjali could spread her designs on it. Reluctantly she showed them her drawings, which were more like landscape paintings of each area, colors and all.

"These are nice, *beta*," her mother said after giving them a cursory look. "Very artistic."

"But not professional. I'm not sure how to go about showing the dimensions and all that technical stuff architects do."

Jeevan-kaka looked a little lost as he turned the sheets this way and that. Her father had a slight frown on his face. It was hard to say what they were thinking.

She glanced at Rishi, who was studying them with narrowed eyes. She was most nervous about his criticism. For some reason his opinion mattered. Of everyone present, he seemed to be the most knowledgeable about store design and also the most sophisticated. Besides, he owned boutiques in some of the swankiest malls and shopping centers of the world.

"This is pretty good, Anjali," he said finally.

"But not great, right?" She looked at him for confirmation. "The contractors wouldn't know how to go about following my ideas?"

He shook his head. "On the contrary, your sketches should be useful in giving them a good bird's-eye view of what we want. Once we have the basic structure laid out, then we can go into what you have here, the shelves, cabinets, and displays in the colors we want . . . the colors *you* want." He put a hand on Jeevan's shoulder. "Don't you think so, Jeevan-kaka?"

"I agree. Isn't your usual architect sending someone from New York to look at the place?"

Rishi nodded. "Our man in London has a contact in New

York City, someone he works with in this part of the U.S. I happen to know the man."

Jeevan asked his brother about building permits.

"I've already taken care of that," said Mohan.

"Excellent." Rishi turned back to the drawings. "Now, let's discuss these lovely designs, shall we?"

Pleased with his remarks, Anjali felt emboldened to mention her color scheme. "Am I allowed to stick with the cream and blue?"

"Yes."

"But I suppose you guys are going to change the name of the store?" She was so afraid they were going to give it some tacky handle that she had obsessed over it the previous night.

Rishi lifted an eyebrow. "A little worried about the name, Anjali?"

Despite her resolve to keep this on a friendly level, she couldn't help asking, "Saris and Samosas?"

"Not even close."

It was her turn to raise a brow. "Kapadia & Shah?"

"Silk & Sapphires," he replied with a sly grin.

She stared at him. "You mean we keep the name?"

"Absolutely."

"I never thought I'd . . . well . . . that you and Jeevan-kaka would . . ." She was so relieved she had no words.

Jeevan-kaka laughed for the first time that evening. "Why are you surprised, Anju? Why would we change such a beautiful name?"

She gave him a grateful smile. "I'm glad you think it's beautiful."

Over the next hour they argued over the placement of the different departments. Anjali was adamant about the food being entirely separate from the rest of the store. "I won't have fried food odors in the store. The way a place smells has a lot to do with its ambience and the mood it creates."

"Not to worry," Rishi assured her. "A solid dividing wall will separate the store from the café. Glass doors will be in place for those who want to get to it. Also, customers will not be allowed to take food and drink into the main store for obvious reasons. The odors don't even begin to creep into the store."

"Exactly how much business will this *chai* shop generate, Rishi?" Anjali's father pushed his glasses up his nose and bent over the designs once again.

Rishi pointed to the area marked *café* on the sheet. "When a bride and her bridesmaids and family members are getting their hair and nails done and spend hours at the store, they invariably get hungry and start looking for a convenient place to eat."

"Makes sense, I suppose," murmured Usha. "They can't walk on the street or drive with curlers in their hair and *mehndi* drying on their hands."

"Exactly. Our cafés, particularly in London, are very popular. They're always crowded, not just with customers from the store but also others who come in just to eat the unusual fare we offer. We always serve something different, like finger sandwiches, and on good crockery, too. Even our tea is served English-style with a china teapot and cups and saucers. No unsightly foam cups and plastic stirrers."

"Sounds too expensive for *Desi* tastes," murmured Anjali. "*Desis* are generally a *kanjoos* bunch, tight-fisted."

"I agree," said Rishi, much to Anjali's surprise. "But when it comes to weddings and special occasions they're willing to splurge. Don't forget those are the events where they're trying to outdo each other and make the others a little envious."

She nodded. "Yeah, keeping up appearances."

A large number of Indians and other South Asians had immigrated to the U.S. in the 1970s and 80s and through hard work and scrimping they had become comfortably entrenched baby boomers. But despite their frugality they thought nothing of spending their hard-earned cash on certain things they considered important, like their children's educations and some significant milestones in their lives. Consequently Ivy League graduations, elaborate weddings, christenings, and birthdays had turned into eye-popping status symbols.

In fact, it was precisely that mentality that had led to upscale stores like Silk & Sapphires to appear on the commercial scene.

Usha stifled a yawn and looked at her wristwatch. "It's been a long day. We should go to bed."

Anjali noticed Jeevan-kaka looking drawn. He'd eaten very little at dinner. She wondered if all this stress was getting to him. He might be a tyrant, but he was still her uncle.

She touched his arm. "You look exhausted, Jeevan-kaka. Maybe you should go to bed, too?"

"I will." He stood up and pushed his chair in.

Her parents followed suit. The elder Kapadias went upstairs to sleep, leaving Anjali and Rishi to continue deliberating over the designs. Rishi looked at her. "You think we convinced the three of them sufficiently?"

"It's not those three you should worry about. They seem willing to eat out of your hand. I'm the one that's not entirely convinced." She stacked the sheets of artist's paper and rolled them into a tube. "But then, it's mostly your money that's tied up in this, not mine."

"A skeptic to the core, aren't you? It's a good trait for an entrepreneur, Anjali."

"No kidding," she said.

"I'm serious. You're a good businesswoman. All you need is a little extra help at the moment."

"A lot of help." She slipped a rubber band around the roll of papers. "By the way, I'm glad the store will keep its name."

"Speaking of names, may I ask you something? It's personal, so if you want me to back off, I will."

"Depends on what it is."

"Did you ever change your surname to Gandhi?"

So he knew she was married to a Gandhi. He'd been doing his homework in that area, too. She shook her head. "I kept my maiden name."

"Any particular reason?"

"It was too much trouble to go through the legalities, and Vik didn't think it was important. I personally don't like hyphenated names either."

"I see. I'm sorry."

"About what? That I didn't change my name?"

"That your marriage lasted such a short time. You must have been devastated." He seemed to ponder something for a long moment. Then his gaze came back to her. "Jeevan-kaka told me a bit about your husband."

It was hard to keep her emotions intact, especially since he sounded genuinely sympathetic. "Vik was a terrific guy."

"You were lucky to have found someone you loved."

"Lucky? Or *unlucky* to have lost him so quickly?"

"I said lucky because although it was very short, yours was a happy marriage. There are couples who are married for fifty and sixty years and are miserable."

He almost sounded envious of her brief marriage. "Are you married?" she asked him, wondering how he'd react to her prying into his personal business.

He shook his head.

"Engaged?"

"I was engaged once. Didn't last long."

"Oh."

He looked amused. "Aren't you going to ask me why?"

"None of my business."

"I'll tell you anyway, because you were candid in answering my questions. The woman I was engaged to wasn't a particularly nice person."

"What did she do?"

"She had a problem with a monogamous relationship."

Anjali frowned. "Hmm."

He let out a bitter laugh. "Laura was part British and part Italian, and beautiful. And she believed men and women are born to be promiscuous."

"So why did she want marriage? She could play as much as she wanted without the restrictions of marriage, couldn't she?"

"That's where I came in. She wanted to marry me for my

money. That way she could play in style and not have to work to pay for it."

"What a gold digger!" Anjali felt instant sympathy for him. No one deserved to be treated that way. "You must have been heartbroken."

"Young, hopelessly in love with a callous vixen—and yes, heartbroken. That was sixteen years ago."

"Looks like you glued your shattered heart back together just fine."

He remained silent.

"I gather you've never trusted another woman after that?"

"Not exactly."

"So you've had other . . . uh . . . relationships?"

He was quiet for an awfully long time before he replied, "One or two. I have a girlfriend at the moment. Samantha and I stay together . . . have been for nearly five years."

So he had a live-in girlfriend: Samantha. To Anjali it was as good as being married. "So you decided to trust a woman after all."

"I didn't say I was married to her."

"Isn't living together the same thing?"

"Not at all," he replied. "Staying under the same roof doesn't extend her the right to share in my assets or certain . . . private areas of my life. I've given up on marriage."

"Looking at it from that cynical viewpoint, I consider myself lucky. Vik was the best. He adored me. I don't think I'll ever find another man like him."

"Is that why you're involved with Rowling . . . because you can't find another marriageable chap like Vikram Gandhi?"

She stiffened at his question. The camaraderie of the past hour was gone in an instant. God, he wouldn't rest until he found out more about Kip. He'd probably figured out the nature of her relationship with Kip anyway.

And honestly, she didn't have an answer to his question, even for herself. She still didn't know exactly why she was involved

with Kip. It was one of those things that didn't have any underlying logic. Impulsiveness and the deep physical need to feel a
warm male body against hers were the only reasons she could
think of, because all she derived from it on an emotional level
was a sense of shame and mild regret.

Rishi's eyes had taken on the familiar laser look. But she wasn't
ready to discuss Kip with him. It was too personal. "Good
night, Rishi," she said quietly and headed for the staircase.

All the way up the stairs she could feel those laser-beam eyes
following her.

Chapter 14

Jerry Falcone, the architect-contractor from New York, showed up a couple of days later. Middle-aged, with a shaved head, a lean, well-maintained body, and a distinctive laugh, he was friendly and easy to work with.

He seemed to know Rishi well. "Hey, Rishi Shah, how are you? Long time no see," he said, pumping Rishi's hand with the ease of a man who knew exactly whom he was dealing with. "How's London, buddy? Good to see you doing business in the U.S. of A. for a change."

After the greetings and small talk were over, Rishi made the introductions. "Jerry and I met in London a couple of times on other projects," he explained to the rest of them.

Anjali and her mother spent most of the morning with the men, discussing ideas for refurbishing Tejmal's store. After conferring over the preliminaries, the two women left the men to deal with Jerry Falcone and the technical aspects like building codes, insulation, roofing shingles, and load-bearing walls and beams. Besides, the daily business of taking care of regular customers was still very much the women's job.

Since summer was a popular time for weddings, there were some customers who stopped in for clothes and matching jewelry. But the sales weren't as vigorous as in previous years, and Anjali found it depressing.

Falcone stayed until the end of the day. By early evening it seemed everything had been worked out to their satisfaction. When Anjali heard the estimated cost of the renovations, her eyes went round with dismay. "That's a king's ransom!"

Rishi merely shrugged. "That's what a major restoration costs these days. When was the last time this store was redone?"

"Over nine years ago, when I first joined my parents in the business and we went from a sari shop to a boutique."

"In nine years things have changed and become twice as costly." He shook his head at Anjali. "Don't worry about the expenses. Jeevan-kaka and I will take care of that end."

That was the problem. The more those two invested in her business, the more uncomfortable she became. But it wasn't like she had any other choices at the moment.

The preliminary cleanup started in earnest on Tejmal's store the very next day. Rishi, Mohan, and Anjali began the cleaning process while Usha and Sejal were left in charge of the business. Jeevan-kaka was told to sit in the boutique's office and help with the paperwork since he was in no shape to handle manual labor.

Although Tejmal had succeeded in selling all his inventory to another wholesaler in town, there were empty crates, shelves, old, yellowed paperwork, tattered plastic bags, and a whole lot of spilled grains and debris littering the store.

Dressed in jeans, sneakers, and T-shirts, they arrived early to tackle the job. Seeing Rishi dressed in casual denim instead of his usual business attire was a pleasant surprise. He looked wonderful. She'd have to be blind not to notice what those snug jeans did for his body. The dark blue of his T-shirt also made his eyes look blue-gray, like the Atlantic on a sultry summer afternoon.

When they reached the storage room in the back, they came to an abrupt stop. "Good God, the old man left this place filthy!" Rishi stood with his hands on his hips and grimaced. "I'd hoped he'd have the decency to leave the building in better condition than this."

"Didn't he promise to clean out the premises before we took

over?" Anjali sniffed the moldy odor combined with something that smelled like rotting onions.

"I suppose this is his idea of cleaning," said her father. "He sold his entire inventory and that's obviously all he cared about."

"It's too late to complain. Get ready for some hard work," said Rishi with a resigned look.

Anjali bent down to pick up an old mousetrap covered with lint and dangled it over one finger. "Look what we have here."

Mohan shook his head. "Let's be grateful there's no dead mouse in it. But maybe there are roaches?"

"Eww!" Anjali looked at both men in turn. "We better get this place professionally fumigated before we expand. I'm positively not going to display my merchandise in this dump."

Rishi placed a giant pack of trash bags on the counter and pulled on a pair of latex gloves taken from the box he'd purchased earlier. "Okay, folks, put on a pair of gloves and let's get to work. Meanwhile," he said, looking at Mohan, "Uncle, why don't you have Auntie arrange for an exterminator to treat the place immediately?"

"Okay." Looking relieved, Mohan hastened out the back door to carry out Rishi's instructions.

Anjali had a sneaking suspicion her father was going to take his time returning. He disliked housework, and cleaning was something he never did. In fact, she was surprised to see the immaculate Rishi getting ready to apply some old-fashioned elbow grease to the task. She doubted if he'd ever handled a broom in his life. As if he'd read her mind, he picked up a broom and started to sweep the floor.

It turned into a long, hot day of hard manual labor. Despite the air-conditioning running on high, it was a sweaty job. By early afternoon, Rishi had hauled out something like eleven jumbo-sized bags of trash, assorted crates, broken shelves, and boxes to the Dumpster behind the building.

By late evening, they had the place pretty much cleaned out and it was possible to take a breath without inhaling dust and going into a sneezing fit. They placed a few fresh mousetraps, just in case. The place smelled a lot cleaner, too, after Anjali finished mopping the linoleum floors with an industrial-strength disinfectant cleaner.

Mohan soon left to go next door to take care of the day's receipts, leaving Rishi and Anjali to handle the rest.

When Anjali finally put down the mop and Rishi was ready to haul the bucket of dirty water out to dump it, he turned to her with a concerned look. "Go home, Anjali. You look beat. You've been working nearly nonstop since dawn." He tucked a stray lock of her hair back into her ponytail. The gesture was so unexpected and sweet, it upset Anjali's balance a little and he grabbed her arm to steady her. "You *are* tired."

"So are you, I'm sure. Thank you for everything, Rishi."

"No need for thanks. We're partners, remember?"

"I know." He had worked like a demon. Being the largest and strongest of the three of them, he'd automatically taken on the heavier load. This was a side of him she hadn't seen yet—a more down-to-earth and likeable side. She'd only been exposed to the polished Londoner. "This must be quite an experience for you," she said. "I bet you have cleaning crews for such things."

He looked amused. "I've done more than my share of hard labor. I wasn't always a businessman."

"So what were you before you became a millionaire?"

He tapped her nose with a fingertip in a playful gesture. "One of these days, I'll tell you all about it, Miss Kapadia."

"Never mind, if you have to be that mysterious about it."

"Let's call it a day and go home, shall we?" He carried the bucket out to the back and returned a minute later. Perspiration stains darkened his T-shirt in patches. His jeans looked dirty and a dark evening shadow was clearly visible on his face. She was almost tempted to run her hand through his hair and muss it a little, make him look dangerous.

But she didn't. Instead she agreed with him. "Sounds like a brilliant idea. I'm dying for a shower and a decent meal."

"Come on, then." He reached for her hand. Without a moment's hesitation, she took his hand as he switched off the lights and engaged the burglar alarm. Together they went next door to tell the others that they were heading home in Rishi's car.

That night, Anjali slept like the dead. She was too exhausted and achy for bad dreams or insomnia.

Jerry Falcone's men arrived in a pickup truck the next day with ladders and some fearsome-looking construction tools. Fortunately, the wall between the two stores would be the last to be torn down, so Silk & Sapphires could continue to operate normally until the very last phase. And when the wall finally came down, there would be heavy-duty plastic curtains installed to keep as much of the dust out as possible.

The next few weeks went so fast they seemed to be a blur. Each day, several times a day, Anjali made it a point to stop by next door and check on the workmen's progress. Rishi and her uncle were always there, making sure things were moving smoothly.

Although there was pleasure in seeing the transformation come about, and a certain amount of excitement, there was also that old fear. What if the whole venture crumbled like a sand-castle? God, this time they'd really be in bankruptcy court. The thought still kept her awake at nights sometimes.

But the days were usually so busy she had no time to worry too much. Besides her regular duties at the store, there were fix-tures to be ordered, fabrics, paints, carpeting, curtains, and mannequins to discuss and design and order. Despite the crazy hours they all kept, Rishi managed to put in an hour of exercise at the gym each morning. Another thing Anjali couldn't help but admire: his diligence.

In the midst of all that work, Rishi suddenly had to return home to London—something about an emergency at one of his stores. Anjali resented his leaving in the middle of the project. She'd come to depend on him, become used to seeing him each morning, working beside him.

But then she had to remind herself that he had other respon-sibilities. This was only a very minor part of his business. She couldn't expect him to drop everything else and give his undivided attention to Silk & Sapphires.

And wasn't it only the other day that she'd wanted him out of New Jersey and out of her life? She should have been glad to see him leave instead of grumbling about his absence. As it was, he had stayed with Silk & Sapphires for several weeks and taken care of all the most important aspects of the expansion. He'd done more than his share of work.

Reluctantly she admitted to herself that she missed him. Although he'd moved into a hotel sometime ago, he was still a large part of their lives.

It was that first evening after he left when the rest of them sat down to dinner, that Anjali realized exactly how large a role he had assumed in their lives. The conversation at the table was on the quiet side. It was clear there was a missing ingredient.

Nilesh, in his boyish but practical way, put it succinctly: "It's kind of strange without Rishi, isn't it? It's not much fun around here."

It was Nilesh's remark that made Anjali realize her young, impressionable brother's attitude toward Rishi bordered on hero worship. Why hadn't she seen that evolving over the past few weeks? Practically every night the two of them discussed sports, debated over the latest in computer software and all sorts of topics that men seemed to enjoy. They also spent a lot of time on Nilesh's computer, doing God knows what.

And cousin Sejal seemed smitten with Rishi. He walked on water as far as her little cousin was concerned. It seemed like Rishi had them all wrapped around his efficient finger. Unknowingly they had all come to accept him as family.

Jeevan-kaka looked downright lost as he ate his dinner. "Yes, *beta*," he said in response to Nilesh's remark. "We all miss Rishi. He is such a nice fellow."

Mohan agreed with his brother. "A very clever and successful businessman at such a young age. Very admirable."

What was surprising was to see her mother looking a bit glum, too. "It's a shame that such a pleasant young man is not married."

Jeevan gave a sad shake of his head. "Since his engagement broke many years ago, he is not willing to get married at all. I have introduced him to some eligible girls, but he's not interested. He says his life is too busy."

"Too busy for marriage?" asked Usha.

In Usha's old-fashioned way of thinking, marriage and family had to be a part of one's life, no matter how busy. How many times had she told Anjali that it was time for her to forget Vik and her hang-ups about marriage and settle down with a good man?

But Anjali could easily relate to Rishi's ideas about freedom. After a while, life just sort of fell into a routine, even if it was more like a rut than a routine, and one became comfortable with it. The older one got, the more difficult it was to make drastic changes. In her late thirties if she felt old and set in her ways, she could only imagine how he felt in his forties. And Samantha was obviously fulfilling his other needs. So why bother tying himself down with marriage?

Then her mother said something that brought her attention back to the conversation, something she herself had been curious to find out. "So, Jeevan-bhai, how did you come to know Rishi?" All these days, since Rishi was always with them, it was a question that couldn't be asked, but obviously her mother was taking advantage of his absence tonight.

"It is a long story, Usha," answered Jeevan. "I owe that boy my life, you see. He was only fourteen years old when he saved my life. I can never forget it."

Just then the phone rang, interrupting Jeevan-kaka's story. The topic never came up again.

Rishi sipped his scotch and scanned a financial report on his laptop computer. It was hard to concentrate on work when his mind was on the emergency situation that was taking him to London. An associate from his flagship store in London had called him early that morning, frantic because the general manager, Balraj Singh, had collapsed from a massive paralytic stroke while working in the storeroom.

According to the employee, Shameem Rizvi, the medics had arrived in minutes and transported Balraj to a hospital. But the doctors had told her that Balraj was essentially brain-dead and hooked up to a life-support machine. He was hanging by a thread.

It was hard for Rishi to imagine the energetic man with the hearty laugh dying. Balraj had named Rishi the executor of his will, and it was now up to Rishi to allow the doctors to unplug the machine and let the older man die with dignity.

The only good thing was Balraj had no family. He was a bachelor, so no one other than his friends and coworkers would miss him. He had been with Rishi's enterprise for nearly eighteen years, right from the beginning, the oldest employee and one of the most trusted.

Mostly Balraj was a friend. It would be hard to replace him. But Rishi would have to find a replacement right away.

Unfortunately the emergency had come at the worst possible time, just when the New Jersey project had reached a critical phase and needed Rishi to be there. But the Kapadias were very efficient people. Together they'd do what was necessary.

He shut off the laptop, put it back in its bag, and stowed it under his feet. Then he reclined the seat in the business-class cabin of the airplane, turned off the overhead light, and stretched out to get some sleep during the long flight.

The airline attendant had been fussing around him with food and drinks and he'd managed to get rid of her. He knew women seemed to find him attractive. But he was convinced it was his assets they found more appealing. Hadn't he learned that about women a long time ago?

Laura was the first woman who'd taught him that lesson very quickly, and then there had been others. So now he had Samantha, a woman who was more than comfortable in her own right. She earned a healthy income from her business. She didn't need his money. He'd talked to her on the phone that morning. She'd sounded thrilled that he was going to be in London soon.

But he wasn't looking forward to seeing her. In the past, whenever he'd gone on long business trips, he'd missed her, or at least her lean, soft-skinned body lying next to him in his bed. Nonetheless his longing for her had dulled considerably in the past several months.

And in the recent weeks, his mind had been so occupied with the Kapadia business in New Jersey that he'd had no time to think about Samantha. If he was honest with himself, though, it wasn't only the business that kept his mind occupied. It was something else.

His thoughts turned to Anjali, the enigmatic widow with the prickly personality. Although her attitude toward him had warmed appreciably since that first day when she'd made it clear she distrusted him, she was still very much on the defensive.

Perhaps because he was used to women flirting with him, befriending him, or mothering him, depending on their age, Anjali had taken him by surprise. She didn't fit into any of those categories.

It was possible that, having no children, she had channeled all her attention and energy into the business. He suspected her affair with Rowling was more a way to combat loneliness rather than love or sex. He hoped she wasn't in love with that rogue. God help her if she was. That playboy would break her heart.

Anjali wasn't precisely beautiful or spectacular or glamorous, but she was appealing nevertheless. He couldn't quite pinpoint it, but something about her aroused in him the need to find out more. At first, the interest wasn't sexual, but a day or two later he'd found himself drawn to her. Or was it the challenge of dealing with an unreceptive woman?

That bastard Rowling was a lucky man.

Chapter 15

Rishi glanced at his watch yet again and stifled a sigh. The starched collar on his shirt chafed his neck. The room felt crowded although only half the tables in the restaurant were occupied. Plus the old chap at the piano was playing something soulful and depressing.

He should have been at ease, eating a superbly cooked meal at his favorite eatery, but he wasn't. The evening had barely begun and he was already getting restless. He'd been edgy all day, too. He wanted to go home to his townhouse, get out of his suit and into comfortable clothes, put his feet up, watch a little telly or work on his computer. Anything but this.

Samantha sat across from him. The establishment was just like Samantha—exclusive, elegant, extravagant. The ambience was pure seduction: candlelit tables, mellow wine, and distinctive French cuisine. Samantha was wearing a little silver dress with whisper-thin straps. She was at her most charming, too.

But none of it was working. Rishi's thoughts wandered to Anjali. Was she back in Rowling's bed? Not likely, but the mere thought was enough to set Rishi's blood simmering. Bloody hell! Was she working too hard, or worrying too much over her financial situation? Most of all, was she thinking of him, perhaps even missing him a little?

Samantha noticed his preoccupation. "Something troubling you, Rich?" she asked, tossing her golden hair back from her face.

She'd always called him Rich instead of Rishi. It was perhaps her way of trying to lull herself into thinking he was a white man. She didn't hold a high opinion of anyone who wasn't the same color as she. However, she was color-blind when it came to money. Her clientele consisted of all kinds of businessmen and women—all prosperous and willing to pay the hefty prices she charged for her advertising services.

He shook his head at her question. "Jet lag."

Samantha sipped her wine and gave a husky laugh. "You never suffer from jet lag. In fact, I always wonder how you manage to function so efficiently with all the time zones you travel through."

"I'm not as young as I used to be." Instead of meeting her curious gaze, he let his eyes wander around the room, wondering what the young couple at the next table was celebrating with a bottle of champagne, what serious matter the half dozen businessmen were earnestly discussing at the large round table, and what the two older men in the corner were laughing about over their calorie-laden dessert.

Meanwhile the waiters moved between the busy tables like silent but efficient ghosts in impeccable black uniforms. Rishi was having a difficult time concentrating on Samantha's words. Nonetheless, with some effort he diverted his attention back to her.

"You could put a twenty-year-old boy to shame, darling. *I* should know that," she said with a wink.

He merely brushed off her comment. He wished he could feel something for Samantha, but what surfaced was only the mild urge to get her out of his life, out of his home, and mainly out of his bed. For the past year he'd been feeling confined about the arrangement he had with her.

Dinner was long and wearisome. Samantha talked and he replied in monosyllables. She ate every morsel of her food and he toyed with his. He was grateful when it ended.

Later, when they returned home, Samantha tried her best to draw him out. "You've been too quiet. Are you going to tell me what's ailing you?" She put her lips to his and lingered there for a beat.

"There's nothing to tell," he replied, ending the kiss by pulling back.

"Did you miss me, darling?" she crooned, smoothing her hands over his shoulders.

Samantha's brand of enticement had always worked well in the past. She was a lovely woman. Yet she'd never looked less appealing than she did at that moment. What was wrong with him?

All he wanted to do was pick up his bags and get on the next plane to the States. Instead he shook his head at her. "I'm tired and I just want to go to bed. Alone."

"Oh, come now," she pouted. "This is our first night together in months."

He gently removed her hands from his shoulders. "I'm tired, Samantha. And I don't want to sleep with you."

"Perhaps tomorrow, then?"

"I'm sorry, but I want this to end."

"Want what to end?" Her brow creased delicately.

He deliberated for a moment, attempting to find a kinder way to express himself, but without success. "This arrangement that we have. I've been meaning to talk to you about it for some time now. Our relationship is not progressing. It's remained stagnant for so long."

"But we both like the arrangement," she said.

"You may like it, but I no longer do. All we do is cohabitate . . . like roommates. I don't see a future for us together." He paused. "I'd appreciate it if you'd find your own place."

"What?" Samantha's perplexed look gradually turned irate as his words sank in.

"It's not an impulsive decision, Samantha. I've given this a lot of thought." He raked his hand through his hair. "I'm really sorry."

She merely stared at him.

"I realize it's not easy to find a house quickly, so I'll give you plenty of time to do it."

"Plenty of time?"

"As much as you need. I'll help you move. But please, we need to end this."

"You're tossing me out?"

"Not tossing, for heaven's sake. I'm asking you in a most civil manner. I'll give you whatever help you need."

After a tense moment of silence her eyes narrowed in suspicion. "You stayed in the U.S. all these months just to get away from me," she accused.

"No. There was more work than I'd anticipated."

"More work or more entertainment?" Her perfect eyebrow rose high in a scornful query.

"Don't be silly."

"Is that why you never invited me to join you there for a holiday, like you promised? You were busy with extracurricular activities?"

"I'll not dignify that with an answer." He was astonished at her reaction. She'd never questioned his business trips before, just like he'd never asked about hers. They'd never before made any demands on each other's time or emotions.

"Aren't we all self-righteous," she sniffed.

"Call it what you like." He was too tired to argue the finer points of their relationship—if it could even be called that. Theirs was more of a domestic arrangement, an extension of their business liaison. Roommates, like he'd said.

Then she stunned him further when her eyes filled with tears. "I suppose you're ending our business relationship as well?"

"Of course not!" He'd never seen her weep before. He eyed her helplessly for an instant before taking her hands in his. "You're the best advertising executive I know. Why would I want to change agencies?"

"Who knows what you'll do next?" she said on a loud sniffle. "You're no longer the man I knew some months ago."

"People change; circumstances change. We need to look at this realistically, Samantha. We respect and like each other. But there haven't been deep feelings on either side since the day we met. It's been mostly physical."

She reclaimed one hand and brushed away her tears with her knuckles. "But we've had a five-year relationship. We've shared a bed . . . a home."

He sighed. What had he gotten himself into? He never should have allowed Samantha to move in with him. Stupid, that's what it was.

In a fit of passion, when she'd said the lease on her flat was up for renewal and suggested that maybe she could move in with him since their love life was so mutually satisfying, he'd readily agreed. It wasn't as if he was a naïve and starry-eyed young man at the time. He was thirty-seven when Samantha had set up housekeeping with him, and he'd had more experience in life than a lot of men twice his age. As a matter of fact, so had Samantha; she was a bit older than he.

Nevertheless he held firm. "I have difficulty believing that all of a sudden you're in love with me, Samantha. You've never mentioned love . . . or even affection, and neither have I. We always knew this arrangement had to end, sooner or later."

"That's not the way I saw it."

"Look, we're both mature adults, so let's keep this simple, shall we?" he suggested.

"I was hoping that someday we'd maybe . . . get married."

Rishi couldn't help but frown. "Marriage never entered into our conversations." When and why had she dreamed up marriage?

"Women are different. We've been together so long. It's only natural that we progress to the next level. After a while, a woman feels the need for a husband and home . . . and perhaps children."

"Do you have any idea what having children involves?" he asked. "Children need attention. A child isn't something you put in a box and ship off to a baby minder somewhere across town. A baby needs a mother, a warm, breast-feeding, nappy-changing mother."

He saw her lips curl in disgust, but she recovered in an instant. "I can be all that," she assured him, brushing off his arguments with remarkable confidence. "I could be a splendid mother."

"Perhaps. But not to my child," he said, shaking his head. "I can't go on like this, Samantha. I can't pretend to have feelings that don't exist. I'll give you plenty of time to find yourself another place." An idea struck him. "I have a friend who owns an upscale residential building a mile from here. I'll help you lease one of the best flats there. I'll even get you a good deal on the lease."

Samantha's tears turned to wounded, narrow-eyed suspicion once again. "There's someone else, isn't it?" When he remained silent, she poked one sharp, manicured nail into his chest. "Isn't it?"

"I just want to move on . . . get on with my life." He stepped away from her, out of the bedroom and into the kitchen to pour himself a snifter of brandy. He disliked being put on the defensive.

She followed him to the kitchen, continuing to rage. "I can tell when you're lying, Rich. I bet you found some cheap little tramp in New York or California or wherever it is that old barracuda Kapadia took you."

"Please don't bring Jeevan Kapadia into this," he said quietly, keeping a firm lid on his annoyance. "I don't appreciate you denigrating him in that fashion."

"He's an ill-mannered, doddering old fool. And yet every time he snaps his arthritic fingers, you run. I bet he's introduced you to some strumpet in his family and you're beginning to fall into his well-laid trap. The old man will ruin you, Rich."

That's when Rishi's temper sparked. "Please don't call anyone in Jeevan-kaka's family a strumpet. The Kapadias are respectable, hardworking people."

"Respectable?" she scoffed, with a dubious tilt of her mouth. "They're backward people with probably no manners—and no scruples."

"That's enough!" He put his snifter down with a thud and crossed his arms across his chest. The brandy sloshed over the side of the snifter and spilled onto the granite counter. "I don't want to hear any comments about the Kapadias, especially my uncle," he warned her. He'd been prepared to be generous and understanding with her, but he refused to tolerate her attacks on Jeevan-kaka and his family. "When I return to London in a few weeks, I would appreciate it if you've made plans to move into a place of your own."

"Just like that?" she snapped.

"I apologize for springing this on you," he repeated. "But you can stay here until you find a suitable house. I won't rush you."

She stared at her own toes for a long while. Rishi observed her flushed skin, her quick breathing. He'd seen her temper tantrums often enough to anticipate what would come next. She had a tendency to turn violent, use foul language, and fling things around. He quickly moved an antique porcelain sculpture out of her reach.

"You're a first-class bastard!" she finally spat out and turned on her heel, looking regal and superior, even in bare feet and nothing more than a see-through robe. At least she hadn't hurled anything breakable—yet.

He grabbed the bottle of brandy and the snifter and strode into the guest bedroom. He lay down on the bedspread and stared at the ceiling. His mind was swirling, making him dizzy. Guilt wasn't a pretty emotion.

And damn it all, Samantha was right to some extent. They'd had five years together. But on the other hand, he couldn't live a lie—sharing a home with Samantha when his mind and heart belonged somewhere else. He couldn't feign feelings he didn't have. And dissolving the relationship in phases wasn't exactly his nature either. It was all or nothing with him.

When he thought about it, he'd been more than generous with Samantha. Her entire wardrobe, including her expensive accessories and toiletries, came free of charge from his boutiques. She had stayed in this house rent-free all these years, and he'd paid for the food, entertainment, joint vacations, and everything else.

Samantha had literally saved her entire earnings while she'd been with him. All his advertising needs were handled by her firm—for a standard fee. He'd referred a number of his friends and acquaintances to her as well.

She was a wealthier woman to some degree because of him. She'd never offered to pay her share for anything and he'd never asked. In fact, he couldn't remember a single occasion when she'd even thanked him for any of it. She'd always treated it as an entitlement.

And that thought made him feel a little better about his present decision. If she felt he'd somehow used her, she'd used him more—far, far more.

It wasn't a good idea to drink brandy on top of the two glasses of wine he'd had with dinner. But he sat up and reached for the snifter anyway, took another swallow large enough to make him choke and sputter.

He drank himself into a stupor and remained in the guest room that night, behind locked doors. Then he slept.

The next morning, battling the inevitable hangover, he wandered into the master bedroom and came to a dead stop when he noticed Samantha was gone. Astonished, he surveyed the room. The two matching antique mahogany armoires that housed her clothes and accessories were open and empty—and so were the drawers of the Queen Anne chest she'd taken possession of. Her suitcases and toiletries were missing. He found nothing left that belonged to her, just a faint trace of the perfume she favored.

Opening the two other armoires that held his own wardrobe, he blew a sigh of relief. He'd expected to see all his things slashed and smashed. But as far as he could see nothing had been touched.

He looked at the bedside clock. It was nearly noon. Where had she gone? To a hotel? To a friend's house? He really hadn't meant for her to leave so abruptly. He'd given her plenty of time to come to terms with his decision, to do it at her own pace. And yet it looked like she'd been packing most of the night. He hadn't even heard any noises emerging from the room. But then he'd been in an alcohol-induced coma until a few minutes ago.

He stood with his hands on his hips and surveyed the room. Instead of feeling liberated, he felt a cold prickle of unease. The pounding in his head and the acid churning in his stomach went up a notch. After years of living with someone, he was alone, and yet the freedom didn't feel as good as it should have. If there had been even a sliver of a chance of making a life with Samantha, he would have. He respected her clever mind, but there was nothing else he could give her.

He shut the doors of the armoires and pushed in the open drawers. The place didn't seem like his anymore. Maybe he could sell the townhouse and get another one—and while he was at it, buy all new furnishings, too. What little essence of Samantha was left needed to be erased.

But for the moment all he wanted was to banish the hangover. A foul wave of nausea drove him into the master bathroom. Reaching the toilet just in time, he threw up. Then he brushed his teeth, went back to the guest room, and plopped back onto the bed.

The sense of physical relief was immense. He slept once again.

Chapter 16

Anjali inspected the new windows installed in Tejmal's store, or rather *their* new store. She'd been on her feet most of the day. They'd had several customers—hard on her feet but always good for business.

Only about half of them had bought anything of real value, while the others had been curious about the renovations next door and the "Clearance Sale" sign in the window. But still, the more interest customers showed, the better the chances of luring them back to the store when the expansion was completed. So she'd served everyone with a smile and a welcoming word.

Because of Jeevan-kaka's unusual needs, her mother spent more time at home cooking and cleaning lately, and her father had completely taken over the financial end of the business. So the floor work was mostly hers.

With Rishi in London, Jeevan-kaka was handling the contractors by himself. He was a slave driver. A couple of times she'd heard the workmen grumbling about "that crabby old fart." But he did a good job of keeping a strict eye on them.

She often wondered how Rishi was dealing with his emergency. He'd been gone nearly a week. She couldn't help speculating if Samantha was the reason he was still lingering there.

Lately Rishi and Anjali had been getting along well, though. That night, when they'd had a private conversation after everyone else had gone to bed, things had changed between them. Mainly she had begun to trust him.

At the moment, everyone else had gone home and she was alone in the store, checking on the progress of the restoration work. Every night, before she left for home, she made it a point to take a final look around.

The new display windows facing the street looked beautiful—wide and tall, with the sill made of brilliant, polished oak. Soon the dinginess of Tejmal's store would be gone and the building, with skylights and creamy walls and chandeliers, would be unrecognizable. The outside of the structure was getting a facelift, too. It would stand out like a jewel amidst the ordinary *dookaans* or shops.

A mild thrill of excitement zipped through her. Maybe this could work. Rishi and Jeevan-kaka were so darned optimistic that it had started to rub off on her. She could only pray they were right and it would all turn out well. For her part, she was willing to work any amount to make the store a success.

In fact, she'd been working so hard that she hadn't found the time to visit Kip since that night when she'd run into Rishi at the Rowling Rok. That was . . . when? About two months ago? She was too tired to see Kip these days anyway. And he was a busy man himself. He didn't have time for her until late at night and she couldn't afford to keep late nights anymore.

Besides, the way Rishi had reacted to seeing her with Kip had bothered her. She tried to tell herself his opinion didn't matter, but it did. She could bet those keen eyes had summed up her relationship with Kip in an instant. And they'd left her feeling cheap and uncomfortable. Rishi disturbed her more than she cared to be disturbed.

The puzzling thing was she hadn't missed seeing Kip all that much. But tonight the loneliness was nipping at her. She was feeling the familiar restlessness, the desire to get away from her family for a while and spend some time with Kip. Checking her watch, she noted it was well after 8:00 P.M.

On an impulse, she pulled out her cell phone from her pocket and called her mother. "Mom, you mind if I join my friends for dinner?"

"Dinner's ready and we're waiting for you, Anju," said Usha, sounding irritated. "Why don't you have a quick bite with us and join your friends for coffee later?"

"Please, Mom, I need some time to myself. I haven't seen them since the expansion started."

She heard her mother exhale a loud sigh. "Okay. Don't stay out too late."

"I won't," she promised and hung up. Lies and more lies. This was getting tiring. But how else was she going to do this without upsetting her parents? Sometimes she wished she was born in a liberal family where having an affair, especially at her age, was considered harmless, an intrinsic part of being a woman. Instead, here she was, sleeping with some guy in secret and feeling ashamed about it afterward, like she'd betrayed her family, her late husband, and her heritage.

It being a weeknight, Rowling Rok's parking lot had few cars. Maybe Kip could make some time for her. Since she'd made up her mind to go discreetly through the back door from now on, she went around the building and through the kitchen. Billy was nowhere in sight, so she opened the door that led into the bar area and stuck her head in. She saw Billy at the counter, his broad back to her while he served some customers. Like she'd guessed, there weren't too many patrons tonight.

She went back into the kitchen and up the stairs to Kip's apartment. He was likely to be doing his paperwork. Wanting to surprise him, she tiptoed furtively and tried the door to his apartment. It was unlocked, so she very carefully let herself in. Finding the living room in semidarkness, she stopped for a moment, undecided.

Everything was quiet and the bedroom door was closed. Had Kip gone out? Or maybe not. She wondered if she should knock. But it would be fun to sneak up on him. She'd done it once before and he'd been delighted to see her unexpectedly.

Grabbing the doorknob, she pushed open the door. "Surprise!"

In the next instant the breath was swept out of her. Oh God!

She stood on the threshold, the shock so potent she couldn't move a muscle. Even blinking seemed impossible as her gaze fixed itself on the bed.

The bedside light was on, and Kip in all his naked glory was making vigorous love to a blond woman. On hearing her voice they both turned their heads toward the door.

Kip's face registered the same kind of shock she felt. He froze, his body still attached to the woman lying under him. "Damn!" The familiar sheen of perspiration glistened on his smooth skin. A damp lock of hair had fallen over his forehead. His breath, too, was coming out in hard gasps, the kind that comes with unrestrained sex.

Finally finding the strength to move, Anjali managed to turn around. Without another word she ran through the darkened living room and down the stairs. She heard Kip calling her name, but she didn't stop until she crossed the empty restaurant kitchen, opened the back door, and stepped outside.

Damn it! Damn it! Why hadn't she knocked before barging in?

On the other side of the door, she stopped only for an instant to suck in a breath of fresh, cool air, then continued to run along the side of the building, the same path she'd taken coming in. She was panting by the time she'd covered the length of the concrete walkway.

She wasn't sure whom she was more disgusted with, Kip or herself. What he was doing came as no surprise, but the fact that she'd walked in on him with another woman bordered on sickening. She couldn't get the revolting image out of her mind. How many times had she herself been the woman in that exact same position in his bed?

She managed to reach the parking lot.

As she raced toward her car she stumbled on something, then slammed into a solid wall—of hard muscle. She let out a scream, but what emerged from her throat was a high-pitched squeal. Even that was muffled as her face got smothered by someone's chest. "Anjali!" the man said.

Assuming it was Kip who'd somehow managed to catch up

with her, she pummeled his chest with both fists. "G-get away from me. I don't . . . want to . . . see you again."

The man was big and strong and he grabbed both her wrists. "It's Rishi, not Kip," he said. When she continued to struggle, he grabbed her arms and pinned them to her sides. "Anjali, did you hear me? I'm Rishi."

That's when she recognized his voice. Still fighting for breath, she raised her face to his. "Rishi?" After staring at him for an instant, she crumpled against him in relief.

He gathered her in his arms. "Are you all right?" he asked, stroking her back with one hand. "You're shaking."

It took her a minute before she regained her poise and pulled away from him to step back. "I'm sorry. I don't know what came over me."

"That's okay. I'm glad I was here to catch you before you fell on your face." He inclined his head to indicate the empty Chinese takeout food container on the ground, over which she'd stumbled.

She scowled at him in the jaundiced glow of the parking lot light. "What are you doing here? You're supposed to be in London."

"I flew in a couple of hours ago."

"Oh . . . so you're back." Her mind was still in a tangle. Unfortunately her breath was still wheezy, too.

"I happened to be at your house when you called your mother earlier," he said. "About meeting your friends for supper," he added, maybe because she wore a blank look.

She lowered her eyes to the ground. "And naturally you assumed I was here."

"Naturally."

That one word brought home the realization that Rishi was mocking her—fool that she was. That Oxford-educated brain of his had likely figured out what had made her run like a lunatic, too. "Well, now that you've found me, why don't you go your own way and I'll go mine," she said and fished her car keys out of her pocketbook. Her hands were shaking so much the keys rattled.

"No, you won't." He caught her wrist before she could unlock the car door.

She glanced up at him. His face was chiseled in stone. He wasn't kidding. "I need to go home, Rishi."

His expression relaxed a bit but his grip on her wrist didn't. "Look, you seem to be upset over something. I don't think you should drive home yet. Let's go someplace where we can talk." He must have seen the wariness in her eyes, because he added, "I'm only trying to help. Obviously something happened here tonight and you're shaken."

She turned away from his penetrating gaze. How could she tell him, a man she'd known only a short time, what she'd witnessed? How humiliating was it to tell someone she'd caught her lover in bed with another woman?

"Did Rowling hurt you?" His voice was soft and measured, but she could sense the undercurrent of fury, something primitive and male. Her instinct told her Rishi was ready to have Kip hanged from the nearest tree.

"No." She drew a long breath and willed her rigid shoulders to relax a little.

His grip on her wrist eased. "Then what is it that had you running?"

She closed her eyes and took another calming breath. He wasn't going to let it go. "Oh, what the heck. You really want to know? I'll tell you," she said. "The whole tawdry story."

"Good. But not here." He shifted his hand to her elbow and led her to his vehicle, settled her in the passenger seat, then got into the driver's side. "Is there a place nearby where we can talk?"

She shook her head. "Can't think of any at the moment."

"Then we'll go to my hotel and you can tell me why you're so upset." He scowled at her. "Don't look so petrified. I'm not going to take advantage of you or anything."

"It's not that. It's my car; I can't leave it here."

"We'll come back later and pick it up. The pub's open late, isn't it?"

She nodded and he put the SUV in gear and drove them to his

hotel. She sat stiffly in her seat, intensely aware of the tension pulsing between them. Not a word was exchanged. He kept his eyes on the road and she let her gaze remain on her clasped hands. Minutes later, at the hotel, she meekly let him escort her across the atrium-style lobby and into the elevator.

In the polished chrome walls of the elevator, she caught her reflection. Her hair had a wild, windblown look and her expression was that of an animal caught in the headlights. No wonder he'd concluded she was too upset to drive on her own. And he was probably right.

When they got off on the fifth floor, she noted it was a nice hotel, with wide, plush-carpeted hallways, potted plants, and tasteful art on the walls. His room turned out to be a suite with a sitting room, office area, and kitchenette separated from the bedroom and bath. It was bigger than the apartment she and Vik used to have in Queens.

He gestured toward the bathroom. "Go ahead. Take your time." He'd obviously read her mind about needing a few private moments.

Grateful for his perception, Anjali locked herself in the bathroom, splashed some cold water over her face, and dried it. When she felt a little calmer she combed her hair and fixed her makeup. Her eyes still looked a bit dilated. She was still wound tight. She needed to sit down, so she sat on the rim of the bathtub.

Her cell phone began to ring. Pulling it out of her pocketbook, she checked the number flashing on it. Kip! She quickly shut off the power. She never wanted to talk to him again.

What was he going to say to her? *Sorry, babe, I was only doing what I'm programmed to do: screw as many women as possible.* It hurt to think of it in such crude terms, but it was true. He was doing what came naturally to some men. They were probably wired that way at conception. Besides, Kip had never promised her anything other than a romp in his bed.

Up until that moment of discovery she hadn't ever kidded herself that she was Kip's only paramour. On the evenings she wasn't around, she knew he was providing his brand of therapy to any number of lonely women. Her occasional half hour with him was equivalent to reclining on a psychiatrist's couch. Just like her, other women used the same couch and went home feeling better. And yet, seeing it with her own eyes had stung like an ornery wasp.

Now that she'd had a few minutes to deliberate over what had just occurred, she was beginning to comprehend why she'd reacted so emotionally to something so predictable. What had sickened her more than anything was the fact that she had become involved with a man like Kip in the first place. She, a mature, levelheaded woman, had thrown common sense and caution to the winds and hooked up with the most unlikely man.

That bothered her more than what she'd discovered earlier. That and the important fact that *she'd* always gone to him, gone to his bed willingly. He'd never come to her.

Well, there was a positive side to this evening's episode. It had finally opened her eyes. It was time to sever her ties with Kip completely.

She powered up her cell phone again. Mercifully, Kip hadn't left a message. She sent a text message to him—polite and to the point—that she wouldn't be seeing him again. On an impulse she added a line to thank him for his past kindness. No matter what his other faults, he'd always been a good listener and he'd offered her friendship and support when she'd needed it.

Then she shut off her phone a second time and shoved it into her pocketbook. It was the end of a slightly disturbing chapter in her life.

After giving herself another moment to settle, she left the bathroom. When she returned to the sitting room, Rishi motioned to her to sit on the couch and brought her a glass of water. Then he sat next to her. "Want to tell me what happened?"

She sipped the water, the cold liquid slowly trickling down and settling in her stomach. It felt good. She realized her throat was parched. "There's not much to tell."

"Most women don't sprint like mad hatters in the dark if there's not much happening to them," he said matter-of-factly. "It has something to do with Rowling, I presume?"

"Since you're such an Einstein, why don't you figure it out?"

Instead of taking offense at her sarcasm, he eyed her with enviable calm. "Did you and Rowling have a fight?"

"Hardly."

"Then what is it? Does he have a new girlfriend?"

She set the empty glass of water on the coffee table. "Hmm."

"I see. Rowling's playing the rolling stone." He gave her another long, speculative look. "Did you find him in bed with someone?"

She chose not to answer. He'd hit the nail on the head within three guesses.

"I get the picture. That's why you were trying to escape from the scene." He was silent for a minute, seemingly absorbing the news. "It's hard to face the truth, isn't it, Anjali?" he said finally.

"Rub it in some more, why don't you?"

He touched her face. "I know all about it. I've been there."

"You couldn't have."

"Remember I told you about Laura? It hurts like the dickens, doesn't it?" His hand moved to cup her face.

Maybe it was his soft, sympathetic tone, or the tender way he rubbed his thumb over her cheekbone. For some unknown reason her eyes filled with tears. When the first one slid down her cheeks, he shifted closer and placed his arms around her. "The man's not worth your tears. He's a playboy. He was toying with you."

"Don't you think I know that? I'm not stupid." She was ruining his nice shirt, but it felt good to be held by a strong man. He smelled of warm summer breezes and that elusive aftershave. And he had a nice, wide chest that felt so comfortable to lean into.

"Are you in love with him?"

"No. Kip's not exactly a lovable sort."

"Then what sort is he?"

She had to take a moment to think. "He's . . . a ladies' man. He's charming and sexy and treats women and sex as competitive sports."

"I suppose he's an avid sportsman and competes frequently?"

"You could say that."

"Then why in heaven's name are you wasting your tears over him, Anjali?"

"Why?" She pulled away from his arms, but he kept his hands on her shoulders. She blew her nose with the tissue she'd picked up in his bathroom. "Maybe because I went there for some TLC and received shock treatment instead."

"There, you've answered your own question." He stopped for a beat. "Why were you looking for TLC from Rowling when you have such a kind family to turn to?"

She rolled her eyes inwardly. Was he deliberately acting dense or was he poking fun at her again? Did he really think she meant TLC in the literal sense? Well, maybe he'd had his own brand of TLC with Samantha in London and couldn't understand other people's need for it.

"Maybe I can give you the TLC you need," he said. "I've even got some chocolates around here somewhere if you'd like. I've been told chocolate has a calming effect on women."

Realizing that he was indeed clueless, she snickered. "Do you even know the meaning of 'tender loving care'?"

He raised a single dark eyebrow at her, but there was a hint of humor in his expression. "You don't think I have warmth and sensitivity?"

She shook her head, thinking once again what a fine man he was. Too bad he wasn't exactly her type. Although at the moment, with him close enough for her to feel the warmth radiating from him, she was beginning to feel something clearly sexual. Right now he looked good enough to . . . Oh dear! It had been a while since she'd been in Kip's bed, but this was ridiculous. She was beginning to hallucinate.

Before she could utter another word Rishi's expression changed. He caught her face between his hands and his mouth descended on hers. It was a gentle brush of lips.

This was unexpected. But it felt nice. Better than nice.

His heartbeat felt a little erratic under her open palm. His lips were soft and warm. So she relaxed, a little reluctantly at first, but he must have sensed her surrender, because he deepened the kiss. In a minute his tongue was diving into her mouth, urging her to respond. And she did. It was sweet and tender and erotic all at the same time.

Warmth *and* tenderness.

Kip had rarely kissed her in the real sense, because he went straight to the main course without any appetizers. But this was different. Rishi was an expert kisser and he was making her feel like a woman—a desperate, hungry woman who needed compassion as well as male strength. And God knew this guy was giving it to her now. Suspending all other thoughts from her mind, she slipped her arms around his neck and returned his kisses with equal ardor. She hadn't been kissed like this . . . since . . . Vik.

Vik! Oh God! Abruptly she drew back. "I can't do this."

Rishi stared at her. "I'm sorry."

She extricated herself from his arms. "No. I'm the one that's sorry. I was asking for it. Shameless, that's what I am." She used her balled-up tissue to wipe away the moisture from her lips.

"You're not shameless."

"You don't know me well enough to say that."

He shook his head. "You're a passionate woman and you've been a widow far too long. Every woman needs love in her life. You're doing what comes instinctively to every woman."

"Is that what it is, instinct? Then what was *your* reason for kissing me? Instinctively missing Samantha?"

He got to his feet, went to the refrigerator, and got a couple of cans of soda for the two of them. "Samantha and I are no longer together."

She frowned at him. "Not long ago you told me you two were a couple. When did this occur?"

"During this trip. I think it was inevitable. It was going to happen sooner or later, and my visit to London proved to be the ideal time to put an end to it."

"What exactly happened?" She wasn't sure if he was going to answer that.

But he did. "I wasn't happy with our living arrangement any longer and told her so. Then she accused me of trying to stay away from her deliberately. And she may be right."

"Oh?" She couldn't wait to hear why.

"When I left London more than two months ago I had told her she could join me here, and that maybe we could take a nice holiday somewhere."

Pulling the tab on her soda can, she took a long swallow. "So why didn't you invite her?"

"I didn't feel like it. I told her that, too."

"She didn't take it well?"

"Not at first, but in the end I think she understood why I had to do what I did. Samantha is a practical and smart woman."

"Precisely why did you do it, Rishi?" Anjali asked, curious to know everything about it.

He turned that laser look on her, suddenly making her feel like her bones were about to disintegrate. "The truth? Because I didn't want to encourage her anymore since I saw no future for us. Because I had no deep feelings for her. Because I met someone more interesting in the U.S. And because I'm hoping that lady will return my sentiments."

She turned suspicious eyes on him. "Sejal? Eww! She's almost young enough to be your daughter."

"I know that." For the first time since she'd met him, Rishi actually rolled his eyes. "Are you that blind and naïve? Or has Rowling's tomfoolery made you suspect all men? The lady I spoke of is *you*, you daft woman."

"Me?" She sat up straight. "But you hardly know me."

"I've known *about* you. Jeevan-kaka's been telling me about his talented American niece for years."

"My uncle says nice things about all his family. He's a bit prejudiced when it comes to the Kapadias."

"That's what I'd thought all this time. I hadn't paid much attention. But after I met you I realized he was right."

She twirled her soda can between her fingers. "What exactly did he tell you about me?"

"In his own words, 'I am telling you, *beta*, our Anju is *bahu soondar, bahu saras.*'" Very pretty, very good.

Anjali melted into amused laughter at Rishi's Indo-Brit imitation of Jeevan-kaka. "Where did you learn to do that hilarious imitation of my uncle?"

Rishi started chuckling. "I've known him long enough for his accent to rub off on me."

"Exactly how long have you known Jeevan-kaka?"

"Curious about my relationship to your uncle, are you?"

She angled a narrow-eyed look at him. "You're not by any chance his . . . um . . . love child or anything, are you?"

It was his turn to explode into laughter. "Do I look like I'm even remotely related to Jeevan-kaka? Besides, he's very faithful to his wife, so illegitimate children are highly unlikely. And why would I call him Jeevan-kaka if he's my father?"

"Precisely what is he to you, then?"

His response was total silence.

Chapter 17

Anjali could see Rishi wasn't about to reveal anything regarding her uncle and himself—at least not right away. He had an entirely different agenda and she was waiting for it to unfold.

Instead of discussing Jeevan-kaka, he said, "I want you to tell me something first." He reached out and took her hand. "Did you feel anything at all when I kissed you?"

He was a clever one—trying to steer her attention away from what she was dying to know. But she humored him anyway. "Couldn't you tell?"

"Yes, I could. You gave back as enthusiastically as I took. Am I right?"

"Um . . . I guess. So . . . what are you saying?"

"That we're both free individuals. I'm no longer with Samantha and you're no longer with Rowling, so I'd like to kiss you again. I want to see if there's any chance this could go further."

She shook her head. "I have no desire to take this further. Just because I'm still reeling from discovering my boyfriend with some woman, I'm not going to hop into another man's bed on the rebound. I'm not that kind of person." She rubbed her forehead for a moment. "I don't even know why I was having an affair with Kip. It just sort of . . . happened."

"You were lonely, Anjali," he murmured, stroking her wrist with his thumb. "There's nothing wrong in being human. Don't punish yourself like this. Vikram died, what . . . ten years ago?"

"But he was my husband. I loved him." Loved him so much that the ache in her chest was almost physical at times.

"And I'm sure you miss him, but getting involved with another man is not betraying him or his memory in any way. Wouldn't he have wanted you to find happiness again?"

"Having sex is not finding happiness. Each time I fulfill my need for sex I feel awful. I go home feeling like—like a whore."

"I'm not asking you to go to bed with me. I respect you too much for that. You're a lady and I'm asking if you'd allow me to see you socially."

"Even when you know I've been sleeping with another man?"

"I was sleeping with another woman until recently myself. In our own way we were both fulfilling our basic needs and nothing more." He quirked a brow at her. "Do you think we stand a chance?"

She sighed. "We have nothing in common, Rishi. You're a jet-setter with businesses scattered around the globe. Women seem to find you wildly attractive. I'm just a middle-class widow with a struggling store that you and my uncle are trying to save. My life's here in Jersey. I can't give it up just to sleep with a guy like you every now and then, whenever you're in town."

"Bloody hell!" He startled her. Sparks were flying out of those awesome eyes. She'd seen them cold, hard, angry, but not livid. "I'm not asking you to sleep with me *every now and then*."

"Then what are you asking of me?"

"I'm asking you to open your mind a little . . . accept me as a man with possibilities. If nothing else, we could be friends. Maybe we could give this a chance. Jeevan-kaka's been hinting for years that we'd be perfect for each other."

"Jeevan-kaka's a conservative old man who thinks in terms of marriage and family, not in terms of sleeping with each other to scratch an occasional itch."

"Will you just listen? After meeting you, I've been thinking about Jeevan-kaka's hints—more and more in the past few weeks, especially since you and I had that little talk about your life with Vikram Gandhi."

"So you're propositioning me?" She was angry now. How dare he pretend to comfort her at first and then solicit her? Just because he'd guessed she was having an affair with Kip and she was upset over his infidelity, this guy could just assume she'd be available . . . as a convenient call girl of sorts?

He gave a long-suffering sigh. "Good God, Anjali, didn't I just say I respect you too much to proposition you?" He shut his eyes for a moment before turning to her. "Tell me, how did you and Vikram meet?" His voice had softened. The annoyance had clearly subsided.

"We were introduced by mutual friends."

"Then what happened?"

"He asked me out."

"Did you go out with him the first time he asked?"

"Yes," she said warily.

"How long were you seeing each other before you fell in love?"

"About four months. What is this, an inquisition?"

He ignored her question and continued. "Then he proposed to you?"

"Yes." She sent him a piqued look. "Where exactly is all this leading?"

"I'll tell you in a minute. When did you get married?"

"About six months after the engagement."

"So, approximately four months after you started dating you fell in love, and six months after that you married the man."

"Yeah. So what?"

"So, that's what I'm doing now: what Vikram did. I'm asking you out so we can get to know each other, like two independent, modern, well-bred, single individuals. Who knows, maybe we'll end up finding we have plenty in common, that we're compatible."

"You mean you . . . I . . . we . . ." Was he saying what she thought he was saying? "Didn't you tell me you'd promised yourself you'd never settle down?"

He took an impatient sip of his soda. "I changed my mind."

"I thought *women* were notorious for changing their minds."

He scrubbed his face with one hand, like he was tired. Maybe he was exhausted and jet lag was setting in after his long flight from London. "I'm beginning to reassess my life lately."

"You had an epiphany?"

"I wouldn't call it that, but my forty-second birthday had me thinking. I feel I need an anchor, maybe even a child."

"Then you're talking to the wrong woman. I'm going to be thirty-eight soon. My biological clock is dying a slow and silent death even as we speak."

He shook his head. "How old was your mother when she gave birth to Nilesh?"

"Nearly forty."

"Exactly my point, darling," he said. "It's not uncommon for women in their forties to bear children these days."

"Don't call me cute names you don't mean, Rishi."

"Who says I don't? When I called you darling, I meant it."

All of a sudden he was talking commitment and children, kissing her senseless. He was going at breakneck speed, too. She was getting dizzy with this kind of talk. She needed to slow down and take a breath. That meant she needed to change the direction of his thoughts, give herself some time to absorb all this.

"Brits tend to call everyone *darling*, even their hairdressers and cleaning ladies. It doesn't mean anything," she said, grabbing the first trivial argument that came to mind. Swallowing the last of her soda, she put the can on the coffee table.

"Not this Brit. And I'm not entirely Brit, as you well know. I'm Indo-Brit."

"Who're you kidding? All you have to do is open your mouth and say words like *dah-ling* and *bahth-room* and *shed-dule*. It can't get any more Brit than that."

"All right, then, I'm a Brit." He took her hand in his again, sending little electric sparks up and down her arm. "Now may I kiss you again, Miss Kapadia—the old-fashioned English way?"

Despite the humor in his words, his eyes had taken on that

smoky, heated look. "I know you enjoyed it the first time. And don't say you didn't."

"I'm not denying it. You're a very attractive man and a polished kisser. I guess you've been around the block a few times."

"Around the block . . . ?" He lifted his brows at her quizzically.

"It means you've been with several women, that you're practiced in the art of kissing and . . . other things."

"I didn't realize kissing and making love were arts." He grinned unexpectedly, making her feel like her bones were turning to jelly with no solid mass left. "Just goes to show one learns something new every day." The grin disappeared just as quickly. "I've been intimate with only four women, and that includes Samantha and Laura."

Anjali sighed aloud. "*Only* four, he says."

"Enough quibbling over numbers." Before she could say anything else she was being kissed thoroughly, proving her right once again. He was well versed in the business of kissing. So where did that leave her? She'd kissed only two other men before, one of them being her late husband. But she couldn't resist the warm tug of Rishi's mouth on hers. So she gave in to the kiss.

He left her breathless. She was right about the other thing, too. No one had made her feel quite so soft and feminine and desirable since Vik. There was such warmth there. Such need. But it was also frightening. He was beginning to look more attractive by the second.

When he finally let her go she leaned her head against his shoulder, weak and shaking. The kiss had stirred up certain emotions she'd kept locked up. She couldn't afford to fall in love. She pulled away from him once more.

He watched her withdraw from him. "Did I frighten you, Anju?" he asked.

She shook her head even though it was a lie. She was scared to death of the way she was feeling. And he'd called her Anju for the first time. Only close family called her that. Once again she realized this was moving much too fast for comfort. She should leave right away, she thought, while she still had her wits about her. She didn't want to leave, but she should.

"I think I better go home now. Despite my advanced years, my mother worries if I stay out too late," she told him, trying to work in a casual smile.

"I'll tell her you were with me—that we accidentally ran into each other at the restaurant . . . with your friends."

"You're going to lie to her?"

"Despite the wisdom of your advanced years, *you've* been lying to her, haven't you?" he remarked dryly. "And this time it's for a good cause." He leaned over and raised his hand to caress her face. "Will you let me take you to dinner tomorrow night? I promise to be a perfect gentleman."

She was tempted to say yes. But getting involved with him wasn't without complications. She needed time to think it over—needed a moment to regain her sense of balance.

Meanwhile, a change of subject was needed to help dispel the sexual energy flowing between them. "Only if you promise to tell me here and now everything about you and Jeevan-kaka," she said, finding a way to get him off the topic of dating and on to something that was almost as important.

"I promise."

"Who *are* you? Why are you and my uncle so tight-lipped about your relationship? And since when has Jeevan-kaka started to take on business partners?"

"You know what happened to Pandora when she opened the box?"

"Uh-huh. I still want to know. Now that you mentioned Pandora, I'm even more curious to learn the truth."

A heartbeat passed. "Very well, then."

Chapter 18

"First, I want to know who you are." Anjali settled a little more comfortably in her seat.

"My father was Jagdish Shah," Rishi began. "My mother was Ellen Porter, a British woman who left her native England for India some forty-five years ago to work as a nurse amongst the poor and sickly in Indian villages."

"Was? So they're both deceased?" Anjali instinctively put her hand in his and he curled his fingers around it.

He shook his head. "My father is deceased. My mother's retired and stays in England."

"When did your father pass away?"

"When I was a teenager."

"I'm sorry, Rishi." Anjali was surprised at the depth of her sympathy for him. An hour ago he was an annoyance and a bully. Now she ached for him. A teenager shouldn't have to lose a parent.

"It was a long time ago," he said with a shrug.

Her attention was immediately riveted on his tale. At last, she was going to find out who this mystery man was. She wanted to know all about him, especially now that she was discovering a whole new and exciting side of him.

"My father managed Jeevan-kaka's dairy farm near Gamdi," he continued. "At the time, Jeevan-kaka and his family used to stay in the city of Anand, where Jeevan-kaka managed his cloth mill and his other urban businesses. My mother worked for a rural clinic run by a Christian charitable organization. Much of the farm labor went there for treatment. Whenever my father drove his sick and injured laborers to the clinic, he had an opportunity to interact with my mother. Eventually the two fell in love."

"Love happened to conservative Gujarati men in those days?" she asked, amused and intrigued by the possibility.

"It happened to my father forty-five years ago. To hear my mother tell the story, Papa was the most handsome man she'd ever met. She said he worked extremely hard and she admired his work ethic. Jeevan-kaka was his close friend besides being his employer."

"Jeevan-kaka didn't have something to say about your father marrying a white woman? I'd have thought he'd have some issues with it."

Rishi chuckled. "I'm sure he did. That's probably why it took my father two whole years to work up the nerve to ask my mother to marry him. Besides valuing Jeevan-kaka's opinion, he was also intimidated by him."

"So . . . if they got married forty-three years ago, you were born a year later."

"Your powers of deduction are amazing." He gave her a teasing grin.

"Very funny, Einstein. So, were there any more children after you came along?"

"No. Mum tells me she had a couple of miscarriages." He looked wistful as he stroked the back of Anjali's hand with his own. "I was raised a Hindu. My mother was old-fashioned that way. Although she was Christian, she firmly believed my father's faith should be mine."

"Interesting."

"Nothing but Indian food was served at home, too. I stayed on the farm the first few years and attended the local Gujarati school while my mother taught me English at home. But then my parents sent me off to a boarding school at the age of nine."

"That's so sad—a little nine-year-old boy going so far away from home. I'm assuming there weren't any good schools in the immediate area?"

"My parents wanted the very best education for me, so they had no choice but to send me away to a residential school."

"Were you and Jeevan-kaka close even then?"

"Not really. To me he was the rich and powerful boss. I respected him, but I also resented him—mostly his big house in the city, the servants, the cars, and everything else that surrounded a wealthy businessman. We weren't poor, but we lived in a small house on the farm. We had one woman-servant who took care of me during the day, cleaned, and cooked while my mother worked at the clinic."

"So money was important to you?"

"Back then it was. But now that I have some money and the things it can buy, it seems like an entirely foolish thing to focus on. There's so much more to life than money, isn't there?"

"Easy for you to say," she scoffed. "You're not the one whose business is teetering and could ruin you for life."

"Your business will not be ruined, Anjali. I promise you that. I'll help you get the store back on its feet. That's what I do for a living. Teetering businesses are the backbone of my consulting business."

"I'll hold you to that promise, then." She tried to reclaim her hand by tugging on it gently, but he held firm. The warm current of electricity flowing through her pulse and going directly to the rest of her body was messing with her brain. "So then you went away to school," she prompted.

"I went home during holidays, and as a teenager I helped my father with the bookkeeping and paperwork. I did a lot of farm labor, too. I liked working with the dairy processing machines and driving the milk delivery trucks."

"Even as a young boy you had a head for business?"

"Remember I told you I discovered at a very early age that I liked it? Whenever Jeevan-kaka came to visit the farm he seemed impressed with my business acumen. He even solicited my opinion on some things. I was flattered that such a rich and powerful businessman thought I had something valuable to contribute."

Anjali figured that's probably how the old man and Rishi had struck up a friendship. "Did my uncle offer you a job then?"

Rishi laughed. "No. I still had years of schooling to complete. But I began to like Jeevan-kaka more and more."

"Did you always call him Jeevan-kaka?"

"Yes. My parents wanted me to call him that and his wife kaki. The families were close."

Anjali recalled something her uncle had said the other day. "Jeevan-kaka said you saved his life. What's all that about?"

"It's a rather long and depressing story, Anju."

"I'd like to hear it. What exactly did you do to save a man like Jeevan-kaka?"

Rishi inhaled a deep breath as if to fortify himself. "When I was fourteen and home for a brief holiday, Jeevan-kaka came to visit. He stayed with us whenever he came down to check on the farm. We'd been having some trouble at the farm off and on: skirmishes with some of our laborers. My father was forced to dismiss a particularly disruptive and violent worker during the week Jeevan-kaka was visiting."

Anjali could feel Rishi's hand tensing up. She had a feeling this wasn't a pleasant subject for him. Nonetheless she remained silent, hoping he'd continue.

"That night, when we were all asleep, someone started a fire in our house. Most likely it was the man who'd been fired earlier by my father. The man had made some veiled threats. He must have used petrol, because the blaze was incredible and the smell of it was everywhere. The house was surrounded by fire." Rishi's breath became a little uneven.

"Arson! Did everyone make it out of the house okay?"

He shook his head. "My room was across from my parents', so I instinctively rushed into theirs. My mother was a thin woman, so we urged her to jump out of the narrow bedroom window. My father couldn't, since he was a large man. And I was nearly as big as he. I thought Papa and I would manage to get out of there together somehow, but . . ."

"You couldn't?"

"Didn't. Instead he ordered me to get out immediately and save myself while he would see to Jeevan-kaka. Amidst the chaos, I'd forgotten we had a guest. By then the house was filling up with smoke. As I crept through the passageway I heard Jeevan-kaka coughing, so instead of running to safety like I was supposed to, I rushed to help him myself."

Anjali noticed his knuckles were white as they held hers in a death grip. "It was a very brave thing for a young boy to do," she said. Most boys that age would have taken care of themselves first.

With his spare hand Rishi pinched the bridge of his nose. "Hardly. I resented Jeevan-kaka's presence in our home at a time when we couldn't afford it."

"And yet you helped him."

He shrugged. "Despite the smoke I managed to get to the farthest bedroom and to Jeevan-kaka. I found him sitting on the bed, dazed and gasping for breath. I grabbed his hand and led him through the long passageway and to the drawing room. Meanwhile I could hear my father coughing somewhere in the back of the house. I couldn't assure him that Jeevan-kaka was with me. Opening my mouth meant swallowing smoke, choking on it."

"Did you know if your father had at least made it out of his bedroom?"

"I couldn't really tell. It was difficult to think rationally at the time. I believe my father succeeded in making it to Jeevan-kaka's room after the old man and I had already reached the drawing room. I assumed he'd find Jeevan-kaka missing and conclude that he'd saved himself. By then the flames were everywhere and I wasn't sure if we were going to get out alive. Jeevan-kaka was wheezing hard and so was I.

"I thought we'd choke to death if not burn. I couldn't quite see the front door but had to feel my way around the furniture through the blinding smoke. Finally I managed to get the front door open and literally shoved Jeevan-kaka out. I saw him fall on his face and groan in pain. That was all I could remember."

Anjali could picture the scene in her mind, feel the tension mounting. "What did you do?"

He went silent for a moment. "Opening the door brought in fresh air to fan the flames. The fire got worse. Just as I turned around to go back for my father, a flaming wooden beam came flying from somewhere in the ceiling and slammed into me, throwing me on my back. It pinned my leg to the floor."

"Oh no!" She winced.

"I don't remember how I managed to free myself but it must have been pure adrenaline. The pain was excruciating. All I could do was drag myself on one leg and keep dragging till I got away from the inferno."

"And then you had to watch your home burn down."

Rishi withdrew his hand, leaned forward, and buried his face in his hands, probably reliving the hell he'd experienced. "I wish that was all my mother and I had to watch. My father . . . he never made it out of there. With my injury and multiple burns I had no hope of going back inside for him. I was in agony and weeping like a baby. Besides, the house was engulfed by fire. Papa must have choked on the smoke and collapsed in the passage-way."

Anjali's heart broke over what she was hearing. Rishi was hurting badly and she hurt for him. She placed a hand on his shoulder. "I'm so sorry, Rishi."

He stayed with his face in his hands for a long time. "So am I," he said, finally raising his head. "They found his charred body right outside Jeevan-kaka's room. Apparently he'd made his way there to save his boss and friend. Even when he knew he was dying, his first concern was Jeevan-kaka."

"Your father was obviously a very caring and selfless man."

Rishi hesitated. "He was no saint, mind you. He had a volatile temper and could be unreasonable at times—a slave driver with the laborers. He was harsh in punishing the errant ones. There were reasons why they resented him."

"I'm sure Jeevan-kaka appreciated that stony side of his personality."

"The main reason he'd employed my father in the first place," said Rishi with a wry smile. "But Papa was always loyal to Jeevan-kaka—loyal to a fault."

"So were you."

"No. I hated Jeevan-kaka for years afterward. He was the one who should have died that night, not my father." He stared at the carpet for a minute. "Took me a long time to forgive the old man."

Now it was all clear to Anjali. No wonder her uncle was so attached to Rishi. Something else became obvious, too. She turned to him. "Is that why you favor one leg?"

"Favor?" he snapped. "I have a distinct limp, Anju."

"Not really."

"I nearly lost the leg, but my mother's nursing skills kept it in one piece until they could transport me to a hospital. And then the around-the-clock care she gave me for months afterward was nothing short of a miracle."

"Your poor mother. I can't imagine the nightmare she must have gone through."

"Neither can I. To this day I don't know how she handled the gruesome death of the man she loved, a serious injury to her only child, and the loss of her home—all in a single night. Besides, she had cuts and bruises on various parts of her body to contend with."

"Remarkable woman," agreed Anjali.

"And resilient woman. She managed to overcome her grief. She eventually remarried."

Anjali captured Rishi's hand once again and held it between hers, more for herself than for him. A man like him would be repulsed by pity, so she wouldn't give him that. But she could give herself some strength from holding on to him. She was shaken from hearing the story. She'd never heard anything quite so tragic or horrific.

How had Rishi managed to pull himself out of it? How had his heartbroken mother managed to recover? After Vik's death Anjali had functioned like a zombie for months. To some extent she still was. She hadn't allowed herself to feel real emotion for any man.

As if in answer to her silent questions, Rishi glanced at her. "Took me months to realize my father was gone. And even longer for my damned leg to heal."

"Did you need surgery?"

"Several. Afterward, when I still couldn't walk normally, my mother decided to return to England to find better surgeons for me. Two of my operations were performed in London by orthopedic specialists who were considered experts in the field."

"Must have been terribly expensive. How'd your mother manage that?"

"Take a guess. You're a bright woman."

"Jeevan-kaka?"

"Correct. He had no more than some bruises and minor burns, and a concussion from falling on his head, but his gratitude was endless. Next to my mother and myself, I think Jeevan-kaka grieved the most. He was inconsolable. My father's family didn't even come close. My mother had only an elderly father, who couldn't travel all the way from England to India to comfort her."

"I can see why Jeevan-kaka is beholden to you for life. He's alive because of you."

"I wouldn't go that far, although at the time I believed it myself. He probably would have managed to grope his way out somehow. He's always believed he would've died if I hadn't dragged him out and that my father would have been alive if he hadn't gone looking for him. But Jeevan-kaka has heaped me with gratitude, more than I deserve."

"How?"

"He paid for my exclusive private school in England, sent me to Oxford, and footed all my expenses while I was a student. And when I wanted to start my first store, he literally bought it for me."

"Just like that?"

"Just like that. When I offered to pay him back, he refused the money, saying it was only a tiny fraction of what he owed my father and me."

"For my stingy old uncle to do all that, he had to be stupendously grateful. As far as I know he doesn't have that kind of generosity in him."

"But he does, Anju. You don't know him like I do," argued Rishi. "He's extremely generous in his own way. You just have to get to know him better. He's been a father to me for many years. He's given me most everything I have today. The gratitude goes both ways."

"He's making it up to you, Rishi." Now that she knew all there was to know, she could clearly see why her uncle and this unfathomable man were so close. They weren't just friends; they were father and son—a bond that was forged that night, when a young boy had saved a grown man but lost his father at the same time.

Why hadn't she seen that before? Rishi was the only person who could reason with her uncle. Jeevan-kaka probably loved this man dearly. And Rishi did him proud. Not only was he personable and bright, he was way more successful than any of Jeevan-kaka's sons. His biological sons diligently took care of the business empire he'd created, but they were neither motivated nor talented enough to take risks and expand it.

Tears burned Anjali's eyes. She glanced at the scar beneath Rishi's eyebrow. "Is that from the fire, too?" she rasped.

"That's from a sports injury." A surprised look came on his face. "Are you actually crying for me?"

She didn't answer him but placed a hand on his bad knee, leaving it there till she could swallow the lump in her throat and bring herself to speak. "How bad is your leg now?"

"There's a metal implant that keeps the knee rotating with remarkable efficiency. I'm every airport security guard's nightmare." His smile was wicked. It obviously gave him a great deal of satisfaction to make those security people crazy. "The metal detector drives them mad." He stretched his leg out in front of him. "See that little protrusion there? That's the implant."

Gingerly she touched the hard bump. She could clearly feel it through the fabric of his pants. "A man with steel in him, huh? Amazing what they can do with high-tech orthopedics."

"The leg still aches like the devil if I don't keep it moving and exercise it regularly. That's why I joined the gym as soon as I got a chance the other day."

"I'm a member of that gym myself. But I haven't gone there in weeks."

"You mean since Jeevan-kaka and I arrived." He studied her for a long moment. "I had a feeling you work out to keep in shape."

"Something puzzles me," she said in an attempt to deflect his attention from her. His close scrutiny was making her self-conscious. "How come we never heard about that fire or any of what you just told me? I'd have been old enough to remember something like that. In fact, I'd never heard about a Jagdish and Ellen Shah ever."

"Well, your father was already settled in the U.S. when the fire occurred. And I don't think Jeevan-kaka told anyone other than his wife and children about the episode. I always got the feeling it was something private. Maybe he didn't want to burden the extended family with what happened that night. Even now he hardly ever talks about it. I think it's left a permanent scar."

"Poor Jeevan-kaka."

"He eventually built another house to replace the old homestead, and hired a new manager. Now that he's semi-retired, he and Chandrika-kaki stay on the farm and his sons and grandsons manage the city businesses."

"That much I know. So exactly when did you two become business partners?"

"About two years ago, when Jeevan-kaka decided he wanted to invest some money outside India."

"I see. And his holdings outside India are substantial, I presume?"

"He's a wealthy man. He and I own a couple of businesses together."

"And they're doing well?"

"Very well."

"About that gun he's been carrying around. What's that for? He scared us to death when he brought it to the dinner table."

Rishi looked a little hesitant. "A few years ago, his house was broken into by a band of dacoits. They were traveling from village to village, looting rich landowners' homes. Jeevan-kaka was assaulted. Thank goodness he and Kaki weren't killed, because there were servants in the house and they fended off the attack. But there have been a few killings in some rural areas."

"He wasn't kidding about it, then?"

"No. Dacoits have made a comeback and crime has increased in India. There's even highway robbery occurring lately."

She pulled in a sharp breath. "That's regressing to primitive times."

"It's because of India's population explosion," he explained. "Too many poor people with no hope of jobs. They resort to crime to put food in their bellies."

"It still constitutes extreme violence," she retorted. "Were my uncle and aunt badly hurt?"

"Jeevan-kaka suffered a dislocated shoulder in the attack. That's when he became paranoid and decided he needed a gun to protect himself. He's also hired some extra *Gurkhas* as security guards. Personally I think it was a good idea. I feel better knowing he's got some protection." Probably because he noticed her wary expression, Rishi added, "He has a license to own the gun—and training in how to use it. He's safe to have around your house."

"A safe gun-toting septuagenarian Indian is an oxymoron."

Rishi merely smiled at her remark.

"Tell me, how did Jeevan-kaka manage to smuggle it into the U.S.?"

"He didn't smuggle it; he got special permission from the American embassy. He has some clout with them. They allowed him to bring it as long as he carried his papers and packed the pistol in his checked luggage."

"He's got friends in the most unexpected places."

"But the authorities don't take it lightly. I'm sure the FBI and CIA are watching him and me very closely while we're here."

Her eyes opened wide. "You mean our house and store could

be under government surveillance because of an old man's gun?" That's all they needed to compound all the other problems that hounded them. It spooked her to think their phones could be tapped and cameras could be focused on their every move. She should have known her crazy uncle would come with plenty of baggage.

Rishi shrugged again. "I tried to tell him the U.S. was relatively safe, but he's convinced there are dangerous elements lurking everywhere."

"I'm not surprised. When Jeevan-kaka gets a bug in his ear, it's hard to get rid of it." But Anjali was still puzzled. "My uncle's change in personality is amazing. With a gun in his possession he's turned into a much softer man, and yet years ago, without a gun he was nastier than a pit bull. He used to be so unkind and thoughtless whenever he visited. He nearly gave my mother a stroke the last time he was here, and Sejal still trembles in his presence."

Rishi laughed. "I've noticed. The poor girl's terrified of him. I don't know why. She has no reason to be frightened. Jeevan-kaka is mostly bark and no bite. He just likes to play the tough patriarch."

"He plays the role to perfection. I used to be deathly scared of him, too. But not anymore, and neither is Nilesh."

"You should encourage Sejal to get over her fear."

"She'll get over it in her own time. She's smart and talented and she's already beginning to blossom into an independent young lady."

"You sound like a mother hen."

"What can I say? I feel like one when I'm around Nilesh and Sejal. They're so young compared to me."

"Stop thinking you're old, Anjali. You're young and pretty and full of energy. In today's world, anything under sixty is considered young and vital. Enjoy your youthful looks and good health."

"Amen, Reverend Shah. Thanks for the sermon." She smiled at him. "But you know what? I'm glad you told me all about you and Jeevan-kaka. I think I've found new respect for my uncle. He's all right in my book . . . except for possibly bringing the FBI to our door."

"He's been all right in my book for many years," he said.

"Talk about radical changes." She turned to him with a bemused look. "Is it just old age or something else that's altered his personality?"

Rishi remained silent.

"So what is it you're not telling me?" she asked.

"I just told you everything."

"Not quite. There's an undercurrent of something between the two of you, I can sense it at times. I just can't quite put my finger on it."

"Is ESP also one of your talents?"

"I'll keep hounding you till you tell me everything. I'm family; I have a right to know."

"But it's not my place to tell you anything about your uncle."

"What are you hiding?" Why was he always stonewalling when it came to information about her uncle?

"I'm not hiding anything," he assured her.

"God, you're infuriating."

"If you're that curious, you should talk to your uncle about it."

"Oh, I will. Believe me, I will." She got to her feet and picked up her pocketbook. "Now, if you don't mind, I'd like to go retrieve my car and go home."

"So, would you like to go to the gym with me tomorrow?" he asked, rising from the couch.

"Why?" She narrowed her eyes with suspicion.

"To work out, of course," he replied mildly. "You just said you haven't exercised in a while."

"Okay, then. What time do you usually go?"

"Seven in the morning."

"You're kidding, right?"

He shook his head. "I'm an early riser. When do you exercise if not in the mornings?"

"Afternoons on Mondays, when the store is closed, and two other days after work—very late in the evening." She noticed his

look of disapproval. "I know it's bad to exercise just before dinner and bedtime, but there is no other time."

"There certainly is: early in the morning."

"I'm not a morning person. I'm a grouch until noon."

"I know," he said, laughing. "I noticed the expression on
your face that morning when Jeevan-kaka disturbed you with
his bell. You looked like a hibernating bear that had been poked
with a sharp object."

"Jeevan-kaka's our very own Dennis the Menace."

"So, you want to find out if maybe you can stand my company early in the day?" When she sighed, he said, "It's one way
of finding out what I look like first thing in the morning."

"All right, wise guy, I'll meet you at the gym tomorrow." She
didn't want to give him the satisfaction of telling him she sort of
looked forward to it.

He already looked a little too smug.

Chapter 19

When the alarm went off at 6:30 A.M., Anjali groaned and hit the shut-off button. Reluctant to open her eyes, she buried her face in the pillow, wondering why she'd promised to meet Rishi at such an ungodly hour. The man was nuts.

But a promise was a promise, and she certainly didn't want him to think she was lazy, or that she was a quitter. So she sat up and willed the sleep out of her eyes.

A minute later she trudged to the bathroom, got the essentials out of the way, and put on a pair of gray gym shorts, a matching sports bra, and a pink T-shirt to cover it. After securing her hair into a ponytail she put on a touch of lipstick. She'd had her gym bag packed and ready the previous night, so she picked it up and went downstairs.

Jeevan-kaka and her parents were already in the kitchen, drinking steaming cups of tea. Three surprised pairs of eyes came to rest on her. Her mother was the first to ask, "What are you doing up so early?"

"I'm off to the gym."

"But you never work out in the morning," her father said.

"Well, with the contractors taking up our Mondays these days, I've decided to go in the mornings," she said with a straight face. She wasn't about to tell them she was going mostly because of Rishi.

"Why don't you eat something before you go, Anju?" Jeevan-kaka suggested.

She shook her head. "I'll eat *after* working out." Before the three of them could say anything else, she strode out of the house and toward her car.

It had rained in the early hours of the morning. Beads of moisture clung to the car and the roads were wet. The cloud cover was still thick, making the air feel like a steam bath. She got to the gym in just ten minutes, but she was already late—it was a little past seven o'clock. Several cars were already in the parking lot. Morning people made her feel inadequate, especially when her eyes still felt gritty and she was tempted to turn around, go home, and climb back into bed. But she kept going forward.

A promise was a promise.

She caught sight of Rishi standing at the reception desk, talking to the young man behind it. Rishi had his back to her but the powerful shoulders, lean legs, and narrow waist were unmistakable. He wore black gym shorts and a black T-shirt.

Walking up to him, she wished him and the other guy a sunny good morning.

Rishi turned to her with a sardonic smile. "Good morning. You made it." Then he looked pointedly at his wristwatch.

"Did you have any doubts?" she said, feigning a carefree grin.

"One or two." He waved at the other guy. "Thanks for the information, Jeff." Then he ushered her toward the treadmills. "Want to walk a little first? Maybe it'll wake you up."

"Are you saying I look like I just rolled out of bed?" she asked him testily. He smelled clean and manly and his face look freshly shaved. Not a hair on his head seemed out of place.

"No. You look fresh as a daisy," he teased and powered up one of the treadmills for himself.

Before she had a chance to respond, he started the slow, warm-up pace on the machine. That's when she noticed his leg. A jagged diagonal scar ran right over the kneecap—about ten inches long, at least an inch wide at the center and gradually tapering toward the ends. The skin surrounding it had the puckered look of severe burn damage. The size of the scar made her wince. It had to have been hell to have a burning beam pin his leg to the floor. And he was only a boy when he'd suffered that.

He was a brave man. She was beginning to find that out—little by little.

She caught his eye when she looked up and felt the embarrassing heat climb into her face. How could she have let herself stare so long? But he didn't seem disturbed by it. She quickly climbed on the treadmill next to his and started her own warm-up rhythm before the more vigorous walking could begin. Within the next five minutes they were both walking at a brisk pace.

Some thirty minutes later, sweating and exhausted, she started to wind down, but Rishi was still going strong and looked like he'd been on a long stroll instead of the high speed he'd been keeping. The perspiration was running down his face and arms but he wasn't gasping for breath like she was.

She noticed something else. Despite his impediment he managed well on the treadmill. He watched her shut off her machine. Ignoring his questioning lift of the brow, she stepped down and went to the adjoining room where she'd noticed the aerobics instructor conducting a class.

Although the class was more than halfway through its routine, she joined the two women in the last row and started going through the motions. She sometimes took the late-evening version of the same class, so she knew all the moves. The session lasted about fifteen minutes, but Anjali realized it felt good to stretch and bend and roll. She'd always enjoyed dancing, and the lively musical accompaniment made the aerobics workout more fun than a treadmill or any other mechanical apparatus.

When the final steps were over and the perky young instructor took them through the cooling-down process, Anjali was dead on her feet. She'd been away from the gym too long. Forced to admit to herself that Rishi's idea had been the kick in the butt she'd badly needed, she bent forward with her hands braced on her knees, trying to catch her breath.

Grabbing her gym bag, she pulled out a bottle of water. After she gulped most of it down, she headed for the showers. On the way there she passed by the glass-enclosed area that housed the bench presses, converging arm machines, full-body exercisers, and a bunch of complicated equipment.

She saw Rishi using one of the full-body machines, his jaw clenched tight as he pitched his strength against the awesome-looking contraption. It had to be sheer torture on his leg when he pushed it to the extreme like that.

He couldn't see her because he had his profile to her. Beads of perspiration rolled down his temple. His shirt was soaked and clung to his shoulder. Standing there for a second, she studied the corded muscles in his arms and legs flexing rhythmically. Such dogged concentration. Most men with a serious leg injury would have used it as an excuse to let their bodies atrophy, but not Rishi. He wouldn't let something like a shattered knee get him down. She turned around and went on her way.

The hot shower felt wonderful, soothing the aches and pains of exercising after a long hiatus. Dried and dressed, she went out to the lobby and found Rishi seated on one of the comfortable, overstuffed chairs, legs comfortably crossed, reading the *New York Times.*

"Hello there," he said cheerfully. "You look splendid after your workout."

"You don't look so bad yourself," she told him, secretly pleased at his appreciative expression. He was back in his signature designer wear: lightweight tan pants, cream cotton shirt, and brown loafers. His hair looked a little damp from his shower.

Why hadn't she noticed earlier what a hunk he really was? She knew why: she was too busy looking for reasons to dislike him. Now that she'd run out of reasons, she was realizing she felt madly attracted to him. So why couldn't she have found a happy medium between the two?

"See, wasn't it a grand idea to get some exercise early in the morning?" he said, putting the newspaper down on the coffee table.

"I wouldn't call it *grand*, considering I'm in pain." She pulled a face. "I didn't know I had so many muscles in my body."

He stood up. "I'll buy you breakfast. You look like you could use some nutrition. A shot of coffee will banish the pain."

"If you're buying, Mr. Shah, then I'll order something big and expensive."

"You're on, Miss Kapadia." He held the door open for her. "The restaurant in my hotel serves a decent breakfast buffet. Want to try that?"

"Sounds like a plan."

Outside, the clouds lingered and the temperature had risen further. It promised to be a steam-room-type day. By unspoken agreement they went to their respective cars. She got behind the wheel and followed his SUV out of the parking lot.

Inside the hotel's restaurant, a waiter served them piping-hot coffee the minute they got seated. Anjali took a sip of hers and closed her eyes. "Mmm . . . I feel the aches slipping away already."

"Good. Now for the nutrition. Come on," he said, pushing his chair back, "let's go find something nice and healthy at the buffet table."

They both returned with plates loaded with food. Being a vegetarian, Anjali had fresh fruit, pancakes, and wedges of cheese, but Rishi didn't appear to have any such restrictions. Anjali watched him tuck away eggs, ham, sausages, and toast.

She smiled at him. "Now I know why you were in such a hurry to move to a hotel."

He looked bemused. "Why?"

"At our house it's veggies all the time," she replied, pointing her fork at his plate. "You're a man who likes his meat."

"I like meat but I enjoy vegetarian food just as much. I'm not fussy about food."

"I've noticed." He'd always had generous helpings of her mother's cooking.

"It comes from boarding schools, traveling around the world, and growing up as a product of a mixed marriage."

"What do you eat on a regular basis?" She speared a piece of cantaloupe and popped it into her mouth.

"You mean when I'm at my home in London or Delhi?"

"You have two homes . . . on different continents?" He was wealthier than she'd thought.

"London's more my home than Delhi, but I do spend a month or two during the year there. In London it's a townhouse but in Delhi it's only a small bachelor flat."

"So you cook for yourself or does the . . . did the lovely Samantha cook for the two of you?"

He looked vastly amused for some reason. "Samantha doesn't know the way to the kitchen. I'm not bad at rustling up fried eggs and toast once in a while, but that's where my talent ends."

"So you two ate out *every* day?"

"Just about. But then, with our erratic schedules we rarely ate a meal together," he said. "There are some places in London that serve healthy food, you see," he added, probably because of her disdainful expression.

"I can't imagine eating out every day. I'd be fat as a whale." But then she recalled that she and her family did eat a lot of restaurant food before Jeevan's arrival.

"You'd never be fat," he assured her. "You have good genes. Look at your parents and your brother. They're all slender people."

"Genes are funny sometimes. I could easily have inherited Jeevan-kaka's tendency for chunkiness." She paused to look at him. "But we all noticed he's dropped a lot of weight. Is he on some kind of diet? He eats like a bird compared with the portions he consumed the last time he was here."

"It's possible."

"And what's all the fuss about having bland food and no tea? He drank rich *chai* at least five times a day some years ago and loved hot, spicy food. Has he finally come to recognize that excesses are not good for him?"

"Maybe." She noticed Rishi quickly changed the subject. "So, are you a good cook?" he asked her.

"Mediocre." She took a sip of her coffee. "I did most of the cooking when I was married. Vik was a good helper, though— so intense yet funny." Suddenly the images of her small kitchen in New York flashed before her eyes. She and Vik had some wonderful times in that kitchen, which wasn't much bigger than a telephone booth.

Although he couldn't cook if his life depended on it, Vik had always liked chopping and dicing and he'd taken great pride in his skills with a knife. He'd even had his own chef's knife: a humongous, shiny-bladed thing he'd sharpened regularly, and a special peeler and grater. He'd called them his tools of the trade.

When that image of a laughing, teasing Vik arose before her, she couldn't help the tears pooling in her eyes. It hit her like that sometimes. All of a sudden she'd recall something sweet and sentimental from her life with Vik and the emotions welled up. She tried hard to think of something else, but she couldn't.

"Anjali?" Rishi said to her. "Are you all right?"

She nodded and grabbed her napkin to dab her eyes. "I—I'll be okay. It's just that . . ."

"You still miss him." Rishi's eyes were warm with compassion.

Perhaps because of his sympathy, the tears only got worse instead of better. Despite her desperate attempts to stop them, they were running down her cheeks. She was making a scene, embarrassing both herself and Rishi. The people at the next table were throwing strange glances at her. "I'm sorry, Rishi."

"Don't be sorry." He pulled out his key card from his shirt pocket and handed it to her. "Here, go upstairs to my room and pull yourself together. I'll sign the check and come up later."

Grateful for his solicitude, she took the key and hurried out of the restaurant, past the wide-eyed waiter and the bemused hostess who'd seated them earlier. She'd forgotten about Rishi's room upstairs. She badly needed some privacy. The key was a godsend.

Inside his suite, she headed straight for the bathroom. It looked neat and spotless and smelled faintly of a mixture of pine cleaner and Rishi's cologne. The stack of towels, soaps, lotions, and shampoos looked newly replenished. The king-size bed was made, too. It appeared that the maid service had been there within the last hour or so.

She studied her face in the mirror. The mascara she'd applied after her recent shower was smudged. The lipstick was gone. Her stomach was still a little queasy. What was the matter with her? Why was she so emotional all of a sudden? Was she sliding into very early menopause? It couldn't be. Her monthly cycles arrived with near-perfect regularity. In fact, her period had started only the previous day. She still had cramps to remind her of the fact. And her body ached.

After washing her face thoroughly, she decided to leave it devoid of makeup. What the heck, she was only going to the store to work, and some of it in the dusty construction area. Going out to the kitchenette, she got a painkiller out of her purse, poured herself a glass of water, and swallowed the caplet to still the cramps and the rest of the aches.

A minute later she heard a knock on the door and went to get it. It was Rishi. He eyed her with cautious concern as he came inside and shut the door behind him. "Feeling better?"

She nodded. "I apologize for embarrassing you in front of a roomful of people."

"You didn't." He stepped forward and put his hands on her shoulders. "And don't ever apologize for having feelings. *I'm* sorry for bringing up a topic that's upsetting to you. I had no idea."

"It's not your fault. We were talking about cooking. How emotional a topic is that?" The heat from his large hands felt good on her shoulders, comforting. Who would have known that the man she'd disliked only weeks ago would be the source of so much solace?

"Would you like to rest a little or something? You can rest here by yourself and join us at the store when you feel better. I'll tell your parents you have a headache."

"No need for that. I'm fine, really. It was just an attack of self-pity."

"Are you sure?"

"Absolutely."

"You ready to head out, then?" he asked, removing his hands from her.

She nodded. "Thanks for the nice breakfast . . . and for the use of your suite."

"Glad to help." He stopped for a moment to look at her before he grabbed the doorknob.

The expression in his smoky eyes was tenderness laced with desire. Her pulse kicked up in response. That's when she realized he spelled trouble with a capital *T*. She was in danger of falling in love with him. Was that why she'd reacted to him with such intensity the first time she'd met him? Had her subconscious known right away that he could pose a serious threat to her heart?

She'd noticed that magnetic quality about him the moment she'd laid eyes on him. Even Vik, despite his casual good looks, couldn't have held a candle to the kind of raw male sexuality combined with smooth sophistication Rishi exuded. He had what they called a *presence*. Whenever he entered a room, people seemed to notice, like when he'd stepped into Rowling Rok the night he'd caught her kissing Kip. Lots of folks in the crowded bar, especially women, had stopped what they'd been doing to look at him.

But she couldn't fall in love—with Rishi or anyone else. She didn't want to love and lose again. Going through that nightmare again was just not possible.

She picked up her pocketbook. "Let's get to the store before my folks think I passed out from exercising too much."

Chapter 20

Anjali walked her last customer to the door, then closed and locked it. Through the glass panel she watched the woman walk to her car in the parking lot and drive away.

A jagged streak of lightning lit up the angry gray sky. The clouds had thickened in the last hour. The wind was picking up, too. The forecast storm was approaching. It had been overcast and humid all day, clearly signaling a major downpour.

This was unusual weather for October, when the trees, kissed by cool nights and sunny mornings, were cloaked in the most gorgeous shades of red, gold, and orange. The air should have been nippy by now, and the first frosts of the season should have covered the grass at dawn. Instead the day had felt more like late August.

The clap of thunder following the lightning bolt made her jump. Quickly she pulled the shade over the glass and drew in a steadying breath. Thunderstorms made her uneasy.

However, in spite of the weather it had been a good day business-wise—busy and lucrative. Sundays were usually like that, with the weekend shoppers crowding into Little India. For most *Desis,* weekends were typically reserved for setting aside the American-style business suits and donning *salwar-kameezs* or *kurtas,* putting on *bindis* and sparkling bangles, shopping in noisy Indian stores, eating super-hot curry, and dousing the heat with fresh-squeezed sugarcane juice or tangy yogurt *lassi.* A good Hindi movie with all the essential elements of high drama, gyrating dances, and music often rounded off the weekend.

The last few weeks had been crammed with even longer hours of work for Anjali and the family. But the results were worth it. The outside of the building was looking very attractive after the finishing touches had been added. The fresh coat of paint, the reworked brick accents, and the repaved parking lot were already bringing in a spate of customers. The cheerful "Grand Opening" banner announcing next weekend's event combined with the advertising blitz helped to attract the curious.

She pulled out the folder she'd pushed underneath the counter. It contained responses to the "Help Wanted" sign she'd posted in the store's window. A handful of young women, mostly high-school and college students, had stopped in to apply.

Amongst five applicants, only one looked promising. She was a housewife, a newlywed just arrived from India, living nearby and looking for a job within walking distance because she and her husband could afford only one car at the moment, which he used to commute to work.

Anjali had spoken to the young lady, Nilima Sethi, over the phone. She was available for full-time work and sounded enthusiastic. The interview was set for the next day.

The beauty salon staff and *mehndi* artist had already been interviewed and hired and would start work on Friday. A good part-time photographer for the bridal studio and a *mandap* and floral designer had been lined up as well.

The café was pretty much set, too. Rishi had discovered a talented chef named Anwar Ali in some obscure New York City restaurant. Besides the usual Indian fare, apparently Anwar made unusual snacks like *paneer* and lamb turnovers, sweet potato *knishes* with ginger sauce, sandwiches with *tandoori* meats and veggies, Indian vermicelli with cilantro pesto, and a long list of interesting items.

Anjali was happy to let Rishi and her uncle deal with the café, which they'd named Neela Chai, or Blue Tea. She was thrilled that Rishi had ordered the cream potteryware with a bold blue design she'd had her heart set on. He seemed to have whole-heartedly embraced the theme of Silk & Sapphires.

At the moment, Rishi, Jeevan-kaka, and her father were somewhere in the back of the store. She could hear them talking, her uncle's voice drowning out the other two. Her mother had left a while ago so she could have dinner on the table when they all got home.

After locking the door and hanging the "Closed" sign, she crossed over to the other side, the new wing. Turning on the lights, she glanced around. She had to admit all the weeks of putting up with construction noise and pollution and then installing the fixtures, decorating, and stocking up were worth it. She took a deep, appreciative sniff. The place smelled of fresh paint, new carpeting, and wood polish. Gone were the musty odors of Tejmal's grocery shop.

Surrounded by the gleaming new expanse, she felt like a little girl looking at her secret fantasy come true. Of course her workload would double, too. But she was prepared for it. No dream came without a price tag attached.

As the big day drew nearer, she felt the tension mounting by degrees, like her skin was slowly being stretched and pulled taut. So much was at stake here. It was their last chance for success. She prayed the opening weekend would be sunny, unlike today's weather. As if to remind her, a clap of thunder sounded really close, startling her again and rattling the windows.

"Satisfied with everything?"

She jumped at the familiar voice behind her and turned around to find Rishi.

"More than satisfied," she assured him. "It's beautiful."

"I hope so. You've worked very hard on this."

"And you haven't? Between handling your businesses around the world and taking care of this store, you've hardly had a moment's rest in the past few months." In the last couple of days she'd noticed the fine lines of exhaustion around his mouth and eyes. She inclined her head toward the back of the store. "Where are Dad and Jeevan-kaka?"

"They just left for home, hoping to beat the storm."

"I'm glad. I like spending a few minutes alone here when everyone's gone. It gives me some private time to gather my thoughts and check on the day's progress."

"Sharing a home with so many people can't be easy." He came closer. "That's something that puzzles me. Why do you stay with your parents when you're such an independent and modern woman?"

"A lot of reasons. At first I needed to be with my family . . . you know . . . when I was grieving. My parents were convinced I'd sink into a deep depression and never come out of it if they didn't keep a close eye on me. Then I put all my savings into expanding the store, so I didn't have much money to live on my own. After a while it became a habit—the three of us as a team, with Nilesh an occasional fourth. We do everything together."

"I see."

"Once or twice I'd thought about getting my own apartment, but what purpose would it serve? Other than to sleep and bathe, what else would I need it for? Besides, after so many years, if I suddenly decided to go off on my own they'd be confused, even hurt. They seem to need me as much as I need them."

"Hmm." He didn't belabor the point. Instead he walked over to the just-installed arch that formed the doorway to the women's department. He ran his fingers over its frame encrusted with shimmering beads and flowing gold designs. The sign above it read Zanana. "I like this. It's both stylish and whimsical."

"Thanks." She rather liked it herself.

"What made you think of it?"

Zanana was a Persian term for an area exclusive to women, a harem concealed from male eyes, but Anjali had thought here in the store it'd be a rare and captivating lure for shoppers. She'd figured people could walk through the archway with its beaded curtain to discover the enticing secrets hidden behind it. She smiled at Rishi. "I'm hoping it'll attract more males rather than keep them out. What red-blooded male can resist taking a peek into a mysterious female universe?"

"And it's exotic enough to stir the curiosity of non-Asians, too—the treasure trove effect." He turned away from the arch. "Aren't you the least bit curious to see the café, Anju? I noticed you've stayed away from it the last few days. You've been using the front door."

"I wanted it to surprise me. Sometimes I wait to see the finished product without seeing the in-between stages. It's so much more fun that way."

"It's finished now. I'll give you a grand tour if you'd like."

"You're on."

Shutting off the lights, she took the hand he held out to her. Their relationship had settled into one of quiet camaraderie, with some hand-holding, occasional pecks on the cheek, and an arm around the shoulder now and then. After that day in his hotel room, where he'd kissed her with both passion and promise, nothing significant had occurred.

They were rarely alone. Most often she and Rishi closed the store at nights together and went home in their separate cars to eat dinner with the family.

Once a week, usually on a Sunday night, the two of them went out to dinner—to discuss business. At times they met at the gym. The elders seemed to approve of it. More and more Anjali had begun to see a smidgen of optimism in her mother's eyes. She could tell that her parents and Jeevan-kaka were secretly hoping for something serious to blossom between Rishi and her, but it hadn't happened yet. It wasn't because Rishi didn't want it. It was *she* who couldn't afford to indulge in an affair with a guy like him, a ship that wandered about the world with no anchor.

Having a fling with Kip Rowling had been safe in many ways; her heart wasn't at risk. With Rishi, however, it was a different matter. She suspected she was already in love with him to some degree. He'd been in Edison for nearly four months. If she succumbed to her need to get physical with him, there'd be no turning back.

She appreciated the fact that he didn't push her. After that candid talk about giving themselves a chance to get to know each other better, he hadn't brought up the subject again.

Maybe he was giving her time to mull over it. She respected him for that. It was all the more reason why he was growing on her, too. She was afraid she was beginning to like him too much.

How could she have judged him as cold and unfeeling? As she'd come to know him better, she'd learned he was a man of integrity despite being a tenacious and sometimes hard-nosed businessman. He couldn't have become a success if he weren't. But he was fair at the same time. He didn't suffer fools, yet he was generous in many ways.

Above all else, he treated her fussy uncle like a father and all the Kapadias like family. He and Nilesh had become close, too. He'd even attended a couple of college baseball games with Nilesh.

She forced her thoughts back to the present as Rishi ushered her through the glass-paneled swing door. The words Neela Chai flowed across it, the letters constructed from blue, jewel-tone stained glass. She waited till he turned on the lights.

With a delighted breath she let her gaze wander across the room. The cream granite counter was long and curved, designed so customers could observe Anwar perform his culinary magic. The five small tables had matching cream tops. The chairs were wrought iron with padded blue seats and backrests. The floor was made of gleaming cream tiles and the walls were covered with rich textured wallpaper. Indian folk art mounted on cream mats and framed in vibrant cobalt blue frames brought the walls alive. The hanging light fixtures were filigreed brass domes.

"This is gorgeous, Rishi. It's more beautiful than I'd imagined." She couldn't help giving him an exuberant hug. "Thank you so much . . . for everything."

"You did all the planning and designing, darling. I'm only the facilitator."

"But you're the one who made it all possible. You and Jeevan-kaka."

He lifted a brow. "Is it safe to assume you don't dislike me and Jeevan-kaka anymore, then?"

"Yep." She angled a sly look at him. "In fact, I've decided I like you a hell of a lot."

"Well, I'll be damned!" He took her by the shoulders and placed a quick, hard kiss on her mouth. "I've waited four long months for the persnickety Miss Kapadia to change her mind about me."

"You're calling *me* persnickety? As if *you* weren't distant and disdainful the day you arrived here."

"How else was I supposed to react when your mother and you looked at me like the snake that had crept in from the wilds of India?"

"What can I say? We were nervous about Jeevan-kaka's visit, and then to see a stranger arriving with him was a bit . . . unexpected."

"And unpleasant?"

"I wouldn't say that."

"Yes, you would," he teased. "And you've actually begun to like me now. Imagine that," he murmured, the lighthearted tone gradually turning serious, seductive, silky. He tightened his hold on her and kissed her again, slowly and softly this time. His lips glided along the sensitive area between her earlobe and her neck, sending a tremor of pleasure through her.

She closed her eyes and sighed. Good God, but the man knew how to get a woman turned on. His hands coasted ever so leisurely up and down her back. They appeared to search out every little nerve that reacted to his touch like a live wire. Instinctively she pressed against him. She couldn't get close enough. The devil knew exactly what he was doing.

Anjali had no idea how long they stood in the room or how long they kissed. All she knew was she wanted him. With his beard-roughened jaw and his eyes taking on that hungry predator look, he was mouthwateringly male.

It was impossible not to respond to what he was doing to her, what he was silently asking of her. He was no doubt feeling the same things she was. She deepened the kiss, lingering over it as much as she could.

"Be with me tonight, sweetheart," he whispered against her lips, his voice sounding urgent.

His words took her by surprise. "I can't."

"Why not? It's obvious you want me as much as I want you."

"Wanting is not the same as . . . as . . ."

"As what?" He broke away from her mouth to look at her.

She blinked. "Physical love can last only so long." She couldn't tell him she was falling in love with him.

"You won't know unless you try it."

"I tried it with Kip."

He loosened his hold on her as if she'd flung cold water in his face. "Forget that odious bloke, will you? He's not the average man. I'm not like him."

"Exactly what kind of man are you, Rishi?"

"I believe in family . . . loyalty. Is that so bad?"

She blinked again. "So what are you saying?"

"Why don't we take this relationship a little more seriously and see where it goes? Then we can both decide whether we want it or not. I know I could use a little stability in my life. I'll let you decide if that's what you want in yours."

"So you think sleeping together is going to help us decide?" She had a feeling this was all some strange dream. Since Vik's death she'd become a believer in the well-known adage, *Man proposes and God disposes.* Every time she started thinking of the distant future, she curbed herself. What was the point in planning something if none of it materialized? Or worse, it got destroyed?

"Maybe," he said, "because chemistry between two people matters. And we have plenty."

She couldn't deny that. The attraction between them was so potent it set off a minor nuclear blast every time they touched. Most of the time all he had to do was look at her and her nerves started to spark.

He cupped her face in his hands, kicking up her heartbeat. "I'm getting serious about you, Anju. I've never come across anyone whom I've felt so strongly about."

"I'd have thought you'd be a magnet for most women. You're in the fashion industry. The gorgeous models alone must be in the dozens."

"To me they're models, nothing more. Besides, I grew up in a mixed culture. The women I've met so far have been either purely Indian and very conservative or totally European and much too forward for me."

"Really?"

"Laura and Samantha are perfect examples of the latter. But now that I've met you I've come to realize I want someone who represents the best of both worlds."

"What do you consider the best of both worlds?"

"Old-fashioned Indian values combined with—I don't know . . . a confident and independent attitude?"

"And you think I have those qualities?"

"Yes. I'm old enough to know what I want."

And persuasive enough, she thought as she met his gaze and felt herself drowning in the melting gray pools of his eyes. "You have such seductive eyes."

He looked surprised. "Despite the unsightly scar above my eyelid?"

"It's not unsightly. It gives your face character. Your eyes are like liquid smoke. They can go from cold to angry to contemptuous to warm to sexy just like that," she said.

"No one's ever described my dull gray eyes quite so glowingly."

"Then they don't know you very well."

"And *you* do?" He looked amused.

"Well, yeah, somewhat—in the past few months."

"Since I have such seductive eyes, will you spend the night with me?" he asked with a laugh. When she sighed, his amusement vanished. "You don't know how difficult it is to work with you so closely day after day and not get my hands on you, Anju. I've tried to keep my instincts under lock and key, but you've become a distraction for me."

"And I bet you don't like distractions messing up your orderly life." He was clearly a goal-oriented man who single-mindedly went after what he wanted. She had yet to see him falter or change course once he'd made up his mind.

"Damn right. Distractions drive me mad."

She knew exactly how that felt. Her life had been tidy and

free of distractions, too, but then he'd come sailing in, a thorn in her side at first. And now her physical need to be with him was not only interrupting her work but causing major emotional upheaval. Ever since he'd kissed her that day she'd lain in her bed night after night, wondering what it would be like to make love with him. She'd built fantasies around him but was afraid to act on them.

She stayed silent.

"What'll it be, darling?" he prompted. "Yes or no?"

She rolled it around in her mind, examined it from various angles. He'd been involved with another woman until recently. Did he still have certain feelings for Samantha? Would he compare her to Samantha and find her lacking? On the other hand, he'd said he was getting serious about her, hadn't he? What more did she want?

Rishi was gazing at her with those amazing eyes and she knew she was sinking. Fast. Maybe if she slept with him this once, she'd get him out of her system. Better yet, despite his apparent refinement there was the possibility he could turn out to be a lousy lover, and she'd discover he wasn't the right man for her. Then she could kiss him good-bye without hurting like hell. "Okay, I'll go with you."

"You will?" He blinked, seemingly surprised.

"But what are we going to tell my family?"

"That we're going out to our usual Sunday dinner and then a movie. We'll tell them not to wait up for you. We'll have to lie again, won't we?" he said with a wink.

"You're a very corrupting influence on me." Then she thought of something. "Wait a minute. We can't; we don't have any . . . um . . . you know . . ." She meant to say *protection* but couldn't. This was already beginning to get awkward. How was she going to handle the rest of the evening at this rate?

He chuckled, apparently reading her mind. "Nothing a trip to the hotel's convenience store can't resolve. Leave it to me."

"Okay." She should have known a smart and practical man like him would take such things in stride. But it all sounded so cold and clinical, like they were entering a formal pact of some kind, similar to the business contract they'd signed not too long ago, making them partners.

Nonetheless, in some ways tonight's plan was indeed a short-term contract, especially the way he'd explained it. *Why don't we take this relationship a little more seriously and see where it goes? Then we can both decide whether we want it or not.* Yep, it was a contract: a trial arrangement with room for negotiation if both parties were satisfied and wanted to extend it.

He turned off the lights and engaged the security system. In the parking lot, the brisk wind lifted her hair and tossed it in her face. Rishi raised a hand and brushed it back. "Feel like you're facing an execution, Anju?"

"No. Why?" Her breath came out shaky, belying her words.

"Because you look like you do."

"Sorry." She tried to smile. "Nerves, I guess."

"I understand." He nudged her toward her car. "You'll be all right, I promise."

The thunder and lightning were still putting on a sound-and-light show but the forecast rain hadn't arrived yet. She shivered a little when once again lightning ripped the sky, too close for comfort.

Climbing into her car, she waited for the sound of thunder to pass before cranking the engine. Her hands were trembling. She noticed Rishi was already behind his wheel and had the motor running. But he hadn't moved. He was obviously waiting for her to go ahead of him so he could follow her to the hotel.

Well, Anjali, you may be on your way to heartbreak again, she told herself. *After next week's opening he'll leave for London or Hong Kong or wherever and you'll be left here in Jersey, pining away for a globetrotter whose first love is his business.* Was she prepared to leave herself vulnerable to that kind of hurt and desolation?

But she knew she couldn't avoid Rishi if she tried. She was the fish that was hooked and getting reeled in quickly. The only difference was she wasn't thrashing around resisting. She was stepping into this affair, or relationship, or whatever it was, with her eyes wide open. He'd made it clear he wasn't holding a gun to her head. She was free to turn down his invitation and go home to her own bed.

But she wasn't going to her own bed. She was going to his.

Chapter 21

In the hotel's parking lot, Rishi parked his vehicle next to Anjali's and glanced up at the sky. The first plump drops of rain were beginning to fall. It threatened to turn into a deluge within the next minute or two.

Alighting quickly and locking his vehicle, he went forward to open Anjali's door. He noticed the taut look on her face.

"Are you all right?" he asked, taking her hand.

"I think so." She shut the car door and hit the lock button on her key. A couple of raindrops landed on her face, making her blink. "Uh-oh."

"We better get out of here," he said, urgently tugging on her hand.

Together they raced across the parking lot and toward the entrance, trying to beat the swelling rain. Lightning split the sky once again, and the downpour started in full fury. The automatic glass doors parted and they barreled inside the building.

Rishi let out a low whistle as the crash of thunder assaulted their ears. "Now that's what I call a right wicked storm. Reminds me of the beginning of the monsoon season in India."

Anjali silently brushed the rain off her face and hair. The pinched look on her face still remained.

Well, at least they'd made it inside the hotel in the nick of time, reflected Rishi with some relief. They'd beaten the worst of the rain. He handed Anjali his key card. "Go ahead and wait for me in the suite. I'll be right up."

"Thanks." Her eyes were on the floor. She seemed reluctant. Maybe she was rethinking her decision about coming here with him, and she was embarrassed on top of it. "Just a few minutes and I'll join you straightaway," he assured her. Unfortunately he had to make that very essential stop at the hotel's convenience store. He wondered if she'd behaved like this with Rowling. Somehow he doubted it. He'd seen her with that man briefly and he hadn't noticed anything like this undecided woman standing before him.

"I'll give your parents a ring and tell them not to wait up," he told her.

"Thanks."

That was the second time she'd thanked him for trivial reasons. She was definitely wound tight. He'd have to find a way to relax her. "Go on, Anju," he said gently. He watched her walk toward the elevator before he turned to go to the store.

Inside the convenience store, he found there were no other customers. Thank goodness. He hoped they had what he needed. The rain was now pounding and he didn't want to go looking for a drugstore.

He stood on the threshold and looked in all directions for the appropriate aisle for condoms. He hadn't made such a purchase in years. It was a bit awkward.

But it was a good thing Anju had mentioned it. He was so anxious to have her that he hadn't stopped to think of the consequences.

Samantha was permanently on the pill and he hadn't had to worry about anything as mundane as birth control. Besides, he reflected, Samantha wasn't one to be caught with an unwanted pregnancy. She was neither maternal nor willing to give up her career and freedom for anything, least of all a child.

But now he'd met Anju and come to know her. He was astonished to find a woman who in some ways still grieved for her late husband, so many years after his death. It meant she was capable of loving wholeheartedly and remaining faithful. That wounded look in her eyes obviously came from losing Vikram.

The thought brought a pinprick of jealousy with it. Rishi promptly dismissed it. How foolish was it to be jealous of a dead man?

Despite her affair with Kip Rowling, Rishi was convinced Anjali was a fiercely loyal woman who was only satisfying the basic human need for intimacy. Even Rowling was someone she'd hooked up with after many long years of celibacy—an insanely long time for a healthy young woman. Her involvement with Rowling was entirely understandable, he reasoned.

Although he'd felt a powerful attraction to her since the day they'd met, it was only after he'd kissed her in his hotel room that he'd realized how much he wanted her—in his bed, in his life. The need for a more stable lifestyle with a wife and home had crept up on him stealthily.

As he strode through one of the aisles, he noticed boxes of diapers, feeding bottles, and various other baby needs. A baby. How would it feel to be a father? What would it be like to share in the miracle of making and then raising a tiny human being? The image was very alluring.

He tried to blink the picture out of his mind and kept walking. It was too soon to see that far into the future. He had a few major hurdles to overcome before he could think of *that*.

Was he falling in love with Anju? It had to be love if he thought about her constantly, and was visualizing marriage and children with her. Whatever it took to do it, he'd make her feel the same thing he was.

He'd make her fall in love with him, he promised himself.

When he made love to her, he'd take it slow, discover every little nuance about her and revel in it. He would love her like nobody ever had, not even her late husband. He'd wipe her mind clean of every other man she'd been with, until there'd be only he.

He knew he could do it.

It was a minute before he noticed the condoms displayed on a shelf next to the cash register. After making his selection he paid the young man behind the counter as quickly as he could. With a polite thank you he hurried out of the store, tucking the package into his jacket pocket. There was no gracious and discreet way of buying something like condoms.

As he strode toward the elevators, he realized a man of his experience should be above feeling embarrassment at such things. In Anju's words, he'd "been around the block" a few times.

Inside the elevator, he remembered his promise to Anju and pulled out his cell phone to call her parents. He explained to Usha that he and Anju were going to grab some dinner and then take in a movie.

As expected, Usha sounded a little surprised about the movie, especially because of the wretched weather. But thankfully she didn't ask any questions. And Rishi didn't offer any explanations. Lying was complicated enough without having to provide details.

Upstairs in the suite, Anjali took off her jacket and dropped it on one of the chairs in the sitting area. Her palms were damp with perspiration. Her heartbeat was racing. Placing a hand on her chest, she tried to still her anxious heart. She felt like a teenager anticipating her first taste of sex.

She glanced around the room. What was she doing here, in Rishi's suite? At her age it should have been anything but this. Was he feeling the same way or was this pretty much routine for him? But then, the fact that he didn't already have something like condoms on hand said he wasn't the type of guy who was ready and prepared for sex at a moment's notice. It also meant he hadn't taken her consent for granted. That said something about his character.

Finding it impossible to sit down, she paced the length of the room. If anything, it made her even edgier. She went to the window, parted the drapes, and took a peek outside. The sheeting rain was so thick and impenetrable she could barely see a foot beyond the glass. Luckily she and Rishi had managed to avoid its full fury. Rain-soaked clothes would have compounded her anxiety.

She turned away from the window and wiped her hands on the seat of her slacks. Her pulse hadn't slowed down one bit. This was pathetic. If Rishi didn't get here quickly, she'd probably have a heart attack. Had he found what he was looking for, or did he have to go out in this flood to find a drugstore?

Just then she heard the door opening and turned around.

Rishi stepped inside and took one look at her face. "Still nervous?"

She nodded. Actually, nervous didn't even begin to describe her jitters.

He took off his jacket and tossed it on top of hers on the chair. Then he gathered her in his arms and buried his face in her hair. "Don't be tense, darling. I'm right here with you."

She clutched at the front of his shirt. "I know."

"You're shaking. Do I frighten you that much?"

"No. I'm just a little jumpy, that's all."

"Relax. It's me—someone you know well." He kissed the top of her head. "You're not a virgin, Anju. We're both experienced adults and we're friends. This isn't some cheap one-night tryst between strangers."

"I know, but this feels kind of different."

He lifted her chin with a finger, forcing her to face him. "How?"

"It's hard to explain."

His eyes narrowed on her. "Because your emotions may be involved in this relationship?"

"Perhaps," she murmured, swallowing to keep her throat from drying out.

"Then it's a good thing. A little nervousness means you care." He didn't wait for her response, but wound his arm around her waist and ushered her into the bedroom. "I have an idea. Since you're so stressed, why don't I pour us some wine?"

"Wine sounds good." It would give her a few minutes to prepare herself. The alcohol would help. Her mouth felt parched and hot.

She watched him step outside the bedroom. Noticed the limp. And yet he remained on his feet for hours. He was quite a man.

A few minutes later he returned with two stem glasses filled with a deep red wine. His sleeves were rolled up. The two top buttons on his shirt were undone, offering her a glimpse of his upper chest, a striking expanse of smooth skin over taut muscle, with a sprinkling of dark hair.

Gratefully she took her glass. He tapped his glass against hers in a toast and sat down on the edge of the bed. "To us. To this evening."

"I'll drink to that." She sat down beside him and took a fortifying sip. It was excellent wine, not too dry, and the flavor was mild and nutty. "This is delicious. What is it?"

"It's a French Merlot. It's a good vintage, too."

He probably knew a lot about wines. And he was right about its soothing quality. After several sips, she felt the tension ebb from her shoulders and her heartbeat return to a more normal rhythm. The alcohol was going straight into her bloodstream because she hadn't eaten anything since lunch. Rishi was beginning to look even more seductive as he gazed at her with his rain-dampened hair and that look of longing on his face. The wine seemed to be relaxing him, too.

Slowly he removed the glass from her hand and put it on the bedside table, then placed his empty one next to hers. "Feel better?" he asked.

"Uh-huh."

He rose to his feet, went into the sitting room, and returned with a small plastic bag—his convenience store purchase. Then he turned down the bedside lamp to its lowest setting, bringing a muted glow to the room. He was clearly setting the stage for the next step in his grand seduction.

Her breath came out in a quiet sigh when he sat back down and lowered his lips to hers. His mouth was warm and gentle and tasted of wine. Her lips parted to accept his kiss. Gradually he increased the pressure and tilted both of them backward to lie on the mattress. Her legs dangled over the edge.

She knew he was an expert kisser, and he didn't disappoint her now. When his lips shifted from her mouth to drift over her jaw, she moved her head to the side, allowing him access to her neck and shoulders. He lingered at the base of her throat. "So soft," he breathed, "so feminine."

His hands were cruising over her now, making her shudder. He unbuttoned her blouse, very carefully, one tiny silver button at a time, like he had a hundred years to do it in. And while his fingers made their unhurried progress on the buttons, his lips glided down by degrees over her newly exposed skin. Finally he pushed away the open flaps to reveal her torso. With the utmost gentleness his fingers explored it, slowly but surely setting her nerves on fire.

He had marvelous hands. They were warm and persuasive and slightly rough, reminding her that he'd worked on a farm in his youth. A few raised scars, probably from the fire he'd battled, remained on his arms. Underneath that suave exterior there still lurked a farm boy. And that made him more human, more desirable.

"Rishi." She reached out to pull him toward her, so she could feel his lips on hers again, feel his weight on her chest. He came to her without hesitation, his mouth as ravenous as hers. She wanted him. Now.

He left her for a moment and leaned down to slide her sandals off. They fell to the carpeted floor with twin thumps. Then he unzipped her slacks, and slid those down, too—again, at a lingering pace. She lay back and let him undress her. She hadn't had this kind of erotic pampering in a long, long time.

The wine was giving her a pleasant buzz. Despite the fact that all she had on now were her panties and an open blouse that exposed her flimsy bra, she didn't care. His eyes were on her, the hot, molten pewter in them telling her he liked what he saw. She felt the flush of excitement reaching her neck and face.

"Get up a moment, darling. Let me turn down the bed," he said and she obeyed. When she stood up, she swayed a little, but he held her firmly against him with one hand while he turned down the covers with the other. Then he slid the blouse off her and tossed it aside. He laid her back on the clean, cool sheets. "You're a beautiful woman, Anju," he murmured.

She noticed the slight tremor in his hands as he sat on the

edge of the bed and discarded his own shoes and socks. Then he shed his trousers. And she watched with growing awe as the shirt came off. He seemed to have no inhibitions about undressing while she watched. When he pulled off the black boxers and tossed them, she inhaled sharply.

All her fantasies paled in comparison to the real man that stood before her, his need to take her so obvious, it left her fighting for breath.

He lowered himself to the bed to lie beside her. His weight made the mattress groan a little. In the next second she was encompassed in his arms. Like magic he got rid of her undergarments. Until that moment she'd had no idea her need for him was so deep, so desperate.

He began to stroke and knead her skin once again. "Anju, I swear I've never wanted another woman like I want you. I want to make love to you again and again and again." His mouth was an inch away from hers. "I want to make you forget every other man in your life. I want you to remember only me." He gave her a moment to absorb that. "Only me," he repeated.

Like a sponge she soaked up his whispered words. She knew he was telling her the truth. He hadn't lied to her thus far and wasn't likely to be doing it now. She let him lead the way. He was so darn good at it. In return she gave with abandon, letting herself savor the sensations that flooded her as he worked on her like a master musician plucking the strings, making her hunger for him gradually escalate into desperation. And all the while his gaze held hers in the pale light.

Then she heard the familiar sound of a foil packet being ripped open.

"Now?" he queried, rising above her. His voice was barely above a whisper.

"Now."

It was a while before Anjali summoned the strength to open her eyes. She found him watching her, a hint of a smile playing around his mouth. He lay on his side, one hand splayed on her stomach and one heavy leg lying across both of hers. She was pleased to discover he wasn't the type to make love, then turn around and start snoring.

"Hello, beautiful," he said in a low, intimate murmur.

"Hi." She smiled at him but didn't move. She didn't want to move. Her body felt fluid and boneless. She wanted to lie there forever and relive the moment. So much for thinking he'd be lousy in bed and she could tuck him away in some remote corner of her mind, then forget about him. On the contrary, he was awesome.

"Are you all right?" He traced the line of her jaw with a finger.

"What do you think?" she asked him lazily.

"I think you look like a woman who's eminently satisfied. In fact, I believe you have the look of a cat that licked up the last drop of cream."

"You're right." She reached up to touch his face. "Thank you for going slow with me, Rishi, and for making it special." She knew he'd kept an iron control over his own needs. He'd deliberately kept up that leisurely pace to allow her to get over her edginess, to become comfortable with him, to get to know him intimately.

"That was my intention," he said. "To give you time to relax and adjust to me—to focus on us."

"You came out with flying colors," she said, snatching his wandering hand and placing a kiss on his palm.

"I don't know about you, but all that talk about cream is making me hungry," he said, a smile tugging at the corner of his mouth. "You feel like eating something?"

"Hmm . . . Now that you mention it, I could—"

She never got to finish her sentence because his mouth was on hers again, more urgent now, more demanding—a contrast to the first time, when everything had occurred in slow motion. Within seconds they were making love. But she was ready for it—more than ready for the speed and sizzle. This time she knew without a doubt that she'd never been loved quite like this.

It was a while before their sated bodies separated. Finally serious about his need for food, Rishi picked up the phone from the nightstand and ordered room service. When it arrived, they ate at the small glass-top table in the kitchenette. He wore his navy monogrammed silk robe and lent her one of his polo shirts. It was huge on her, so it served as an adequate wrap. And it was made of the softest blue cotton.

She had vegetable soup and a salad while Rishi consumed a gargantuan roast beef sandwich and french fries, or chips, as he called them. When she remarked on his appetite, he grinned. "Love is hard work, Miss Kapadia." When she blushed, his grin widened. "Besides, I need the energy to make love to you again."

Her eyes went wide. "Again?"

"Didn't I say again and again?"

"I didn't think you meant it literally."

"I'm a man of my word, darling," he said and rose to his feet, pulling her up with him and catching her in a tight embrace. "See, you fit perfectly in my arms."

"No, I'm too short for you," she countered, tossing her head back to look at him. "I'm barely five foot three, and you're what . . . six?"

He pulled her face back into his chest and parked his chin over the top of her head. "I like it that you're petite. I can easily carry you."

To prove his point he hoisted her in his arms and took her straight to bed, surprising and delighting Anjali at the same time.

Settling her head over his shoulder, she gave a contented sigh. "I feel like a princess."

"That's the general idea." As he laid her down and settled himself beside her, he glanced at her legs. "Have I mentioned you have lovely legs, Princess?"

She pretended to search her mind. "I vaguely recall something of the sort." Putting a hand on his bad knee, she looked at him, her expression turning serious. "Speaking of legs, all this activity must take its toll on yours, Rishi."

"Exercise is good for it," he said.

"Not *this* kind of exercise."

"Exactly this kind of exercise." He pushed her down into the mattress and covered her body with his.

Sometime later, she stirred from her nap, every nerve in her body still tingling from the intense lovemaking she and Rishi had indulged in. The air conditioner hummed steadily beneath the windowsill. The sound of rain hammering on the window was no longer there. The storm had apparently subsided. She could hear the drone of traffic on the ever-packed Garden State Parkway less than half a mile away.

Rishi was asleep on his side, facing her. His breathing was even and soothing. The light was off but the red glow from the bedside clock-radio provided enough illumination for her to watch him sleep. It was well past midnight.

On a wistful breath she closed her eyes. A torrid affair with her business partner wasn't what she'd wanted, but she'd stumbled into it anyway. She wasn't entirely oblivious to its potential repercussions, either. Deep down she'd known she was vulnerable to him long before this. Making love with him had only increased her vulnerability. But she wouldn't trade what she'd had with him during the last few hours for anything.

Gently she shifted over to the other side of the bed so she could use the bathroom. He remained sleeping. Poor baby was exhausted. No matter how much he joked about it, that injured leg had to be hurting. She'd had ample opportunity tonight to study that scar up close, and each time she'd winced, not from revulsion but from anguish. She wanted to put her hands on it and smooth it away, dispel the pain associated with it. Of course, she couldn't do any such thing. He could mistake it for pity.

She picked up her clothes from the floor and entered the bathroom. Within minutes she was dressed. While she stood before the mirror, pulling a comb through her tangled hair, she couldn't help noticing the glow on her face—the afterglow—color blooming high in her cheeks. Her eyes virtually sparkled.

"Enjoy the euphoria, Anjali," she whispered to the starry-eyed woman in the mirror. "He'll be gone in a week and you'll be crying your eyeballs out." Despite all that talk about needing stability in his life and wanting to see where their relationship would go, he hadn't said one word about it all evening. It had been mostly physical, skin to skin, breath to breath. Desire and lust—nothing more.

It was surely going to hurt when he boarded that plane and vanished from her life. He could even return to Samantha once he was back in his familiar milieu.

What was worse was that he'd probably drop in once or twice a year to check on Silk & Sapphires, his American investment. Naturally he'd charm the dickens out of the whole family as well as the employees, tease and tantalize Anjali, and then disappear once again. She couldn't imagine that kind of "occasional sinful dessert" relationship with him.

But it was too late to undo what she'd already done. She'd have to find a way to live with the consequences.

When she returned to the bedroom, she found the light on and Rishi sitting up in bed, the sheet pulled up to his waist. "You disappeared," he remarked in a gravelly voice.

"I was gone only a few minutes."

"So I missed you for those few minutes," he sulked.

"I have to go home, Rishi."

"Not yet." He held out his arms. "Come here."

She shook her head. "I'd love to, but if I come back to bed I know what's going to happen. You're a slave driver, Shah." She kept her voice light and teasing. Best to keep her bleak mood to herself.

Obviously pleased by her remark, he smiled. This Rishi was so different from the cool, controlled businessman dressed in custom-tailored suits. This one looked disheveled and roguish. But she loved the pouting, boyish look, and she really had to curb the need to go to him.

He stepped out of bed and gathered his clothes from the floor. "All right, then, I'll drive you home."

"Don't be silly. I can get home on my own."

He already had his boxers in place and was pulling on his

trousers. "I'll follow you home and make sure you get there safely." He started to button his shirt.

She plucked her car keys out of her pocketbook. "I've been driving myself since I was a teenager. Go back to bed. You need your rest."

"*You* need rest more than I," he insisted. He came to her, studied her for a moment, and brushed his knuckles against the side of her face. "I wore you out, didn't I? You look bushed."

"I'll live." The gentleness and warmth in his voice and eyes were killing her. She'd never in her wildest dreams thought he was capable of such tenderness. He'd shown her a completely different side of him tonight.

"You better. I've got plans for you, Miss Kapadia," he said in low growl, as they proceeded to the sitting room.

"Oh?" She put on her jacket and watched him shrug into his. "What kind of plans?"

"Let's just say you better take your vitamins and build up your strength," he replied with a mysterious smile. "Tonight's only a small taste of what I have in mind for you." He hooked his arm around her shoulders and led her out of the suite and toward the elevator before she could ask any more questions. He put a finger over his lips, reminding her that the other guests were sleeping in their rooms.

Outside, the rain had stopped, but a brisk, damp wind tossed wet leaves into their path as they walked across the parking lot, his arm still locked around her shoulders. He followed her car all the way home. Then he insisted on walking her to the door like a proper gentleman.

Just before she went in, he gave her a lingering, soul-stirring kiss. "It's Monday, so sleep late and rest up."

"Not too late. I have that salesperson interview scheduled for this afternoon." She noticed the drawn look on his face. "You better get some sleep, too."

He waited till she was safely inside before taking off. From the family room window she watched him drive away. She wasn't surprised at the tears burning her eyes. The first stab of pain was already blooming. All these years she'd managed to keep that steel armor around her heart intact. But there was a weak spot somewhere and Rishi had managed to sneak past it.

After tonight she had no armor left. She felt more emotionally naked than she'd ever felt. Even with Vik, she hadn't felt this painfully stripped, because she'd been young and inexperienced and had dived into the relationship with complete abandon. In those days she hadn't known that life was full of surprises—many of them unbearably heartrending.

She'd known all along that making love with Rishi would be her undoing—and she'd done it anyway. And it wasn't just the sex, although that was incredible. She was still feeling the warmth and scent of his body locked up with hers. The urge to hop right back into her car, return to his hotel, and accept his invitation to stay was compelling. She missed him already.

One thing she knew for sure—she was in trouble.

Chapter 22

Rishi took his time driving back to the hotel. He didn't like going back alone. He'd wanted Anju to stay with him the rest of the night. He wanted to wake up with her beside him. It made no sense, but he'd never felt this kind of aching need for a woman before. He'd appreciated his lifestyle until now, with all the freedom it afforded.

He'd come to the States to do a job—do it quickly and get out. It was mostly a favor for Jeevan-kaka. The favor had turned into a four-month project. Then there was that unexpected little matter of developing a mad attraction for the old man's niece. Rishi hadn't factored that into the equation.

The more Anjali had withdrawn from him, the more he'd wanted to break down her defenses. It was the proverbial red flag waved at an untamed bull. He'd wanted to get her one way or the other. And he had—at least into his bed.

It should have been a victory for him. Strangely, it didn't feel like one. Because while he was trying to win her over, he'd become so bloody attached to her that she was becoming an obsession. And the odd thing was, his tastes had always run more toward Caucasian women—white skin, light hair and eyes. Anjali Kapadia didn't fit that mold.

She was unique—a woman with a generous heart. And he wanted her. Lately it was more need than want. It wasn't as if he hadn't attempted to expel her from his head. He'd truly given it his best attempt while in London. And he'd failed.

As the multistory hotel abruptly came into view Rishi realized he'd been driving with no thought to the roads and traffic signals. Good thing it was the dead of night, with little to no traffic. Within seconds he was turning into the parking lot.

Reluctantly he went up to his room. Since he was too wide-awake to sleep he booted up his computer. A friend in London had referred an American client to Rishi, a California man who owned a chain of specialty gourmet bakeries that catered to an elite customer base. Rishi had talked to the bakery owner a few times over the phone in the last couple of weeks, so he had some idea of the financial mess the baker had landed in.

Opening up the documents from the West Coast client, he started working. He'd promised the baker he'd fly out to San Francisco after the Silk & Sapphires opening to discuss business in person.

Making himself a cup of tea in the kitchenette, he studied the sales figures, made notes for himself, did research on baking and bakeries, the market for certain types of baked goods, the kinds of people who consumed what the California man produced, and made comparisons to other areas of the U.S. and Europe. He worked steadily for a while.

When he finally felt he'd done enough, a purpling dawn sky was blossoming outside his window. Traffic sounds on the highway had picked up in the past hour, too.

He wondered if it was too late to grab some sleep. But his eyelids felt heavy with fatigue. If he could manage to get three hours, he'd be ready to face the day. He'd just have to skip his daily trip to the gym. He shut off the computer and strode toward the bedroom.

Tossing his clothes aside, he fell into bed. The pillows smelled of gardenias and strawberries. Anjali's presence was everywhere in the room. He dragged one of the pillows close to his chest, pulled up the covers, and shut his eyes.

And while he lay in that twilight zone between wakefulness and sleep, a plan began to take shape in his mind.

Chapter 23

Anjali and her mother chatted with Nilima Sethi, the young lady who'd just been offered the sales job at the store. She had accepted right away.

"Welcome aboard, Nilima," Anjali said to her, shaking her hand. "We hope you'll like working at Silk & Sapphires."

"Thank you, Anjali," Nilima said excitedly, "and Mrs. Kapadia. I'm looking forward to working with such beautiful things. I love your designs."

Anjali smiled. "You're very kind."

They walked Nilima to the front door. It had been a long interview. They had talked for an hour or more, then gone on a tour of the store. Anjali had used that as an excuse to see how much the young woman knew about the type of merchandise they sold. In the end, Nilima had passed not quite with flying colors, but she showed potential. She had a pleasant personality and she seemed eager to learn. The rest would have to come with experience.

After they bid Nilima good-bye, her mother started walking toward the office, where Jeevan-kaka and her father were arguing over the best method of dealing with India's corrupt and bureaucratic Customs and Central Excise department.

Deciding against taking part in the debate, Anjali picked up a box of price tags and the tagging gun and headed for the children's department. She unpacked a carton of toddler clothing. Tagging the garments, she put them on hangers and placed them on a carousel. They were adorable, the tiny *sherwanis*, *kurtas*, and *churidars* for the boys and the daintiest little *chania-cholis*, *salwar-kameezes*, and even miniature, made-to-size saris for the girls.

She gazed at a tiny pink *choli* with silver beads sewn around the midriff. Maybe she and Vik should have planned a child early in their marriage. If they had, she'd have had a boy or girl around eleven years old by now. He or she would be wearing some of her best creations. But then . . . she'd be facing the trials of single parenting. It wouldn't have been easy, not with her working hours and her travel schedule.

From the corner of her eye she saw movement and looked up. It was Rishi. He stood some ten feet away, a thoughtful look on his face.

"Hey, how long have you been standing there?" She acknowledged the warmth spreading in her belly—but suppressed the need to rush into his arms.

"A second or two," he replied. "I like watching you work. You have such a contented look."

"I happen to like my work." She hastily put the *choli* on a hanger. But she had a feeling he'd seen the look of yearning on her face. Those keen eyes missed nothing.

"I knew that even before I met you." He came closer and studied her face. "Looks like you got some rest."

"Some," she said. "How about you?"

He put a hand on her cheek, urging her to meet his eyes. "I missed you. Couldn't sleep after you left."

A smile tipped the corners of her mouth. He'd missed her. She let his words sink in, let the pure joy spring to life inside her. She'd missed him, too. And it wasn't until almost sunup that she'd been able to fall asleep. It was noon when she'd forced herself to rise and take a hot shower to get the fatigue out of her system. He was a demanding lover but he gave twice as much as he took.

When his hand slid to her shoulder she stiffened. "They're in there," she whispered, inclining her head in the direction of the office.

"They're so busy arguing they're not likely to notice us."

"Don't count on it. Mom has the instincts of a brand-new razor blade."

Rishi chuckled. "You're right about that. But I saw her leaving a few minutes ago. Something about grocery shopping for tonight's dinner."

"Oh yes, dinner." She sighed. "God forbid Jeevan-kaka should have to eat something bought at a restaurant."

"Why don't you and I have a quiet dinner somewhere?"

"Two nights in a row would make them suspicious." She studied the look in his eyes. She knew what that meant. She wanted the same thing he wanted: a rerun of last night. But it was dangerous. She could so easily get used to sleeping with him and fall into a pattern. "Let's take it easy for now?"

"If that's what you want." He didn't look happy about it but he was too much of a gentleman to prod her.

"Maybe in a couple of days, okay?"

"All right." He thrust his hands in his pockets. "I'll go join the men in the back."

"You do that." She picked up the tagging gun once again, her hands unsteady. "By the way, Rishi . . ."

"Yes?"

"I missed you, too."

He nodded but said nothing.

She watched him walk away. Was he upset with her? But then all she'd said was she couldn't continue to sleep with him. It wasn't as if she didn't want it. She wanted it desperately and was thrilled that he wanted it, too. But at the same time she couldn't continue to ignore reality. She belonged to a conservative Gujarati family that would be shocked if they discovered what was going on. In fact, despite all their Americanization, they could very well be living in nineteenth-century Gujarat. Some things never changed in her community.

She couldn't handle the idea of more or less living together. If she started going to his room every night, it would be tantamount to living with him. With his liberated European ideas and having lived with Samantha, he was probably under the impression it was as easy as asking for it and getting it.

That wasn't going to happen with her. She couldn't give in to his every whim. And there'd been no hint of anything long-term in their relationship. He hadn't said one word about loving her either. At least if he'd said the L-word, she might've had something to think about.

Oh well, it would be good for him to sleep alone in that giant hotel bed. Maybe he'd miss her so much he'd realize he was madly in love with her . . . so madly in love that he'd be forced to give up London and move to New Jersey. *Yeah, right! Dream on, Anjali.*

For now she'd take it one day at a time. No sense in looking too far into the future. She had no time to look that far. In the short term, the grand opening on Saturday was looming large.

After that, if he still lingered in New Jersey, maybe . . . just maybe she'd think about where this relationship was going.

Chapter 24

On Saturday, the Kapadia household was up at dawn. Although everyone went about their business quietly, there were undercurrents of tension and excitement in the air.

They had to leave early for the store to perform the *pooja*: religious rituals to invoke the blessings of Lord Ganesh and Goddess Lakshmi.

Anjali picked an outfit that was an interesting East-West combination: a golden rust silk pantsuit. She'd designed it herself. The sandals and jewelry she'd bought in India during her last trip matched the ensemble perfectly.

Just as she started on her makeup there was a knock on her door. "Come in," she called as she smoothed foundation on her face. The door opened and Nilesh walked in, wearing a gray suit with a rumpled white shirt and no tie. His black shoes had obviously never seen anything that resembled shoe polish. He looked pathetic.

"Hey, Anju, do you know anything about ties?" he asked.

"You mean what matches with what?"

"I mean how to knot a tie."

She nodded. "I did it for Vik sometimes." She studied her brother's sloppy getup. "Honey, first of all, your shirt needs some serious ironing. Haven't you heard of an appliance called an iron?"

He shrugged, looking clueless. "There's an iron somewhere in my closet."

She helped him out of his jacket and unbuttoned his shirt. Memories of doing this for him when he was a little boy flashed through her mind. He hadn't changed much in his dress habits. Of course, now he was several inches taller than her and there was some hard muscle developing beneath the undershirt, reminding her that her little brother was no longer so little; he was a young man.

"Let's get the shirt ironed first," she said, going to the ironing board and plugging in the appliance. "While I do this, go borrow Dad's shoe polish and get working on those shoes."

"You want me to polish my shoes? Now?"

She gave him one of her big-sister scowls. "Now. Then we'll pick something suitable from your tie collection."

"Okaaay." He trudged out of there, whining. "So much crap for nothing . . ."

Anjali smiled to herself as she started to press the shirt. The boy needed to learn some dress sense. He seemed to like Rishi a lot, so maybe she could request Rishi to guide her naïve brother toward acquiring a decent wardrobe. Well, at least Nil had remembered to shave, thank goodness.

Several minutes later, he strode in with four ties and tossed them on her bed. "Which one do you think?"

She looked at his shoes. They looked a shade better than they did before.

Once the ironed shirt was buttoned and tucked neatly into Nilesh's waistband, Anjali picked a coordinating tie and helped him knot it just right. After he slipped on the jacket she threw him a comb and stood back to observe as he neatened his hair. "Not bad, kiddo. You clean up nicely. You actually look like a decent, professional man."

"I *am* a decent, professional man," he growled. "Why do men have to wear monkey suits anyway? A good, clean pair of jeans should be plenty if you ask me."

Anjali went back to finishing her makeup. "Nil, everything you own is faded, frayed, and wrinkled."

"That's your girly opinion. You and Mom own a boutique; your heads are filled with nothing but fashion." He threw the comb back on her dresser and studied his image in the mirror, looking somewhat surprised and apparently liking what he saw. "So, you think I look good enough to attract some chicks?"

She pinched his face and grinned when he grimaced predictably. "You look handsome enough to attract a truckload of chicks, baby. Just remember to keep those scuffed shoes out of sight and they'll find you irresistible."

"So stop calling me baby already!" He stomped out of her room.

"Then start dressing like a man," she yelled after him and grinned again. Her brother was taking an interest in girls? It wasn't all that long ago that he'd spit up all over her graduation gown and then some years later screamed till he was hoarse when she'd dropped him off on his first day at kindergarten.

He was growing up too fast, the little stinker.

It took Rishi a few seconds to realize he'd been dreaming. He sat up in his bed and glanced around in the darkness. The nightmare was back! And it was so damn real. He could have sworn the smoke was right there, inside the hotel room, mixed in with the stench of charred hair and skin. The hot, explosive feeling in his lungs felt like he'd swallowed the flames.

He'd clearly been thrashing around. The sheets were badly rumpled. He was perspiring.

The nightmare hadn't troubled him in months. Now it was back—in all its grimness. It would never really go away. He was sure of that. It was too deeply entrenched in his subconscious to vanish. For the rest of his life he'd probably continue to wake up yelling at his father to get out of the inferno and save himself.

Looking at the bedside clock, Rishi realized it was only a few minutes before the alarm would go off, so he shut it off and headed for the bathroom. A hot shower was generally a good way of washing away the lingering bleakness of a nightmare. A hearty English breakfast would be even better. So the minute he got out of the shower he picked up the phone and called for room service: eggs, sausage, bacon, toast with marmalade, and a pot of strong tea.

Half an hour later, he thrust his feet into the black loafers the valet delivered to his door. They were polished to a brilliant shine. Allowing himself a final glimpse in the mirror, Rishi headed out. The cobwebs from the nightmare were almost gone. For the moment.

Despite having done this a dozen times in the past, the nervous tremor in his stomach was still very much there. Every time a new store was about to open, the doubts set in. Just because his businesses in other countries had done well it didn't guarantee success in the American venture. And he had a lot more vested in Silk & Sapphires. It was personal.

He'd promised Anju he wouldn't let her down. He couldn't let her down.

On his way to the store he made a brief stop at a florist shop. For Usha he picked a dozen yellow roses and for Anjali he decided to go with an exotic bouquet of mixed orchids.

Pulling into the store's parking lot, he decided to stop in the front for a minute. He wanted to get a good look at the building, try to see it from a customer's point of view. Keeping the engine running, he studied the storefront. Everything looked fresh and sparkling. A *bandarwal*, the traditional Indian doorway decoration and welcome symbol made of colorful fabric, gold braid and tiny bells, hung above the door. Nice touch.

Despite two straight days of wet weather, this day had fortunately dawned clear and cloudless. It was late October, but the temperature was still remarkably warm.

His gaze moved to the display windows. The mannequins dressed by Anjali looked uncannily real. Both Anjali and he had agreed that the models, while attractive in face and figure, had to look realistic in terms of skin tones, facial expressions, and hair. The other stores had dummies with pale alabaster skin, some with glassy eyes and unnatural-looking hair that practically screamed nylon wigs. They looked like dummies. In comparison, Silk & Sapphires' mannequins looked lifelike.

Anjali even had models of an older couple in one of the windows, an authentic Indian grandmother and grandfather with graying hair, dressed in traditional apparel and posing with their grandchildren, a boy and a girl. Anjali wanted both genders and all age groups represented, thereby welcoming everybody to spend time and money in the store.

Nodding in approval, he drove toward the rear parking and shut off the ignition. He noticed the Kapadias' van was already there, and so was Anwar Ali's.

Mohan and Jeevan-kaka were standing by the door, chatting. Both men wore formal suits—an unusual but cheerful sight.

Jeevan-kaka noticed him first and waved him over. "Looking good, *beta*." He cast a pleased eye over the flowers. "You bought flowers for Anju?"

"For Auntie *and* Anju." He held the door open for the two men. "Shall we go in?"

As soon as they entered the building and stepped into the café, Rishi caught a whiff of something delicious cooking. Anwar was probably making his famous shrimp and *paneer samosas*. The café looked inviting. Nilesh sat at one of the tables, a plate heaped with a variety of finger foods in front of him. He was happily stuffing himself. He grinned at the three men.

Anwar was in the kitchen, working with a tray of something that looked and smelled appetizing. "Good morning, Rishi-saheb," he called and gave a mock salute.

Rishi returned the salute. "Everything in order here, Anwar?"

"Yes, sir. You want to taste some chicken-asparagus spring rolls?"

So that's what smelled so good. "A little later, thank you. Let me go inside and see what's happening there first."

"All right, sir."

"Nilesh, you can eat later," Mohan said to his son. "We have to pray now. I think your mom is ready for the *pooja*."

Reluctantly Nilesh wiped his mouth with a napkin and followed them out of Neela Chai.

The men went directly to the office, where they found the women lighting the lamps. Rishi stood on the threshold for a minute. His gaze immediately went to Anjali. She had her back to him, so she wasn't aware of his presence until Mohan spoke. "Are we ready to say our prayers?"

Anjali turned around and saw the four of them standing at the door. Her smile was luminous. She looked lovely in the silky outfit. The unusual color suited her honey-tinted complexion.

"You guys look fabulous!" she said. "I can't resist men in formal wear."

"Thank you, kind lady," said Rishi. Stepping into the room, he handed her the bouquet of orchids. "To wish you luck."

She took them with a puzzled smile. "For me?" When he nodded, she buried her face in the blooms for an instant. "They're beautiful. Thank you." Her eyes were misty when she lifted them to him. He wondered if he'd brought back certain memories. Had Vikram given her flowers?

He offered the roses to her mother. "For you, Auntie."

Usha looked equally taken aback. "Me, too? Why, thanks so much, *beta*. You shouldn't have. You've already done so much."

Rishi gave her a brief hug. "It's a minor token of my appreciation for your hospitality. You've been a most gracious hostess."

Usha blushed very becomingly. "Don't be silly, dear. Cooking is something we women do. Besides, we should be the ones grateful to you and Jeevan-bhai for all this." She made a sweeping gesture with her free hand.

He shrugged. Despite their initial misgivings about him, they'd slowly embraced him as one of their own, and for a man without much family other than his mother, stepfather, and Jeevan-kaka, it was a splendid feeling. He looked at Usha clutching the flowers. "Would you like me to find a vase for those?"

"We have some vases near the cash register," offered Anjali. "I'll get them."

"I'll help you," he said and plucked the roses from Usha's hand. This was an ideal opportunity to get Anjali alone for a minute before the day started in earnest. He followed her. "Anju."

She turned around for a moment. "Yeah?"

"You look beautiful, sweetheart," he whispered. He noticed the color rising in her face.

"Thanks." She touched the sleeve of his Nehru jacket. His suit, too, was an East-West blend of conventional black trousers paired with a close-neck jacket that had just a bit of embellishment in gray and silver threads around the collar. "Nice."

He took her hand and brought it to his lips. "Your hand feels cold."

"Last-minute nerves," she replied, reclaiming her hand. "But I'm grateful for your support." She resumed walking toward the register and slipped behind it. Bending down, she retrieved two tall, clear glass vases from the cabinet below.

He took one of them and she picked up the other. "Let's go to the kitchen and fill them with water. Gives us a chance to sample some of Anwar's delicacies, too. They smell scrumptious."

"And fattening," Anjali chimed in.

"I know that. I've been doing nothing but eat since I arrived in the U.S."

She gave him an appraising look. "Looks like you tucked it away in the right places."

"Glad you approve, ma'am." It was funny how her compliments both pleased and touched him, especially when such remarks from other women had never had the same effect. He winked at her. "You think you could show your approval tonight?"

A sly smile was all he got. "We'll see about that, Shah. It all depends."

"On what?"

"I prefer to keep you guessing."

With an exaggerated sigh he used his elbow to push open the café's door and let her glide through. "Women!"

He watched her chuckle all the way to the kitchen, her arms full of orchids and her hips swinging just that tiny bit to make it a subtle come-on.

The rear door burst open and the other Kapadias walked in: Naren, Varsha, and Sejal. Every one of them was dressed to the nines. And they looked handsome. He rewarded them with a cheerful greeting.

Nilima Sethi followed them in, also dressed in a *salwar-kameez* made of burgundy silk, with a tense look on her face. Anjali introduced her to everyone around.

A few minutes later, the family lined up in front of the makeshift altar to pray. Usha invited Nilima to join them. The elders knew their Sanskrit *shlokas* by heart but Anjali, Nilesh, Sejal, Nilima, and Rishi stood with their eyes shut and their palms joined in silent prayer.

This was something Rishi hadn't done in years. The last time was some eight years ago at Jeevan-kaka's house in India, when he and his family had a *Diwali* party and Rishi had spent the weekend with them. It was heartwarming to pray with family.

When they finished the *pooja*, the clock read 9:46 A.M. It was almost time to open the doors. Rishi stepped onto the floor to turn on the lights while Usha went to check on the two women who were setting up the beauty salon.

He noticed Anjali walking over to the Zanana, which was her area of expertise, and request Nilima to handle the sari department. Usha would take care of the jewelry counter and Rishi put himself in charge of the men's section. As expected, Mohan and Jeevan took their places by the cash register and Sejal went toward the children's area. Nilesh looked a little uncomfortable. This wasn't his environment of choice. But he'd promised to help out, so Rishi placed him near the front door, where he could direct traffic and answer simple questions.

Anwar and his young helper were already setting out complimentary trays of food at Neela Chai and pitchers filled with exotic fruit drinks. Anwar had even come up with the idea of making a blueberry-flavored iced tea with a hint of blue food color in keeping with the whimsical blue tea theme, much to Anjali's delight. The rich aroma of *masala chai* was rising from the silver urn sitting on a small table in the café's corner.

Rishi took one last look around and threw open the main door.

The new Silk & Sapphires was officially open for business.

Chapter 25

By late evening Anjali knew their opening day was a success. At least a dozen customers had remarked on how unique and beautiful the store was, so different from anything they'd seen in the neighborhood or elsewhere. Gratified, she'd held on to that praise and passed it along to the others in the family, and of course to Rishi, knowing they'd all worked equally hard in making this whole thing come to life. Nearly all day she'd floated on a cloud of excitement.

No doubt they'd have their share of bounced checks, returned merchandise, and complaints about the quality of the goods or any number of things. She'd been in business long enough to learn there was no such thing as pleasing everyone.

Nevertheless she thought of the opening as a success.

Now that she had a chance to slow down and think about it, her feet ached from all the walking and standing she'd done in her new super-high-heeled sandals. Being a career saleswoman, she should have known better than to use footwear that hadn't been broken in yet. But she could hardly pass up the opportunity to wear something so pretty, especially when it was a perfect match for her outfit.

Between sales, fittings, minor alterations, and catering to window-shoppers and curiosity seekers, she hadn't had a chance to grab a bite to eat. That, too, was something that hadn't hit her until just now. Somewhere in the middle of the afternoon, her mother had insisted that she drink one of Anwar's rich pa-

paya juice concoctions, which had tasted delicious. She'd hidden the cup under the counter and sneaked an occasional sip between customers.

She had watched Rishi working just as hard as she, maybe more. Out of the corner of her eye she'd noticed him talking to people, shaking hands, offering advice, and laughing with them. He had also sold a whole lot of merchandise.

Rishi seemed to get along famously with customers. It probably came naturally to him, just like his other business skills. Many of the folks he'd been talking to had walked out with multiple bags filled with purchases.

It gave her immense satisfaction to see people carrying those familiar blue and white bags displaying the store's logo throughout the day. The sound of the cash register ringing up all those sales was even more satisfying. Her father and Jeevan-kaka had been busy at the counter.

Even Nilesh appeared to be doing a fine job greeting people at the front door and directing them to the right place despite his earlier grousing. His youthful looks helped to complete the poster-boy image. She had smiled and waved at him once or twice when she'd caught his eye. He'd rolled his eyes at her good-naturedly. She'd also noticed he'd been eyeing every young and personable female entering the store. And there had been a steady trickle of those.

Anjali's guess about the Zanana concept had been right on target. The psychology of forbidden fruit never failed: make the entryway attractive and hint at some deep, dark secret behind it, and they were sure to come. Once they found out how lovely it was on the inside, with its willowy mannequins dressed in the most interesting fashions, the men were likely to buy something for the women in their lives. Sure enough, lots of men had visited the Zanana, and she had helped many of them with their purchases.

Almost every customer had stopped for several minutes to watch the informational video she had made with interesting facts about the origin of certain types of ethnic Indian clothing, how silk was produced, and a collage of clips of the fashion shows she had put together in recent years with appropriate background music. She'd even included demonstrations on how to wear a sari the right way, the multiple ways to wear a *chunni*, and the various means to enhance a plain outfit with the right accessories. She'd tried to make it a mini documentary combined with entertainment.

Customers seemed to love watching the fifteen-minute video that was set to play over and over all day. Although Anjali had had some doubts about it at first, she was glad she had introduced it after Rishi had assured her it was a refreshing and bright innovation. To her delight, it appeared to be the star attraction in the store. Many had stood to watch it more than once, then proceeded to order something they'd seen on the screen and liked.

Sejal seemed to be the belle of the ball. Anjali had noted with satisfaction that her cousin seemed to enjoy the day's hectic pace. Anjali had even caught her flirting with some young man with long hair and enormous brown eyes. The good thing about Sejal's interest in the young man was that she hadn't been gawking as much at Rishi.

Anjali didn't want to feel that stab of jealousy every time she saw Sejal drooling over Rishi. It was childish to feel that way, especially when she knew Rishi thought of Sejal as just a kid with a crush on an older man. But Sejal's fresh youthfulness often reminded Anjali of her own age—and the painful fact that she herself was used goods at best.

Her mother was everywhere, a nervous hen tending to her chicks. But she was in her element. Playing boss was her favorite role in any case. She had plenty to keep her running. In spite of all the policing, an elderly woman had managed to smuggle in a glass of juice into the clothing area and spill it on the carpet. Between Nilesh and her mother they'd mopped it up, and Varsha-kaki had been permanently posted by the Neela Chai door as a security guard.

Later, a child was caught hanging on the Zanana arch, tilting it dangerously, and Rishi had to bring a step stool and perform some quick repairs. "All in a day's work, Anju. Nothing that can't be fixed," he'd whispered to Anjali when she'd lamented over the damage to her precious Zanana.

Every time she'd panicked about something, it had been Rishi who'd calmed her down. A couple of times he'd stopped by just to check on her. His baritone voice had whispered to her, "Why don't you take a break and get something to eat?" Although she didn't need that kind of attention and didn't expect it, it was nice to know he cared enough to do it.

"Maybe later," she'd replied. "At the moment, food's the last thing on my mind."

He'd secretly squeezed her hand. "Promise?"

"Promise," she'd said. She hadn't realized she'd missed that kind of thoughtfulness until she'd seen the look of concern on his face. "What about your leg? You've been on your feet for hours."

He'd given her a veiled smile. "Maybe you can do something about it later?"

"Um . . . if . . ."

"No ifs or buts, Miss Kapadia. I'm taking you to my room tonight and that's that." He'd left her frowning and staring at his back.

Had he turned bossier lately or was he always like that? She'd realized she rather liked it. She had resented his brand of assertiveness in the beginning, but it had grown on her. Maybe she was so crazy in love with him that she'd begun to look at him in a different light.

At nearly 9:00 P.M., there was still one last customer browsing in the aisles. Anjali caught her mother's impatient look. The doors were supposed to close at 8:30 P.M., but opening day was special. It was the one opportunity to make a dazzling and lasting impression on customers, and have them spread the word. Anjali realized she was dead tired, and so was the rest of the family, but until the last customer left, the store would remain open.

Naren-kaka, his wife, and Sejal had left a while ago. Mohan

had taken Jeevan-kaka and Nilesh home and then returned to help clean up. All the employees were gone, too.

Rishi was on his cell phone out in the parking lot. She'd been watching him through the window for the past several minutes, pacing as he spoke into the phone. He was in the habit of walking while he handled business calls. His limp looked a little more pronounced than it had that morning. She'd begun to notice the subtle changes in his gait, like when he was tired or he hadn't exercised in a day or two.

Sometimes she wondered how he'd managed before the advent of cell phones. He used his constantly and it stayed on night and day since his other businesses were in different time zones. It interrupted him frequently. But he'd promised her he'd keep it off when they were intimate together. And he'd kept his promise the other night. That phone had remained silent all the while she was there.

It was a little past nine by the time she rang up the lingering customer's purchases, saw her out, and locked the front door.

Usha came out of the office. "She finally left?"

"She bought quite a bit, Mom—well worth the extra half hour," Anjali said.

"Thank goodness." Her mother looked around. "Where's Rishi?"

"He's on his phone in the parking lot."

"In spite of his other concerns he worked so hard today, did you see?" Usha looked out the window before shifting her gaze to Anjali.

"Yeah, can't say he's merely a silent partner. He's definitely hands-on."

Usha's eyes on Anjali sharpened. "Did you notice how well he got along with the customers?"

Anjali knew where this was leading. "Mm-hmm." Better nip it in the bud before her mother started reaching silly conclusions, she decided. "I better clean up." Picking up the handheld vacuum cleaner stashed in the office, she proceeded to do spot cleaning wherever she saw the need. From the corner of her eye she noticed her mother returning to the office.

A few minutes later, Rishi walked in through the café door, pocketing his phone. "So, are we ready to call it a day?" he asked Anjali.

"I guess so. Check with my parents, will you?"

He threw a cautious glance around before approaching her. Without warning he picked her up by the waist, gave her a quick whirl, then placed her back on her feet, taking her by surprise and leaving her breathless. "Congratulations! You did it, darling!" His hands remained circling her waist.

"With your help and Jeevan-kaka's," she reminded him, trying to recover from his unexpected exuberance.

"I'm taking you to dinner for a private celebration."

She gently removed his hands. "I'm not sure it's a good idea."

"Why not?"

"It's been a long day and everyone's tired." She gave the place one last glance. "Besides, shouldn't this be a joint celebration? All of us are in it together."

He mulled over it for a second. "You're right. We'll all go out together. After that, we'll see if we can find some time alone."

"Jeevan-kaka can't stand to eat restaurant food, remember?"

He dismissed it with a wave. "I'm sure we can find something nice and bland for him. Your poor mother's ready to drop from exhaustion. It's not fair to make her go home and put a meal on the table at this hour." He looked at his watch and whipped out his cell phone. "I'll call Uncle Naren and invite his family. They worked almost as hard to make this a success." Just before he dialed, he looked at her. "Does India House restaurant sound okay to you?"

"Sure."

Rishi waited for his telephone to connect with Naren Kapadia's. Leaning against the counter, he watched Anjali go about her chores: picking up this and straightening out that. She clearly couldn't relax. He sensed the nervous energy vibrating around her. She needed to unwind soon or she was going to snap.

He knew the feeling of working for months toward a goal and then watching it unfold. It was an emotional high that was hard to descend from. Sometimes, depending on the stakes, it stayed for days, even weeks, but you had to let yourself step down from it and walk away for a bit, or the mental overload could break you in half.

He'd hoped to take her to his suite right after the store closed, help her relax, but she obviously had other ideas. However, she was right: it should be a joint celebration, a family venture, and it would be selfish on his part to keep it private.

When Naren finally picked up the phone, he seemed reluctant to get out of the house. "We are all changed and ready for bed, Rishi," he grumbled. "We ate some leftovers after we got home. Usha gave us plenty to bring home."

"What about Sejal? Does she want to join us?"

"Sejal is studying; she has an exam on Monday."

"Never mind, then. How's tomorrow night for you?"

Naren sounded more eager about that. "That sounds good. So where are we going?"

"I'll make reservations at India House. We'll meet you there after the store closes."

Concluding his conversation with Naren, Rishi made the reservations, then went into the office. He found Mohan and Usha getting ready to leave for home. Usha smiled at him. "I was just on my way to get Anjali."

"Would you mind if I took Anjali out to dinner, Auntie?"

Usha threw an uneasy glance at her husband and then at Rishi. "Umm . . . isn't it a little late to go out?"

He laughed. "A storeowner calls this late?" But he noticed Mohan looking just as edgy as his wife.

"Well, it's just that . . . you know . . ." Usha had a furrow between her brows.

"Auntie, are you worried about Anju and me seeing too much of each other?"

She threw another quick glance at her husband. "Yes and no."

"What does that mean?"

"We'd like to talk to you privately about it sometime, Rishi. There's something we need to discuss."

"Is it urgent?"

"I wouldn't call it urgent, but it's important. Jeevan-bhai and I had a chat the other day and he told me a few things . . . about his relationship to your family and you . . . how much he owes you and your father."

"I see."

"He also told me you have a *live-in* girlfriend."

Rishi noticed the subtle emphasis. "I'll be happy to talk to you tomorrow." He could tell from Mohan's expression that he didn't want to be included in the conversation. "You name the time, Auntie." When she agreed, he added, "By the way, I'm taking everyone out tomorrow to celebrate at India House. I've already cleared it with Naren-kaka and his family. How about you?"

Usha's face brightened. "That'll be nice."

"I believe you're long overdue for a break from kitchen duty."

She sighed. "You're not kidding."

"So, is it all right if I take Anjali out tonight?"

"I guess . . . if it's okay with her." Usha followed her husband out the door. "Make sure you bring her home, okay? She doesn't have her car here."

"I'll drive her home."

Rishi stood for a moment, mulling over Usha's request for a private talk. She was clearly worried about whatever was brewing between him and her daughter. And he found that surprisingly endearing. It was a mother's prerogative to be concerned about her children. But what was he going to tell her? He had a whole list of plans, but none of them had been discussed with Anju. If she balked at them, every one of them would pop like soap bubbles.

He shut the door to the office and went in search of Anju.

He expected her to be dusting or mopping or some such thing. He needed to rescue her from that kind of obsessive-compulsive behavior. Instead, to his amazement, he found her sitting on a low footstool inside the Zanana, her knees drawn to her chest and her arms hugging them. He came to a standstill. With mostly her back toward him he couldn't see her expression, but she seemed pensive, melancholy.

That aura of sadness never seemed to leave her. Even when she laughed, the despondency seemed to hover just beneath the surface.

Staring at nothing in particular, she sat motionless, oblivious to his presence. In fact, she was so still she could easily pass for one of those mannequins she'd meticulously dressed. His immediate instinct was to go to her, find out if she needed comforting. But he watched her silently for a minute. Would he ever be able to eliminate the lurking shadows from her life? He sure as hell wanted to try.

Reluctant to startle her, he called her name softly. "Anju."

She turned around. "Hi."

"A penny for your thoughts. Dollar? Euro?"

She gave a sad shake of her head, the gesture tugging at his heartstrings. "Priceless. Did you round up the clan for dinner?"

"No. Everyone's gone home. They all seemed disinclined to go out, so we're set for tomorrow night at India House." He stepped forward and offered his hands to help her rise to her feet. "What were you so deep in thought about? Still worried?"

She slid into his welcoming arms as naturally as he'd hoped. "I was decompressing. After all the excitement of the last several weeks it's finally happened."

"And what a smashing success it was."

"Some months ago, when Dad mentioned bankruptcy, I panicked. I was going to lose everything I'd worked for over a decade."

"I'm sorry."

"And now . . ." She took a long, tremulous breath. "Now I look around and I can't believe all this is partly mine. It's so beautiful—what I'd dreamed about for years. Vik and I had planned to start an international chain of boutiques someday. He was going to be my financial manager and I was going to be the designer queen. We used to talk about it often." Her smile was the saddest Rishi had ever seen. "Only it never happened."

"But it's happening now. And the rest of it will happen, too, if you keep that dream alive." He traced the outline of her lower lip with his thumb. "I could make it all come true for you."

"Most of it is the clichéd pie-in-the-sky. Besides, you've already done too much." She stood on tiptoes and placed a light kiss on his lips. "Thank you. I hope I can fulfill my end of the bargain—keep this business healthy."

"You will. And there's something else I want to discuss with you later." He didn't like to see the distress in her eyes, but he could do something about erasing it. Maybe it was that unexpected quality of vulnerability that had attracted him to her in the first place.

The other women he'd been involved with hadn't needed him, whereas Anjali did. He'd never before considered himself a protective sort of man, but now he wanted to do it all—for this one woman.

He was in love with Anjali. For the first time in forty-two years he could honestly say he was in love.

His mother would get a good chuckle out of that, he thought with an inward smile. She'd always warned him that love was a strange thing. She'd told him how, as a pretty young woman with a good nursing career ahead of her, she'd been offered love and marriage by at least two good-looking men. She'd turned down their offers and gone off in search of adventure and to answer her calling. Then she had gone against her devout Christian parents' wishes and married a Hindu.

She often said to Rishi, "You'll stumble into it when you least expect it."

He'd looked into his mother's twinkling gray eyes and laughed. "Mum, I'm over forty, in case you haven't noticed. If I haven't found it yet, it's bloody well never going to happen."

"Look what happened to me," she'd pointed out. "The Lord took your father, but years later he put another good man in my life." With that she'd sent her husband, Charles, an affectionate glance. Charles Mallory was an upstanding, solid man. Rishi was genuinely fond of his stepfather.

And now Rishi had *stumbled* into love. But convincing Anjali of that was going to be a major hurdle. Besides, he had no idea how she felt about him.

Chapter 26

Anjali lay with her head resting on Rishi's shoulder, wondering how she'd ended up in his bed again. She'd managed to keep away from his suite for an entire week despite his efforts to entice her. The temptation had been fierce. If it weren't for the loads of work at the store, she would have given in to the urge and let the future take care of itself.

Tonight had been a repeat of that other night. Rishi had been a tender and ardent lover. He'd offered her a glimpse of bliss again and again. He had shown her what physical love combined with emotional love could be. The only problem was he was in it for the short term. Very short.

He hadn't said when he was leaving, but it had to be soon. The store was on its feet and he'd done his part to make sure everything was running smoothly. Jeevan-kaka hadn't said anything so far either. Tomorrow was probably when the two men would make an announcement about their departure.

She dreaded it.

It hurt like hell to think Rishi would be leaving soon. But it didn't mean the end of the world, either. She'd survived the loneliness before and she'd survive it again.

"Why the frown?" Rishi's voice drew her back to the present. "Was it that bad?" He'd been lazily running his fingers up and down her arm.

"It was fabulous, and you know it," she said. "I didn't realize I was frowning."

"I thought you were contemplating how to let me down gently."

"Funny how we were both thinking the same thing."

"So you *were* planning on jilting me."

"No, I was wondering if you were going to say something like, 'It's been mah-velous knowing you, dah-ling. I'm returning to London tomorrow, so it's—'"

"I love you."

"—ta-ta for now—" She sat up, unmindful of the sheet sliding down to her naked waist. "What did you say?"

"I love you."

"You don't mean that."

His eyebrows snapped together. "I most certainly do."

"Well . . ." She'd hoped for it and dreamed about it, but now that he'd said it, she was speechless.

"Is that all you can say?" He folded his arms across his chest.

Pulling the sheet up to her chin, she took two deep breaths. "It's a little unexpected."

"After the two nights you've spent in my arms, it's still unexpected, Anju?" The scowl eased a little but he looked puzzled.

"Why are you so surprised at my reaction?" she said. "I thought you'd be telling me we could be friends and that if you happened to be in the U.S. on business in the future, and if we can make the time, we could sleep togeth—"

He reached over and clamped a hand across her mouth. "Marry me."

She caught his wrist and slowly lowered his hand. "Marry?"

Tugging on her hair, he gently urged her to settle back on the pillow. "Yes, marry me." He studied her face for a long moment. "You look like I just asked you to jump off the nearest cliff."

It hit her then, sending her brain into a tailspin. Love. Marriage. She knew he wasn't lying. Those eyes looked as sincere as anything she'd ever seen. He didn't seem like the kind of man who'd lie—at least not about something like this. And yet, despite the heart-busting euphoria, she couldn't really follow through with it.

Ordinarily, this would have been a dream come true: marry

the man she was giddy in love with, someone who'd come along when she'd least expected it. He was smart, good-looking, sophisticated, funny, and a dynamite lover. Was he a little too perfect?

When she didn't respond, he said, "We'd be good together. We're in the same sort of business. Since we both travel we could do it together most of the time. We could complement each other personally, professionally, in every way."

"Sounds delightful, but I . . . I can't marry you."

"Why?"

"I have obligations here. My parents can't run the store by themselves."

"They're more capable than you give them credit for, Anju," he said in rational tone.

"But now there are multiple departments and new employees and so much more floor area and merchandise," she pointed out. "Mom's bright and fashion oriented, but she's not into it as much as I am."

"I've thought about all that."

"When?"

"Since I fell in love with you that's all I've been thinking about, making plans for the future, seeing how you could expand your talents to other areas."

She threw him a wary look. "But my talents are needed here."

"I know that, but you could start designing clothes and accessories for our other stores in other countries."

"You mean your fancy boutiques will accept my humble designs?"

"They're not humble; they're very appealing and they're versatile enough to grab the attention of mainstream stores, the ones that sell standard western clothes."

She angled a puzzled look at him, the first faint stirrings of excitement kicking in. "You mean my clothes could make it on the international circuit?"

"I could make it happen for you."

"You'd do that for me, Rishi?"

"I'd do that and a hell of a lot more. I'd even move here if I could, but the bulk of my business is in London. Besides, the U.S. government makes it nearly impossible to gain permanent domicile in the States." He paused, giving her a moment for thought. "On the other hand, living in London as a British citizen's wife won't be a problem for you."

"I suppose so," she said, chewing on her lower lip. She'd known this relationship was complicated right from the beginning. It wouldn't come without its obstacles. No relationship was simple.

"I love you," he repeated. "I'm offering marriage, so you'll be my partner in every way. We can make your dream of having a chain of Silk & Sapphires boutiques come true. You and I," he said, drawing her close. "We can do everything you ever wanted to do." One suggestive eyebrow climbed up. "We could even . . . make a baby."

"Oh." Her wildest dreams could come true. And all of that was being offered by the man she was in love with. "Did you say baby?"

"I did."

"How are we going to make a baby at our age, much less raise it?"

"Like other parents in the world. Like your own parents." He pushed the hair off her face. "Did you ever think about having children?"

"Yes. Vik and I thought we'd get around to it when we had some money saved. We were young; we had plenty of time to have children. Or so we thought." She looked away. "Pipe dreams."

"This time around it needn't be. We could have a child right away. I know you'd make a superb mum."

"What do you base that on?"

"I've watched you interact with Nilesh and Sejal . . . and children in general. Didn't you tell me you took care of your brother often when he was a baby?"

A smile tilted her mouth. "I've done diaper and bottle duty quite a bit. He was a cute little devil despite spitting up and peeing on me. Nilesh is like a fungus: he grows on you eventually."

Rishi laughed. "He's grown into a rather likeable mushroom." He tweaked her nose. "You, on the other hand, darling, I happen to love."

"You're sure what you feel for me isn't lust?" she asked.

"Positive."

"Going for weeks without sex could make a man mistake one for the other, you know."

"No mistake here. I know you don't return my sentiments, but I jolly well plan to make you fall in love with me. I know this is egotistical on my part, but I'm a hard worker and I almost always get what I want."

She threw her arm around his neck. "You don't have to work hard; I'm already there."

"Are you saying what I think you're saying?"

She tugged his head down to touch hers. "That's what I'm saying."

"Then will you please say it clearly, for mercy's sake?"

"I love you."

He gave her a mock frown. "And when exactly were you planning to tell me?"

"Never, if you didn't reciprocate my feelings. No point in humiliating myself."

He kissed the tip of her nose. "You should know by now how I feel about you. I wouldn't have made love to you if I didn't care deeply. Sleeping with you isn't a casual pastime for me."

"That makes two of us."

"So, what's your answer, Miss Kapadia? I wouldn't mind if you decided to keep your maiden name like you did the first time. You'll have all the independence you want if you marry me."

"Sounds like a dream life . . ."

"Do I hear a *but* there?"

She gave him a helpless shrug. "This is all going too fast for me. I'm not prepared for this. Until two hours ago I was only thinking about how I was going to organize tomorrow's workload at the store. Now I have a marriage proposal. I have too many things on my plate . . . too many complications."

"Don't worry; I'll think of a way around those. It's my job to solve business problems. People pay me handsomely to do it."

He surprised her when he said in perfect Gujarati, *"Jaynoo kaam thaynoo thhaai."* Leave it to the expert.

Perhaps because she continued to look overwhelmed, he said, "Haven't I kept my promises so far?"

"You have, but . . . there's still . . . you know . . . Samantha."

"I made a clean break with Samantha."

She paused. "I'll accept that. However—"

"For now, just think about my proposal. You don't have to give me an instant answer."

"All right." Her stomach was bunched up in a tight ball.

"Come on, let's eat something first," he suggested. "Maybe some food will mellow your thoughts about marriage."

"I doubt that. I'm not even hungry."

"We've just had a fantastic workout and you haven't eaten a thing all day. I'm going to order something to be brought up." He picked up the leather-bound menu from the nightstand and handed it to her. "I'm going to have their broiled swordfish. What about you?" He smiled. "Should I think optimistically and order a bottle of champagne?"

"Not yet." She studied the menu. "I'll have a grilled cheese sandwich and decaf coffee."

"We'll forget the champagne for now." He put the menu back on the nightstand, all the while studying her expression. "Take all the time you want to think about my proposal. I don't want to rush you."

"Okay." She badly needed some private time to digest his proposal and reflect. She couldn't think straight when he was too close. So she slid out of bed and dragged the T-shirt he had lent her over her head. "Mind if I grab a quick shower?"

"Go right ahead. It'll be a while before our food arrives," he said, picking up the room phone.

She could feel his eyes following her. What was going through his mind? Was he wondering why she'd behaved the way she had? What woman on the wrong side of thirty-five would turn down such a dream of a man and the added fantasy of a business she'd always wanted?

While the hot water rained over her, she kept going over and over what Rishi had just said, but she couldn't think of a way to accept his proposal and still remain active in the business. London was too damn far, and he was constantly on the move. She had her own work. Ironically, Silk & Sapphires, the thing that had brought them together, would likely be the very thing to keep them apart.

And then there was that other matter—as troublesome as the first, if not more. Although he'd said his affair with Samantha was over, it was unclear whether or not Samantha still had a place in his life. Was she still living in his house? Would their business relationship continue in the unforeseen future? He hadn't said a word about it when he'd proposed.

It had all happened so abruptly that it had caught her by surprise, making it impossible to ask the more practical questions. Now, very slowly, the relevant issues were beginning to surface. And Samantha was a significant relevant issue.

Minutes later, when she came out with a towel tucked around herself and her hair still damp, she found him in the sitting room, talking on his cell phone. She stood behind the partly open bedroom door and observed him. He had his trousers on but no shirt. He was pacing the floor in bare feet.

She was tempted to sneak up from behind and throw her arms around him, but the conversation sounded like business, so she refrained from following through on her impulse. He had on that familiar intense look and his tone was crisp and authoritative. He was all business when he was like that.

Her stomach rumbled, reminding her she was hungry after all. She wondered if their food had arrived yet. A quick glance around the sitting room through the crack in the door showed no sign of it.

She turned around and went back to the bathroom to dry her hair and fix her face. After putting on her slightly rumpled pantsuit and sandals, she returned to the door and opened it fully this time. He was still on the phone. But he noticed her presence and motioned to her to sit on the couch. He joined her there and hooked an arm around her while he talked.

She knew it was his way of including her in his life. His conversation continued for several more minutes. She waited patiently—understood the pressures of work.

He handled work with the same calm efficiency he reserved for everything else. She had yet to see him go completely berserk over any situation. Even when his most valued employee had taken ill unexpectedly and Rishi had to rush to take care of the emergency, he'd gone about it in the most rational manner.

When the conversation finally ended, he put the phone on the coffee table and turned to her. "Sorry, love, but that was important." He explained to her about the new consulting project in California. "I'll have to fly out to the West Coast very soon. I'll be gone for two or three days."

"I completely understand."

"That's another reason why I think you're so good for me. You understand the demands of business." He nuzzled her neck. "Smells nice. It's not your usual scent, but it'll do for now."

"I had to manage with the hotel's supplies."

"But you look just as beautiful." He wiggled his brows at her. "Want to go back to bed?"

"You have a one-track mind, Rishi Shah."

"That's why you love me." He grinned at her, the dimple appearing in his cheek. He was irresistible when he looked like that.

"You're such a good bullshitter. No wonder you manage to charm the tusks off those Indian elephants."

He laughed. "And those elephants aren't exactly congenial, I'll have you know." In an instant his expression turned nostalgic. "That reminds me of something. I should take you on a safari to Gir Forest in Gujarat."

"Safari?"

"Seeing the wild cats in their natural habitat is an extraordinary experience. There's nothing like it in the world."

"I can see you still love Gujarat very much."

"It's my childhood home. I go back to the farm and spend time with Jeevan-kaka and Chandrika-kaki whenever I get a chance. I know you'll come to love it, too." He studied her face. "Did you think about what I said earlier?"

"Hmm."

"I had a feeling you wanted a little time to yourself. It's the only reason I didn't join you in the shower."

"I'm still deliberating."

In response he curled a hand around the nape of her neck and kissed her, thoroughly and competently. "That ought to help in making a decision," he murmured against her mouth. "By the way, they say a Gir safari can be an incredible honeymoon adventure."

She chuckled. "Lions and leopards wandering into the honeymoon suite."

His cell phone started to ring, interrupting them. Rishi apologized to her again and picked it up.

His voice came out in a surprised murmur. "Samantha!"

Chapter 27

Anjali stiffened and pulled away from Rishi the instant she realized it was his girlfriend on the phone. It had the effect of ice cubes sliding down her back.

His expression told her Samantha's call was important. He'd told Anjali he had made a clean break, and yet his girlfriend was calling him at this hour of the night?

Rishi rose to his feet and paced in his usual fashion as he listened and spoke into the phone by turns. "So you got over your temper tantrum . . . I'm glad . . . No, Samantha, I mean that . . . I understand that part as well . . ." He paused. "Where are you now?" He waited to let Samantha speak. "Don't be silly. Of course I care," he said at one point.

Ah, so Samantha had thrown an angry fit, had she? Anjali mused. Interesting. Rishi had made it sound casual, like he and Samantha had separated on amicable terms. And he'd just admitted he cared.

"How critical, Samantha?" he asked. He listened for a long minute to Samantha's explanation of whatever it was.

Wishing she could hear both ends of the conversation, Anjali sat in her corner, watching Rishi's expression—knitted brows, eyes on the floor, as he walked up and down again and again. That was the look he usually had when he was on a business call. And yet something in his concerned, soothing tone told Anjali this was personal. Very personal.

The call lasted over ten minutes. It obviously had something to do with money. And Anjali began to wonder about it. If Rishi had truly broken off with his girlfriend like he claimed, why was he discussing her private finances? Why was he so solicitous in his attitude?

The jolt of jealousy that ripped through her was startling. She'd never considered herself the catty type. She'd had plenty of doubts for sure. What normal woman in love wouldn't? But corrosive jealousy? Was she capable of it?

"I'll ask my accountant and solicitor to look into it," he told Samantha. "You'll probably hear from them in a day or two."

Finally he shut off the phone and turned to Anjali. "Sorry, sweetheart. I had to take the call."

"Of course you did," she said. "It's your girlfriend."

He gave her a measured look. "Ex-girlfriend."

"Same thing."

"Definitely not."

"Former girlfriends don't usually call at nearly two in the morning."

"It's nearly seven in London," he reminded her.

"Still a bit early to call an ex-boyfriend, don't you think?" Anjali's eyebrows rose. "Unless of course she called to say she's missing you."

His silence said it all.

"Are you missing her, too?"

"Don't tell me you're—" His eyes widened. "Are you actually . . . jealous, Anju?"

"What do you think?"

"But you have no reason to be," he insisted.

"Oh yeah? Here you are, supposedly proposing marriage to me, and your girlfriend from London calls with some cockamamie excuse just so she can hear your voice first thing in the morning."

"That's absurd. It was a business call."

Anger replaced jealousy in an instant. "Don't insult my intelligence, Rishi."

"She's having some cash flow problems because a few of her large accounts went to her competition recently. She asked if I could help her with her predicament."

"Predicament," she repeated blandly. "Sure."

"All right, damn it! Yes, she said she missed me. Is that what you want me to admit? It was just a friendly remark. A friend missing a friend."

"I also asked you if *you* missed *her*, Rishi."

"Not in the least."

Anjali pulled in a breath, trying to bring her simmering emotions under control. "Assuming she's genuinely in financial trouble, can't she go to a bank for help?"

"She could, but banks take an awful lot of time to process loans. With me she can get help quicker."

"How convenient." She angled a snide glance at him. "Do you specialize in rescuing women in dire financial straits?"

He gave a deep sigh. "Look, Anju, you're exhausted and hungry. You'll see this differently after you've eaten something." He sat on the couch again and reached for her. "Come here, darling. Let's talk this over rationally."

She scooted away to the far end of the couch. "All this time, while I was considering your proposal, I was pondering mainly whether your work and travel could ever mesh with mine. I certainly spent some time thinking about Samantha as well. But I was more concerned about my responsibilities here in New Jersey."

"As you should be," he allowed.

"But now I'm beginning to wonder more about your personal life. Every time your former girlfriends call, you're probably going to run to them?"

"You're jumping to conclusions once again. This is an unusual circumstance."

"Sure it is."

"I can't just ignore a plea for help from Samantha. We did stay together for a while."

"As if I need reminding," Anjali sniffed. "From what I gather, Samantha is a beautiful, successful woman—"

"So are you," he interjected.

"—and yet you're asking a plain woman like me to marry you. It makes me wonder."

"About what?"

"If you want a real marriage. I could just be the convenient little Indian wife who could give you a child and be a mild asset to you in the merchandising area, while you go around the world and . . ."

"Sleep with every attractive woman I come across?" His eyes turned to ice as he completed her sentence. "Is that what you were going to say?"

She didn't respond.

"I'm amazed at you, Anju. Don't you know me a little better than that by now?"

"I've known you all of four months. During that time, you've had one trip back to London. I don't exactly know what happened between Samantha and you then. As far as I know she's still shacked up in that townhouse of yours."

His jaw tightened visibly, a mark of suppressed anger. "She moved out of the house while I was still in London—right after I told her we had no future together. I didn't even know where she'd disappeared to until now. She just now informed me she's staying with a friend while she's looking for another flat."

"Then why is she still calling you?"

"Like I said, it's business. She handles all my advertising and public relations." He leaned back against the sofa cushion and shut his eyes briefly, like he was too tired to argue. "She means nothing to me anymore, Anju."

"I find that hard to believe."

"I assure you she and I will simply be two individuals who work with each other occasionally."

Anjali gave it some thought. Something about Samantha's call was very troubling. Why had the woman called about business when she knew Rishi would be sleeping, unless she suspected something and had deliberately timed it that way?

But despite her reservations Anjali wanted to believe him. Earlier, while in the shower, she'd tried to banish the tiny, niggling doubts. Until that phone call she'd almost succeeded, too. But now, Samantha encroaching on their lives had gone from a possibility to a certainty. Instinct told her Samantha wasn't going to let go of him easily. It wasn't something Anjali was sure she could handle. And with the kind of magnetic man Rishi was, there would likely be other women in the future.

All at once she was plagued with doubts. It had been one shock after another on top of a very exhausting and emotional day. Was she simply overreacting?

After a quiet minute he glanced at her. "Are you still angry with me?"

She rose to her feet. "I don't know."

"Does that mean you don't even want to consider my proposal?"

"I said I don't know. It's a lot to think about." She picked up her purse. "I want to go home, Rishi."

"At least eat what you ordered before you go. You're going to collapse from starvation, Anju."

"I'll be fine," she assured him. "I thrive on adrenaline."

"As you wish." He rose to his feet. "I'll drive you home, then."

"No need. I'll call a cab."

His annoyance seemed to return. "Stop acting childish, Anju. I'm going to drive you home." He must have noticed her expression. "Don't argue." He picked up the phone and instructed room service to leave the food outside his door.

During the drive home Anju remained silent. She could sense the coiled tension humming inside Rishi. He drove without a word, but she could tell he was fuming. He was a man of action, a pragmatic and organized man who planned and plotted and executed his ideas with flawless precision. This time around, precision and timing weren't cooperating, and he didn't like it. Well, too bad.

For once, why couldn't he understand *her* feelings? He wanted everything his way. He wanted her to give up her life in the U.S. and move to London. His life was to remain the same while hers would turn topsy-turvy. On top of that he wanted to maintain contact with his ex-girlfriend, and yet he expected Anju to understand and accept it. Exactly how reasonable was that?

Maybe despite her American ways she was still an old-fashioned Indian woman who looked on total fidelity and trust as the cornerstones of marriage. Even if he wasn't going to sleep with his ex, it still wasn't right. How would he feel if she continued in "a friend missing a friend" relationship with Kip? Surely he'd have a problem with that?

He couldn't have it both ways. If he wanted to marry her, he'd have to cut off all ties with Samantha. It was the only way she could accept his proposal. And if he refused to give up Samantha? Then what? He'd break Anjali's heart, that's what.

Oh well . . . everything about his proposal had been too good to be true anyway. She'd known there had to be a catch. And now she'd found it.

When they arrived at her house, he walked her to the front door like he'd done the other night. Except this time she didn't wait for him to kiss her.

"I'll ring you to make sure you eat and get some rest."

"No need for that." She was in no mood for caring gestures.

"I'll ring, anyway."

She bid him a terse good night, let herself into the house, and went directly upstairs to her room.

She could feel her heart beginning to splinter already.

Chapter 28

Anjali lay on her bed and fumed and wept alternately. When the tears and rage receded she was still undecided about her feelings, and what she should do. Meanwhile she'd developed a tension headache. And nausea. Rishi was right. She was just about ready to collapse from hunger and exhaustion.

At the moment she needed some aspirin, but if she took it on an empty stomach it would only aggravate the nausea. She had to eat something first. Changing into comfortable pajamas and bedroom slippers, she took the aspirin in her fist and padded downstairs to the kitchen to look for food.

She found the café's leftovers in a foil-wrapped platter in the fridge. Carefully she lifted some of Anwar's grilled vegetable finger sandwiches onto a plate. After filling a glass with apple juice, she took the meal to the table and sat down to eat.

Now that she'd vented her emotions, a strange numbness was settling in. It felt like a fog descending—gray, damp, heavy. She'd probably stay awake all night and suffer for it the next day. Hopefully there'd be plenty of customers and she wouldn't have a single second to nurse her heartache.

While she nibbled on her sandwiches she heard footsteps. It was probably Nilesh, looking for a snack as always, she concluded, and continued to eat. Hearing her name, she turned her head.

Jeevan-kaka stood in the doorway in rumpled white pajamas.

A sigh escaped her. That's all she needed to round off her evening: her bossy uncle prying into her personal life.

"Jeevan-kaka, why are you up this late?" she asked him.

He shuffled toward her and pulled out a chair. "I was so tired earlier that I went to bed without eating. Now my stomach is hurting." He stopped and leaned forward to study her face. "What happened to your eyes?"

"Soap got in while I was washing my face."

"So why don't you use Indian herbal soap instead of some commercial brand with chemicals?"

"What a clever idea," she quipped. But he looked so old and tired he touched a chord of sympathy in her. "I'll fix you something to eat."

"Can you make some *masala* milk?"

"Sure." She set the milk in a pan on the stove and started adding the spices. While the milk warmed up, she turned to her uncle. "Are you feeling all right?"

"Just exhaustion and indigestion. All this excitement is too much for an old man like me."

"The past few weeks have been hectic," she agreed, observing him carefully. It wasn't just the wrinkles and the weight loss. He looked beat, as if he'd been fighting a long, losing battle. The way he clutched his stomach sometimes, or clenched his teeth, he looked like he might be in pain. "Are you sure you're not hurting or something?"

He shrugged and looked away.

"Jeevan-kaka, is something wrong with you?" she demanded. He gave her a wary look. "Why are you asking?"

"You don't look well. Since the day you arrived I've been wondering about you. Rishi seems extremely protective of you . . . like he's worried about you or something."

"Rishi is fond of me, Anju."

"That doesn't explain why he changes the subject when I ask about you." She gave him a pointed look. "It's okay if you don't want to tell me, but you should at least tell Dad. He's your brother. He cares about you."

"I care about your dad, too, *beta*. You know I raised him and all my brothers and sisters after our parents died."

She stirred the milk as it came to a slow, frothy boil, watched the spirals of steam rise and perfume the air. "Yeah, I've heard about how you single-handedly nurtured your siblings." *And terrorized them in the process.*

As if he'd read her thoughts, he sighed. "I know I was strict with them." He stared at his hands for a beat. "I regret that sometimes."

"You do?" She'd never heard that tone in his voice: remorseful, despondent. It was hard to imagine the word *regret* existed in his vocabulary.

"When our parents died, we were all young, Anju. I was the oldest and I had to take care of all of them. They were children and naughty sometimes. I had to use strict discipline to make sure that they went to school and studied and made a good life for themselves." He rubbed his eyes, looking more spent than ever.

Anjali had never had a heart-to-heart talk with her uncle. She hadn't considered the fact that he was scarcely more than a child himself when he'd been saddled with four younger siblings and a large business to run. What a burden for a boy who was merely twenty years old. At the time, her two aunts were teenagers, her father was eight, and Naren-kaka was a toddler. The only way Jeevan-kaka could probably fulfill his responsibilities was by becoming a control freak.

"I'm beginning to see your point," she admitted. "You wanted to make sure they all stayed on the straight and narrow."

"Exactly."

"If you love your siblings so much, then you know they love you right back. It's all the more reason why you should talk to Dad if there's something wrong with you. Don't you think he has a right to know?"

"I will tell him before I leave for India."

"When is that?"

He shrugged again. "Next week . . . maybe."

She strained the milk into a cup and put it in front of him. In the light coming from the multibulb overhead fixture, his skin looked parched and mottled.

"Jeevan-kaka," she said softly, "why don't you tell me what's wrong?"

"There is not much to tell, *beta*," he said on a sigh that sounded a lot like defeat. "I have cancer."

Anjali drew in a ragged breath. "Not *much* to tell?" He'd made the announcement about as calmly as going on a short vacation.

"I have advanced colon cancer. My doctor says I have maybe one more year . . . maybe less."

"How long have you known?"

"About two years."

Anjali pulled out the chair next to his and sat down. "And you never told us?" No wonder her uncle looked like hell.

"What is the use of telling? Everyone will become sad unnecessarily."

"But that's part of being a family. Don't you understand?"

"Of course I understand," he said crossly. "Why do you think I sacrificed my own education and gave it to my brothers and sisters? How do you think they all got college educations when I got little more than high school? Why did I work day and night to make sure my brothers got into good businesses and my sisters got good husbands?"

"Okay . . . okay, I'm sorry," she said, patting his arm. "I didn't mean to preach. But when Dad finds out you've been hiding this from him for two years, he's going to explode."

He took a cautious sip of his milk and made a face. "Too much cardamom."

"Oh, stop complaining." She angled a frown at him. "It can't be all that bad."

"You used to be scared of me at one time." He eyed her suspiciously. "You have changed."

"It's called growing up," she said. "And don't try to change the subject. How can you be casual about something as serious as cancer and imminent death?"

"Everyone must die of something. How long can anybody expect to live?"

He had a point, but it didn't diminish her concern. "Tell me everything about it. And you have to promise you'll tell Mom and Dad first thing tomorrow."

Taking another sip of his milk, he nodded. "Why are you so angry?"

"I'm not angry; I'm distressed. Now I know why you've given up spicy food and your multiple cups of tea and everything else you used to enjoy."

Jeevan exhaled very slowly. "Spicy food does not agree with me anymore. For many years I was suffering digestion problems. I think the cancer was probably growing at that time."

"Probably." Guilt was starting to nip at her. While she was sitting here, feeling sorry for herself because some guy was toying with her heart, her uncle was grappling with a death warrant. "Are you on medication now?" she asked him gently.

"Not much at this time. Just something to keep the pain under control. I went through surgery, chemotherapy, radiation, and all kinds of treatment in India. Rishi even forced me to see a specialist in London."

"Do you have to wear one of those . . . bags?"

"You mean a colostomy bag?" He shook his head.

He seemed reluctant to discuss it, so she let it go. It was a delicate subject.

"I tried everything, including ayurvedic and homeopathic medicines," he continued. "But it kept spreading to other parts."

He must have noticed her look of despair, because he raised a hand and patted her arm with unexpected tenderness. She'd never known her uncle to be soft in his touch. Her throat constricted.

"Why are you looking so sad? I am an old man," he reminded her. "My life has been very good. I have no complaints if I die now."

"And Rishi is your added blessing?" When Jeevan looked at her quizzically, she nodded. "He told me everything: the fire, his father's passing, and your continued generosity toward him."

"He is a good boy." Jeevan smiled. "A special blessing."

Too bad he turned out to be her special headache, she reflected, but decided not to bad-mouth Rishi to his staunchest champion. Instead she said, "Dad and Naren-kaka and your sisters are going to be devastated when they hear about your illness."

He sipped some more milk. "I am planning on telling your father and Naren before I go back to India. After I reach home I will telephone my sisters in England."

"Don't wait till the last minute. Do it right away." She took a deep breath to keep her crumbling emotions under control. "This might be the last time we'll be seeing you?"

"God will decide that. This is why I wanted to come and help Mohan and Usha and you. When your father telephoned me, I thought I might as well help him and do something useful before I die. Also, this was a good chance to spend some time with my brothers and their families."

She touched his hand. "Thank you for coming to our rescue. We couldn't have done it without you. You've been more than generous." And to think she hadn't wanted him to come, hadn't wanted him in any way involved in their lives. By this time next year he could be dead.

"Why are you thanking me? Most of the help came from Rishi. He is the one who plans everything and offers advice." He narrowed his eyes at her, clearly forgetting his own problems for the moment. "Rishi told me he was taking you for a celebration dinner. Where did you go?"

She gnawed on her lip. "We didn't."

"Why?"

She wasn't about to discuss the earlier fiasco with her old uncle. It was too private, too painful—and complicated. She was having difficulty sorting out her feelings herself. So many deep needs, so many doubts, and so many responsibilities to so many people.

The last thing an ailing old man needed was to know his niece had been struck by a case of jealousy and heartbreak, and that the cause of her pain was his protégé, a man he obviously loved and admired very much. Besides, compared with Jeevan-kaka's problems, hers were trivial.

He remained silent with his brows raised, clearly waiting for an answer, so she replied, "No particular reason."

"But you just came back from somewhere. Rishi drove you home, didn't he?"

So he'd heard the sound of Rishi's car and then her coming home. Maybe it was time Jeevan-kaka learned the truth. It was bound to come out sooner or later. "We went out . . . talked a bit . . . but we didn't have a chance to eat dinner."

"Why not?"

"Rishi's . . . uh . . . girlfriend called him unexpectedly."

Jeevan-kaka's bushy brows descended in a scowl. "Rishi didn't tell me that Samantha was still in contact with him."

"I don't think he was expecting her call." Rishi's surprise at hearing his girlfriend's voice was definitely genuine. Anjali had sensed the instant tension in him the moment he'd picked up the phone.

"Did you hear their conversation?" The scowl was fiercer now—Jeevan-kaka's trademark look.

"I was there, but I obviously couldn't hear her end of the conversation. Samantha was *supposedly* asking for his help with money." The pungent sarcasm was hard to keep out of her voice. "And he readily offered it to her."

"It doesn't mean anything."

"Wake up, Jeevan-kaka. If he didn't have some feelings for her, why would he let her take advantage of him like that? She still has a hold on him . . . for whatever reason." She wondered if it was love or just sex, like her own relationship with Kip had been. No matter what, it was still bothersome.

"Samantha is not suitable for Rishi," Jeevan informed her with supreme confidence.

It was so typical Jeevan-kaka that she couldn't help chuckling. "Does Rishi agree with that opinion?" She finished the last bite of her sandwich then washed down the aspirin with juice.

He snorted at her remark. "Rishi knows she is unsuitable. He told me that."

She noticed his milk was almost gone. "Do you want any-thing to eat?"

He shook his head. "He also told me he was breaking up with her."

"He tells you about his personal life?" Why would Rishi tell a conservative old man all about his love life?

"Oh yes. He is like my son." Jeevan smiled at her unexpect-edly. "He also told me he was going to ask you to marry him."

"Told you that, too, huh?"

"Yes, Anju, he told me everything," said Jeevan. "You like him, don't you? If you marry him, you will be happy. You two are perfect for one another."

Her eyes narrowed suspiciously. "Was it you who suggested he ask me to marry him?" She wouldn't put it past the old man to coerce Rishi into taking pity on his poor, lonely, widowed niece—offer her marriage and put her out of her misery.

"No, *beta*. Rishi is an extremely independent boy. He told me he was interested in you and that he was going to talk to you about marriage." He raised his hands in a gesture that looked curiously like surrender. "All I want is to see everyone happy."

"Well, he did."

"He asked you to marry him?"

"Uh-huh."

Jeevan-kaka's eyes took on a hopeful gleam. "You said yes?"

"I didn't say anything." She recalled that scene in bed earlier, when Rishi had made his unusual proposal. Her throat and chest began to tighten again as she remembered every word, every expression that had passed between Rishi and her. Darn it! She couldn't cry in Jeevan-kaka's presence. It was bad enough that he thought all women were weaklings and needed a man to take care of them. She didn't want to prove him right.

"Why?" he demanded.

The tears started to well up despite her best efforts to sup-press them. "Before we could discuss it in detail, Samantha called."

Jeevan-kaka reached across and took her hand. His felt

rough and hard and cold. "He does not love that woman, *beta*. He wants to marry only you."

"But from what I gathered she won't give him up." Grabbing a paper napkin with her free hand, Anjali dabbed her eyes. She wasn't usually such a crybaby, but her tear ducts seemed to be working overtime tonight. In fact, she'd been weeping a lot lately.

"That is not true," he argued. "One thing I will tell you, Anju, Rishi does not lie or cheat. If he told you that he has no relationship with that woman anymore, then he does not."

"How can you be sure of that? He could even have other girl-friends and you'd never know." For a clever old man her uncle was hopelessly naïve when it came to love and sex and relation-ships in the modern world.

"Trust me, Anju. I have known Rishi since he was born. He is a very honorable fellow."

"I don't want to talk about him anymore, Jeevan-kaka." After blowing her nose noisily, Anjali tossed the balled-up nap-kin in the trash can. "I know I'm stuck with him to some extent because he's my business partner, but I don't want to have much to do with him on a personal level."

"Anju."

Startled, Anjali turned her head toward the doorway once again. "Mom!" Oh great, now her mother was here to grill her. Soon her dad would show up and then all three elders would in-sist on offering unsolicited advice.

"Shouldn't you be sleeping?" she asked her mother.

Usha ignored Anjali's question. Instead she looked suspi-ciously at her brother-in-law and then at Anjali. "What's go-ing on?"

"Nothing. Jeevan-kaka and I are having a conversation." An-jali withdrew her hand from Jeevan's.

Usha glanced at the kitchen clock. "An odd hour for a con-versation."

"I needed something to eat and Jeevan-kaka needed milk, so we talked while we ate."

"Why didn't you wake me up?" Usha studied the crumbs on

Anjali's plate. "I could have fixed you something more substantial than junk food."

"Mom, I'm not a kid. I wanted junk food. Besides, I'm capable of fixing a simple meal." She tried to smile, but the tears were still there, the shakiness in her voice lingering.

"If it was just a casual chat, why are you crying?" Usha asked.

"It's been an emotional day. The strain from the last few months seems to be catching up with me tonight."

"Don't lie to me, Anjali Kapadia."

Usha's tart rebuke brought back memories of her teenage years, when Anjali used to try to pull a fast one on her mother. The way Usha was glaring at her now, Anjali felt like an errant teenager again. She couldn't lie to her shrewd mother convincingly then and she couldn't do it now.

"I'm not lying, Mom. Jeevan-kaka and I were really having a conversation."

"Did you have a nice dinner with Rishi?"

"I didn't have dinner with him, period."

"Why not?"

Anjali rose to her feet and placed her plate and glass in the sink. "Why don't you ask Jeevan-kaka? He knows all about it."

"Does he now?" Usha looked at her brother-in-law like she was seeing him for the first time.

But then Anjali, too, had glimpsed a side of Jeevan-kaka tonight that she hadn't before. Her mom was in for a surprise.

"I'm sorry." She squeezed Usha's shoulder. "I just don't feel like explaining it all over again."

Usha's expression softened. "Are you okay, dear?"

She shook her head. "If you must know the truth, I'm not okay at the moment."

"You poor child, what—"

"It's all right, Mom," Anjali cut in. "I'm not going to fall apart like I did some years ago. I just need a little time . . . by myself."

Usha's face was distraught as she patted Anjali's cheek. "Can't even talk about it to your mother?"

"Maybe in a day or two. Not right now." Anjali headed for the door. "Jeevan-kaka will explain it. While he's at it, why don't you ask him to tell you about his own problems?" She tossed her uncle a meaningful glance before striding out of the kitchen.

She heard her mother say in her schoolmarm voice, "Jeevan-bhai, you better tell me everything. What's going on with Anju and that boy? I will not tolerate anyone hurting my daughter."

Chapter 29

Rishi wheeled the food cart into his suite and sat down to eat his solitary meal. The fish had turned cold, with the juices beginning to congeal around the edges. The salad looked unappetizing. He managed to eat a few bites, then pushed the cart away. His hunger had vanished. He didn't even want to look at the cold grilled cheese sandwich Anjali had ordered.

He locked the door to the suite and prepared for bed. However, sleep wasn't likely to come any time soon. His mind was consumed with Anju.

He could only hope she'd eat something at home. With the grim mood she was in when he drove her back, he doubted that she'd eat or sleep. He still couldn't understand why she was so upset over a simple business transaction. How many times had he told her that Samantha meant nothing to him?

And for mercy's sake, why was Anju still analyzing his job and hers to death? Hadn't he promised her that he'd take care of all the logistics? In this day and age, intercontinental business was as easy as hopping on a plane or picking up the phone or booting up a computer. Didn't he himself do it all the time? It wasn't as if London and New Jersey were worlds apart. The distance wasn't much more than that between New Jersey and California.

And damn Samantha for calling at the most inopportune moment. If she'd just waited until she'd started her working day, everything would have been okay. He'd have found a way to explain things to Anju in a rational manner about what was going on with Samantha. As a businesswoman with financial problems of her own, Anju would have understood. But the unexpected call at that particular instant, when Anju was seriously mulling over his surprise proposal, was a disaster.

Bad timing was what it was.

Something struck him in that instant. Timing. Good heavens! Could Samantha have deliberately called him at that hour, wondering if she'd catch him with another woman in his bed?

Suddenly he began to wonder if there was more to the call than a plea for help. Was this Samantha's perverted form of revenge? She'd been livid when he'd broken up with her. She'd more or less accused him of having another woman in the U.S. Now all of a sudden she'd sounded rational and almost . . . forgiving.

Her abrupt overnight move from his house had left him feeling uneasy, especially because he knew her well. He'd seen her operate on both a business and personal level. Samantha was tenacious—and just a hair short of devious. It wasn't like her to do anything without a motive, or walk away from anything she wanted badly without a fight.

Was this her way of thrusting herself back into his life in the most insidious way, by playing on his guilt and his sense of loyalty? As far as he knew, her business was thriving. So why was she suddenly experiencing problems?

Had she planned all this the morning she'd packed up and left him? Or had she really deluded herself into thinking he'd miss her so much that he'd regret his decision and welcome her back with open arms? Crying financial problems could be just a ploy, a way to keep her claws firmly inside his skin. A business loan could bind them for years. Could Anju have sensed the deceit before he had? Woman's intuition?

If Samantha was indeed up to dirty tricks, she couldn't have plotted her revenge better.

He thrust his hands into his pockets and paced the length of the room. He hadn't been this conflicted and frustrated in years—not since he'd been in a hospital bed with a shattered leg, wondering whether he'd lose a limb.

But all was not lost yet. He had resources, more resources than a lot of men, at his fingertips. If Samantha was plotting to make a fool out of him, he could stop her right now. And he would. One way or another he'd find out the truth.

Picking up his phone, he pressed the button for his solicitor, Arthur Rush. Arthur's secretary answered, so it was a minute before he got Arthur on the line. Rishi didn't waste time on polite talk. "Arthur, I need a favor. Could you discreetly check into Samantha Harrington's finances for me?"

Naturally Arthur was cautiously curious. "Any particular reason?" Arthur also knew about Rishi's relationship with Samantha.

"She called a little while ago asking for financial help because of cash flow problems, but I'm almost positive her business is doing extraordinarily well. Before I commit myself to loaning her money, I want to make sure her claim is genuine."

"Uh-huh," said Arthur, in his stolid solicitor voice. "Are you very sure you want to do this?"

"Without a doubt."

"It is highly confidential information, Rishi. It's not easy to obtain."

"I realize that. But it's extremely important, or I wouldn't have asked you. Try your best, Arthur." Rishi paused. "And keep it discreet."

"I'll see what I can do," replied Arthur. "Give me a day or so."

"Thanks, Arthur. You can ring Harry if you need to," said Rishi, referring to his accountant. He shut off the phone and headed for the bedroom. Despite his wide-awake state of mind, he needed to rest, rejuvenate. Exhaustion was slowing him down, and his knee ached.

Resisting the temptation to call Anjali yet again, he forced himself to go to bed. She hadn't answered the two voice mail messages he'd left her within the past ten minutes.

It was probably best to give her time to simmer down, let her sort it out on her own.

When the bedside phone in his room began to ring, Rishi groped for it in the dark. Disoriented, he couldn't locate it right away. Damn it, he'd hardly had a chance to close his eyes.

The clock read 6:18 A.M. It couldn't be Arthur this soon. It couldn't be Anju either, not after the way she'd been sulking. It was probably Samantha again, whining about her finances.

"I wish you'd stop ringing at such ungodly hours, Samantha," he said wearily.

He grimaced at the familiar voice on the phone. It wasn't Samantha.

"This is not your girlfriend." Usha's words were clear and rapier sharp. "This is Anju's mother."

He sat up in bed. "Oh, Auntie, I'm sorry. I . . . It's been one of those nights."

"No doubt."

Hurriedly gathering his wits about him, he said, "What can I do for you?"

"Some explaining, that's what. Mohan and I need to meet with you. Jeevan-bhai will be sitting in on the meeting."

"First thing in the morning, Auntie. I'll stop by as early as you'd like." He could hear the suppressed anger in Usha's voice. He'd come to know her rather well in the past few months.

"It is morning now. I want to discuss this right away."

Bloody hell! She wasn't angry; she was livid. "All right, then. I'll come over now."

"No, you stay right there. We'll be coming to your hotel room. I don't want Anju or Nilesh to hear any of this."

"Yes, ma'am." He let out a troubled sigh. "My room is 505."

He replaced the receiver and shot out of bed. He had just enough time to brush his teeth, shave, and get dressed—if he hurried. There was no time for a shower.

It was bad enough that Anju was enraged at him, but now he'd gone and compounded a difficult situation by incurring the wrath of one more woman, Usha Kapadia.

Instead of the pleasantly exciting night he'd envisioned, a night of celebration, marriage proposal, hours of making love with Anju, and hopefully waking up with her, it had turned out to be one unexpected and unpleasant surprise after another.

For a man who prided himself on his pragmatism and sense of balance, he had completely lost control of the situation. *Jolly good work, Shah.*

He pushed the food cart out the door and into the hallway, then called the front desk to have it removed at once. Going to the kitchenette, he poured himself a glass of wine and drank it down in three gulps. It was too early in the day for alcohol, but he needed some fortification to face the Kapadias. He'd need every bit of his strength to defend himself.

He was well aware of the damage each one of them could inflict as individuals, so when they joined forces and put up a united front, they were sure to be formidable.

Minutes later, when he opened the door to his suite and took one look at the grim faces of the three Kapadias, he knew there was trouble ahead.

Usha looked neat and proper as always. But her expression was an entirely different matter. If looks could kill, Rishi would have turned into a tiny mound of charred remains by now. She glanced about the room, taking in the furnishings . . . or perhaps looking for clues. Very little escaped those discerning eyes. Mohan looked gray and exhausted. Jeevan-kaka appeared more haggard than he had a few hours ago. Obviously Anju's emotional state had been worse than he'd thought for her family to be this upset.

He invited them in with a polite nod. "Please come in. Sit down."

Mohan took a seat on the couch and Usha sat beside him, her back held rigid. Jeevan found the nearest chair and sank into it, looking relieved at being able to rest. Rishi wondered if the old man had lost even more weight within the past few days. He'd been eating next to nothing. Clearly the illness was spreading quickly. How long would this continue before he succumbed to it? Rishi didn't want to think about it.

He quickly forced himself away from his thoughts and faced his guests. "Is there anything I can get for you folks? Tea or coffee? Breakfast?"

"No, thank you," snapped Usha. "We're not here to socialize."

Mohan ran his fingers through his hair and shook his head. He must have been raking his hair for a while from the way it was standing at attention. Jeevan-kaka motioned to say no, too.

Rishi's immediate instinct was to put a hand on Jeevan's shoulder. "Are you all right? You look a little . . ."

Jeevan gave Rishi a resigned look. "No need for being so secretive, *beta*. They know about my cancer now."

Rishi eyed the other two. "I see." He wondered how that news, too, had happened to leak out on this, the worst of nights. Everything was beginning to come to a head at once. It had to be one of those cursed new moon nights or something, *Amavasya*, when some of the undesirable events occurred, sometimes in multiples.

"Naturally we are upset that Jeevan-bhai didn't see fit to tell us earlier," said Mohan, eyeing his brother with a mix of irritation and sadness.

"I tried to convince Jeevan-kaka that he should share the news with all his family," Rishi said. "But he felt he wasn't ready for it yet." He patted Jeevan's arm. "And I respect his wishes."

"You could have at least given us a hint, Rishi," scolded Usha. "We're family."

"It wasn't my place to do it, Auntie. It was Jeevan-kaka's wish to share that when he wanted to."

Jeevan made an imperious and dismissive gesture with his hands. "Enough about me. We have more important things to discuss."

Usha cleared her throat. "Yes, we do."

"Sit down, Rishi," ordered Jeevan. "Mohan and Usha are worried about Anju. I have explained some things to them, but they want to talk to you in person."

Rishi sat down in the only chair left in the sitting room. "All right, then. Let's talk."

As expected, Usha came straight to the point. "Is it true that you proposed to Anju?"

"Yes."

"Why?"

"Because I'm in love with her, Auntie. I believe I could . . . make her happy."

Usha's eyebrow flew up. "Did you invite your British girlfriend to live with you because you believed you could make her happy, too?"

Despite her deliberate sarcasm Rishi decided to keep a lid on his temper. He shook his head. "I never actually invited Samantha to live with me. She suggested it and I agreed. And if you're wondering whether I kept Samantha a secret from Anju, I did not. I mentioned Samantha to her and the nature of our relationship some time ago. Anju had no problem with it. At least that was my impression."

"If you already had a relationship going in London, then why did you start one with Anju?" Mohan's voice sounded more tired than angry. His wife had probably woken him early and dragged him here against his wishes. Of course, he'd just found out about his brother, too. It had to be hard on a man his age—coping with all that on top of the stress of opening a new business.

"Uncle, please understand that I didn't *plan* to start anything with Anju. I came to the U.S. at Jeevan-kaka's request to help you with the business issue. But then I met Anju. The more I saw her, the more I liked her, and fell in love with her. You have a lovely and talented daughter with a captivating personality. However, I started seeing her seriously only after I broke up with Samantha. Until then, I didn't date Anju, and nor did I tell her of my intentions."

"And you never once thought that by playing with her emotions you'd be hurting a vulnerable girl whose life has been blown apart once before?" The distress in Usha's voice was sharp enough to affect anyone, even a strong man.

Rishi felt his stomach tighten. "Auntie, I had no intention of hurting Anju. Precisely for that reason I didn't pursue her until I made a clean break with Samantha. When I was in London recently, I told Samantha that our relationship wasn't progressing and that it was time for us to part."

"Samantha obviously didn't think so," Usha quipped.

Ignoring Usha's barbed remark, Rishi continued, "I made sure there was nothing of hers left behind. In fact, I even thought about selling my home and all its furnishings if Anju agreed to marry me. I wanted us to start fresh, with no ghosts from our respective pasts."

A frown settled over Usha's face. "Then why is your girlfriend still calling you in the middle of the night?"

"She's facing some financial problems." He was beginning to have doubts about Samantha's claims but he couldn't tell the Kapadias that. Not yet anyway. "For some unknown reason she called me for help."

"What do you mean, *unknown* reason?" retorted Usha. "In our culture, when a man and woman live together like husband and wife, then they're expected to be husband and wife. And apparently you and she lived together for several years."

All Rishi could do was nod. He knew enough about the values she was talking about. "I understand, but I wasn't entirely steeped in that culture, Auntie. I've lived most of my life as a white man in England."

After his long silence Jeevan joined in the conversation. "That is true, Usha. Did I not tell you that although he has a girlfriend, he is basically an honorable fellow?"

Rishi glanced at the old man. "Thank you. It's kind of you to offer your support."

"So exactly what are your intentions toward Anju now?" asked Mohan, when his wife sent him a pointed look.

"My intentions are still the same, Uncle: I want to marry her; I want to encourage her to market her designs to reputable international houses of fashion; I want to help promote her career; and by the grace of God I hope to have a child with her." He put on his most humble face. "I want to do it honorably and with your blessings."

He noticed with some satisfaction Usha taking a deep breath and settling back a little. Maybe he'd put her mind at ease to some extent. Or maybe not. He couldn't be sure.

"But you know Anju has obligations, Rishi," Usha said after several seconds of uncomfortable silence. "She has deep roots here in the U.S."

"I realize that, but doesn't she also deserve a life of her own? How long do you expect her to live as a widow and let the business occupy her entire life?"

"She's our partner and she's the one who has managed most of the design and merchandising," answered Mohan. "If she marries you, how will she manage the business?"

"I've thought about that, Uncle," explained Rishi. "Sejal's graduating soon and she seems to be extremely interested in co-managing the store. I've talked to her about it briefly and I think she's a natural for the job. I'm not saying Anju has to remove herself completely from the boutique; she'll still have much to do with it. She can visit you several times a year, spend a couple of weeks each time, take inventory, set up the new fashion lines, et cetera. She'd still remain your fashion expert and strategist, but Sejal and Auntie and you can manage the daily operations."

"What about you?" Jeevan raised his brows at Rishi. "You are also our partner in Silk & Sapphires."

"I'll be just as active as Anju. I manage to keep an eye on all my businesses and this one is no exception. It's Anju's store. How could I not be involved?"

That particular remark seemed to earn him a little clemency from Usha. "Really?"

"Yes. I want to make her dreams come true—at least some, if

not all." He looked at Usha. "Did you know Anju had dreams of starting an international chain of Silk & Sapphires stores?"

"She told you that?"

Rishi nodded. "Apparently she and Vikram had some long-term business plans?"

"She had dreams, all right," Usha conceded.

"She still has a chance to realize them," Rishi emphasized gently. "She seems to love children, and I could give her that as well. Before it's too late."

Usha glanced at her husband, probably wondering what his feelings were. But Mohan still appeared a little dazed.

It was Jeevan who took the initiative. "We understand that you want to marry Anju, but how are you going to convince Anju of that? She says she doesn't want to see you again."

"I know she's confused and angry."

"Very," said Jeevan.

"But she has absolutely no reason to be. I didn't get a chance to explain things to her clearly. A minute after Samantha called Anju jumped to certain conclusions and then decided to go home." He looked at Usha and Mohan. "I could use your help in convincing her."

"She has a mind of her own, Rishi," said Usha. "When she's hurting she withdraws into herself. After Vikram's death it took us a long time to draw her out. Although she's very outgoing and friendly, she's a very private person when it comes to certain things. When she eventually comes out of it, she throws herself into her work till she's ready to drop."

"I know. I've observed her." He rose to his feet and paced, hoping to ease the increasing stiffness in his knee. For a minute he mulled over how to deal with Anju, then came up with an idea. "What if I went away for a while? I'm supposed to meet a client in California within the next few days. Instead I'll leave immediately. That might help, don't you think?"

Usha gave him a dubious look. "You mean that age-old cliché about distance making the heart grow fonder?"

He shrugged. "Anything that'll work in my favor. If nothing

else, my absence will give her the time and space to put things in perspective."

"Does she know anything about your trip to California?"

"I told her I was planning on leaving sometime within the week."

"I will talk to Anju," offered Jeevan. "She might listen to me."

"Thanks, Jeevan-kaka, but I think it's best if Auntie talks to her, woman to woman."

"I'll do it, Rishi," said Usha, "on one condition. I never want to hear about any girlfriends from your past or present. If you have anything sneaky going on in your life, you can forget about Anju. She's had enough heartache to last her a lifetime. Besides, we don't tolerate extramarital affairs and things of that nature in the Kapadia family."

"I understand. Other than Samantha I have no other issues in my life. Any future contact with her will be purely business."

"You promise to take good care of our daughter?" Usha shot him one of her cutting looks.

"Yes, ma'am."

"If you make her unhappy in any way, you'll have me to answer to."

Rishi stopped in his tracks and turned to her. "You have my promise, Auntie. I'll take care of her as best as I can. If she'll have me, that is."

"And that's a big if." Usha rose to her feet and gestured to the two men to do the same. "Now let's go home and deal with the next problem—Jeevan-bhai's condition."

"Thank you for allowing me to state my case," Rishi said to all three of them.

"So you are leaving for California in the morning?" Jeevan asked him.

"Yes, sir. I'll check airline schedules straightaway." He gave the old man's arm a reassuring squeeze. "I'll ring you when I get there. I should be back in a couple of days."

"We'll take good care of Jeevan-bhai in your absence," Usha assured Rishi as she opened the door.

Despite the gravity of the situation, Rishi couldn't help smiling as he watched Usha sweep out of the room with Jeevan-kaka and Mohan trailing behind her. She would have made a formidable CEO. He had no doubt about her management abilities. It gave him great satisfaction to know she'd have no problem managing Silk & Sapphires without Anju.

But convincing Anju to accept him was going to be one hell of a challenge.

Chapter 30

Rishi was gone. Anjali learned that nearly two days after she'd had her spat with him on Saturday night. On Sunday, the store had been extremely busy. Most everyone who had wandered in had bought something. That was the only redeeming feature about Sunday.

Although she was wrapped up in serving clients all day, Anjali had noticed Rishi's absence, felt it keenly. How could she not? He was all she'd been thinking about, and she hadn't slept much for two nights in a row.

There was no sign of him. Every time the door had opened and the chimes had sounded, her eyes had flown to the door, looking for him. And every time, her shoulders had slumped when a customer had walked in instead.

Rishi was the one who'd thought of celebrating at the Indian restaurant and made the reservations for Sunday night, and yet he'd remained conspicuously absent. Anjali had convinced herself that he had flown back to London and Samantha after realizing he didn't belong here. The thought had made her ache, the kind she'd experienced once before, from having loved and lost.

When Naren-kaka and Sejal had asked why Rishi wasn't there for the celebration dinner, Jeevan-kaka had replied, "He is busy with a new project."

Yeah, a new project called Samantha, Anjali had concluded bitterly, *or more like an old project he can't let go.* By the time she and her family had gone home, it was nearly midnight. She had fallen into bed exhausted, and then slept fitfully.

How could she have been so blind about Rishi? But then he'd been convincing in his proposal, so earnest, so persuasive. When he had a sophisticated and successful woman like Samantha, why would he want to settle for Anjali, who was about as exciting as tepid tea?

Today was Monday, and Jeevan-kaka, Anjali, and her parents had arrived at the store in the morning to take inventory, restock, and clean up after the hectic opening weekend.

While Jeevan-kaka and her father had taken care of the paperwork, the two women had unpacked and organized the new shipments in the storage room. Lunch had been a hurried affair with some takeout food from the restaurant down the block. Fortunately, Jeevan-kaka had wanted only a glass of warm milk, and that was easy enough to rustle up in Anwar's kitchen.

After lunch, Anjali and Usha went about taking care of the large number of special orders they'd taken over the weekend. It meant contacting the fabric suppliers in Bangkok, the tailors and embroiderers in India, and then trying to coordinate their pickup and delivery with the shippers. With the differences in time zones, it had taken up the better part of the afternoon to accomplish everything the way they wanted it.

It was nearly six o'clock now. It had turned dark outside a while ago. Rishi still hadn't shown up. Where was he? Back in London with Samantha? Supposedly arranging a business loan for her . . . or something else?

She didn't give a damn where he went or with whom, Anjali tried to tell herself. She really didn't.

Picking up her sewing kit, she settled on a stool behind the counter to shorten the hem of an ensemble someone had bought the previous day. At least with a needle and thread and beautiful silk fabric in a rare shade of plum draped over her lap, she could keep her mind occupied.

Her mother worked nearby, polishing some silver jewelry. The two women worked side by side in companionable silence, as they often did. Anjali sensed Usha's gaze on her every now and then. She could tell her mother was curious to know what was going on.

Anjali knew her parents and Jeevan-kaka had gone out early Sunday morning and met with Rishi. Having remained awake all night, she'd heard the sounds in the house: her parents and uncle having a whispered dialogue, and later the three elders going out the door and driving off. From having overheard her mother's heated words to Jeevan-kaka in the kitchen the previous night, Anjali had concluded that they had gone out to confront Rishi.

When her mother was on the war path, there was no stopping her.

But despite her curiosity Anjali had refrained from questioning her mother about it. And none of the elders had volunteered any information. It was all very strange, like the code of silence surrounding the emperor's new clothes. Everyone knew that the others knew and yet no one talked about it.

And Rishi had mysteriously disappeared, just as inexplicably as he'd appeared in their lives. No one talked about that either. Had her parents, in their attempts to protect her, told him to get out of town and leave her alone? Or had Rishi decided he was better off returning to London?

Anjali wanted to know, and yet on some level she didn't. It would hurt even more if she discovered he had indeed gone back to his former life and lover.

Usha threw her another curious look. But Anjali was in no mood to discuss anything deeply personal at the moment. However, there was one thing she was sure of: this time around she wasn't going to allow herself to fall to pieces. Life had taught her a tough lesson, and she was older now, more mature, more philosophical.

And she wasn't going to think about tomorrow. The business seemed to be back on its feet today, her family was with her today, and there was work to be completed today. That's all she needed. Today.

Suddenly her mother said something that interrupted Anjali's thoughts. "I wonder how Rishi is doing with his California client." She made it sound matter-of-fact, but Anjali knew better than to take the bait.

So that's where he was. Anjali worked her needle and thread silently over the buttery fabric. He'd mentioned going to California sometime soon, but he hadn't said anything about leaving right away.

Usha claimed her attention directly this time. "Did he mention when he was coming back?"

Anjali shrugged. "Why should he mention anything to me?"

"You two are friends. You go out to dinner on Sunday evenings and all that."

"We discuss business."

Usha tossed her a wry look. "I'm sure you talk about more than that."

"He doesn't discuss his itinerary with me, Mom. I didn't even know he was going to California—at least not this soon."

"What I meant was, since you and he are friends and partners he may have mentioned it to you in passing."

"He doesn't answer to me or anyone else. And we're partners, nothing more."

Obviously finished with her chore, Usha put the polished silver back, shut the display case, and locked it. "He said he was leaving for California yesterday morning to meet with some new client."

Anjali had assumed he'd stayed away from the store to avoid her. For that she was both disappointed as well as grateful. She still didn't know what she wanted. She needed to see him and yet she wasn't sure if she could stand to look at him anymore. She needed to feel his touch and hear his voice, but she didn't know whether she'd cringe at both. She'd never experienced such conflicting emotions before.

She was startled when she heard her father calling urgently. "Usha! Anju!"

Her mother was the first one to start running. Anjali dropped the garment and followed on her heels. Something was clearly wrong.

When they got to the office they found Jeevan-kaka sitting on a folding chair, doubled over and clutching his middle. Her father looked frantic. "He suddenly started complaining that his stomach is hurting," Mohan explained. "I took him to the bathroom a minute ago. He threw up."

Anju went down on one knee beside the old man. "What's wrong, Jeevan-kaka?"

"I have this pain . . . in my abdomen." The old man's face was pale and slick with perspiration.

"Have you been taking your medicines regularly?"

"Yes."

Anjali and her father exchanged a glance. She could see the panic rising in her father's face. They had no idea what kinds of complications advanced colon cancer could bring on.

"Has this happened before?" Usha asked.

"A few times," replied Jeevan-kaka, trying to catch his breath.

Anjali turned to her father. "Dad, call 911. He needs a doctor."

Jeevan-kaka put up a hand to stop him. "No! I don't want to go to a hospital, Mohan. Your *Amreekan* hospitals are going to charge a lot of money for giving me aspirin and sending me home."

"But you're seriously ill, Jeevan-bhai. You need medical help."

"Just take me home. My pain tablets are in my bag, and I will take those."

Usha glared at her brother-in-law. "I don't care what it costs. We're taking you to an emergency room."

Jeevan shook his head. "Usha, I have been in a hospital so many times in the last two years, I can't even count anymore. They can't do anything for me. Just take me home. I will eat something and take my prescription tablets and then I should be okay."

"This is my fault," rued Usha. "I should have brought something homemade for your lunch instead of letting you drink a glass of milk. An empty stomach is what's causing this, isn't it?"

"No, no. This kind of thing can happen with or without food. Don't blame yourself," scolded Jeevan-kaka. "Rishi knows this for a fact."

Anjali rose to her feet. "Rishi has seen you through these episodes?"

"At least two times."

"I better call Rishi, then," Mohan said and started to dial Rishi's cell phone number. "Maybe he can tell us how to handle this."

"Don't bother that boy when he's busy with a client, Mohan," pleaded Jeevan-kaka. "He can't do anything for me. I just need to take my medicine and get some sleep."

"From now on, you better not come to the store," Anjali told him firmly. "You shall stay home and rest."

Ignoring Jeevan-kaka's directive, her father called Rishi. Meanwhile Anjali and Usha helped the groaning old man out of the chair and gently led him out the back door to the car. "Are you okay?" they asked him a few times until they got him settled in the backseat. Anjali slid in beside him and her mother got into the front passenger seat.

A few seconds later, Mohan came out of the store and got behind the wheel. "Rishi said it is no use taking him to an emergency room."

"Then what are we supposed to do?" queried Anjali.

"He said we should make sure Jeevan-bhai eats something soft and starchy like plain rice with *dal* and takes two of his pills. After that we should force him to rest."

"When is Rishi coming back?" asked Usha, throwing an anxious glance over her shoulder at Jeevan.

Mohan started the car and pulled out of the parking lot. "He's planning to catch the earliest flight he can get."

"But he needs to be with his new client," insisted Jeevan. "Why did you force Rishi to come back for my sake? It is a waste of his time."

"He says the tour of the facilities and most of the discussions with his client are over and everything else can easily be done on the phone and computer. So he's going to check on flights right away."

"Thank God." Usha leaned back in her seat. "He seems to have such a calming effect on Jeevan-bhai."

Anjali reluctantly agreed. Rishi did seem to have that effect on her uncle. In fact, he seemed to have that effect on everyone, except her. When he looked at her intensely with those magic eyes of his, or touched her, he got her pulse scrambling madly. But the man was the personification of calm confidence when it came to business. If it weren't for his steadying influence, she'd never have survived the grueling tension, the fear and excitement of the last few months.

She didn't want to see Rishi again, but she had no choice. When he flew back from San Francisco, he'd be sure to rush to Jeevan-kaka's side. She'd have to tolerate his presence. The important thing was to set aside her personal hang-ups and think about what her uncle needed.

Sitting beside Jeevan in the backseat, Anjali kept a close eye on him. He sat with his eyes shut and his head thrown back against the headrest. The pain was etched on his face. It was frightening to see him like this.

Two nights ago, when he'd mentioned the cancer, it hadn't hit her with such ferocity. Cancer was just a clinical term, a condition, but now she could see the disease was devastating enough to bring a strong, willful man to his knees. The man who'd seemed so invincible all her life now looked like he was ready to drop. The thought of him dying made her squirm in her seat.

When they reached home, the first thing they did was to coax him to eat a little rice and bland *dal*, and take his medication. An hour later, reclining on the family room couch, he claimed he felt better, and the color was nearly back in his face. So her father helped him up the stairs and to bed.

When Nilesh came home, he found the three of them seated around the kitchen table. They had just sat down to what amounted to dinner. They'd hastily thrown a few things into the microwave, but no one seemed interested in eating.

Nilesh took one look at their faces and stopped short. "Who died?"

"That's not funny, Nilesh," his mother chided him.

"I didn't mean it literally," he shot back. "What's wrong?"

"It's Jeevan-kaka," said Anjali.

"What happened to him?" Nilesh washed his hands and wiped them on the kitchen towel.

That's when Anjali realized that Nilesh hadn't been told what was going on with their uncle. The poor kid was clueless. "Sit down, Nil. We'll explain," she said and got up to get him a plate.

Helping himself to generous portions of the rice, *dal*, and vegetable *shaak*, he sat down. "Where is he?"

"Resting in his room." Usha explained everything to Nilesh as succinctly as she could.

Anjali watched the expression on her young brother's face progress from relative nonchalance to shock to genuine regret. "So he's, like . . . dying?"

"He says he doesn't have much time left."

"Shit!" Nilesh murmured under his breath. "So that's why he got so thin and he drinks nothing but milk." He took a forkful of food and chewed on it for a while. "What's going to happen to him now?"

Poor Nil, reflected Anjali. He didn't really know what death was. He was four when their maternal grandfather had passed away. As far as grandparents went, only their maternal grandmother was still around, and she lived in India with her son— Usha's eldest brother—and his family.

When Vik had died, Nilesh was a nine-year-old. But now he was old enough to know about death, and yet still too young to accept it so close to home. Anjali patted his hand across the table. "Rishi's on his way back from California. We'll figure something out when he returns."

"I didn't know Rishi was in California," said Nilesh. "What's he doing there?"

Anjali shrugged. "Beats me."

Her mother gave her a sharp look. "I told you he's there to see a new client."

"So you did." Anjali rose to her feet, dumped the uneaten food from her plate in the garbage can, and put the plate in the dishwasher. Why was her mother defending Rishi all of a sudden? Usha was too smart to fall for a lame excuse like a business loan to an ex-girlfriend. But then Rishi was an expert at working his charm, especially on women.

A minute later her mother joined her with the rest of the dishes, and the two of them silently cleaned up while Nilesh and her father went upstairs to check on Jeevan-kaka.

That night, Anjali and her parents decided to take turns watching over Jeevan in shifts. Although he was sleeping at the moment, they weren't sure if it was safe to leave him alone. Mohan volunteered to take the first shift.

Anjali relieved her father a little after 1:00 A.M. She made herself comfortable in the armchair by the window, turned on the gooseneck lamp, and settled down to read a book. She noticed her uncle slept in fits, but he didn't complain of pain anymore and seemed oblivious to her presence.

When he woke up and found Anjali in the room, he blinked at her. "What are you doing?"

"Making sure you're all right."

"How long have you been here?"

"Just a few hours," she told him.

"I don't need a private nurse. Go to sleep," he murmured with an ornery scowl.

She got to her feet and approached the bed. "How're you feeling?"

"Much better. There is no need to worry. This happens sometimes." He turned his head to look at the bedside clock. 4:37 A.M. "Do you know when Rishi is returning?"

"He called Dad to say he managed to get a seat on a late flight. He's supposed to arrive in Newark later this morning."

Jeevan-kaka surprised her by patting the spot on the bed beside him. "Since you are awake anyway, sit here. I want to talk to you."

"About what?" She sat on the edge of the bed.

"Something important." He shifted a little to make more room for her. "I may die tomorrow, or I may die next year, but before it happens, I want to tell you a secret."

Chapter 31

Anjali studied her uncle's face. It was hard to read his expression. "All right, what's on your mind?" she asked him.

"I know you are angry at Rishi, but please don't be, Anju."

"I'm not angry anymore. I'm hurt that he didn't tell me he still had ties to Samantha. He said it was all over between them after he broke up with her during his trip to London."

"He told you the truth. He cares about you."

"Fine way of showing it, right? He didn't even tell me he was going to California."

"How can he inform you about his trip when you refuse to take his phone calls?"

She looked away to gaze at her hands. She hadn't bothered to listen to Rishi's voice mail messages. She'd deleted them without hearing a single one. Perhaps he had mentioned California. "Maybe he's realized it's a mistake proposing to me after all."

"No. Your parents and I had a talk with him."

"So you did visit him the other morning like I suspected."

"Yes. He said he still wants to marry you and he has nothing to do with Samantha anymore."

"And you believed him?" Friendship and loyalty were admirable traits, but in this case Rishi had brainwashed her uncle to the degree that Jeevan-kaka had become blind and deaf to Rishi's faults.

A dry laugh emerged from Jeevan's throat, ending in a mild coughing fit. "Anju, I have believed in that boy since the time he was born," he rasped. "I am willing to put my life and all my money in his hands. He is more than a son to me. He takes better care of me than my sons."

"I don't doubt his love and devotion to you. It's the other part of his life I have reservations about."

"Has he ever told you any lies?"

"I don't know. I haven't had a chance to test him yet. But tell me this: why would a practical, intelligent woman like Samantha call him for help instead of a bank, and in the dead of night, unless they still had some ties to each other?"

"They have business ties. Her company does his advertising and public relations."

"What does that have to do with Rishi loaning her a huge sum of money?"

"Rishi is a kind fellow and very loyal. Don't you see that?" Jeevan sounded testy.

"I'm trying."

"So try harder." He gave her a moment or two to chew on that. "Do you want to be alone for the rest of your life, Anju?"

She turned the question over for a minute. Did she want to live alone? Did she want to die a lonely, frustrated old maid, using the Kip Rowlings of the world to appease the occasional need? At the same time, was it worth marrying a man she had a difficult time trusting, just so she could have a husband?

"No woman likes to be lonely," she allowed. "But sometimes it's better than living with a man who might break your heart."

"Remember one thing, *beta*: everyone has to make choices in life. Sometimes we make good ones, sometimes bad, but every choice comes with . . . uh . . ." He seemed to fumble for the right word.

"Consequences?" Anjali prompted.

"Yes. You must trust someone in your life besides God, should you not? Otherwise what is life?"

"You're a wise man, Jeevan-kaka, but I'm too afraid to take a big step like marriage once again . . . especially to a man I can't trust."

"Do you love Rishi?"

She had barely acknowledged the fact to herself, let alone told anyone else about it. It took her a whole second to reply. "Yes." *Desperately*.

A small smile touched Jeevan-kaka's parched-looking lips. "I knew that."

"How?" Was she that transparent that even her uncle could read her?

"I'm not blind, you know."

"Jeevan-kaka, can I ask you something?"

"Sure."

"Did you ask Rishi to accompany you just so you could bring him and me together?"

The old man closed his eyes for a moment. "Yes and no," he admitted. "He is excellent at solving business problems, so I wanted him to help you with the shop. I also think Rishi needs a good wife and you need a good husband." He smiled at her, the missing tooth reminding her of the gap in their backyard fence that had yet to be repaired. "And I believe you are suited well for each other."

"Did Rishi know why you asked him to come to the U.S.?"

"He knew it was business related, but I don't think he knew about the personal reasons."

"So while you've been pretending to be here solely to help us out of a financial jam, you've been doing some serious match-making."

Jeevan dissolved into laughter—something unusual for him. It also meant he was feeling better. "Jam is a good word—just like in our language we say *chutney*." It took a second for the mirth to subside. "Anju, if I tell you a secret, can you keep it to yourself?"

"Depends on what it is."

"I want you to promise me that you will not tell this to your parents until after I die."

She narrowed her eyes at him. "Exactly what devious plot are you hatching now?"

"*Beta*, you know the money I invested in your—"

"I know," she interrupted. "It's a lot, and we're very grateful for the loan. Don't worry; we'll make sure we return it with interest as soon as we can. I promise."

Tears appeared in the old man's eyes. Gone was the earlier amusement. "The money is not a loan; it is a gift to all of you. I don't want you to return it."

Anjali sat up straight, her eyes wide. "What are you talking about? We can't take your money."

"This is my last wish for my brother and his family, Anju. I am planning to give some cash to Naren also. I want him to pay off the mortgage on his motel. But I don't want any of them to know."

"Then why are you telling me this?"

"Because you worry too much about the store and the money you think you owe me. You will refuse to marry Rishi and go to London just for that reason. You will insist on staying here and making sure you pay me back. At least if I tell you the truth, you can stop worrying about your financial obligations."

"I see." He was right. The huge debt was one of the major reasons for her wanting to remain in New Jersey. But according to her uncle it was no longer a debt. Guilt was a mild word to describe what she felt in that instant. For all the rotten names she'd called Jeevan-kaka and all the accusations she'd made against him, she wanted to shrivel up and die. In his own way, he was one of the most generous men in the world. "I feel awful about taking your hard-earned savings."

"I have plenty of money, Anju. My children, my grandchildren, and their children have enough to lead a luxurious life. It makes me happy to help my brothers to become more secure. If I am to die soon, I want to do my duty to my family—and to God."

"What about the money Rishi has invested in the store?"

"All the cash is mine. Rishi's contribution was to come here, stay at his own cost, and provide free advice."

Mulling over that for a while, Anjali wondered exactly how much Rishi had spent—and was still spending on this venture. He'd been in an expensive hotel for weeks, he had leased an automobile, and he traveled strictly in business class. Considering all those things and four and a half months' worth of his valuable time, his contribution was sizeable. It probably added up to somewhere in the same range as Jeevan-kaka's share, perhaps more. She had no idea what Rishi's standard consulting fees were.

It was too much for her to accept as charity.

However, at the moment, her uncle's sad and pleading eyes compelled her to consider his offer. He used the sleeve of his shirt to dry his eyes. The simple gesture brought a lump to Anjali's throat. She tried hard to swallow it, but couldn't.

"In that case I accept," she murmured. "And I promise not to tell Mom and Dad until . . . until . . ." Now that she'd had a glimpse of what lay deep inside Jeevan-kaka's heart, she wanted to hold on to him a while longer, get to know the man she'd despised all her life, make it up to him in some small measure if she could. Instead, she sat beside him and cried her heart out.

"Why are you crying so much, *beta?*" He looked more tired than ever when he spoke again. "Get married, Anju. I can't promise that God will be kind to you. Nobody can promise that, but take an old man's advice. My life would be worthless without my wife and my children and grandchildren. A business will not give you a family, and hard work will not give you true contentment. You listen to me now, okay? Get married, have children, be happy."

Watching his parchment-like eyelids begin to droop, Anjali slid off the bed. "I'll think about it."

"You do that. Now go get some sleep." He turned onto his side, clearly dismissing her.

She adjusted his blanket. "Rest well," she whispered. Within a minute he was snoring lightly. She watched the gentle rise and fall of his shoulder. Despite all the outward gruffness and bluster, he was a man with a heart. The sad thing was she hadn't thought to look for it all these years. Now that she'd finally discovered it underneath those crusty layers, it was much too late. Rishi, on the other hand, had glimpsed it when he was only a boy.

The door opened softly and her mother stuck her head in. "How is he?" she whispered.

"*Fine,*" mouthed Anjali and put a finger over her lips to shush her. She tiptoed over to the lamp and shut it off before stepping outside and closing the door.

"He talked to me for a while and then went to sleep," she whispered to her mother, hoping the dark hallway would keep her puffy eyes hidden. "I don't think it's necessary to watch him anymore. Why don't you go back to bed?"

Usha shook her head. "But I'm wide-awake now."

"So am I." Any thoughts of sleep had vanished after that emotional talk with her uncle.

"I think I'll make some tea." Usha looked at her. "You want any?"

"Sure. I'll keep you company." Feeling a sudden chill, Anjali pulled her robe closer around herself.

They walked downstairs together and Usha put the water and milk on the boil. She turned to Anjali and stared for a second. "You've been crying."

Anjali shrugged. "Had a rather emotional tête-à-tête with Jeevan-kaka."

Usha's eyebrows were raised. "Must have been serious if he made you cry."

"I'm beginning to think I misjudged him all these years."

"So am I." Usha let out a deep sigh. "I feel terrible about it."

"I know. That's why I was crying. I've never really talked to him in the real sense. He's a good man when you get to know him."

Adding the right blend of spices to the pot, Usha glanced at her. "Are you sure it's okay to leave him alone?"

"He's asleep and snoring." Anjali got out the cups and the sugar.

"Hope he doesn't insist on getting out of bed soon and performing his *pooja*," Usha said. "He needs his rest."

Meanwhile Anjali rummaged through the pantry for a light snack. Finally settling on an oatmeal cookie, she started nibbling. "I think he's too exhausted to wake up anytime soon. Our little talk seemed to tire him out."

"What did you talk about?" Usha absently added the tea leaves and stirred the pot, but Anjali heard the probing note.

She hesitated. "Mostly about Rishi."

"You mean about Rishi and you."

"He mentioned your conversation with Rishi the other day." She eyed her mother, who was still busy pretending indifference. "Want to tell me about it?"

The tea came to a boil and the froth rose to the top. Usha stirred it again to let the bubbles settle before shutting off the burner. "You really want to know?" She deftly strained the tea into the two cups Anjali had set on the counter.

"Uh-huh." Carrying the steaming cups to the table, Anjali set them down and pulled out a chair for herself and another for her mother.

Settling in the chair, Usha took a sip of tea and studied Anjali for a long, speculative second. "Rishi told us that he asked you to marry him."

"Jeevan-kaka told me that part."

"Then you already know what we discussed."

"Not really. I know Jeevan-kaka's all enthused about Rishi marrying me. But let's face it, he's an old man who thinks all of mankind should be in pairs, and if his adopted son ends up marrying his niece, it'll all be in the family." Popping the last bit of cookie into her mouth, Anjali picked up her cup and held it in both hands, letting its heat seep into her cold palms. "I want to hear what you and Dad talked about with Rishi. I want to hear *your* side of it."

"I think your uncle is right. Rishi's a decent, solid, and dependable man. He'll be good for you."

Despite her gloomy mood, Anjali smiled. "You make him sound like a sturdy station wagon with an eight-cylinder engine and a roomy luggage compartment."

Laughter bubbled out of Usha's throat. "You know what I mean, you silly girl."

"I know what you mean." In their culture, Rishi was the ideal potential husband. Most women would need to have their heads examined if they thumbed their noses at a gem like Rishi. Anjali angled an amused look at her mother. It wasn't often that her mother laughed with abandon, so it was nice to hear the sound.

"Plus he's so nice-looking," her mom reminded her.

And sexy as ever. Anjali's mind drifted to the two brief nights she'd spent with him. "Sure," was the extent of her response. It wouldn't do to use the word *sexy* to describe Rishi to her mother.

"And don't forget he's well-to-do."

"There is that." It was an important criterion for a potential Gujarati groom. A healthy income made him all the more attractive.

"In all seriousness, I think he'll make a good husband," stressed Usha. "He didn't lie to us or hide anything about his relationship with Samantha. He said it was just something that happened between two single people, but now he's met you and he wants to marry and settle down."

"Since when have you become a champion of casual relationships?"

"I don't condone his past relationship with Samantha, but I realized I don't have a right to judge him either, because I don't know much about the younger generation born and brought up in western cultures. Their values are a little different from ours, and besides, his mother is British."

"I suppose you're right." Kip Rowling came to mind. If her mom were to discover that Anjali had been having a *casual* affair with an acknowledged womanizer, God knows what she'd do.

Usha cupped Anjali's face in her hand. "Rishi has promised to put all that behind him and be faithful to you. That's all that matters to your dad and me. We want you to have a good life. You've suffered so much these last few years. Don't give up a chance for happiness because of jealousy and distrust."

Anjali continued to hold the cup in the circle of her hands. She needed the warmth. "What'll happen to the store if I go off and live in London? Who's going to help Dad and you with all that extra work that comes with a bigger and better store?"

"Your dad and I had a store since before you were born. We managed then and we can manage now. Besides, we have Sejal and a full staff. Rishi reminded us last evening that in a few months Sejal will be graduating, and she definitely plans on working at the store full-time."

"She told you that?"

"Rishi has already talked to her about it, and she's very eager to take on more responsibilities."

"When did he talk to Sejal?"

"When he fell in love with you and started to think about asking you to marry him. He knows you're worried about the future of Silk & Sapphires; he had to have a possible solution to all your objections before he proposed to you." Usha explained to Anjali some of what he'd said that night.

"So he's worked out all the details, has he?" Anjali wasn't surprised. He always seemed to have answers to business problems. But that didn't address the personal ones.

"You see, that tells me Rishi's a very practical man and has taken into consideration every angle, every contingency. That's why he's such a successful businessman and consultant."

"All that may be true, but I'm still scared, Mom. I'm so damn scared."

"Of what, dear?"

"Loving a man again . . . and possibly losing him. Again."

Chapter 32

"So you're in love with him." Usha paused to study Anjali's face for a moment. "My guess was right."

Her mother's expression was so loaded with maternal love that Anjali put her cup on the table and instinctively leaned forward to rest her head on her shoulder. "I'm crazy about him."

"Nothing wrong with that, honey," said Usha, rubbing Anjali's back.

Anjali buried her face in the soft fabric of her mother's robe. It smelled like vanilla musk and the spices she'd just put in the tea—a homey, comforting scent. "And I miss him so much. In a lot of ways, I think I love him even more than I loved Vik. I don't know why. I just know I do."

"Maybe because you're more mature now and have the capacity to love more deeply," suggested her mother.

"Hmm."

"But isn't it a *good* thing that you're able to put the past behind you and learn to love again? I've wanted that to happen to you and prayed for it for so long."

"Mom, you don't understand. I know the kind of agony loving someone and then losing them can bring."

"Of course I understand, dear. I have similar fears about losing your dad."

"It's not the same. What if Rishi leaves me? What if he gets tired of me and decides to go back to Samantha or get himself another girlfriend? I'm just a simple Indian woman with middle-class tastes. He's a wealthy Indo-Brit man with a certain lifestyle. How long do you think he'll be happy with someone like me?"

Usha wrapped her arms around Anjali. "Don't underestimate your beauty and charm, *beta*. And never put yourself down like that. You're a talented girl and you have a big heart. Rishi has obviously recognized that. He's no fool. And don't forget he was born and raised in a very humble home in India. He wasn't always rich."

"But what if . . . you know. I can't lose another husband. I don't know if I can survive that."

"Life never comes with guarantees, Anju. We all know that."

"Yeah, but it does come with *some* guarantees, like you and Dad and Nil. No matter what, I know you guys will never abandon me."

"That's true, but then death could take away one of us from you at any time. Dad and I won't be around for Nilesh and you forever. Besides, Nilesh will want to get married in the future and start his own family. What are you going to do when that happens? Wouldn't you want someone to love you, keep you warm, and console you when you're sad?"

"I wanted all that, so I married Vik. And look what happened."

"We can only hope it won't happen again." Usha held Anjali in her arms for a long time. "There is a God, so we can both pray to Ganesh—pray for the best." Smoothing Anjali's hair away from her face, she said. "Who knows, maybe you can even have children."

"It's too late for that."

A soft chuckle vibrated through Usha's chest. "You're talking to the woman who had a baby late in life."

Pulling away from her mother's shoulder, Anjali faced her. "Was it hard? Pregnancy and childbirth at that age?"

"That part wasn't bad. It got tough after the baby came, especially the sleepless nights and the crying." Usha raised an eyebrow. "Surely you were old enough to remember that?"

"Oh yeah, I was ready to choke that screaming brat a few

times." She recalled something that made her smile. "I didn't want to admit it in those days, but Nil was rather cute."

"He was adorable. And your dad and I think of him as our special late-in-life blessing. Both of you are blessings. I can't imagine life without my kids."

"You think there's hope for me, then?"

"There's always hope. And remember this: a child can soften the blow of losing a spouse."

"Yeah?"

"Responsibility for a child automatically brings with it emotional strength. Children have a way of keeping us sane."

Anjali silently pondered that for a second. Perhaps if she'd had a child when Vik had died, she wouldn't have gone off the deep end like she had. A baby would have kept her on a more even keel. Her smart mom was probably smarter than she'd imagined.

"Do you know why we named you Anjali?" asked Usha.

"Because you and Dad liked the name and it was easy for non-Indians to pronounce?"

"That, too. But after an exhausting childbirth I took one look at your face and realized you were worth all that pain. *Anjali* means gift or offering. You were God's gift to your dad and me. Plus you looked like a tiny angel."

Anjali beamed at the warmth in her mother's expression. Kip called her Angelface, too. How was that for a strange coincidence?

The phone rang, making both women jump.

Usha was the first to recover and dive for the phone. "Hello." Her brows snapped together as she listened to the caller. "Oh my God!"

Anjali's heart missed a beat. She glanced at the wall clock, then watched her mother carefully. If someone was calling at 5:13 A.M., it had to be an emergency. She raised a questioning brow at her mother.

"*Rishi,*" her mother silently mouthed.

Wasn't Rishi supposed to be on a plane? Anjali rose to her

feet. Had something happened to him? Was it the airline calling?

"Emergency landing?" Usha's knuckles looked pale as they gripped the receiver.

Anjali listened with mounting alarm. Something *was* wrong. Emergency landing could mean a fire or accident . . . or hijacking. Or God forbid . . . a terrorist bomb.

Not again, God, she prayed with a sinking feeling. *I can't lose another man I love. I haven't even had a chance to spend some time with him. Please don't take him away, not when I've just realized I need him in my life.*

"Jeevan-bhai's much better, *beta,*" she heard her mother inform the caller. "He's sleeping now." Usha chuckled in response to something the other person said. "No bell-ringing this morning. Not yet anyway."

That's when Anjali realized the caller was Rishi and not some stranger. He was alive. She sank bank into the chair, weak with relief.

"We made sure he ate something," continued Usha, giving Rishi a brief update on Jeevan's condition. The conversation went on for a few more seconds. Then Usha said something that penetrated through Anjali's thoughts. "Rishi, I want you to talk to Anju . . . Yes, she's awake. In fact, she's right here. Let me ask her, okay?" She motioned to Anjali to come to the phone.

Anjali's feet felt like lead as she stood up and walked around the table.

Usha placed a hand on the mouthpiece. "He thinks you're still furious with him and you'll refuse to talk. Is that true?"

Anjali shook her head. She was experiencing all kinds of emotions, but fury wasn't one of them. "I'm just worried sick about him," she whispered, unable to keep the angst out of her voice.

"Then tell him that. Tell him you care about him."

On a shaky breath Anjali took the receiver. "Rishi."

"Hello, Anju," he said warily. "I didn't think you'd agree to talk to me."

It felt so good to hear his voice—so damn good—like a long drink of water after dehydrating for days. "Are . . . are you okay?"

"Yes."

"Thank God!"

"They detected a minor mechanical problem and decided to make an emergency landing in Omaha. They have another flight leaving in half an hour. Boarding doesn't start for a few minutes. I thought I'd check on Jeevan-kaka and let you know I'll be arriving very late."

"I'm glad you're safe and you're . . . all right."

"I'm better than all right, now that you're talking to me." He sounded genuinely elated. "I missed you."

It took her a while to react to that. "What about . . . ?"

"Samantha? It turns out she lied about her situation. I had my solicitor check into it and it's all bogus."

Anjali's sigh of relief was long. Her instincts had been right after all. "Where do you go from here?"

"I'm terminating my account with her company as soon as our contract comes up for renewal. I want nothing to do with her."

"You're positive you want to do that?"

"Absolutely. I don't tolerate lies and deceit." After another brief moment of silence he added, "Samantha's out of my life."

"For good?"

"For good."

Anjali could clearly hear him breathing, like he was standing beside her instead of more than halfway across the U.S. "I'm glad."

"You know how I feel about you, don't you, Anju?" His voice was warm and intimate and filled with promise.

"I know." She noticed her mother sneaking out of the kitchen and heard her footsteps going up the stairs. "How's your knee holding up with the long plane ride?" she asked him.

"Surprisingly well. And here's something that'll make you smile. I found that San Francisco badly needs a Silk & Sapphires boutique. The Indian shops there are mediocre at best."

She had to smile. "Do you ever stop thinking about business?"

"Sure, when I'm thinking about you."

"What time will you be home?" she asked him, still smiling.

"Do you really want me home? *Your* home?"

"Yes . . . very much."

"The flight is expected to arrive in Newark around 10:30 A.M. By the time I pick up my car from the parking lot and drive home it'll probably be close to noon." He paused. "Will you be waiting for me, love?"

"I'll be waiting." She would have loved to keep talking, but he had a plane to board. For now, he was safe, and that's all that mattered. "Have a safe flight, honey."

She didn't feel like going to bed after the call ended. She was too keyed up to relax. Instead she went into the family room and switched on the lights. In a corner was the low stool that held Jeevan-kaka's silver idols of Krishna and Ganesh.

On an impulse she lit one of the many tea lights set in front of the idols. The little silver bell he loved to ring in the mornings sat silently beside the incense holder. She stared at the idols for a while.

Dear God, she had so much to be grateful for. Why had it taken her so long to realize it? But like her mother said, it was never too late to pray. And offer thanks to the Lord.

Going down on her knees, Anjali bowed her head, shut her eyes, and joined her hands in prayer.

Author's Note

Dear Reader,

After writing two novels set in India, both of which have stories woven around hot-button social issues, I decided to set *The Sari Shop Widow* in the United States. I felt it was time for me to explore the Indian-American experience, to take my readers on a different kind of journey by offering them a rare glimpse into the lives of Indian immigrants.

Nonetheless my deep interest in women's issues resonates in this book as well. Here I have painted the portrait of a young Indian widow in an American suburban setting, and have shown how, despite her westernization, the traditionalist culture still impacts every facet of her life.

To give you a taste of India right here in the United States, I made the backdrop for *The Sari Shop Widow* a fashionable boutique set in the heart of New Jersey's "Little India." It was the perfect avenue for me to introduce the colors, textures, scents, and fashions of India into my story, and also the diverse lives of a particular ethnic group.

After reading this romantic tale, I hope you will be tempted to visit your Indian-American neighborhood and try some spicy *pakoras* or curry, and indulge in the shopping experience. Trust me, shopping for a *salwar-kameez* outfit, or a hand-embroidered purse, or some colorful Indian jewelry can be loads of fun. Most often, you can even have the pleasure of haggling over the price of an item, something you cannot do in most mainstream American stores.

I sincerely hope you enjoy this book as much as I enjoyed writing it. As always, I wish you Happy Reading and Good Karma.

Warm Regards,

Shobhan Bantwal

THE SARI SHOP WIDOW

Shobhan Bantwal

ABOUT THIS GUIDE

The suggested questions are included
to enhance your group's
reading of this book.

DISCUSSION QUESTIONS

1. Anjali Kapadia is a Hindu widow from a conservative family. Is her life different compared to the lives of widows from other cultures? Discuss the uniqueness of her situation.

2. Is a sari and jewelry boutique a good backdrop for a book set in the United States? Could it have been a different background, something that could have given the story an entirely different twist?

3. Jeevan-kaka, Anjali's uncle from India, is an autocratic man with an agenda of his own. Discuss his entry into the lives of Anjali and her family, and the consequences.

4. What role does Anjali's brother Nilesh play in this story? What does he bring to the plot?

5. Discuss Anjali's lingering feelings for her dead husband and how they influence her actions and emotions throughout the book.

6. Why do you think Anjali has picked an unlikely man like Kip Rowling for a secret boyfriend? What kind of impact does he have on her life and the story?

7. Rishi Shah is the reluctant and unwelcome third party when he is introduced to Anjali. Do you think her overtly hostile reaction to him is justified?

8. What are some of the consequences of a widow falling in love with a man of mixed race, a man who does not even live in the same country?

9. Discuss Rishi's relationship and eventual breakup with his girlfriend, Samantha. Compare and contrast that with Anjali's relationship with Kip.

10. Does the grand opening of the new Silk & Sapphires store offer any insights into the planning and running of a large and diverse ethnic business? What about the cultural elements introduced as part of the opening festivities?

11. Jeevan-kaka has a couple of deep secrets, which are revealed toward the end. What do you think of the motives behind his actions, and some of the ramifications of his disclosures?

12. Discuss the unique Hindu family structure as portrayed in this story. How is this domestic arrangement different from that of western cultures? How does it affect Anjali's present life and her potential future with Rishi?

13. Could the story have ended any other way? As a hopeless romantic, I naturally gravitate toward happy or hopeful endings, but you could discuss some other, highly interesting possibilities. And the possibilities are always endless. . . .